Paul Ho.....   .... of the
senior censors   .lassification.
His first novel,   available in
Black Swan paperback.

Acclaim for *The Wisdom of Crocodiles:*

...on on a grand and ambitious scale ... inspires
...sations of terror, nausea, bemusement and
...ilaration'
...*ly Telegraph*

...lliant ... utterly intoxicating ... Hoffman has set
...self an awesome task, nothing less than a general
...ry of everything. Moves with the pace of the best
...lers'
...*sendent on Sunday*

...man appears to be writing *Bonfire of the Vanities, The*
...*:e of the Lambs* and *Invasion of the Bodysnatchers* all at
...ame time'
...*dian*

Also by Paul Hoffman

THE WISDOM OF CROCODILES

and published by Black Swan

THE GOLDEN AGE OF CENSORSHIP

A Novel

Paul Hoffman

BLACK SWAN

TRANSWORLD PUBLISHERS
61-63 Uxbridge Road, London W5 5SA
A Random House Group Company
www.rbooks.co.uk

THE GOLDEN AGE OF CENSORSHIP
A BLACK SWAN BOOK: 9780552771740

First published in Great Britain
in 2007 by Doubleday
a division of Transworld Publishers
Black Swan edition published 2008

Copyright © Paul Hoffman 2007

Paul Hoffman has asserted his right under the Copyright,
Designs and Patents Act 1988 to be identified as the
author of this work.

A CIP catalogue record for this book
is available from the British Library.

Addresses for Random House Group Ltd companies outside the UK
can be found at: www.randomhouse.co.uk
The Random House Group Ltd Reg. No. 954009

The Random House Group Limited makes every effort to ensure that the
papers used in our books are made from trees that have been legally
sourced from well-managed and credibly certified forests. Our paper
procurement policy can be found on www.randomhouse.co.uk

Typeset in 11/13 Giovanni Book by
Falcon Oast Graphic Art Ltd.

Printed in the UK by CPI Cox & Wyman, Reading, RG1 8EX.

2 4 6 8 10 9 7 5 3 1

Mixed Sources
Product group from well-managed
forests and other controlled sources
www.fsc.org Cert no. TT-COC-2139
© 1996 Forest Stewardship Council
FSC

For Alexandra Hoffman

For herein may be seen noble chivalry, courtesy, humanity, friendliness, hardiness, love, friendship, cowardice, murder, hate, virtue, and sin.

William Caxton, Preface to *Le Morte D'Arthur*

The solution to every problem is another problem.

Louis Bris, *The Wisdom of Crocodiles*

Opening Credits

> For everything I describe I have seen; and if I may have
> been deceived when I saw it, I am most certainly not
> deceiving you when telling you of it now.
>
> Letter to Marie-Henri Beyle

IT IS THE THIRD of September and Nick Berg has been dead
for just over four weeks. All the more odd, then, that as we
begin this story he is standing at the back of a large bar in
the Royal Opera House attending his own memorial.

You're thinking, perhaps, that this is a story about a
fraud or somesuch – a mid-life crisis tale of a man who's
faked his death and turned up just to see what they would
say. Nick, let me tell you, is unambiguously dead. He is in
the Royal Opera House listening to various people saying
what a good man he was. The more subtle eulogists drop
in a few caveats about his saintliness and his occasional
imperfections with both taste and wit. One of them in
particular gets it just exactly right – no mean feat, as you
will agree if you've ever had to deliver a eulogy yourself.

Nick hears himself being praised by people who liked
him, admired him and some who clearly loved him. The
laughter has been as warm as only the most deeply

affectionate human laughter can be. New sides were revealed to people who had known him for years. It turned out he had done charitable works of real merit, all the more impressive in that he had diligently observed the biblical injunction not to let the left hand know what the right hand did. They speak of his work with sick children and the old who were born with mental handicaps (why do you never hear anything about them?). There were more than one or two of his detractors present who had to squirm with the odd sensation caused by being obliged to recognize that someone you looked down on was clearly, even if only in some respects, your superior.

What Nick was feeling was low, low in a special way particular to the lately dead. Think of the most anti-climactic moment of your life and add eternity to it and you might have some idea of what he's going through. What did he expect? How could it be different? These are not rhetorical questions. Imagine yourself in his position. It's not as if you're reading an obituary (we'll get to them in a bit). Nearly everyone present liked you to a greater or lesser extent, some loved you. But at such a gathering as this even the ones who hated your guts (and we'll go into this later because there were many who hated Nick) wouldn't dare to speak out. Well, it just wasn't going to happen. Just as it isn't going to happen to you. When *you* stand at the back, when it's your turn at the pyre or the deep hole, nobody is going to say horrible things about you. People are pretty decent on this score, or at any rate too cowardly to break with the narrative conventions of funeral orations.

But you can imagine how listening to the sum of what he had done and all he was ever going to do would be a fairly dismal experience, an occasion it might be better to miss. One of those things that are better left if not unsaid then probably unheard. But none of us, I'm afraid, has a say. Ghosts like Nick, ghosts like you'll become in time, don't have much in the way of choice until the Day of Judgement (sorry to let that one drop on you out of nowhere. Perhaps I should keep that for a climax, the fact that shortly you will be called to account by eternity for everything you have done or failed to do). Do you like to be in control? Nick Berg did. He liked control a lot. And the control that Nick had and which I suppose is the core and centre of this book he desired above rubies, beyond beauty or fame or love or sex. And he got it. Perhaps since the age of democracy began no one in all the democratic world had such mastery of the thing that he coveted the most. And it was because of this command that on the occasion of his sudden death (probably unlike you and definitely not like me) every paper in the country carried his obituary.

I Spit on Your Grave

THOSE OF YOU who've seen more than a couple of horror films in the last twenty years will know that it's a staple of ghost films that ghosts are the souls of people who don't know that they are dead. It may come as no very great surprise to you to know that this, like almost everything in films, is completely wrong. Obviously enough, suicides catch on pretty quick while apparently healthy twenty-five-year-olds who die in their sleep find it a bit more difficult. But not even the healthiest and most youthful cretin could fail to realize what had happened to them in less than half an hour.

The circumstances of Nick's death were nothing very unusual – a heart attack. Although it should be said that had he been attended by an even moderately competent doctor and been given an injection of streptokinase on admission (standard practice for victims of cardiovascular trauma), then he would probably have lived for another ten or twenty years. At any rate Nick realized within five minutes of undergoing the final spasm of his cardio-vascular earthquake exactly what his predicament was – though I acknowledge that predicament is a particularly feeble way of putting it. As you will imagine this is an unnerving time and an uncertain one. There's no one to tell you what to do next, to give you the low-down or score. You just have to wait. What dawns on you over the next few days is that there is something shaping the things that happen to you as a ghost. And happen is what they do. A ghost has no control, they are wafted here and there so that they can prepare themselves for the Day of Judgement that the more intelligent begin to guess is coming. Ghosts drift on strange currents that take them to places where they might pick up a thing or two about the nature of their eventual fate.

After a few hours' hanging around the hospital, Nick found himself being floated into a large number of places where he would very much rather not be. To his enormous discomfort, Nick found himself drifting in and out of innumerable newspaper offices ranging from the *Daily Telegraph* to *The Stage*. Given Nick's considerable antagonism towards the papers this journey was something of a via dolorosa. It became quickly clear to him within a few minutes of entering the most infamous of our daily tabloids that he was going to be obliged to read his obituaries almost as they were being written. Nick Berg, late chief censor, entered the editorial offices of the *Sun* to be greeted with its final summing up of his life's hopes and works in the headline: MOVIES' MR SEX IS DEAD.

What follows is how the fourth estate brought Nick Berg to the bar. Imagine for the next few pages that you are reading these final verdicts about yourself, these absolute decrees, these knowing summings up, and consider how you would feel. Though, of course, and please don't take this the wrong way, this is a fate unlikely to be yours. Perhaps when you've finished reading what follows you might be grateful for your anonymity.

Here then is the life of a man – let it be said, one of the most devious, strange, lying, cheating, brilliant, kindly, nasty, malicious, generous, appalling . . . Well, words, words fail me when it comes to Nick, which is why I have to show rather than tell. Here they are then: Nick's obituaries in order as he experienced them starting some three hours after his death had been announced.

In the offices of the *Sun*, the shade of Nick Berg had time only to read the following line:

The man who sat through more movie sex than almost anyone else has died.

The use of 'almost' is interesting here – qualification of any kind normally being alien to this paper's house style. Perhaps there was a moment of unconscious honesty at work, the writer acknowledging that Nick would, even as a professional, have had to sit through a very great deal of porn if he were to compete with, say, the average *Sun* journalist, gifted scopophiliacs as most of them are. Unsurprisingly the line about how much sex Nick had watched was not only gracelessly disrespectful (to be expected) but also completely wrong (similarly to be expected). As we shall see, Nick's control of policy on sexual matters bordered on the deranged. But he no more sat through sex films than Colonel Sanders cooked chicken in the back of a Kentucky Fried franchise or Stalin personally shot anyone after he came to power in 1929. This last comparison may not turn out to be quite as broad as you imagine. Let's crack on.

Former Director of the British Film Secretariat, Nick Berg, has died suddenly of a heart attack at the age of sixty-two. Famous for giving certificates for *Reservoir Dogs*, *Rambo* and *The Last Temptation of Christ*, he was also responsible for banning *A Clockwork Orange* [completely untrue] and *The Exorcist* [also not true, but also, paradoxically, absolutely correct]. Noted for his elegantly tailored grey suits, despite twenty years of viewing the most extreme material he admitted that his favourite film was *The Philadelphia Story*.

Nick gave a ghostly sigh at these inaccuracies and, though they were distortions, so was his irritation at them. I'll go into these invariably drawn-out sagas of misinformation as we come to them but the thing to keep in mind is that Nick had a strange way with the truth. I don't just mean that he was a good liar, I mean that he had the ability to distort the truth in the same way that a black hole has the ability to distort time and space. It wasn't something he did, it was something he was. When you were in his presence the truth had a way of not looking the way it was supposed to look.

Whoosh! And Nick is at the *Telegraph*.

When Nicholas Berg came to the BFS in the early seventies it was an organization in crisis. It was almost bankrupt, its offices epitomized the seedy, its liberal decisions on such films as *A Clockwork Orange*, *Straw Dogs*, *Last Tango in Paris* and *Emmanuelle* had caused such outrage that local authorities who then had the ultimate say in what was shown in local cinemas were rejecting the Secretariat's decisions from Land's End to John o'Groats.

Not bad this – we've managed to read something in a newspaper of more than seventy-five words without coming across an error – although I couldn't really say whether there actually was a cinema in John o'Groats.

What it does not go on to say is that by the time Nick retired, the BFS had changed from occupying three-quarters of a floor – and a slimy and dingy floor at that – to owning the whole building. On the day he closed the door behind him for the final time, this monument to himself looked like a particularly successful advertising agency or the minor palace of an evil dictator blessed with moderately good taste.

He became a target throughout his controversial career for the opprobrium, both of pro-censorship groups for his liberal attitudes, and of libertarians for his de haut en bas condescension.

I admit that I had to look it up myself, but I can tell you that a superior or patronizing manner was a very long way from being his worst fault.

In his blue suits and frameless glasses [he didn't wear glasses], Berg attempted to present himself as a neutral, even slightly dull, technocrat [very astute this – the greatest trick the devil ever pulled was persuading people he was a neutral technocrat with a blue suit and frameless glasses – which in Nick's case he didn't wear].
He was vehemently against films which depicted violence towards women and regarded the sexual abuse of children as beyond the pale [as opposed to those of us, presumably, vehemently in *favour* of films depicting violence against women or who believe that sexual abuse of children is merely regrettable]. Despite his admiration for such challenging directors as Scorsese and Cronenberg, his favourite film was *Singing in the Rain*.

Reading this recognition of his firm stance against bad

16

things soothed at least some of the misery that Nick was feeling as he struggled to come to terms with his present state: the dreary implications of what death really meant in ordinary terms as well as eternal ones: the lack of a gentle kiss, the taste of soft white bread, the laughter and conversation of friends, the pleasure of his wife's company. His next station of the cross, the offices of the *Daily Mail*, snapped him out of it. Its opinion of Nick could easily be gathered from the headline: **FILM CENSOR BLAMED FOR FLOOD OF SLEAZE DROPS DEAD.**

The rest was pretty much as expected except for the sentence: 'He had a lifelong interest in pornography'. This unforgivable (yet perhaps understandable) error was amended in subsequent editions (without apology) to: 'He had a lifelong interest in photography'.

Then it was the *Guardian*. He wafted in through an open window with little enthusiasm, expecting, no doubt, some de haut en bas condescension. He was not disappointed.

Nick Berg boasted of being a 'film lover and a film buff'. But the middlebrow nature of his tastes was only too clearly revealed in his favourite film, *Wonderful Life*. Often attacked by the right for his alleged liberalism, this was a carefully constructed reputation with little real substance. It's true that Berg banned many fewer films than his predecessors but he preferred simply to keep controversial titles 'under consideration', sometimes for years. Faced with less intellectually gifted and devious film censors, an astute director could rail indignantly against being banned and raise a storm of lucrative publicity over their work. It was much harder to protest against Berg's more subtle approach. On being accused by one film maker of suppressing his work, he was greeted with a pained sigh and the claim that his work had not been suppressed, it was undergoing a careful review. But if Berg hoped to create the image of being libertarian *and* conservative, in the final analysis he neither fooled nor pleased anyone.

Not that the media have ever thought it worthwhile to say either generous or unpleasant things about me, so I'm only guessing here, but I imagine that the angry frustration Nick was feeling had little to do with his being a ghost, nor with this being the last word on his character. In a sense, I suppose, if you read something unpleasant about yourself in a newspaper it probably doesn't make much difference whether you're a ghost or flesh and blood. You can't protest in any serious fashion either way. All newspaper articles are really obituaries. Journalists think of the people they're writing about as, in a way, dead. Theirs is always the last word because *you* don't get one. Even if what they say is a half-truth or a barefaced lie, who's going to know? When was the last time you read a retraction or cared even if you did. It isn't fair, journalism. Journalists are the Chams, Liliths, Babeals and Beelzebubs of our times. But these malignant minor deities are very far from omniscient – I mean they hardly get anything right. What you will come to think of Nicholas Benedict Berg we shall see. But he deserved – no that's not right – it was required, it was needful, it was an obligation in the case of Nick to find and weigh and consider what was the case with him and come to a verdict only then. It is not because Nick deserved better – we'll see in time what Nick deserved – it was that the truth deserved better. But I am bound (as in compelled) to try to give you what you need to sentence not only Nick but also me. Every judgement is a pronouncement both on the accused and on the one who weighs them in the balance. And if I do this well, perhaps I will be forgiven.

This, then, is pretty much the sum of what was said of one man's life. You get the picture. Except there is one more line I want to bring to your attention. It was a line that made me shout aloud in shock – and I have pretty much seen it all. It shocked me because it was wrong. No, that's not really good enough. It shocked, it staggered me because I have not in all my many days encountered such wrongness, such total and absolute and utter error. It's so pure in its untrueness that it should be in that place in Switzerland where they keep the standard metre rule that defines the perfect absolute measurement for all other measurements. And they should keep it next, also, to that clock, the one that keeps the perfect time against which all other time has to be compared. This pure sentence of the erroneous, the fallacious and the inaccurate came in the obituary in (what else?) the *Guardian*.

Berg's greatest problems were brought about by the introduction of the Video Recordings Act in 1984.

The Limits of Disgust

Censorship in the United Kingdom is a slow dance along
the edge of taste and custom.

Louis Bris, *The Wisdom of Crocodiles*

BEFORE THE TERRIBLE CRISIS that brought Nick to power the
British Film Secretariat had been a body trusted far and
wide as a safe pair of hands that could always be relied on
to regard film as an utterly worthless medium suitable only
for the great unwashed. The depth of the contempt in which
the only new art form of the twentieth century was held was
most precisely indicated by the fact that the first person to
run the BFS, Geoffrey, Lord Ryle, was blind. I don't mean, let
it be clear, that he was in some way lacking in discernment
or perception (though he was) but that he was sightless, as
in he required a white stick to get about. I am not making a
lame joke here, this is a matter of record. And while you may
be horrified that a man afflicted in such a fashion should be
given such power (and this was in the silent era when films
were an entirely visual experience) it didn't, in fact, make
any difference at all – whoever had been appointed, the
films would have been treated in exactly the same way, with
capricious and unmitigated contempt.

Not wanting to be tainted by the notion of government censorship, Parliament had decided that each local authority should have control of the licensing of films. The local authorities, bemused by this unexpected offer of power, readily agreed to sub-contract their new and confusing responsibilities to a body paid for by the film industry and in so doing avoid the trouble and expense of doing the job themselves. If they had any doubts about the determination of the BFS to clean up the film industry such reservations were soon eased by Lord Ryle's cutting nearly everything that might possibly cause offence to anybody – by which it should be clear that this meant anybody who mattered, such as Parliament, quality newspapers, educated society and, amongst others, the Gas Board. I was particularly taken when I first went to the Secretariat by an outraged letter in the archives from the latter indignantly protesting about a scene in one film of the early twenties where a woman tried to kill herself by sticking her head in the oven. They objected to this on the grounds that it would seriously damage their reputation for providing a family product. As it happened the sightless aristocrat was able to please morality as well as Mammon, by cutting the scene both because it gave a bad impression of a utility vital to the nation's well-being and also because it set a bad example to women. Lord Ryle was from the first convinced that women were particularly vulnerable to the malign influence of films, this despite the fact that he had never actually seen one, and, short of a miracle, was never likely to. Determined, nevertheless, not to be at a disadvantage to his examiners he began a practice at the Secretariat that was to remain standard procedure, though for very different reasons, for many decades. Lord Ryle ordered his film examiners to write down every scene of every film they watched in a book

21

bound in red leather. At the end of the day the examiners would enter his office, sit down and then read him the films they had just watched.

Already distrustful of both films and women as he was, these daily readings began to disturb him deeply and his concerns about the effect that the cinema might have on the female psyche gradually extended, first to negroes, then the working class, then to communists and liberals and, by the end of his first year, almost everyone in the country. This growing distrust widened even as far as his film examiners whose morals he was sure must be suffering as a result of actually witnessing things that it was bad enough just to hear about. In this way he began a history of suspicion between the Director and his examiners that was, a lifetime later, to end in ruin and death. Blindness, Lord Ryle was increasingly convinced, was not a handicap in this most all-seeing of jobs but a saving grace.

Given that his reign set the tone for the way the BFS was to deal with films, it was hardly surprising that the Secretariat was considered a safe pair of hands for the next fifty years. How then had an organization so steeped in such deadly caution descended to become by the early seventies despised and disdained through the length and breadth of the country for suddenly releasing a tide of violent filth on an unsuspecting nation? So majestic was its collapse that numerous outraged local authorities decided to take back the power to censor films and exercise their long moribund right to do the job themselves. The reason for this epic loss of confidence was that just before he retired in the early 1970s, the then Director of the BFS had decided to pass, almost uncut, a slew of cinematic poisoned chalices: A Clockwork Orange, Straw Dogs, and The Exorcist descended barely retouched on an astounded public. There was delight from some, but

22

mostly there was shock and dismay. Why had he done it, you may ask? Some said it was an act of irresponsibility by a man who had grown cynical about the point of doing the job at all and who knew that someone else would have to take the rap. Others insisted it was an act of spite, that he hadn't got the pension from his employers that he thought he'd deserved and so he'd got his own back by letting gratuitous sex and violence teach them a lesson. A third opinion is that the job destroyed his sanity – and perhaps by the time I've finished you'll have an opinion as to which of these seems most plausible. But whatever caused his collapse into reckless tolerance it was sudden, almost overnight. As late as 1970 he wrote a letter to one film distributor banning a film they had submitted:

> SUCCUBUS is decadent and degrading, and it contains scenes of sex and sexual perversion and violence that are totally unacceptable and go beyond the limits of disgust. I have therefore decided to refuse it a certificate.
> The fee for viewing this picture is £76. 0. 0 and I shall be glad to receive your cheque.

A nice touch, that, adding, as it were, an invoice to the injury, and as close, I suppose, as we are likely to get to the Chinese custom of making the relatives of a condemned man pay for the bullet used to blow his brains out.

What struck me at first about the letter formally banning *Succubus* is that the idea there could be any alternative way of interpreting the film is simply not considered. But I now think I was mistaken: the letter goes beyond the author simply knowing public opinion and regarding himself as the champion of its values. The question of whether or not there might be alternative opinions to his own was quite possibly perfectly clear to

23

him but, regardless, he was part of an establishment quite ready to impose its standards and, in all senses of the word, to do so without apology. We all recognize now that persons on the Clapham omnibus will be many and various and they all have rights and are prepared to sound off about them. The real difference between now and then is that now everyone with power is obliged to care about what the many and various think. Harder, then, to be a censor these days when there are so many temperatures to be taken and your patients are no longer willing to defer to Matron. I cannot say for sure, of course, whether or not the Director left the Secretariat in 1973 with revenge in his heart, but there's no doubt that it's hard to think of a legacy more certain to destroy his successor. And given that he had kept the lid on criticism of the Secretariat so skilfully and for so many years, how could he not have known?

And this was how, with the foaming of much blood and buggery and horrorshow violence, Peckinpah, Bertolucci and Kubrick ran amok the length and breadth of Albion. It wasn't surprising that the dogs of outrage and disgust were loosed to hunt them down and the Secretariat and its new Director found itself facing complete collapse. Liberals amongst you might consider this no great loss but when local councillors bypassed the Secretariat and watched the films themselves, they turned out to be even more witless and arbitrary than their unelected predecessors. They cut, slashed and banned with the enthusiasm of serial killers granted a licence to kill. A few Labour councils in London took the view that censorship was a repressive tool of the state and refused to ban anything. There was uproar as an endless series of chaotically ludicrous and incoherent decisions were made – films banned in Wetherby, by local watch committees chaired by portly northern gentlemen who pined for the re-introduction of hanging, were at the same time being passed for teenagers in Camden by Marxist Labour councillors. Conservatives were outraged as were libertarians, the press alternately thundered and mocked, and a reluctant government secretly let the film industry know that something had better be done or it would be the worse for them. First, of course, the hapless incumbent and blameless successor to the man who had caused the problem was asked to retire to the snooker room with a revolver. He having been duly dispatched, a replacement was desperately sought.

And the film industry was wise in their choice, for Nicholas Berg turned out to be as cunning as a polecat: handsome, charming, clever, witty and serpentine. Berg was a man who calmed and reassured in every way. You trusted Berg because Berg trusted himself. His meetings, whether with the truculent communists of NW8 or the portly northerners of Wetherby, were like a feeding. Nick could take the five loaves of concern for moral standards and the two fishes of alarm for civil liberties and turn them into a banquet in celebration of his integrity. You were in safe hands with Nick; all your anxieties whether for morals or for freedom of speech seemed to drift away when he spoke, although afterwards you were not able exactly to put your finger on anything he actually said. Nick Berg was here. Everything would be all right.

During the next ten years things went well for Nick. They also went very badly. First, the good news.

A Pol Pot of the moving image, he decided that the clock would be set to nought. Year Zero for censorship would begin with the appointment of Nick Berg. During the next ten years its prior history of blindness and sheer

stupidity was to be eradicated. Nick sowed salt into the traditions it had sustained throughout its history: films were to be treated with respect if they were considered to have merit, and with carefully articulated condemnation if they did not. The punishments to be meted out by the Secretariat were no longer to be summary executions thoughtlessly arrived at and carelessly dispensed. The bullet in the back of the head was still to be delivered (and still to be paid for), Nick was no libertarian, but neither was he a fool and he knew and cared about films. Now offending images were to be struck down only after due process. The black cap of censorship was to be worn by a man who weighed and considered and who sent those who had offended to their deaths with an articulate explanation of their sins. Nick wanted to explain himself because he wanted those who had offended his eye to know exactly why they should be ashamed. The BFS was going to be a place forged in his image.

But like all radicals he had an inheritance to overcome – the examiners who were to serve him were none too happy with his reformation. He continued the practice of obliging the examiners to write every scene down in a red book because he believed that these real-time novel- izations concentrated the minds of those who watched and gave them a careful record of what they'd seen – it was of course too expensive for the film companies to provide the Secretariat with a copy of their films in celluloid. The carefully written record was a useful tool. What horrified his examiners was that they were now required to write a report on every film. The first paragraph was to detail the narrative of what they saw; the second and more important was to explain why they made the decision to pass it 'X' or 'U' or to justify the very frequent command to cut what they had seen. Of course they were horrified.

Imagine, if you can, the shock they felt. Imagine the work *you* do. Imagine that the way you do it has been so for fifty years. Then imagine if someone came and said that everything that underpinned the way you work must change. Where before you just decided and it was done, now you have to justify yourself. No aristocrat used to telling the hungry poor to turn to cake could be more aghast discovering that suddenly he had to get their vote; no Pontiff, his infallibility ordained by God, informed that he must talk to focus groups to get a sense of what the faithful thought could be more horrified. They muttered and resisted and most of all they failed because they didn't understand that they were living in another world. But these were jobs for life (remember them?) and he was forced to wait until they died or they retired. It took Nick years to rid himself of his angry and bewildered inheritance and slowly gather round himself people who would and *could* do what he wanted.

It was not Nick's fault that his first decade in office saw a serious fall in revenue for the Secretariat. Money was so tight that, like some unprovided-for widow, he was obliged to rent out several rooms to an editing company. The brown lino became browner and more frayed, the paint grew more phlegm-like in its glossy green, everywhere it smelt of failure. Anyone could see it. This was a dead-end of an older world of disapproval. The justification for the existence of the film censor was rooted deep in the belief that the public's desire for filth was almost infinite. Without a regulator to police the nasty link between desire and supply, it was assumed that there was bound to be a tidal wave of dross to fill the hungry cesspit ruling the caverns of the human heart. But mostly people didn't want to see sex and violence quite as much as the moralists or Hollywood believed. No one went to the flicks in the seventies all that much – and when they did it was to seedy cinemas with terrible sound and scratchy film. In the once welcoming dark of the local picture house, the gloom now hid the sight, if not the sound, of crunchy, sticky things beneath the feet.

Sometimes there was only a film a week for the Secretariat to watch. And as its revenues came solely from every foot of film that flickered through its projector you see why the place looked like such a dump. Meagre as the pickings were, if it hadn't been for the distributors of porn to keep it going, the Secretariat would not have made it through that woeful decade of decline, of three-day weeks, and strikes and all the paraphernalia of an entire culture hitting the skids. On Monday they watched a blax-ploitation film followed on Wednesday by a weedy sex comedy and then on Friday a seriously hardcore film that had to be entirely gutted before it could go out to the customers who gathered in the public dark of the Prince Charles. Every city had one of these – a place for desperate men to gather miserably in the gloom for a communal act of masturbation over films that had been entirely . . . emasculated, I suppose, would be the word. How quaint it seems now, the idea of sex cinemas, of groups of wretched men in public trying to reconstruct the fucking on the screen from what was left after the BFS had done its work. Like palaeontologists of filth these crepuscular cinemagoers tried to reconstruct a dismembered creature from a bit of bone, a foot, a fossilized impression in the mud. It was hard work in the quarries of lust in the 1970s. Difficult to imagine now, when everyone has access to the broadband pornotopia in the spare bedroom. Another age entirely, and yet it was hardly any time ago.

Anyone making a judgement of Nick's empire would have seen only, like England itself, the management of inescapable and not so slow decline. But they would have been wrong. Nick might not have been busy watching films, but he had been busy earning the trust, the moral capital with which he was such a skilled investor. How could he have known during this time that his hour would come? But that's the way, I suppose, of visionaries. They believe. They *know*.

And it was then, just as the money was finally running out, that Nick hit his gusher in the shape of a device that recorded pictures on two playback heads mounted on a rotating drum spinning at 1,800 revolutions per minute. What dreary techno-speak to describe an instrument that according to the *Daily Mail* raped our children's minds. By the early 1980s there were again horrified demands that something must be done. But this time it was seen that only Nicholas Berg could do it.

When Alexander the Great was shown the Gordian knot and told that no one had ever been able to unravel it he solved the problem on the spot by cutting it open with his sword. Had it been Nick he, too, would have solved the puzzle that had bewildered cunning minds for centuries. But Nick could have undone it with his fingers. Some would have said that the reason for such success could have been found in the fact that it was Nick who'd knotted it in the first place. What I want to put to you is that the comparison with Alexander stands. You must grasp that being great is not a matter of scale, of vast lands and deadly battles. I want you to see it as I do: that Nick was a Napoleon, a Peter the Great, an Ozymandias, King of Kings. There are always visionaries around us just as great as these. Sometimes they are stalled in their greatness in a piping, weak and complicated time of peace; but others build empires bounded by the distance between their ears. As you read this there are epic struggles going on inside the bedroom of the house next door or in the office selling paperclips you pass each day on the way from *your* bedroom to *your* office. Matters of life and death rage over the coveted promotion, battles are won and lost over the vast landscape of where she will allow your hand to roam. The big is everywhere. Sub-plots are a device for books.

When he saw that he had no more worlds to conquer, Alexander sat down and wept. His hour had passed. But not so for the Alexander of the BFS. His Gordian knot is called The Video Recordings Act, and today behind his desk he contemplates an empire just within his grasp. But befitting the shape of things to come, this empire is not a place of vast lands, subject peoples, of spice and mine. It is a virtual empire. Before his time he sees that the battle over right and wrong and good and evil will not take place in trench and tank. The fight will not be on the beaches, nor will the war be in the air. This new invasion will be an invasion of the heart and mind. And he alone, Nick is convinced, can save the world. Out of the wilderness like many a saviour, false and true, he has come. The office in which he works is grubby, down at heel – it needs more than just a lick of paint to put things right. It seems an unlikely place for a messiah. But then this is the way of living gods in human history – how often they are forced to slum it at the lowest rung.

And then the call.

But who is calling for this cool and clever visionary? And what rough beast is Nick to save them from? Unquiet things are on the move, disturbed by the power of technology to dig and delve at everything the human heart desires.

Consider the video cassettes in 1984 available to anyone of any age from the local shop for 50p: *Cannibal Holocaust, Faces of Death; The Gestapo's Last Orgy* and *Eaten*

Alive; Human Experiments and *Blood Spattered Bride; SS Experiment Camp* and *I Drink your Blood*; and *Psycho from Texas* and *Snuff*. You get the drift. Some of it is feeble stuff, it's true, the experience, as with so many films, failing to live up to the hyperbole; hysteria abounds as the morally outraged claim the video nasty has replaced the conjurer at children's birthday parties. But the inferno of the moronic contains its talents, too. Four of these, at least, would make you retch. Unsuitable for kiddies, even the most relaxed would say. Even the majority of liberals, while wringing hands, could not gainsay that something must be done.

Who better than bright and reassuring Nick? Who could be more acceptable to left and right, to the outraged *and* the civil libertarian? He was, of course, extremely careful never to talk to either in the hearing of the other. In public he perfected the art of the self-cancelling vacuity. His convictions were firm but somehow in precise ways slightly out of reach. He was *for* protection of the young and vulnerable: he was against knee-jerk reactions that would offend our civil liberties. Everyone was sort of happy then, and as there was no one else to do the job, inevitably, like a ripe apple from the tree of the knowledge of good and evil, it fell with a comforting slap into the palm of our hero's hand. And with it came money – and with money came the means for Berg to realize his dream.

For it was a golden apple. Where before there were tens of films a month, now there would be hundreds, and therefore many thousands of chargeable feet of videotape a year. Licensed to print cash, Nick would pay wages that would attract the cream. And not just any cream. The cream that rises to the surface of the cream would be his aim. There would be a competition. A test. An Olympiad of cultural commissars. Only the very best would do. In every paper in the land the call went out – to psychiatrist and teacher, lecturer and wife at home; to left and right, to conservative male and staunchest feminist. To anyone who wished the chance would come. But they would have to fight. And only the fittest would survive. Only the very best. This Darwinian ruthlessness would give the Secretariat and Nick (and were they not the same?) something he had long desired. His real vision. Not just power, but a *just* power. Not just control, but a control legitimized by the fact that no one to the disapproving right and no one of the chattering left could stand against his acolytes of excellence.

Events moved quickly. Legal instruments were laid before Parliament. With a dazzling talent for minutiae, Nick baffled and bewildered politicians and civil servants as he fixes, alters, slides and tricks his way through every clause of the impending Act to give himself the power to do exactly as he wants. They learn, as many others will in time, that an argument with Nick Berg involves one usually in defeat, at best a numbingly perplexing draw. This was not because of the majestic nature of his predicates, the beauty of his axioms and dialectic genius. It was attrition that did it. He could coin an opening sentence with enough subordinate clauses to make Henry James weep with envy. He was a Hereward, a General Giap, an Erwin Rommel of negotiation. He would lead you into swamps of grammatical circumlocution, jungles of multi-layered analysis, deserts of parenthetical vast eternity. Ten minutes into a disagreement with Nick Berg and you did not feel as if you were losing the argument, you felt as if you were losing the will to live.

Then the great search began for his elite. The jobs were advertised. Three days a week his censors will work. But they are to get full-time money for this part-time job. They will be cosseted and rested – the two days free a week will keep them in touch with reality, with the common world. There will be seven hired.

And seven thousand applied for these seven jobs. And Nick was pleased. The Olympiad began. First the weeding out of applications. Thousands were culled, the no-hopers and the plainly mad. Then the remainder were re-read. And hundreds more were slaughtered even before they hit the beach. But there were massacres still ahead, for many were called and amongst the competent and thoughtful there were a dazzling array of talents and aptitudes – but even the excellent were scythed.

Then the interviews. Another cull. More interviews. Another massacre.

Finally there were fifty left. Over a week, they came in groups of ten and spent a day watching the unwatchable: guns blaze, knives slash, flesh tears. Every orifice is filled with every unimaginable thing. Hour after hour of demonic murderers and cannibals and pimps and sluts. And then the reports. What would you cut or pass? And how? And why? Prove to Berg that you are worthy of his trust.

Twenty were considered deserving of a final interview. And what an interview it was. Thirteen must fail at the very last.

And then it was done. Nick called the seven at home himself. Begin in a month, he said. And I was one of them.

We were quickly dubbed The Magnificent Seven by the examiners whom Nick had chosen during the previous ten years and who in turn had chosen us. Infected by his vision of a great union of minds he'd included them in the selection process; the interview board we faced consisted of all ten of them. This was smart because there was room for real dissension here. Nick had hired them through the years on word of mouth or a chance meeting with someone who'd impressed him. But they had not fought as had the Seven for their places and against such odds. By making them part of the process he'd given them a sense of power over us that was a useful balance to their sense of inferiority. I imagine all this stuff about how wonderful we were is getting on your nerves by now. Perhaps you've never been regarded as belonging to an elite – how many of us have? Not me before this I can assure you. So for a moment imagine what it would be like to have won your reputation in such a demanding way and to be seen and talked about as if you were special – and I mean in front of you, so you could hear. I ask you to be honest and admit that it would be pretty fine. So suppress your irritation with them and me for a few more pages – and not just because you know it would be nice to be regarded in that way yourself but also because it was to lead us into a fall as great as our present ascendancy. And even if you think it serves them right, spare a thought for me. Why? Because in good time you'll see that my pleasure at this unexpected goldenness was going to exact a terrible revenge.

Within a week Nick revels in the knowledge that he's been right. We are everything he wants and more. Our reports astonished in their brilliance and their wit. And strange as it may seem, no one seemed to envy or resent us. There was a sense from everyone that we were part of something that had never existed before. What Nick was setting out to do was to create an ideal state where for the most serious task of deciding what others could or couldn't see only the best was good enough. It was a Round Table, laugh if you will, and we were its knights and Nick, you had to hand it to him, was its king. I believed then that when we gathered for our first meeting this was as noble an enterprise as any ever set in place: a civilization speaking to itself – throughout its history the office of censor had been a byword for abuse of power, panic, fear and thoughtlessness and now it was about to change. The place founded in blindness was finally about to see.

That this must be a good thing you will agree no doubt. But you might want to consider that there are worse things than blindness – madness, for example, or death.

The Magnificent Seven

WHEN I APPLIED TO join the Secretariat I was working with the Civil Service at the Department of Education. I had spent five years as a teacher before joining them and had done well, moving quickly to a senior grade. I have an unusual talent. I'm good at everything. If this sounds vain, try to accept that I'm simply being honest – I took the greatest pride then in seeing things as they were, both about myself and certainly about others. I accepted straightforwardly that I was not outstanding perhaps, truly outstanding, at any one thing in particular, but much more than a jack of all trades. And, unusually, certainly for a man, I could keep track of many things at once. Why did I leave? Because I was bored and also because I fancied the idea of being well paid to watch films three days a week – who wouldn't? There was nothing more to it than that. I was pleased when Nick himself rang me to tell me that I had got the job but surprised when I told my colleagues where I was going. From the moment I explained what my new job was, people expressed interest, their eyes widened with something I had never seen in the eyes of anyone when I was talking to them about myself: fascination.

Perhaps you do an interesting, an unusual job, that makes people pay attention to you. Certainly no one had ever reacted to me in that way when I told them I was a teacher or a civil servant. I learnt a deeply unfamiliar satisfaction in answering the question, 'And what do you do?' at social occasions knowing that for the first time in my life I could almost amaze people. No one, no matter how superior they felt to me, no matter how much condescension was in their manner, could survive my answer with their smugness intact. No one had ever met a censor before, no one in a room of doctors, journalists, writers, architects and whathaveyous could claim to do something, no, more than that, to *be* something, so strange and so suggestive of arcane power. Go round the table at the last dinner party you were at and deny you would have been fascinated if one of them revealed they had the power to tell you what you could or could not see. Only a secret policeman might get the same response – but of course he would have to keep his interestingness, his power, hidden. Let me be clear that this was not why I had applied to the BFS – I had no interest in lording it over anyone; I wanted to watch films for a living and get paid a full-time wage for a part-time job. I'm just telling you what it was like once I had taken it. It was as if I had become visible to other people for the first time. I've had to think hard about what I felt and found myself slightly ridiculous (if it's any comfort) for realizing what it was. For the first time in my life I was experiencing what it was like to go into a room and become the centre of attention. I had become, in a minor way, I grant, but there is no other word for it, special. What had begun as an application on the off chance, a job for whose central purpose I had previously had only mild disdain, was beginning to work a curious magic on my soul. But curious is, as you will see, not the right word. Terrible, perhaps.

Because of the complexities of my job at Education it took time to finish off some of the projects I'd been working on and so I arrived for my first day at the Secretariat about two weeks after the others. It has been said that hindsight is an exact science. It isn't. I am telling you this story from a long time in the future and from the privileged position of ghost. I know many things now that I did not know then. But while I promise to tell you the truth as far as I know it, there are still things that are unclear because even though I am a ghost I am the remains of something that was once human. As I write I do so to purge myself of all self-delusion and to tell it to you straight. And all I can promise is to try to give you the best picture that I can.

That first day I was brought into the largest viewing room to meet the other six by the Assistant Director, Walter Casey, a welcoming pleasant man in his midforties. The six of them looked at me, interested and friendly enough.

Descriptions of people's physical appearance in stories are for me a bit like road directions: I forget them as soon as I hear them. But I'll try to give you something of the impression that I had of them as I faced them like a new boy at school. They were arranged around a large table and as Walter went from left to right then so will I.

First was Emma Saward. Her fine looks, to be honest, only struck me later. What I remember was her clothes. She seemed to have on too many. I don't mean she had on a heavy coat in a warm room, but that she was layered in waistcoats and tops and a long and frilly dress. To complete an outfit that spoke of a rather girly femininity she was wearing pink tights. The odd thing was that the hair on her shins was so thick she can't have shaved her legs for many months.

Next to her was Thomas Farraday. His hair and his moustache leapt out at me. It wasn't a modern face. It was the kind of face that stared out at you from imperial paintings of the nineteenth century – a look of absolute and confident belief in his presence as he sat surrounded by admiring brown people. There was no self-doubt in that weighing-up look of his, no neurosis. He was all there, solid as a tree.

The woman next to him is clear in her impact on me even now. Molly Tydeman was a stunner by any standard. This was not because she had made any effort with her appearance. She looked as if she had come from a funeral that was both laid back and yet required everyone to wear black. Black T-shirt, trousers, waistcoat, socks and shoes. Blackest of all were the pupils of her eyes – wide and fierce. Oh, and to be fair, to be open, even the shapeless cotton shirt couldn't hide that she had wonderful breasts.

Then Allan Rhys. I took a mild but instant dislike to him. Everyone of course was giving me the once-over, but he was trying too hard to show that he was doing it. And he had a beard, one of those devil goatee things.

Rob McCarthy stood at the far end pouring himself a cup of coffee. He nodded pleasantly as he sat down. But what made him different from the rest was how at ease he was physically. The others, with the exception perhaps of Rhys, gave off a sense of serious self-confidence. But McCarthy was different. I don't mean confidence so much as a pleasant detachment. He wasn't huge or obviously muscular, he just filled the space differently from the others. Yet even now I have difficulty recalling what he looked like.

And finally, Sadie Boldon. To be honest again, I had an

eye on her from the moment I walked in. And why wouldn't I? Sadie was a star, the apple of Nick's eye, his black and golden girl. She really was special and everything about the way she held herself, the smile with which she looked at me declared it so. It was not arrogance because she was a genuinely sweet person – it was something she just knew. And everyone else knew it, too. I can't be quite sure but I think that very deep down something moved inside me as I smiled at her, the beginning perhaps of all that happened subsequently. But I can't be sure, for Sadie's annihilation was such a complicated thing.

What was it like to be a censor then? It was bliss.

Have you ever been happy at your work? I mean truly excited almost every minute of the day. Was the cause of our delight the ecstasy of being killjoys, the pleasure in preventing the pleasure of others, the zeal of doing good by telling other people what to do? Certainly there was moral zeal at times but you'll see it was of an odd and convoluted kind. Just think for a second, there's nothing to it. Here were seven people being paid to watch the most disturbing films of the last ten years and sit and talk about them. During the next three months Nick wouldn't let us make decisions, he just wanted us to watch and write. But from the first he wanted us to be more than neophytes. We were, and he made it clear to us, to change the way things were done. We seven were meant to smash for ever the habit of repression, of thoughtless disapproval and of stupidity that hung around the office of censor. Nick had many talents but one of the greatest was his gift for encouragement.

'I don't want you to think like censors,' he said amiably the first time he came to talk to us, 'because I want you to change what it means to be one. I want to see what's possible. Don't worry about what I want or about the fuss going on in the press. That's my problem for the moment. Let's see what you can do.'

And that was what we did. We wrote down everything we saw in our red books – total immersion in violence, sex, depravity, controversy of every kind, all of it went down. Thump, splatter, howl, kiss, fuck, smash, splat, rip, beat, thump, screw, clash, bang, bash, belt, box, crack, knock, smack, sock, wallop, whack. Then we'd talk and then we'd write. At the end of the week he gathered all the examiners around the big table in the old boardroom and he read our reports to the others. There were two things to note about this. First, that he was excited. It's really quite something to know that the man or woman who's employing you is thrilled by what you do. You don't experience that kind of thing much in this country. People are mean here with praise, worried in case you might get above yourself or something I suppose. But it's the cheapest way I know to get people going – that bit of work you did was bloody good. It works better than money and yet it hardly ever happens. Think what it was like then to have a man like Nick reading the highlights from the preceding week and clearly delighted with every word.

The fact that Nick was also doing something else rather less generous didn't mean he wasn't entirely sincere. The thing about Nick was that he was *always* sincere, totally and absolutely, even when he was defending two or even three completely incompatible points of view. What else he was doing besides being nice about us was warning the others that there was a new way of doing things. And that they'd better realize it and raise their game.

The odd thing was, I don't recall there being any jealousy from the other examiners. Raising their game was what they did. They responded to Nick's vision and began

41

to write in a new way. The reports, much to the annoyance of the secretaries who had to type them up, became longer and longer. Then Nick would read out the results and then hand them around in batches thick as a Russian novel. The sense of doing something that had never been done before in a place like this was with us constantly.

During the first few weeks one thing that struck me was the skill with which Nick had made his choices. There were three women and four men and throughout the examining body he always kept it balanced between the sexes, or genders as Saward relentlessly reminded (it was a term I couldn't bring myself to use). But he balanced us in many different ways: there were conservatives with a big and a small C, feminists with a big and a small F, libertarians, *Guardian*-reading vegetarians, *Telegraph* readers who hunted with the hounds. But the thing is, despite the explosive mix of temperaments and attitudes, it was, in the early days, such fun. There was an agreement in the air to set limits on the importance of being right. It's hard to imagine zeal lying down with comedy, fanaticism cohabiting with wit. But here for a while they did – there was self-righteousness around and plenty of it but the laughs were able to keep the absolutes at bay. It was in the end a place of extremes and, as it turned out, of extremists. But for a while and for a long while they agreed to disagree, to go easy on the right to feel affronted. Here, for a time at any rate, it felt like being part of a civilization that had not forgotten what it meant to talk. That this round table fell apart was inevitable, but that it lasted as long as it did was rather touching in a way.

What did we see and talk about? Everything and anything. Blasphemy, sex (of course), violence (of course, as well), manners, morals, men and women, boys and girls, reason and intuition, modes of representation, blood and guts. And always in the end what the public would wear. I don't of course mean just the man or woman in the street, I mean the press, the cops, the politicians and anyone else who wanted to cause Nick grief. There were plenty of them. The censors' slow dance along the edge of taste and custom was always shimmying to a new and tricky tune. But it would have to be a tricky melody indeed to get the better of Nick's swerves and dips.

I like examples myself, so let me give you some. Within about three weeks we all began to notice trends and one of them was what we always referred to as the forcible exposure of breasts.

The Forcible Exposure
of Breasts

A WOMAN IN HER late twenties is moving through the rooms of her house. She is brunette and very pretty, a nice face, not stunning, but there's a sweetness in her, a real niceness. Her clothes reflect her pleasant simplicity. Her skirt is long, carefully pressed, her white blouse with pearlescent buttons is tucked carefully into her belted waist. She's neat, this girl. She moves around her living room tidying here and there and humming softly to herself.

Someone is watching. A shadow moves unseen. And then we have the watcher's point of view. The girl now seen through eyes that have no room for anything but envy. Envy of her neatness, her sweetness of temper, the bloom on her, something that he can never taste.

She hears something. Puzzled she moves to the kitchen and calls out. Is anyone there? But there is no reply. Nervous she moves towards the door to check it's locked.

Then something jumps in front of her. A scream. And then a laugh. It's just the cat. Sighing with relief she turns.

A man is standing in front of her. Too scared, too horrified to move she stands – her pretty eyes go wide. Terror. Rigid, she backs against the kitchen door. 'No,' she says. 'No, please don't, please don't.'

And then the hands reach for the white and buttoned blouse, slowly, deliberating. 'Please don't. Please.'

He puts his fingers carefully to the line of buttons on the front. Suddenly he tears.

At once her breasts spring into view. So white, so large, so unexpectedly voluptuous, the nipples darkest red against the whiteness of her blouse and skin. She tries to cover herself but he is irresistible and pulls her hand away. Her breasts heave and shake, the rest of her so prim, the breasts so white and then . . .

The picture freezes and it cuts to black.

'Tell me what you think,' says Nick to the seven of us.

There was a moment's hesitation, broken by Farraday.

FARRADAY

We should definitely cut it. I thought it was incredibly sexy.

The slight air of tension eased completely as the others laughed.

NICK

Anyone else agree?

MCCARTHY

I thought it was a disgraceful attempt to eroticize violence against women.

MOLLY TYDEMAN

In other words, yes.

MCCARTHY

Don't think I'm not ashamed to admit it, Molly.

Neither Rhys nor I did anything but smile, both of us less at ease with the women than Farraday and McCarthy. Emma Saward, however, looked annoyed.

45

SAWARD

I'm not sure as a woman I think it's all that funny. It's not a turn-on for us.

Farraday, as usual, was unfazed by the attack.

FARRADAY

What's the point of changing what's true? I mean it when I say it should be cut precisely because I can feel exactly what it's trying to do.

Rhys sniffed primly.

RHYS

I don't think it necessary, Tom, to be excited by this kind of thing. Its intentions are obvious, in my view. Whether it excites you or not. After all, the women here can tell exactly what this is doing without, as Emma says, being stimulated by it in any way.

MOLLY TYDEMAN

Since we're all being so honest, I have to say I was a bit turned on.

Everyone looked at her, McCarthy and Farraday with delighted interest, Sadie with surprise and Saward with both disapproval and confusion.

MOLLY TYDEMAN

Look, it's not men who buy bodice-rippers, is it? The idea of being swept away by a big strong man is clearly a pretty common fantasy.

SAWARD

Swept away is one thing, raped is another.

46

TYDEMAN

Women have rape fantasies too, Emma.

SAWARD

Some do – but they don't go out and get themselves raped, do they? That's the difference. Women, some women, have rape fantasies but that's all they are. Men fantasize about rape and then they go and do it.

Nick interrupted, soft and provocative.

NICK

Are you saying all men are rapists, Emma?

SAWARD

I'm saying that *some* men are rapists. I can accept that people can fantasize about all kinds of things they have no intention of doing. But some of them are clearly ready to act them out. This kind of thing takes it out of their heads and makes it public. It's for a male audience and it's clear what the pleasure is and it's an illegitimate pleasure if it's given a public space by being taken out of the private one.

I thought it best to say something, just to make my presence felt.

PURCELL

So we should ban bodice-rippers?

SAWARD

I can't see why people would want to read them myself, but it's women who read them not rapists. The plain fact is that there are plenty of them out there and I don't think we should be helping to break down the barriers between what they fantasize about and what they *do*.

SADIE

I agree. I must have seen four or five videos last week where

47

a woman was raped and screamed and resisted and then started enjoying it. That's a pretty rancid message to be putting out, and a pretty simple one. When women say no they mean yes.

The argument had settled down to one between the three women. But it was clear that something more than a difference of opinion was going on. I'd noticed on a number of occasions that Molly was irritated by Emma's way of co-opting her into the women's view. I doubt if she had any real disagreement with Emma over the rape scene; she was drawing a line between herself and the assumption that she belonged to a particular point of view just because she was a woman.

TYDEMAN

I'm sorry, but while, of course, I agree that on some occasions 'no' means 'no', it's just not human to say that it always does. Sometimes it means maybe. Sex is about power and it is dangerous and full of awkward feelings. The problem I have with blank assertions like 'no means no' is that they're so ... I don't know ... puritanical. They're not human.

The uneasiness was back now. Nick moved over to the VCR, replaced the tape and then sat down. 'This is the cut version,' he said and hit the remote.

There was the same build-up. The sweet young woman, innocently tidying the house in her modest but fetching clothes, the noise in the kitchen, the cat and then the turn to see the man standing in front of her. The violent and dramatic struggle was still there, but no sign at all of any interference by Nick, except that the sight of her blouse being ripped and her breasts, her beautiful and so soft

48

breasts, being exposed was gone. So skilfully had Nick erased it that you would have had no idea of what had once been present – where there had been a rape, explicit and prolonged, there was now only homicide.

He switched it off. 'Any comment?'

TYDEMAN

Look, I'm not bothered that you've done it. But it strikes me that you've gone beyond being a censor, beyond marking out society's disapproval. This isn't a cut rape scene, it's an ordinary murder. You haven't just removed something, you've changed it into something acceptable.

FARRADAY

Molly's got a point. Shouldn't you let the people who would have enjoyed this—

MCCARTHY

People like you?

FARRADAY

Exactly. Shouldn't you let *us* know you've cut it, that you're on to us and that you're here watching and making it clear these pleasures are unacceptable and they . . . I mean *we* . . . should be ashamed of ourselves?

Nick laughed and looked at his watch. 'Interesting point,' he said 'but I don't have time to answer you. Thank you,' he said to us all. 'Very stimulating.' And with that he was gone.

Shock Corridor

ABOUT A WEEK LATER Rob McCarthy found himself with five minutes to spare before what was referred to as 'morning prayers' began – a short meeting when the censors got together and the day's work and any news was handed out. He quickly ran up to the fourth floor, knocked on Nick's open door and popped his head around. Walter Casey and the Deputy Director, Beth Ackroyd, were both there. They stopped talking immediately as if they were doing something shameful.

'Can I help you, Rob?' said Nick, oddly but still pleasantly enough.

'Here's the book I was telling you about.'

Nick looked at him blankly.

'*Both the Ladies and the Gentlemen*.'

'Oh, thanks.'

It was obvious he had forgotten about their conversation the week before.

'Better get to work,' said McCarthy.

Downstairs at the meeting he mentioned the strange way he'd been received and both Farraday and Sadie Boldon picked up on what he'd said immediately.

'I went to talk to Nick a couple of days ago about an

article of mine in *Sight and Sound* . . . whether I should put that I was a censor in it . . . what the form was about such things, and he was really strange about it.'

Farraday too had talked to Beth Ackroyd about a holiday he was arranging at Christmas and she too had seemed incredibly flustered.

It was Allan Rhys who put his finger on what was at the back of people's minds with a kind of grim satisfaction he always maintained when he thought he knew something unpleasant that other people didn't.

'I don't think they're going to confirm all of our appointments when our three-month probation is up. That's why anything about the future has them so uneasy.'

As it turned out he was wrong. But the strange atmosphere increased in intensity over the next few weeks. It came to a head one evening when we came upstairs from the viewing rooms and found that each of us had a white envelope in our pigeonholes. Inside was the contract we should have had when we arrived for our three-month probation, and a long and staggeringly complicated letter with it, although the bottom line was clear enough. We had all been sacked.

You will be able to imagine our shock and horror. What you won't be able to grasp, because I'm still not entirely convinced I've grasped it myself, was the reason why it had nothing to do with the seven's disappointing performance – that would have been at least a comprehensible explanation. The problem, as it turned out, had its roots in something that Nick had neglected to mention at any time during the arduous and lengthy interviews we had all attended, nor at the time when he had offered us the job. The BFS had always been a body set up by the film industry to keep the government off its back in a way that might prove least damaging to its commercial interests. It had no legal status: it was a gentleman's agreement. But while films were still to be governed by this agreement, it was not the case for videos. The infinitely greater danger that videos were held to represent – of which more later – required in any case new legislation. This time the government was not going to be caught out by handing over its powers to a series of local democracies who had only shown a talent for buggering things up. This time it would keep an eye on things by allowing the old BFS – the gentleman's agreement BFS – to continue while the same organization also became a legally empowered new BFS. It would be in the same place, employing the same people and the same bureaucratic structure, but be, in law, when categorizing video, an entirely different institution. Confused? Just wait.

This, of course, required masses of new legislation that had to be agreed between Nick and the government, between the government and Parliament and, of course, the thorn in the side of any modern ruler, the press and the pressure groups.

I have already said something about Nick's genius for legal complexities. I've been involved in some tricky legislation myself as a civil servant and can well attest to the mind-numbing dreariness of even simple legislation. I did some work on the infamous European banana protocol – such a thing exists I assure you – a document so thick with labyrinthine entanglements that it's almost four times the length of *War and Peace*. Consider what it meant, then, that Nick could outbyzantine civil servants who sharpened their teeth daily on this kind of thing. But he did. Bureaucrats who grew faint with pleasure at the thought of a sub-clause on the maximum amount of mechanically recovered meat permitted in desiccated bovine food supplements would emerge from a meeting with Nick feeling like a virgin after a night with one of the undead. But even the greyest bureaucrat has his sticking point, his this-far-and-no-further line in the sand. After a couple of years of being frustrated by Nick they were fed up to the back teeth with him – their horse's head in the bed, their fish wrapped in newspaper, came in the shape of labelling regulations.

Curiously enough their reprisal was only possible because of a quality in Nick I've noticed across the years in lots of people: it turns out that their sticking point, *their* line in the sand beyond which nothing can persuade them to pass is often astonishingly trivial. I've done it myself, got in a no-surrender spat over nothing much. It's usually a last-straw kind of thing, I suppose. You've had enough of backing off and make your stand over whatever issue happens to be around. But that doesn't explain how they put their finger, as it were, on Nick's ability to self-destruct. It was just luck, I think. I didn't understand then and even when I think about it now I ask myself whether I'd missed the point somewhere, that there must have been a serious issue buried in this catastrophic row. But there wasn't.

The row was over this: Nick had decided that all video cassettes and all the boxes they were sold in were to have their certificates – a 'U', a 'PG', a '15', an '18' – printed four times on the box in letters and numbers of a particular size and twice on the cassette itself. Do you care? You would if it cost you your job. The civil servants at first mildly disagreed but Nick, righteously refusing their suggestion to reduce the number of times the certificate was printed and the size of it by a quarter, wrote a lengthy and indignant reply. It was absolutely vital that he had his way on labelling. 'Never let your enemies know what you're thinking,' said Vito Corleone. Wrong, Vito. Limited though my experience of hits and offers you can't refuse might be, it's never let them know what you're *feeling*. The civil servants realized that the labels really deeply mattered to Nick, not least because his written reasons extended to more than ten pages. God knows how. So that's how they stuck it to him. He refused to accept their amendments to the number and size of labels and because of this nail the war was lost. If Nick wouldn't sign off on the labels then the whole legislation couldn't be laid before Parliament to become law. With this session of Parliament about to end, the bill would fail. There would be no law compelling the distributors to pay to have their videos certificated and no one with the legal power to do so if they did.

Although we knew we were on three months' probation, it turned out that Nick had neglected to make it clear to us when we were offered the jobs that they were dependent on the BFS becoming a legal entity in the present Parliament, something that, as we could now painfully see, was not going to happen.

The next morning after we received the letters firing us, we all gathered, angry as hell, in the boardroom and waited for Nick to explain. What, we demanded, was going on? At enormous length we got the story about the labels. You can imagine the mixture of bemusement and sheer incredulity we felt: not only were our jobs going down the pan, but the entire future of the Secretariat itself, and all because of this bloody nonsense about labels. Nick was, and I still can't quite believe this, exasperated at our failure to understand the importance, the absolute *centrality* of the size and placing of the labels. It was *obvious*. The explanation went on and on, and then on a bit more – and all of us, despite the painful immediacy of

54

what was at stake, began to be overtaken by the fog of ideas, the miasma of notions that poured out of Nick. Being subject to one of Nick's explanations when his back was to the wall was like trying to find your way through a labyrinth designed by Daedalus and fabricated entirely out of murk.

It's no easy thing to give you a sense of the numbing nature of someone's conversation without boring you at the same time. And in any case this isn't really an issue of personal dullness because in ordinary conversation he was stimulating and witty. You have to think of him as employing a deadly poisonous logorrhoea fitted to a particular end – he was a cobra who used obfuscation to paralyse his prey. The thing is you could no more get a sense of what it felt like to listen to him by reading what he said than you could get a sense of Mozart's genius just by looking at a manuscript of his Requiem. You had to hear it to understand. But let me try.

QUESTION

But, Nick, why is the size and number of discs detailing the certificate so fundamentally important?

NICK BERG
(patiently)

It is essential that it is clear for the protection of children that at no point can there be any confusion about the certificate that we have given the feature whether it is in the box provided by the rental company or for retail at the point of sale where it needs to be considered that many of those either in the retail or rental outlets will not themselves be eighteen and may be considerably younger. Neither parents nor children nor teenagers under the age of eighteen at the point of sale or rental are under the meaning of the act regulatory zygote coterminous viscosity vituperation amalgamate

55

calumny aqueosaline peroration declivity but umbilical retrograde idealization nomenclature wobble backwards as well as desensitize psychological retroactive legislation in camera episodic ambiguity lifelong terminology intermediate pre-empted 1947 backlog forty nimrod dissent labelling malfeasance derogation consignment obscene publication act test minor blah blah blah blah blah blah blah blah blah blah blah blah blah blah blah blah blah blah blah blah blah blah blah blah blah blah blah blah blah blah blah blah blah blah blah blah blah blah blah blah blah blah blah blah blah blah blah blah blah blah blah blah blah blah blah blah blah.

QUESTION

I'm sorry but I'm still not clear why it's so important that you're prepared to let the bill fall and ruin many years' work.

NICK BERG

Let me clarify that by legislation in camera episodic ambiguity lifelong terminology intermediate pre-empted backlog responsibility labelling malfeasance derogation consignment coterminous guidance blah blah blah blah blah blah blah blah blah blah blah blah blah blah blah blah blah blah blah blah blah blah blah blah blah blah blah blah blah blah blah blah blah blah blah blah blah blah.

It was Farraday who snapped out of this hypnotic disbelief first and berated Nick roundly for firing us on such utterly trivial grounds.

For once, Nick was lost for words. But not, as we thought, because righteous indignation had made him contrite. He looked at Farraday with a strange squint, caught between launching into yet another epic attempt to explain that the labels were in no sense trivial and deep confusion. The latter came first.

'What do you mean?' he said at last. 'Fired you?'

Now it was our turn to be baffled. It was Rhys this time.

'The letters we got in our pigeonholes, Nick. We're going to lose our jobs. We've been fired.'

'You certainly have not,' he said. Again an astonished silence – but quickly broken.

'Will you please explain, Nick.'

'It's very simple. You weren't fired, you were given a contract.'

'I'm sorry, I don't understand.'

'The letter inside was a contract for three months. That's what was in it. I gave you a contract for three months that comes to an end four weeks from now. I certainly didn't fire you.'

'You did fire us.'

He almost laughed in exasperation. 'You have a contract for three months. How is that firing you?'

You can be sure that the meeting went on to become even more heated, but it needn't be repeated here because it never got anywhere. We furiously insisted that we had been fired for something trivial. He more calmly insisted, increasingly more in sorrow than in anger, that labelling was not trivial and that – sigh of exasperation – we had not been fired.

At any rate, our deliverance from redundancy came from an unlikely source. As usual, whenever the British decide that a committee must be formed because Something Must Be Done, sooner or later that most galling of British institutions The Great and the Good has to get its snout in the trough. Nick was obliged to appoint a presidential tier of three people in order to oversee himself and make sure he behaved. What kind of idiot, I wonder, thought it would be useful to allow a man who needed overseeing to appoint the people to oversee him? Nick, of course, chose as carefully as you might expect. They were people who looked good on paper: former Governors at the BBC, children's charities, government committees of this and that. And, because Nick was a bit of a snob, two of them were Peers of the Realm. But he made sure that none of them knew anything about films and that they weren't much interested in any case. Fifteen and ten thousand quid respectively for twelve days' work a year – Nick knew they wouldn't be rocking any boats, and they knew he knew it, too.

Shortly before Nick was to confront the civil servants in a final meeting where he was determined not to budge, his mother had a stroke and he had to rush down to somewhere in Cornwall to be with her. To the meeting in his place went the President, Lord Joyce. Speaking as a life-long republican I loathed him on principle, but I'm glad to say I loathed him personally as well. Joyce had in abundance the one quality you can always find in the English aristocracy no matter how bluff and friendly they might seem: an iron, self-serving ruthlessness. Within twenty minutes of the start of the meeting, Joyce had utterly destroyed Nick's stand and saved our jobs and transformed our lives. Odd that. And the thing is, to be fair, I don't think for all I've said about his ruthlessness, that he did it just to preserve his fifteen thousand pounds. I got the sum of what happened from Beth Ackroyd a few years later at a party when she'd had a bit too much to drink and was pissed off with Nick for something or other. It turned out that after a few pleasantries and some other business, the Home Office officials had coughed, straightened their backs and made their position clear.

'I'm afraid, Lord Joyce, we have to insist that the labelling regulations stay as they're outlined in our proposal.'

'Really?' replied Lord Joyce. 'Oh, very well then.'

And that was it. Our jobs were saved, the future of the Secretariat assured.

Why had he done it? Partly, I think, it was the very thing I loathed about him – aristocratic indifference to what anyone else thought about anything. Nick had given him the same elaborate explanation of why the future of civilization depended on the size and number of the labels in the box and on the video cassette – but though he wasn't stupid he had a limited attention span and it wasn't hard to switch off when you were forced to listen to this kind of lunacy. I think, in the end, he thought it was all total balls, which it was, and he simply couldn't care less what Nick would say.

When he returned and found out what had happened, Nick had a conniption fit. 'Oh really, dear boy, was it important?' said the Lord, charming and insincere. But there was nothing to be done despite Nick's sulks and within a couple of weeks the bill went into law and we got our jobs back. This was not how Nick looked at it – we couldn't get our jobs back because, of course, we had never lost them. We were simply, in his view, given new contracts.

Up till then we'd had every reason to think the world of Nick so this experience dealt our confidence in him a hefty blow. But only half of what happened had any significance as it turned out. Curiously, throughout the next ten years I never saw this self-destructive aspect of his character again. This is pretty odd when you think about it. After all he was not only ready to get rid of us, he was absolutely prepared to see all of his work of the last ten years come to nothing just as he had his hand on this great prize of legal status, absolute control over everything seen on tape in the country and immense power to see his vision of the world happen in reality. How many people, even at a minor level, get to say something and for that something to be so? Yet he was prepared to see his empire fall for nothing. This is a weakness so striking you think it would be bound to dog him all the time. It didn't. He never did anything like this again. I suppose there are things in the human character like knots in wood, they're just there, a malformation in the character of a man or woman that is isolated in some way from the rest of them and only freakish and unpredictable circumstances make you aware of them. A fault that *was* consistent with his character, however, was his horribly wacky attempt to claim he was not firing us. This was no isolated flaw: self-regard was the very grain of Nick's character. He was morally vain through and through and so much so that even something as formally stupid – is there another word for it? – as claiming he was giving us a contract rather than firing us couldn't shake his need to be doing the moral thing. I remember years ago during some interminable television debate over the right and wrongs of abortion – I don't know why I was watching it, I couldn't care less either way – at one point someone said that abortion couldn't be a morally evil thing to practise because as a liberal he would never agree to doing something evil. Whatever your views are on the matter you have to admit this is a pretty bizarre kind of reasoning: *what I'm doing can't be wrong because I'm not the sort of person who does wrong things*. A lot of people I've met turn out to think this way, but Nick was the Babe Ruth, the Pelé of such com-placency. It never ceased to amaze me with what natural ease he took the ethical high ground in any argument. For Nick Berg his moral compass was always pointing north.

So it was back to work. But it wasn't all sex and violence, not by any means. The Video Recordings Act made it a requirement that as well as our seeing all new films the backlog of all the films that had ever been released on tape also had to be seen and certificated within two years. There was lots of sleaze to see, it's true, but in my first year I was actually paid to watch *Citizen Kane* and *The Terminator*.

The problem we were there to solve was this: the police were seizing *Cannibal Apocalypse* (crap), *Zombie Apocalypse* (nasty and crap), *Nightmare Apocalypse* (boring) and *Apocalypse Now* (one of the greatest films ever made). To be fair, after a couple of weeks they realized their mistake but the fact that they made it in the first place indicated something of the problem of putting the police in charge of such matters. The courts weren't any better. A jury in No. 2 Court of Leicester Crown Court at 11.45 a.m. found *I Spit on Your Grave* to be obscene. In No. 3 Court at 3.15 p.m. the jury decided it was not.

When people talk of moral panic there's usually something thoughtless about the assumption – as if it were self-evident that other people are becoming hysterical about something that doesn't exist, like witches. These concerns are usually further condescended to by being explained as displaced alarm about something else. For those who talk about moral panic there is never anything to be worried about, except, I suppose, for the things they worry about which are not, of course, caused by hysteria or displacement. Moral Panic is to the right what Political Correctness is to the left – things rooted in fear, only peculiarly different kinds of fear. People morally panic about witches, communists, race, pornography and violence. People are politically correct about race, of course, but not witches or communism, and they are deeply alarmed about violence but only to women. If you think the latter judgement harsh let me tell you a story. I was out with my wife one evening, celebrating as it happens my appointment to the Secretariat. After dinner we went to a pub and as we were drinking I looked around and noticed a couple in their mid-thirties and on the other side of the narrow room another couple in their early twenties. Both couples were affluent and from their demeanour and clothes appeared to be middle-class. What had alerted me to looking around besides my boredom with what my wife was saying was that the younger couple were having an argument. I don't mean a slanging match but the girl was clearly upset.

Then she picked up a nearly empty pint glass and smashed it in his face.

I don't think I have ever witnessed anything more shocking, I imagine because it was so utterly and completely unexpected. The four of us looked on as the girl, deeply distressed, stood up and ran to the toilets. The man she had struck in this staggeringly violent manner was looking at her, as she vanished, with a mixture of confusion and dawning horror as he really rather slowly absorbed what had happened to him. The blood from his cuts started to pour down his face but all he did was continue to look astounded. Two things happened: the barman rushed to his aid and so did the middle-class woman in her thirties; or so I thought. But she didn't stop at the young man's table but without looking at him rushed after the girl and also vanished into the toilets. The barman, now joined by the landlord, attended to the bleeding young man by holding what looked like a clean white bar towel to his face which soon blossomed with red. The landlord left to call an ambulance and, one presumes, the police. My wife wanted to leave but I said that we were witnesses and ought to stay. Reluctantly persuaded by my completely insincere urgings she agreed.

About five minutes later the middle-class woman returned and pointedly did not look at the glassy-eyed and softly groaning young man in the corner. She sat down and said with the deepest concern and the most sincere reassurance to her partner: 'She'll be all right.'

In defence of her partner, I should tell you that he looked at her as if she were insane.

So having stated my reservations about accusations of moral panic there was nevertheless an atmosphere of moral panic about video and it affected everything we did. I don't mean that Nick let the hysteria get to him because he didn't. But he was playing a pragmatic and political game and all of us began to play it too.

The Secretariat's view went something like this: some of the things we see are reprehensible and dangerous; some of the things we see are reprehensible but so badly done they're ludicrous; some of the things we see look as if they could be reprehensible but in fact are works of merit, great or small. Until The Video Recordings Act came along the job of deciding what was obscene or not was solely the responsibility of the police who brought prosecutions and the courts who decided whether to uphold the charges at the subsequent trial. In law, to put it simply, something is obscene if it is held to have the power to deprave and corrupt the viewer. That's it really. The main defence is that the work in question has artistic merit and therefore . . . well, I'm not quite sure what the law argues after the 'therefore'. I've asked legal authorities about what the real nature of the defence is and there's an assumption that if something which is potentially depraving and corrupting – say the moment in *Gestapo's Last Orgy* where a naked Jewish woman is lowered head first into a glass case of rats – takes place in the context of a film where this appalling scene is meant to make clear to the audience in various ways the depth of the cruelty of fascism, then this would be a defence on artistic grounds. However, if it is present only to pander to the prurient sexual sadism of the audience and there is not, as it were, a redeeming saving grace, then it would be obscene and it's eighteen months for the distributor – take him down bailiff and may God have mercy on his soul.

If you actually had to watch *Gestapo's Last Orgy* (Nazis eat unborn Jewish baby at banquet, mother and daughter tied together and forced to have sex), I don't suppose anyone would be likely to argue that there was much of an artistic defence under the obscenity laws, whatever you might think of the notion. You might reject the idea of obscenity altogether, thunder against the absurdity of the cops and men in wigs judging artistic merit, as being akin to a taxidermist or a ferret-handler judging Olympic high dives or skating on ice. But that's the defence in law and in the case of *Gestapo's Last Orgy* there wasn't one. Therefore it was obscene. Therefore it was banned to the public.

It was only years later when I read the Act more carefully that it occurred to me that there were two ways of interpreting it. The artistic merit clause in the legislation seemed to me to argue that a scene in a film could be depraving and corrupting but if the film taken as a whole was deemed a serious work then, as a whole, it was not obscene. A film not guilty of obscenity could be likened to a husband with one or more moral defects but who, weighed in the balance by his wife and taking his virtues into account, was, taken as a whole, judged to be a worthy spouse.

Nick, on the other hand, simply ignored this interpretation, or rather didn't see it at all. Nick didn't believe, as a court always does, that whoever is in the dock is either innocent or guilty; Nick believed in reform. He interpreted the law as saying a work had to be wholly pure in order not to be obscene, and decided that his function was not to balance the errors of moral judgement in a film against its merits and let a bad scene go because overall it was an honest film. His determination was that such films could be made honest. He would cut and trim the scene so that its merit could shine through unaffected by its moral errors. The films would be banned only if they were seamlessly vile. Nick was a tough-love liberal who believed in improving as many of the cinematic social deviants who came before him as he could. Their moral shivs and flick knives would be taken from them and they would be released into the community without the means to stab or cut. Unlike the cops or courts or his pre-decessors, Nick liked films, he was on their side, he wanted them to be released. But if their morality was flawed in ways he thought would harm, he surgically removed the threat. That was the deal. That was the way it was done. Moral surgery was what we did and the need for an operation, of what kind and how deeply we would cut, was what we talked about. At first the talk was passionate, but then over the years it became heated. And finally, the talk became murderous.

Cutting Up Women's Bodies

It is something of an understatement to say that feminist film critic Laura Mulvey has had an extremely significant impact on academic studies revolving around film, gender and the dominating power of the male gaze. Mulvey states that men have the power, pleasure and active control of the gaze, while women have become the objects of that male-centred gaze. In psychoanalytic terms, this process is known as scopophilia: the focusing on others as if they are objects that exist purely for our viewing pleasure.

Sadie Boldon, 'Feminism and Film: an introduction for the BFS'

'HELLO, SADIE, WE WERE just talking about you.'

Sadie had come into the clapped-out boardroom. It was piled at one end with furniture and TVs because the building hadn't caught up with the increase in the number of people who worked there or the wall of money that was beginning to move into the place and which would, in time, transform its appearance. For the time being the offices in Golden Square were grubby and mostly cramped. Smiling, Sadie sat down with her sandwiches.

'Whatever it was, I'm sure it was generous.'

Farraday looked pained. 'We're fans of yours.'

'Great fans,' agreed McCarthy.

'We were discussing your intro on Feminism and Film.'

'This is a wind-up, right?'

'What makes you think that?'

'I wonder.' She bit into her sandwich, eyeing them suspiciously but not with any great alarm.

'Rob', said Farraday, 'doesn't really understand it.'

'Don't get me wrong,' interrupted McCarthy. 'I know the male gaze is a bad thing. I'm just not entirely sure why.'

'Yeah,' said Farraday. 'We know we should be ashamed but we don't really understand what it is we should be ashamed about well enough to be as deeply ashamed as we ought to be.'

'I mean, we ought to be ashamed, am I right?'

'Definitely.'

'So how do we stop – gazing.'

Sadie looked thoughtful as she took another bite of her sandwich. 'It's too late, in my opinion. You're both too old to change now.'

'That's what I said,' laughed McCarthy.

'There you are, then.'

'But I want to change, Sadie. I want to be good.'

'That's nice – but I mean it, it's too late.'

McCarthy, who always seemed to have a cup of coffee in his hand, stood up and got a refill from the machine in the corner. 'I realize we're beyond help but I'd still like to understand because I'm not clear about the gaze. I mean I've heard loads of women— Hello, Emma.'

Emma Saward came in carrying two huge plastic carrier bags of food from Marks & Spencer. Sadie and Emma had become great friends and without speaking Emma took out a flimsy plastic tray and placed a large ripe peach on the table in front of her. She smiled at the two men. 'Would you . . . ?' They both shook their heads. Sadie took a bite out of the peach and laughed as the sweet juice dribbled down her chin.

'I've just been telling the boys that they're too old to stop focusing on women as if they were objects that exist purely for their viewing pleasure.'

'And don't forget,' said Farraday, 'we also cut women up into parts that we can fetishize and therefore control.'

'We're heartbroken about that in particular,' said McCarthy, mournfully.

'I'll bet,' replied Emma, laughing.

'I was just going to ask Sadie, so I'm glad you're here,' continued McCarthy, 'to explain how come, if it's all down to men looking at women – I mean, how come I've known loads of women who say they don't dress up for men they dress for other women? Explain that. There must be a female gaze. But that's not bad?'

Emma sat down and started to try to open a plastic triangle of M & S sandwiches.

'It's still the male gaze, Rob,' she said, concentrating more on the package which seemed to have been designed not so much for keeping the freshness in as for keeping the customer out. 'The thing is that women who dress for other women, they're just internalizing the role of the one who's defined by being looked at, the role that men have created. The other women, too, they're just carrying the male gaze inside themselves.'

'My God, I never realized I was so powerful,' said Farraday.

'Yeah, that's a bit of a problem for you both, wouldn't you say?' asked McCarthy. 'Doesn't all this make men staggeringly potent and women just passive victims?'

'Not if they start to become aware of the process and refuse to go along with it.'

'But come on, Sadie,' said Farraday. 'Forget women

dressing for women. They look at men too. I saw something on TV a couple of months ago . . . *Horizon*, I think . . . where they strapped a small camera to the side of a woman's head – one of those tiny things, hardly weighs anything. Then they got her – and they repeated this dozens of times with different women – to go into a party where there were loads of men. Before they did this they asked the women what they found attractive in men, what they looked at first and they came up with the usual stuff: eyes, nice face and smile, and the occasional honest one who said they looked at their bum. So off they go with the camera and it's got this little cross-haired thing on it so you could see exactly where they were looking and how often. And, guess what? The first place all of them looked, *all* of them, was the guy's groin.'

Sadie laughed out loud but Emma looked uncomfortable.

'The point is,' came in McCarthy, 'there's a biological imperative to looking, not just a cultural one. Men and women are always checking each other out to see if they'd make suitable mates. Forget Ms Mulvey and start reading Darwin.'

'And there's another thing . . .'

Sadie groaned. 'For God's sake, give me a break, you two. Nick asked me to write a paper on feminist film theory and that's what I did. I didn't say I agreed with it all.'

'But *some* of it!' said Farraday, as if he'd produced the vital clue to a murder.

'Yes, some of it. So what? You're just a pair of old dinosaurs. I wouldn't expect you to take on board something that threatens your sense of superiority.'

'I'm hurt that you should say that, Sadie.'

'I'm more hurt than he is,' said McCarthy. 'I'm genuinely

trying to make up for all the time I've oppressed women but he's just pretending. I don't like to say this about a man I've come, and I'm not ashamed to say this, a man I've come to know and love, but he's unreconstructed.'

They both started giggling at this.

'You're like schoolboys, you two,' said Emma. 'Always whispering and talking at the back of the class.'

'Can we eat our lunch in peace now?'

'Just one more question. Please, Sadie?'

'Get on with it.'

Farraday picked up her report and flicked through it. 'Here it is.' He began quoting. ' "However, Mulvey states that the function of woman as voyeuristic spectacle poses a deeper problem for the male viewer because she does not have a penis. Indeed, in psychoanalytic terms this is a scenario that suggests a threat of castration and therefore 'unpleasure' for the male viewer." '

'Yes,' said Sadie. 'And?'

'Well, the fact that Mulvey or anybody else *states* something doesn't make it true or even plausible. I can *state* that I've got fairies at the bottom of my garden but so what? I mean, come on, you two, you don't actually believe this stuff?'

'Don't we?' asked Emma.

'I don't know. Do you? It's just an assertion, that's all, and a bloody silly one, let's face it.'

'If it was true you *would* say that, wouldn't you?'

'Come on, Emma . . . If the sight of naked female genitalia were really threatening to men because it made them fear castration then why would they spend so much time trying to get into women's knickers, let alone spend so much money buying magazines and videos full of close-ups of them? I mean call me a big girl's blouse if you like but I hate spiders. I don't go obsessively ferreting

70

around in my cellar in order to try and come into contact with them. I don't buy magazines with enormous close-ups of black widows and tarantulas. I avoid things that scare me and so does everyone else.'

Sadie sighed, mildly exasperated. 'Now you've had your fun will you both shut up and let me eat my lunch in peace.' She turned to Emma and rolled her eyes. 'Honestly, what a pair of nags.'

The unusual thing about these debates, and there were many of them, is that they were pretty good-humoured on the whole. But this wasn't the case elsewhere. People have forgotten, I think, how vexed and angry all this was, how puritanical and fanatic. I'm not an optimist. My sense, for what it's worth, is that things, just things generally, are getting worse. It's not just that there's nothing on the telly, but that what is there is poisonous: stupider, more malicious, less intelligent than it used to be. And every-where else, the witless world of celebrities and fame, of nosiness and cruelty. There are those letters for celebrities: A B C – but it's *all* C list. It's a C-list world, C-list ideas, C-list art and C-list eyes to look at it all. OK. All right. I'm just a terrible old git moaning about the way of the world and how it's going to the dogs. But one thing isn't. One thing, I have to say, I am compelled to admit, has got much better. Women and men have got better. I don't mean that they aren't fucking each other up the way they always have, but it's a lot better than it could have been. It's a lot better all round than it was in the eighties, hardly any time ago. Then there was a lot of hatred for men and it was OK. You could say 'All men are rapists' and no one would lock you up. During this time my sister was at university and, in her feminist theatre group, she admitted that she'd shaved her legs. And there were angry scenes.

There were condemnations. She was denounced. My daughter was a toddler at the time. Now she's a teenager, and when I told her about all this she looked at me as if I was mad. As I tried to explain that people were passionate and angry about these things, I started to wonder if I was exaggerating, because what I was saying sounded so ludicrous. But I wasn't. Real hatred was involved in the matter of hairy legs. She thought it was funny. She's lucky to be able to think so. Perhaps what's happened between men and women in little more than a decade shows that it's possible for things to get better, more generous, wiser. And you have to say they are. What if the hatred had won out? It usually does. In 1984 it still looked as if there was going to be a hundred years' war between men and women. But it stopped. I just want to say – not just to convince you but to remind myself – there was a lot of real fanaticism about then which made it seem more touch and go than now seems possible.

The Kingdom of Caring

ALLAN RHYS WAS A libertarian. If this suggests that he was
something of a free spirit it would be understandable.
Liberal, liberator, libertine – all of them have the notion of
freedom from restriction at their heart. He was Welsh,
brought up in a particularly strict form of Calvinism which
held that the notion that God loves everybody is a vile
heresy. He had rejected his upbringing only in the sense that
he no longer believed in God or a prescriptive moral code,
but in other ways he was unchanged: he simply replaced
dour Protestantism with dour licentiousness. He harangued
in defence of his libertarian views with the gusto of any
bible-basher; listening to one of his diatribes was like hearing a sermon from an apostate John Knox, dogmatically and
glumly arguing the case for an increase in the amount of
genitalia in this video, for more gratuitous violence in that.

Let me be clear about this. Allan was not a comparative
libertarian; it was not that he was unusually permissive by
the standards of a censor (in the sense that someone
might be peculiarly tall for a jockey). Allan didn't believe
in *any* form of censorship. I'm not entirely convinced that
he even took the view that its practice was justified in the
protection of children, that if someone had earnestly

suggested to him that no harm would come from, say, an eight-year-old watching *Cannibal Zombie*, he wouldn't have smiled in his you-and-I-know-that-but-do-they manner and shrugged. But I might be wrong. Please be clear that I'm not accusing him of being a hypocrite, or rather I am, but not accusing as such. After all I don't think there were all that many at the Secretariat who had a real belief in censorship. They accepted it, they weren't *against* it, they might even on occasion, such as on the banning of *Gestapo's Last Orgy*, have censored with a certain grim enthusiasm; cutting the protracted rape of women filmed entirely as an erotic display caused no one to have a sleepless night. But there was no eagerness, by and large. Had they not found themselves with the chance to watch films for a living, most of them would never have thought about censorship except, perhaps, to think badly of it and those who carried it out.

So we were all tarred with double standards to some extent. It was not humbug that I would criticize Rhys for. In fact, I'm not criticizing him at all really, except that the complete lack of sincerity in his daily life, even to the often bogus sacred mantra of the protection of children, left him stranded in an unusual way. The thing is, that sincerity is a pretty useful quality in life, not just because it's a good thing to mean what you say but because it's very hard for people to make up something completely out of nothing. To adopt a pose, professional or otherwise, without at least some sense of what it would mean to genuinely be that person is extraordinarily difficult. In my experience even a homeopathic dose of honesty goes a terribly long way when you're telling fibs. But Rhys's life was a lie in a very pure way and this made it very hard for him to do his job. With even a mild concern for the proprieties of children watching things that are unsuitable for them you can easily build a comprehensive and coherent system of concern that is a guide when deciding if this thump is too hard, that sight of a breast too risqué, this use of a naughty word probably inappropriate. Lacking any internal standards of this kind, Rhys was at a huge disadvantage in just a practical sense. He was like some working-class scholarship boy come to Oxford and on his first visit to High Table, gawping at the incomprehensible array of cutlery next to his place: he could recognize the knife but had never seen tongs for holding snails or the pliers used for cracking lobster claws. Rhys was reduced to an immensely sophisticated form of watching what other people did. I don't mean during a particular film or video, I mean he learnt as he went along, imitating the rules that others used. Sometimes it was simple: the use of the word 'fuck' made it a '15'. And he was easily intelligent enough to calculate what a sincere moral response might be even in complex situations and get it right. But it was a profound pretence, like being a double agent, and sometimes he picked up the wrong cue and got things wildly wrong. He was like a trapeze artist who had enormous technical skill but absolutely no *feel* for the art. The result was that sometimes he just fell off.

The most spectacular of Rhys's disasters came a couple of weeks after a Secretariat meeting where Nick had tried to rescue the 'U' classification from being completely swallowed up by the Parental Guidance category. The original idea for there being two types of children's film was based on the perfectly reasonable notion that parents would be able to make a better choice about whether a film was suitable for their kids if the mildly scary, that would be all right for younger children, was distinguished at 'U' from the more disturbing that would suit the stronger nerves of older children, up to the age of the next category at '15'. As this was a pretty broad age range it was no easy task, though clearly a useful one. The problem was that this useful distinction failed to take into account the natural desire of people not to get into trouble. The thing was, if you passed a film 'U' and it had some element in it that might frighten even a small number of scaredy-cats with hysterical mothers, then a fair amount of grief could come your way in the shape of indignant phone calls or outraged letters. Nick had ruled that the examiners responsible for a film complained about should answer the letters personally. This might seem fair enough but the real problem with this was that he insisted on reading the answers first and he inevitably asked for changes. He would then check those changes, ask for more, and so on, a process that could go on for weeks. Given that by making something 'PG' it excluded nobody, imposed no costs on parents or children, and was guaranteed to avoid any comeback, it was unsurprising that examiners gradually slipped into finding any excuse possible to pass a film 'PG'. The result was that the 'U' category had become almost redundant. The idea that the system should give useful information so that most parents could distinguish between the upsetting but manageable (say, Bambi's mother being shot off-screen) and the not quite terrifying enough to ban everyone under the age of 15 (say, Robert Shaw being eaten alive on-screen in *Jaws*) was entirely lost.

Realizing the problem, Nick had given everyone a talking-to in which he explained how he had been influenced by child psychologist Bruno Bettelheim's *The Uses of Enchantment*. Bettelheim argued that the frightening aspect of fairy tales enables children to recognize that by facing up to powerful enemies and dreadful hardships, and overcoming them, they can be helped to deal with the

inescapable difficulties of life. Inevitably enough someone had then pointed out that in 'The Steadfast Tin
Soldier' and 'The Little Match-Girl' nobody overcame
dreadful hardship, they just died. This pointless squabble,
the hazard of having hired so many competitive know-
alls, bounced around for a bit before a (justly in my view)
exasperated Nick pointed out that he was making a really
rather simple observation: that it was perfectly acceptable
that there should be an element of the upsetting even in
'U' films and that we should all keep this in mind.

The trouble was that all he did was urge a change. He
didn't do anything about making the perceived dis-
benefits of sticking your neck out any less weighty.
Examiners took a distinctly non-Bettelheim view that the
best way to deal with this particular problem was to run
away. Not so Rhys. Having, as he saw it, been given
permission for once to follow his natural instincts, he was
instantly converted into a disaster waiting to happen. It
duly did.

Two weeks later he was down in the theatre watching a
Disney short film, *Frankenweenie*, by a new director called
Tim Burton. This is Rhys's synopsis of the story.

12-year-old Victor Frankenstein is mad about horror films
and makes his own versions of classics such as
Frankenstein and *Dracula* on his Father's eight-millimetre
camera. The star of these is always his beloved pet dog,
Sparky. When Sparky is run over, young Victor is heartbroken. But then he has the idea to dig him up and
resuscitate his best friend with electricity. Sparky isn't
quite as good as new now that he has numerous stitches
and a bolt through his neck but remains the best friend a
boy could have. Sadly, he terrifies the neighbours who, in
a reprise of the original film, attack the Frankensteins'

house in order to destroy the devil dog. This time, all ends happily as they realize that appearances can be deceptive and that Sparky is still the faithful and friendly dog he used to be.

The at least notionally senior examiner watching it with Rhys was Jenny Manzi who, when the film was finished, spent five minutes with Rhys discussing how much they admired what Burton had done with his witty replica of the 1930s classic and then proceeded to OK the passing of it at 'PG'.

'Why not pass it "U"?' he replied.

She looked at him, bewildered. She pointed out the scary effects, the death of the dog, the gothic nature of the pet cemetery where Sparky was buried, the bolt through the neck, the scars on his body and so on.

Rhys listened to all this with patient condescension and then pointed out that the film dealt with difficult subjects such as death and the fear aroused in others when they encountered someone different from themselves. By resolving these problems happily, *Frankenweenie* was almost designed to fit into Nick's injunction that the Secretariat should be passing such films at 'U'. When he felt in control of a situation, Rhys shed both his reticence and his tendency to finger-wag, and affected a kind of quietly compassionate bombast. He would nod his head sympathetically at each objection. 'I know,' he would murmur agreeably. 'I understand what you are saying, but don't you think . . .' and then he would proceed to lay out his case in detail and with great skill. But for those who weren't entirely sure of themselves it was the tone that got under them, the sense of feeling slightly stupid, lacking in insight or backbone. Within ten minutes Jenny had signed it out at 'U' and that was that.

Their reports were read, of course, and had it not been Disney, a byword by then for everything unadventurous and bland, perhaps a question or two might have been asked. But, after all, the reports pointed out that it conformed entirely to the arguments that Nick had recently and so forcefully brought to everyone's attention.

The problem was that no one had told the public or the distributors about Bruno Bettelheim. The wishy-washy nature of the 'U' had become part of the culture by this time. And unfortunately for Manzi and Rhys, the distributors assumed the 'U' meant harmless pap and so *Frankenweenie* went out with *The Care Bears Movie*.

The Care Bears live high up in a country in the clouds, a particularly good vantage point for hearing, on the day their film was released, the screams of terror of thousands of tiny tots who had come along to the cinema for an entrancing encounter with Love-a-Lot Bear, Tenderheart Bear and their pal, Cozy-Heart Penguin, only to be traumatized by a confrontation with a dead dog covered in stitches and with a huge bolt through his neck.

Not only were the phones jammed by calls from mothers incandescent with rage but the papers got hold of the story.

THE CENSOR'S LOST HIS HEAD, screamed the *Daily Mail*.

For the only time in its history the Secretariat withdrew a film and raised its category. At the next Secretariat meeting the two hapless examiners were obliged to sit through a showing of *Frankenweenie* while the category issues involved were given a lengthy airing. The other examiners took great delight in the discomfort of both Manzi and Rhys. But curiously, and rather sweetly I thought, Nick was neither mocking nor angry. He recognized that he had encouraged them to be braver in their decision-making and even if he hadn't intended something quite as reckless as this, he only, and very mildly, pointed out that they should have referred such a difficult film directly to him. And that was the end of it.

There was a memorable coda to this fiasco. A few weeks later, as always, we started work with the most important ritual of the censor's day: checking the schedule to find out what we were going to be watching for the next six hours. The hope was that it would be the latest Scorsese in the cinema, the dread (more often fulfilled) was that it would be watching two Bollywood films back-to-back on video.

It was on this very matter that Peter Kyriacou – originally hired to watch Greek-language videos that never actually materialized – was complaining to Walter Casey: 'This can't be right, Walter.'

'Really?'

'You've put me down for three Hindi videos. Christ knows it's torture watching just one of the fuckers.'

Walter looked at the list, at first sceptical and then puzzled. 'You haven't got three.'

'Yes I have. Look.' He jabbed irritably at the list. '*Janam Se Phele Sholay*, then *Deedar* and then *Dheena Duos*.'

Walter started to laugh and called over Mala Ishara, the most senior of the four people who simultaneously translated the vast number of Indian-language videos that came into the Secretariat. He nodded at the list. 'Tell Pete what Dheena Duos means.'

'How would I know?'

Pete looked puzzled.

'It's not Hindi,' said Walter. 'Dheena, I suspect, being made up, and Duos as in coming in twos. I think you'll find when you look at the tape it's being distributed by Double D Productions. It's a sex tape for men who like big tits.'

He turned back into the room and raised his voice: 'Morning, censors,' he said cheerfully. Everyone gathered around and he started handing out various documents and giving out general information. 'And finally before you go, you might like to know the result of a problem raised by Allan Rhys. Obviously concerned for linguistic standards at "U", Allan rightly referred on a sequence in a Tintin cartoon that, despite repeated playing, he couldn't decipher. After considerable efforts by the technical department the offending words turned out to be "mint sauce"'.

Rhys was ruefully gracious about the resulting laughter.

'So,' continued Walter, 'not offensive in any way, unless of course you happen to be a gambolling lamb.'

We dispersed to our day's work. As it happened my partner was Rhys who complained mournfully that he was never going to be allowed to forget the problems over *Frankenweenie*. I wasn't really listening as my day in the cinema consisted only of one film, some piece of what looked like utter drivel called *The Terminator*, yet another thug-brained splatter-fest fuelled by revenge and no doubt needing endless cuts to make it suitable for the viewing by drunken C1s over a six-pack of Carling Black Label and a late-night curry.

Two and a half hours later we emerged from *The Terminator* having not only had a wonderful time, but having been paid for it. This was one of the great pleasures of working there. Because films submitted to the Secretariat often arrived without any publicity, frequently many months before they were released, we came to them with an innocence that is now impossible. These days you've already seen half the film in those ridiculous trailers that give away everything – and if they don't, the reviews do. But imagine what it's like to know nothing about what you're going to see and then watch *Blood Simple, Raise the Red Lantern* or *The Terminator* unfold unexpectedly in front of you.

What I loved, even about the trash, was that you couldn't choose. Everyone else can. In fact you can't avoid it. And there's a terrible limitation in this choice, precisely because you have one. You're always going to consult yourself, *your* preferences, *your* tastes, *your* self. So you only see what's predetermined by who and what you already are. Your capacity to choose condemns you to watch only the kind of things you watch. But someone chose for us. We were assigned our daily films and videos arbitrarily by others and so were obliged to watch things that we would often have chewed off our own arms to avoid. Everyone else had the free will to follow the exact path of what they already were. But our way was full of the shock of the unchosen. It disrupted the predictability of one's inner life, the inevitable blinker ordained by one's preferences for this or that. The censor is at the forefront of an epic anarchy. And if you disagree then wait and see.

So, full of delight at our discovery of *The Terminator*, we collected our stuff and headed back to the video viewing room to watch a couple of episodes of *Mission Impossible* (the TV series), an episode of *Fireball XL5* and a trailer for *My Fair Lady*. As we came into the corridor, we saw Rob McCarthy hiding behind a pillar and staring through the window of one of the viewing rooms, almost overcome with laughter. On seeing us he gestured that we should move forward slowly to join him. As we did so it became clear what had caused him such amusement. It was certainly a bizarre sight.

I had noticed on the work sheet that Farraday had a solo day that consisted entirely of kids' cartoons, including the infamous *Care Bears Movie* that had skewered Rhys. He was not, however, watching a video. He was sitting with a look of intense concentration on his face, pushing a biro in and out of the anus of what appeared to be a moderately sized teddy bear. Rhys and I watched with an open-mouthed astonishment that only made McCarthy worse. Able to contain himself no longer he burst into Farraday's room and shouted: 'You fucking pervert. Leave that teddy bear's arse alone.'

Still shoving the biro in and out of the toy's rear end, Farraday looked at him with distaste. 'It's not a teddy bear, it's a Care Bear and it's broken.' He stopped as the insides of the toy began to click and whirr and in a high-pitched whine it declared: *'My name's Love-a-Lot Bear and I live in the Kingdom of Caring.'*

'Just like us really,' he said triumphantly and gave the biro another shove.

'My name's Love-a-Lot Bear and I live in the Kingdom of Caring.'

Last Tango in Paris

THINGS SETTLED DOWN FOR a while after that, with only a song at the Christmas pantomime to show that what had happened over the dismissals had neither been forgiven nor forgotten. The panto featured skits of varying degrees of skill ranging from the mediocre to the downright embarrassing. But the spoof version of Gershwin's 'Let's Call the Whole Thing Off' written and sung by Farraday and Molly Tydeman as the incompatible lovers was something else again. The first verse went:

> You say 'fellatio'
> And I say 'blow-job'
> You say 'contract'
> And I say 'no-job'

The rhyme was so perversely unexpected – timed with wonderful sweetness by Molly – that the entire room erupted with hoots of delight. Even Nick himself smiled, if barely. But he left soon after.

With the bill now signed into law we were inundated. The video industry had held off sending in their tapes, leery in case the legislation would fail, but now we were desperately trying to catch up with a backlog that stretched as far back as *Birth of a Nation*. (A deeply unsettling film, this, as you realize that the structure of almost every film ever made began here. Its radical sophistication is all the odder as you watch its drunken darkies doing the jigaboo and the Ku Klux Klan presented as saintly heroes.)

Parliament had agreed a complicated timetable for this catching-up process, the upshot of which was that we were trying to do three things at once: pull in the videos like *Zombie Apocalypse* and *Driller Killer* that had never been released on film and were the true target of the legislation; rewatch on video all the films previously seen by the BFS on film and give them a new video certificate; and finally watch nearly everything that was not a film but which was taking advantage of the new life offered by a new medium. What this meant was watching *Postman Pat*, *The Good Life* and made-for-video sex tapes. As a result a typical day's viewing might be: *Zombie Flesh-Eaters*, *The Magnificent Ambersons*, *Nasty Nurses* and *Thomas the Tank Engine*. You may smile wryly at such a specifically modern concatenation of the ghastly, the inspired, the lurid and the infantile – but this daily contact with the inferno of the contemporary led to something more unpleasant than the usual injuries of the workplace.

But stuff like this is still a few years away and for the moment we are watching films and being paid for it. And when it came to *Thundercats* and *Pingu* a careful thumb on the fast-forward button eased the workload which could be pretty stiff if you had a 'problem' video. Some 'problem' videos weren't actually much of a problem to be fair. Videos set in a Nazi concentration camp where the women prisoners were crucified and had their breasts cut off were not much of a predicament. Agonizing, to be frank, wasn't something in these circumstances that we really, any of us, went in for.

But the purity of response offered by a Nazi rape camp video was less frequent than the *Daily Mail* might have you believe. The tidal wave of filth turned out to be more an occasionally heavy swell than a wave, more grubby than revolting. It's not difficult to accept that genius is rare, so why should evil genius be any more common? There's an assumption that ennobling the human spirit is difficult, depraving it is easy. But I've been there on the coal face of the corrupt and most of it is dross: dull, poor, inept and flat. All too often it produced more of a tendency to fall asleep than a tendency to corrupt. Malice is not enough, nor greed. It takes skill to deprave and in the foundry of feculence that was the BFS much of it was sorry stuff. But it took time to write about and most of the time what you had to say was that while *Zombie Biker Sluts* or *Snuff* tries hard to deprave and to corrupt, it really does, it miserably fails. It's too lame, half-baked and badly done. Evil in intent, no doubt, *Nazi Holocaust* or *Driller Sluts* still needs something more to rot and poison the human heart – talent might do it but there isn't any.

So what to be done with the underachievers in the Grand National of filth? With a kind of heavy heart we give them the chop along with the rarer types: the evil good. And why a heavy heart? I suppose because it gives them a seriousness, a gravitas, they didn't deserve. Still they get the bullet on political grounds alone. Witless they may be but they don't *sound* witless. No one at the BFS is unaware that politics is what we're playing with. In a climate of hysteria and panic, wasting such capital as we have on arguing that dross cannot be depraving hardly seems sensible. We keep our powder dry, or so we tell ourselves, for films that might be worth the candle.

Sadie Boldon, however, managed to make these deliberations even more complicated. Sadie was a fan of horror films and refused to allow us to make the distinction between malign and skilful, and malign and crap. There were, she insisted, films of real merit which might share all the obvious features of what she insisted on labelling 'so-called video nasties' (in order to distance herself, as far as possible, from her uneasiness about being the handmaiden of the *Daily Mail* or Mary Whitehouse). She claimed *The Texas Chainsaw Massacre* was an American gothic masterpiece that reflected the fears of its audience. Those who wanted to reject the film, on the grounds that it led the viewer to identify with the monstrous aggressors and to enjoy the infliction of terror and pain on the innocent victims as they are slaughtered by the cannibalistic occupants, were missing the complicated points of view on offer.

She argued, convincingly it has to be said, that it was obvious that even a child watching *Star Wars* was at one level identifying with the heroes but at a deeper level also identifying with Darth Vader as a figure who realized all the negative feelings of hate and destruction naturally felt by any child on a daily basis. Darth Vader costumes were given to little boys at Christmas. This was not some arcane film theory but obvious to anyone who had any experience of children and a point made more or less continuously in *Star Wars* itself about the conflict within Luke Skywalker. And if this is true for the young it's also true for everyone else that in complex ways we also move our identification right across the spectrum of goodies and baddies.

SADIE

The rationale for banning *The Texas Chainsaw Massacre* –
(smiling sweetly)
– which is to say Nicholas Berg's rationale – is that the film
channels the identification of the viewer towards the aggressors, inviting them to derive pleasure from the
terrorization of the helpless. What I've been arguing today is
that this is far too simple a way of defining this particular
film. In parenthesis I'd like to demonstrate my credentials as
a censor by pointing out that such an analysis is, in my view,
entirely justified for such films as *Gestapo's Last Orgy* and
House on the Edge of the Park. These two in particular lie
outside the horror genre and misuse it by appropriating –
one might say pillaging – gangster and rape-and-revenge
genres as well as pornography in a way I'll examine in more
detail later.

The Texas Chainsaw Massacre is a pure horror film, if that
doesn't sound too Leavisite: simply the most successfully
terrifying film of modern times. Detailed in a strikingly
minute way it allows the audience to terrify themselves with
all their worst fears about living in a family. The relationships
between its monstrous and grotesque characters form a
frightening though witty parallel with the sometime horrors
of what we are pleased to call ordinary family life – the
exclusively male-bonded household with its strange order,
the sibling rivalry, the homespun creativity involved in the
carefully arranged but awkwardly built ornaments made
from human remains, and strict demarcation of household
tasks: one brother is the cook and cannot step outside this
role, another is the provider of food, another a long-haired
artist who gets the family into trouble by rebelliously
practising his 'art' in the local graveyard. There is the pride
in the continuing maintenance of proletarian work skills
(grandpa was the best cattle slaughterer at the local

abattoir). These are not glosses on a terrifying or disgusting film but the source of the audience's ambiguous horror and delight. No one who has ever told a ghost story to a group of simultaneously frightened and ecstatic children can fail to recognize this or claim that what I'm arguing is the product of some new-fangled uncommonsensical film theory. Not that I'll hear a word spoken against film theory.

In this last sentence she mocked both herself and the other examiners, chiefly Farraday and McCarthy, who were always winding her up about her passionate belief in the importance of semiology and deconstruction.

She didn't deny that the film was hard to take but her patient mockery of our attempt to write about it as if it were *Pride and Prejudice* was hard to dismiss. The trouble with Sadie was that unlike most of the apologists for this stuff she was smart and she could write. And she convinced as well.

Nick had actually been taught by F. R. Leavis himself, and it's important if you are unfamiliar with this world that you know Leavis was a man admired and loathed in equal measure. Depending on whose view you listened to he was either an influential literary critic who paid such close attention to words and their connections with ideas that he changed the way we read, and who asserted that art must be morally serious; or he was an impossibly authoritarian, claustrophobically book-based literary critic who detested cinema in particular and who asserted that art must be morally serious.

It was entirely clear that Sadie was aiming her jibes directly at her employer. But she had a point. Nick had a tendency to talk about even porn films as if they were Victorian novels with plots and themes and moral out-looks, like once respectable women who had taken to earning a living on their backs. The thing was, Nick adored her and even if he was the object of her criticism, his vanity (he never really believed he was wrong) and her charm (she could imply that anyone who disagreed with her was a conceptual cretin hidebound by outmoded intellectual concepts with so much sweetness that you forgot you were being insulted and instead felt you were being gently teased). She was the beloved daughter and he was, if not her beloved father, then certainly her protector. Sadie liked to be admired, was used to it. Like some beautiful, proud and insolent Siamese cat, she expected to be stroked. It's an odd thing but I've noticed that while powerful people love, of course, to be praised they also like to be teased, as long as it's the kind of teasing that confirms their power and your respect.

A tradition had grown up at the BFS that anyone could respond to something they heard and wanted to comment on by writing a piece and putting it up on the notice board. At any one time there were half a dozen of these conversational pamphlets pinned up. A couple of days later McCarthy had put up a piece gently mocking Sadie about her presentation on the horror film. As he came downstairs for lunch he found her reading it and laughing. She didn't say anything to him but only smiled as he came up behind her and read as she read:

Despite Sadie's elegant claims for the horror film and its subversive role in cinema it strikes me on the contrary, as someone who has only seen large numbers of them recently, how deeply conventional they are. Taken as a whole their rigid sense of social order wouldn't raise an eyebrow at a Hapsburg garden party. Vampires are aristocratic and therefore few in number, as well as being acutely careful about the kind of people allowed to join their ranks. One of the reasons they're prepared to choose the virginal daughters of the upper middle class, like Mina Harker, is because they've never worked for a living and haven't had sex with someone who has. Vampires are exciting and powerful and wouldn't dream of having furniture in their castle that wasn't inherited. The real reason they can't enter a victim's house unless they are invited is because they're terrified that otherwise they might be mistaken for a common burglar. If you want to be safe from vampires you needn't worry about garlic or crosses, just wear a polyester shell suit, or as he's about to bite your neck ask him if he'd like a serviette.

Werewolves, however, are innately less well-bred and tend to be middle-class professionals. Jack Nicholson in *Wolf* works in publishing. No wonder vampires detest them.

Zombies are working class. They slouch and mumble incomprehensibly and have all sorts of disgusting skin problems. They smell of course and absolutely anyone can be a zombie. They breed like rabbits – and, my dear, their shoes!

As for the family in *The Texas Chainsaw Massacre*, the horror they generate lies not in the repressions of the nuclear family but through their dark echo of the social anxieties of the college student victims' upwardly mobile mothers who must surely have warned them about the unpleasant consequences of going into the homes of their social inferiors.

When she finished she laughed and looked at McCarthy. 'You don't think that underneath the surface irony of this –' she nodded at the typescript on the board '– your own fear and self-loathing may be just a little transparent?'

He pretended to be offended. 'Leave my fear and self-loathing out of this.' At this point Farraday came through the door and smiled as he saw them both. 'Please, sir,' McCarthy said to him in the tone of a bullied child, 'Sadie Boldon's showing off again.'

Still, much as we all admired her, her insistence that we treat the nasties with more care meant that watching them took even more time if Sadie and her growing band of devotees were not to chastise you at the weekly meetings. Let me be clear: it wasn't that she was feared but that the place buzzed with the idea that this was someone special, that something new was happening, that Nick's dream of excellence was something attainable. It wouldn't do if you were a believer not to do your best to respond to her. But not all, as it turned out, believed.

At any rate, finding time to write at great length was a priority, so Postman Pat and Tintin were even more prone to the fast-forward treatment. The trouble with mis-behaving, however, was that sometimes you got caught.

'Could I have a word, Tom? You too, Rob.'

Walter Casey beckoned Farraday and McCarthy into his office and shut the door. The two men looked at each other knowing some kind of ticking-off was imminent.

They were an odd couple: the immaculately educated and wealthy Farraday was the last person you would have expected to be such close friends with McCarthy, whose boast was that he was the only person at the Secretariat with a qualification in metalwork. It was confidence as much as anything that made them close – neither of them seemed to have any idea what it was to doubt himself. They were careless about what other people thought. And it wasn't a pose or defensive stance – they really didn't care. But they were nice about their complete arrogance, there was an adolescent innocence about it. For all their intelligence, Emma Saward was right, they were basically the two bigheads at the back of the class.

'Do you two remember,' asked Walter, 'a tape you watched together about three months ago, *Rupert Bear and Little Yum?*'

Both men shook their heads.

'Then let me refresh your memories,' said Walter. 'This is Rob's report.' He picked up a single sheet and began to read:

Rupert chooses to disobey his friend, Officer Growler, and the laws he represents in order to free a rare baby abominable snowman from the influential Sir Jasper. However, it's only when he plays by Growler's rules that Rupert realizes that, although it may seem slow, the law is fair and does punish the wrongdoers.

Comment.
In next week's episode Rupert visits a courtroom and helps a friendly judge sentence the Guildford Four.

By the by, despite Noddy having recently been banned by some libraries because of racist stereotypes (golliwogs to you and me) it's interesting how much more subversive Enid Blyton's Noddy is than Rupert Bear, and not only by comparison. PC Plod, as his name suggests, is slow and stupid and unalterably prejudiced against Noddy who, it has to be said, is a cheeky little sod.

Pass Uc Uncut

Walter switched on his video recorder and a tape began to play of Rupert talking to his father in his study. Walter turned the sound down.

'Anything strike you at all?'

The two men looked carefully.

'No.'

'Come on, Walter, don't fuck about. The suspense is killing me.'

Walter froze the tape and handed McCarthy a magnifying glass. 'Have a look at the books in the case behind Rupert's dad, third shelf down.'

McCarthy did as he was asked. There was a brief pause and then he burst into laughter.

'What?' said Farraday, trying to take hold of the magnifying glass.

'Get off, it's mine.'

'Perhaps,' said Walter, 'you'd like to read the titles aloud.'

'Um . . . *Lesbian Nurses* by D. L. Doe, uh . . . *Spanking Nuns* by Rosy Bottom, and . . . ah . . . *The History of Knickers* by Ivor Pussy.'

All three of them were laughing now as Farraday grabbed the magnifying glass and looked for himself.

'You passed this "Uc" – especially suitable for children.'

'Fuck off. You can't blame us for missing this,' said McCarthy.

'Can't I? I'd like to point out, Trotsky, that if you'd spent less time wagging your finger at the English legal system and more time watching the video you might have spotted it.'

'You bloody liar, Walter. You didn't see this either, did you?'

'Only because I trusted you two to do your job. A trust I can now see was misplaced.'

'Come on, how did you find out?'

Walter handed Farraday a letter that had been lying on his desk. Farraday unfolded it and began to read aloud.

Dear Sir,

Having watched 'Rupert Bear and Little Yum' with my son I am appalled that you appear to believe that the titles of the books in Rupert's father's library are in any way appropriate for children. Perhaps you think that this kind of schoolboy smirking about sex is acceptable. I find it distasteful at any category. I accept that I'm out of touch and old-fashioned but I fail to see how you can justify jokes about sexual perversion in a traditional children's cartoon. Is it too much to ask for an explanation?

Yours sincerely,
Emma Johnson (Mrs)

'The explanation, you mad old bat,' said McCarthy shaking his head, 'is that we didn't see it. The real question is how the fuck did you?'

Farraday looked carefully at Walter who, while amused, seemed to be taking the letter seriously.

'What?' said McCarthy.

'She has a point,' replied Walter.

'You're not serious? We needed a magnifying glass. No one could spot the titles.'

Walter smiled. 'Obviously that's not true, is it? *She* did.'

'OK, mad mothers who watch children's videos through binoculars. How many of *them* are there?'

'There only needs to be one. The point is that a parent has drawn our attention to the presence, however cheeky, of a series of references to spanking, female genitalia and sex toys. The category "Uc" stands for "Universal: especially suitable for children". You passed it "Uc". Frankly I don't see we have any choice but to call the tapes back in and raise it to a "PG".'

'You're kidding!'

95

'Not really.'

Farraday gasped in exasperation. 'If you pass it "PG" how are people going to know what for? There'll be ten tapes or whatever at "Uc" and one at "PG" warning that there are scenes that may be unsuitable for children, but no explanation as to why. Because nobody else is going to spot them, are they?'

'Probably not.'

'Definitely not.'

'You can't be sure of that. I agree it's pointless at one level, but suppose she writes to the *Daily Mail*. Consider the headline: "Censor passes lesbian sex as especially good for children"'. Walter sighed. 'Come on, boys, you know it makes sense. Change the category and one of you writes to Mrs Johnson and apologizes.'

'What?'

'What else do you suggest?'

'It's OK,' said Farraday, 'I'll do it. Something along the lines of . . . Dear Mrs Johnson, I can't tell you how sorry I am that you ought to be in a mental institution . . . that sort of thing.'

'You can sneer, both of you, but strictly speaking it's your job to spot it – and *she* did. If she's mad, what does that make you?'

'So, you want us to watch with a telescope from now on?'

'Bugger off, Walter. You wouldn't have spotted it either.'

'Probably not,' he said thoughtfully. McCarthy and Farraday laughed and admitted defeat. 'You can change the paperwork now and I'll send the letter up to Nick on Friday.'

Farraday looked surprised. 'Christ, it's like being back at school. Don't you trust us, Walter?'

Walter looked at them both and smiled. 'Absolutely not.'

* * *

What really convinced Farraday and McCarthy to back down was the stuff about the *Daily Mail*. Now that most shops on the High Street no longer sell video recorders it's been generally forgotten how deep and strange the fear of them was and how this fear reignited older fears about television and the corruption of children. Why? Well, there were plenty of theories at the time about cultural hysteria, fear of the modern, the reinvention of the demonic in human life and so on – but I won't go into all that now. But it was intense, mad even. There were red triangles on Channel 4 warning anyone who might stumble across a late-night film that something wicked was on its way. It seems now to belong to another era – like having someone walk in front of a Model T Ford with a red flag. And darker fears were on the move. Rape of children's minds was one thing but it presaged a deeper, darker dread. Something much older and stranger was abroad – shadowy threats were coalescing into something solid, something *there*, something happening in England *now*.

Of course, the thing is that any office will be a theatre for dramatic stuff: all workers fight, fuck, make friends, succeed and fail, have breakdowns, betray and are betrayed – oh and have a laugh, enjoy themselves, get paid. But the thing about the Secretariat was that it had all this and then it added what it did, what it was *for*. It was a clearing house for the modern. Pretty much everything that was the case in the twentieth century was funnelled through its doors in one form or another. We swallowed this stuff for years and it isn't good for you at all. I know that now.

I watched an adaptation of Kafka's *The Trial* at work once and I was struck not by its nightmare lack of logic, its arbitrary punishments, its pointless rules, but by how familiar it seemed, how realistic it was. I've worked in offices now for twenty years and reading *The Trial* again a few days after I watched it at the Secretariat it struck me as both funny and hardly exaggerated at all. Mad and absurd it may be but I've come to see the lunatic and the preposterous as typical, day to day. That's how we live, that's how we are. Don't get me wrong. I know the mundane, the ordinary, the normal, the admirably simple, the commonsensical, I know they're just as real – but the customary world lives cheek-by-jowl with the frenzied, the ludicrous, the rabid and the mad. And everybody gets to share in this, no one is free of the hysteria generated by the war between sanity and madness that plays out everywhere around you in offices, marriages, schools and hospitals and pubs and bars and . . . you get the point. All you need are the human equivalent of a spring tide and a bigger than usual storm at sea – that's when the floods swamp and the sea walls fail. It doesn't really take all that much. Just patience.

I like examples myself. So let me give you one.

About two years after the Magnificent Seven had finally been appointed, we were all gathered together in the boardroom to listen to a couple of psychotherapists and a psychiatrist from the Farber Clinic in Islington, a health institute that specialized in the adult victims of child abuse.

After an hour during which they discussed the effects on children of watching video nasties, they began to move the subject to an area that at the time I had never heard of: satanic child abuse.

We listened with astonishment as they told us about one patient, a woman in her early twenties, who had revealed that she had been subject to this kind of ritual cruelty since she was a baby. By the age of six she had been forced to have sex in every conceivable way in front of her own family and that of many others. The older girls in the village, a place entirely given over to these practices, were deliberately made pregnant. The children who were born as a result were either cooked in a microwave and force-fed to other children or kept solely for acts of sexual devil worship. The girl had run away aged nine after she had been tied to a table and had numerous billiard balls inserted into her both vaginally and anally.

There was a complicated silence after they had finished. Some were deeply upset, others disturbed but clearly mystified. Eventually Allan Rhys with an impressive lack of sensitivity spoke up. 'Did you report her claims to the local police?'

One of the shrinks, a woman, looked at him, the expression on her face that of someone who had a taste for instructing others in the depths of human cruelty, for shocking her listeners into silence. 'All the local police were involved.'

To her obvious disappointment this failed to provoke the aghast reaction she had been expecting.

'I see,' said Rhys, matter-of-fact. 'What did the police at regional level have to say?'

This time it was the psychiatrist, a man, who replied. 'A number of the abusers were policemen at regional level.'

'And higher,' chipped in the third woman.

Horrified by what they had said and affronted by Rhys's unwillingness to react appropriately, as she clearly saw it, Emma Saward interrupted to voice her support. 'It doesn't seem to me to be at all surprising that the police should be involved so deeply in this. It's a fundamentally patriarchal organization – look at the way they deal with rape victims.'

There was some head-nodding at this because there had been a huge outcry after a fly-on-the-wall documentary on the Thames Valley Police Force which had exposed a way of dealing with rape victims that beggared belief: cruel, cynical and inept.

Surprisingly, it was Sadie Boldon who challenged her. 'Look, you won't get any arguments from me about the disgraceful way the cops treat rape victims, but I have to say that I'm still reeling from the claims you're making.' She looked directly at the three shrinks. 'I mean, we've got good evidence of the disgraceful way some of the police behave towards victims of sexual assault – but I think you have to provide something pretty solid when you're talking about senior police officers being involved in cooking and eating babies.'

The two women looked affronted, even betrayed, that a woman should doubt them – but the man was more conciliatory. 'I understand what you're saying. I used to be sceptical myself, but I've heard these things too often – seen the terrible psychological damage inflicted – not to accept that what we're telling you is all too horribly real.'

This time it was Farraday who replied. 'We're censors here – of course we take a dim view of human nature – we make a pretty good living out of the belief that people are capable of anything. A great-uncle of mine died at Treblinka so I'm perfectly happy to believe in the bestial nature of mankind. What I want to ask you here is for evidence of this. There must be vast amounts, if it's as large a conspiracy as you claim.'

'We've explained,' said one of the women coldly. 'The police in the area are part of this. How can we get it investigated?'

'Go somewhere else,' said Rhys.

'You don't believe us,' said the man. 'Neither does anyone else.'

'OK,' said Sadie. 'Granted the local and even the

100

regional police are blocking any investigation, not all the evidence is in the area controlled by them. And what about the girl?'

'Woman,' corrected one of the shrinks.

'What about the woman, then. If a child of nine had been penetrated by snooker balls then the damage physically would have been horrendous. That's evidence you could easily obtain.'

For the first time they looked angry. One of the women replied coldly. 'If we force her to go through an examination of that kind we're just repeating the physical invasion of her private physical space.'

But Sadie wasn't having that. 'I wasn't suggesting you force her. Have you asked her if she objects?'

'She's not stupid. All her life people have refused to believe her, just as children all the time in abuse cases are not believed. We know that only too well and we're not going to continue to abuse people who come to us by effectively calling them liars.'

'So what you're telling us,' said McCarthy, 'is that you never, as a matter of policy, try to verify what your patients tell you even when it involves something as widespread and grotesque as this?'

One of the women leant back, a cold, quiet anger clear in her pursed lips. 'I think it's very worrying to have a group of people charged with protecting the young as you are, who are so ready to discount the pain of children and adults who come forward and say this is happening to them.'

'But what if what they're saying isn't true?'

'In my experience most men think that children and women are habitual liars.'

Emma Saward re-entered the discussion. 'There's some truth in that, I agree, patriarchy being what it is . . .'

101

There was a collective grimace from most of the men, although not Nick, who instead nodded a sad agreement.

'But it's a plain fact that *some* children and *some* women *do* lie,' said Molly Tydeman. 'You can't just take someone's unsubstantiated word for accusations of child rape, cannibalism and murder.'

'I think it's more complicated than that.' It was Sadie speaking and she did not notice Molly's irritation at the implication of her interruption. 'Someone who makes claims like this might not be a liar in the usual sense. They might be very disturbed indeed. I have to say it seems to me that it's your primary job to distinguish, surely, between people who need help because they've actually been raped and witnessed babies being cooked in microwaves and those who are so disturbed that they've imagined these events.'

Now the three visitors were boiling, one of the women in particular losing her temper.

'If they believe these things have happened, then there's no difference – they *have* happened.' She was shouting now. Sadie was unperturbed.

'No, they haven't,' she said calmly. 'And your refusal to see the difference between someone disturbed by real events and someone disturbed by imagined ones . . .' She paused with a smile somewhere between mischief and malevolence. '. . . I think it's very worrying to have a group of people charged with the care of the young who have failed to understand that difference. One lot need help to come to terms with terrible betrayals by people charged to protect them; the other to try and re-establish a connection with reality, to understand that what they think happened emerged out of their own disturbed imaginings. They're not liars and they deserve help and compassion – but it's not the same help or compassion that you give to

102

someone who has actually experienced these things.'

Throughout this Nick had remained silent – except for his sympathetic nod against the evils of patriarchy. But now he moved to smooth things over by bringing the meeting to an end, thanking his guests with sad gratitude for the depth of the difficulty of their job and ushering them out of the room to go and have lunch with him in his office.

While they ate, Nick practised some rather more subtle satanic rituals of his own on his indignant guests. He settled their ruffled feathers, pointing out the inexperience of his examiners in such matters, the seriousness of which, he told them, he understood only too well. He was, he made it clear, a sympathetic fellow traveller on the high-way of man's inhumanity to man. Of course he had (he knew they'd understand) many conflicting opinions to negotiate – but they should never doubt that, though there might be some who would instantly reject the truth of their clearly deep, no, more, their *anguished* concern, he, Nick Berg, was not one of them. Nick was an ally. They should keep in touch.

In the past, kings and emperors would often seal alliances with an exchange of gifts, and the lunch between Nick and the shrinks was no different. The trio from the Farber Clinic had brought an offering of their torment to the BFS and now Nick was very ready to do the same for them. This was a practised routine and one where the dramatic power of video made it easy to show just what a burden of care was his. He kept a twenty-minute tape con-taining all the most horrendous cuts from the previous three years. Unsurprisingly, this tape was pretty grim stuff: an anthology of rape, torture, mutilation, bestiality and pretty much any depravity you've ever heard about – and some you haven't. Even the most imperturbable tended to look pretty green around the gills after twenty minutes of this stuff.

The point of this, as with all such exchange of gifts, was that each side was trying to top the other – in this case as to which of them had the greater cross to bear. I'm not saying, don't get me wrong, that the caring and the concerned are always trying to show the scars they wear but in my experience it's an occupational disease, like lung ailments for miners: some moralists like to appal. Christ detested the Pharisees not because they were hypocrites but because they were prone to make an exhibition of their suffering, painting their faces white during a religious fast to make clear the nature of their sacrifice. Concern and care and compassion: they can be as corrupting as money, power and sex.

At any rate, Nick returned without his guests for the remainder of the Secretariat meeting in the afternoon, clearly pleased with himself for having placed the Farber Clinic analysts exactly where he wanted them (which is to say he could call on them as allies if they ever managed to get the ear of the papers or the government – but not get too close in case they turned out to be cranks). Perhaps a little too cocky from all this, he tried to give the examiners in general, and the Soho Seven in particular, one of his more-in-sorrow-than-anger dressing-downs about the reception they had given them.

'Of course you're all very analytical and we prize that very highly here – but sometimes a certain . . .' He paused. A little sigh of regret. '. . . humility might be in order. The suffering of these people is real. Compassion is as important as intellect – more important perhaps. I think we should remember that.'

There was a silence – unusual in that en masse the examiners were a noisy lot, always elbowing each other either to express or, more usually, contradict an opinion. It was an affronted silence – but no one quite knew how to disagree without sounding as arrogant as Nick implied they were. It was Farraday who broke it.

'You know something?' he said, musing thoughtfully. 'My nephew is only four weeks old and my brother has one of those really large microwaves.' There was a careful pause. 'Frankly, I don't think he'd fit.'

Perhaps this comes across as tasteless – but it was the way he said it, a lightness, a puzzlement that hit exactly the right note. At any rate, there was a groan of delighted horror from everyone. And the subject was closed. The thing is, even Nick laughed. Typically, just when you wanted to feel nothing but disdain for him, he'd do something that frustrated you. He was maddening like that.

A Short History of Buggery

Benny Hill speaks the international language of misogyny.

Kay Lewis

If my sketches teach anything, it's that, for the male, sex is
a snare and a delusion. What's so corrupting about that?

Benny Hill

AFTER THREE YEARS OR so the Secretariat had made its
impact. Seizures by the police had slowed to almost
nothing except for pornography and the few notorious
titles that were still doing the black market rounds. If
Nick's solutions were pretty odd at times, compared with
what had preceded us it was hard not to see the result as
a massive improvement. His caution had begun to pay
dividends as alarm about videos faded, and now he was
taking greater risks in passing material he would have
baulked at in '84. The problem was that none of us, still,
was able to understand what kind of a man Nick was: an
eccentric whose weirdness was mitigated by intelligence
and a healthy streak of good sense, or an able and
thoughtful man undermined by the fact that he was
slightly mad.

The labyrinthine nature of his peculiarity came home to me particularly painfully when he appointed me Chairman of the BFS Sex Committee. No doubt you are amused by such a position, perhaps imagining how wonderful to be paid to watch people fucking all day. Others, I suppose, would recoil at such an idea: how *unpleasant* to watch people fucking all day – even if you *were* being paid for it. Let me tell you it was neither exciting nor odious. It was just a bloody nuisance. It was a time when the examiners had successfully encouraged Nick to call a kind of census of BFS practices. Different committees were set up to examine formally what we were doing about sex, or violence, sexual violence, language, drugs and so on. Like one of those films about castaways in boats who draw lots to determine who will be the first to be eaten, everyone was deeply relieved not to be on the Sex Committee. I was the one who drew the shortest straw.

'You poor bastard,' McCarthy said to me later when he heard I had been made chairman. 'What did you do to upset Nick?'

In fact it was a sign of Nick's respect for me. I know this because a couple of days later he came down to the editing room to adjudicate on a split decision between myself and Hoxton Frayn.

Hoxton, shortly to retire, had been at the Secretariat for more than twenty years and was the last of the old school. He loathed Nick, primarily (though there were plenty of other reasons) because he now made him justify his opinions (what for? he bitterly lamented). It was easy to dismiss Hoxton, so that was precisely what we did, but the thing is that he was much closer to the public and its views of how things should be understood than we were. He loathed the Seven almost as much as he loathed Nick, regarding us as a collection of pretentious, overeducated, smart-alecs pontificating endlessly about things that were fundamentally straightforward if you just employed a bit of common sense.

I appreciate that now I'm well into my story you might have some sympathy with this view. Certainly his belief that analysing things, having theories about them, was fundamentally dangerous and wrong-headed remains an almost defining aspect of Englishness. I remember one conversation I had, at a wedding reception I think, as reflecting the widespread nature of Hoxtonism. I had been asked by a clearly intelligent man in his mid-thirties what I did for a living. People continued to react to my answer with a satisfying raising of the eyes in surprise and interest, and to enquire further, fascinated (much to my wife's irritation because she'd heard it all before. As soon as the question was asked she would groan and vanish, knowing that she'd have to listen to the same old stuff for at least an hour.) Nobody on these occasions ever denounced or thundered or demanded what kind of arrogance led me to believe that I had a right to tell them what they could or couldn't see. Or only once, and she was an American.

Anyway, the wedding guest took me through the usual list: How did you get the job? What did we do all day? Would there be any chance if he applied? and so on. After a while we drifted on to the question of whether I enjoyed my work. I started talking at length about the films I liked and why I was interested in them and how being a censor made me appreciate more deeply why I liked them. The wedding guest was, if not shocked, certainly concerned. He clearly disapproved.

'I can see you like films,' he said, reproach drenching the politeness, 'but don't you think that it's wrong for some-one who does your job to be so *very* enthusiastic about them? Surely when you know so much you must get too involved?'

When it comes to the world of ideas, knowledge is a form of incapacity for the English. They wouldn't dream of handing over their new cars to a mechanic whose only training was a bit of common sense, their brains to a surgeon who claimed to have obtained his skills from the University of Life. It's not just that on all other matters you are, as a British citizen, entitled to an opinion even if you don't know anything, but that your lack of proficiency is actually an advantage; erudition, a thorough grasp of things, is a canker on the visionary bud of ignorance.

As you will see the Magnificent Seven eventually managed to fuck things up in an impressive display of self-delusion and lunacy. But if you think that Hoxton Frayn or the wedding guest were better suited for the task consider what Hoxton and I were having a row about.

First you need to know more about the laws on buggery than you probably do at the moment.

In 1533 Parliament passed the first law specifically forbidding buggery: 'a detestable and abominable vice punishable by hanging until dead'. It was repealed in Edward VI's first parliament but restored in 1548. Oddly enough it was again repealed on the accession of the Catholic Queen Mary. But then after her death it was reinstated by her sister Elizabeth. As you can see, the question of anal sex was from the very first a complicated matter – legally speaking I mean. To cut it short: the Sexual Offences Act of 1956 made it illegal to aid, abet or procure an act of anal sex either between men or between men and women. In 1967 this was modified so that it was no longer an offence for two consenting males to have anal sex in private. Again oddly (and this brings us to the nub of my dispute with Hoxton) buggery remained a criminal offence between men and women. The Secretariat's view of anal sex and its visual representation relied upon laws which were hopelessly confused and contradictory.

With all the other problems of press, politicians, the cops and the law that Nick had to face, a more rational approach to buggery than had obtained during the previous five centuries was low on his list of priorities and it got pretty short shrift. Any implication of buggery on a sex tape was ruthlessly excised. If Nick was going to take flak it wasn't going to be over the kind of pervert who liked it up the fart chimney (as Hoxton so memorably referred to it).

This was all pretty unambiguous so Nick was perplexed as to why we'd asked him to come down and break the deadlock over a cut which Hoxton insisted we make and which I was just as insistent we should not.

Nick was not in a good mood for some reason.

'I'm busy,' he said, looking balefully at me. 'You know policy is to cut out any references to anal sex if it's a sex tape.'

Hoxton looked on smugly.

'I know that, Nick, but there have to be limits. Just let me play you the tape – it'll only take a minute.'

He nodded, bad-tempered, and the tape began to play.

A naked woman was lying on a couch while a bald man with a goatee sat in a leather chair listening to her and making notes.

'Doctor,' she said in a pretty good imitation of Marilyn Monroe, 'I keep having these strange dreams where a hairy workman keeps trying to push a pink rolled-up carpet through my back door. What,' she gasped breathlessly, 'do you think it means?'

The doctor considered thoughtfully for a moment then

110

answered in a thick Viennese accent. 'I can see, my dear, that I'm going to have to psychoanalyse you!'

Nick burst into laughter but when I switched off the tape he looked puzzled. 'Sorry, I don't understand.'

'The guidelines – *your* guidelines are perfectly clear,' said Hoxton, looking considerably less smug. 'No references to anal sex.'

'It's a joke,' I said. 'The guidelines are meant to cover references to anal sex as a turn-on. This is just a joke.'

'It's a clear reference to anal sex. Policy is clear,' said Hoxton. 'We should cut it.'

He was shaking with rage now. Nick coughed. There was a pause.

'Um . . . look, Hoxton, I take the point about what I said – but Duncan is right. I meant it to cover turn-on language. I mean, it is just a joke.' He tried to make light of it. 'And a pretty good one for a sex tape.'

But it didn't work. With an angry *slap*! Hoxton shut his notebook and stood up. 'What's the point of rules if you don't stick to them?'

And with that he walked to the door and was gone. Nick and I smiled at each other, mutually condescending.

'I hear you were less than thrilled about being made Chairman of the Sex Committee.'

I shrugged.

'You know I chose you with your particular abilities in mind?'

I liked the sound of this. Nick could do compliments the way some people could do jokes. It was the way he told them. He smiled at me, admiringly, genuine, his approval lighting up his eyes. It made you warm.

'Of course there are others who write better than you – Sadie, of course. And there are better minds – Farraday.' He smiled warmly. 'He's a cheeky sod, but he's got a good

111

brain. But you . . . you have an all-rounder's ability: you handle the paperwork better than anybody, you've got an eye for detail, you're good on the technical stuff. I can't tell you how often I wish I'd chosen more people like you and fewer like them. The sex guidelines are going to be very tricky. You really are the best person.'

And with that he turned and left. What did I think? I was stunned – no, that's not right. I was in pieces. I'd taken a blow that was all the worse for being so un-expected. My defences were down because I was listening to something designed to make me feel good. And that was partly, I suppose, why I felt so bad, so very bad. My sister is an osteopath. She does my back from time to time. She found this spot on the left side of my neck just where it meets the skull. She pressed it and I nearly fainted with the pain. 'Lots of people have got somewhere like that,' she said, 'places where it's incredibly sore for some reason. It's best, I find, just to leave them alone.'

But, of course, to go bad as a human being takes time and not everyone has a knack or taste for resentment. Feeling animosity for me was an unpleasant experience. I thought, or thought I thought, that serious resentment was beneath me. But it wasn't beneath me as it turned out. For the time being I put it away at the back of my mind. No, that's not it – at the back of my soul.

For now I was busy running the Sex Committee. Why was it such a pain? In a word: Nick. If he'd really under-stood the British attitude to sex he would have tried to dump responsibility for porn tapes back on the Vice Squad. But Napoleon Nick (there I go again) couldn't resist the idea of complete control. Somebody or other, I can't remember who, advanced the view that the first law of war was never to advance on Moscow. If they'd been similarly aware of British attitudes to sex they would have said something equally definitive about having nothing to do with pornography. Until Nick became Mr Sex, as the *Sun* insisted on calling him, the law had been administered by the police and the limits of what was accepted as legal or otherwise evolved in as haphazard a way as you might expect of anything concocted by cops. The judicial system was no better: a court in Birmingham could declare a sex shop owner guilty of depraving and corrupting the public on a Monday and duly send him to prison; while on the next day a court in Brighton would set another sex shop owner free without a stain on his character – and this, mind you, for selling exactly the same videotape.

This offended Nick's notion of an ideal censorial state in which nobility of purpose, morally good manners and rationality could be brought to bear on material blatantly ignoble, immoral, ill-mannered and atavistic. In fact, now that I think and write about it, I take my earlier analysis back. Nick didn't take pornography on because he hadn't thought it out properly – I see now that its innate disorderliness, its sordid chaos was a challenge. Enlightened pornography, that was the lunacy he was after; civilized lewdness, sensitive grossness, rational filth.

Having said this, Nick's first attempt at trying to bring all this under control seemed entirely sensible. He devised a special category for sex shops, 'Restricted 18', under which hardcore tapes could be sold legally in a place licensed by the local council. Nick believed that he had squared the circle of censorship: members of the public who wished to avoid such material could simply refrain from entering the one carefully demarcated ghetto where it would be available. Children would be protected. The deviant was, within limits, also granted his rights. The bright light of Nick's wisdom, its civilized realism, would disperse the hysteria of the ranting moralists on the one hand, and the expansionist ambitions of the pornographer (and his drooling customers) on the other. Pornography would be available but at the same time it would not be allowed to taint the wellsprings of public life.

The trouble with Nick was that he believed the only reason that people didn't agree with his ideas was not because they held an opposing view but because they hadn't understood properly what he was saying. This is not to say he had a settled view on everything but that when it *was* settled he knew he was correct. If people disagreed with him on such matters, it must only be because they were either wilfully refusing to accept he was right, or because he hadn't made himself clear. This was the source of his habit of endlessly repeating his explanations. People subjected to one of these multi-layered assaults tended (about ten minutes usually did the trick) to take on the look of chickens shortly after they had been electrically stunned prior to having their throats cut. Nick invariably interpreted the look of vacancy that resulted from one of these parenthetical onslaughts as a sign of growing acquiescence, and hence he was only further encouraged.

When I told him that local councils were more concerned about local voters than his centralist theories and that they wouldn't give licences for porn shops because local people didn't want them next to them, he just smiled condescendingly. They would see this was the rational way to solve the problem. They would come round. I tried again by pointing out that the Vice Squad saw porn as their patch. They regarded pornography, most of them, as depraved and the people who sold it as criminals – a group of people they understandably regarded as the enemy of an ordered state. They were likely to regard Nick's efforts to reconcile pornography with the law in much the same way as if he were to try to do something similar for bank robbery or child molesting.

'Nick, most of the people in the Vice Squad genuinely think that photographs of erections and penetration are wrong, that they're bad for people.'

'But that's ridiculous,' he said.

'According to you and me. But they aren't going to change their minds just because Nick Berg thinks it would be a good idea if they did.'

I thought later that perhaps I'd overstated the case but it quickly turned out that, if anything, the opposite was true. When I had this disagreement with him there were about thirty licensed sex shops throughout the country. Within five months there were twenty-three. I once spent an entire Indian video working out that if you walked every road and street throughout the country you could expect to come upon a sex shop about once in every fifty years. When he dragged me up to talk to a delegation from the Vice Squad in order to try to come to a gentleman's agreement not to step on each other's toes (i.e., do what Nick wanted) – the cops clearly thought that we were a pair of tossers.

After this meeting Nick realized that the Vice Squad dealt with his way of arguing by the simple expedient of not listening to what he was saying. It was clear he was going to have to be extremely careful if his management of the porn issue was not to damage the more important aim of 'maintaining the reputat. n of the Secretariat' so that it was trusted to keep control of films and video. The upshot of all this was that despite his keenness to see an official pornography which left normal sex uncensored (i.e., no S and M, bestiality or anything generally too weird) he decided that the safest policy for the sex-shop category was for the moment not to have very much sex in it (which is to say, no close-ups of labia, no erections and no penetration).

The trouble was, it was impossible for the porn distributors to make money. It cost a thousand pounds to have a tape certificated plus the cost of the rights. And there were only twenty-three shops where they could sell them. The licensed sex shop had become a cultural panda whose fate was all the more precarious because nobody cared about its extinction except the porn barons and Nick. And, of course, the customers – but nobody cared about them.

However, the pornographers were quicker to adapt than poor old Yin-Yin or Yang-Yang. If the 'R18' sex video was a non-runner then they'd ask for ordinary '18' certificates. Even if the results hardly contained any sex at all, they had long been used to selling the sizzle and not the sausage. There would always be punters dumb enough or desperate enough to buy what they had to sell, they would just have to market them with a little less respect for the truth than might be regarded as permissible under the Trade Descriptions Act. After all, how many people were going to drop in on their local Trading Standards Officer and complain their pornography was insufficiently filthy? (Apparently it did happen once and Trading Standards, understandably bemused, referred the disgruntled customer to Nick who duly sent him a long letter explaining why his sex tape couldn't, given the current state of the law, contain any actual sex.)

They could sell sex videos with an '18' certificate in any video store in the country, and, perhaps most importantly, send them through the post – something forbidden to 'R18' tapes by law despite Nick's protestations that this would seriously damage the viability of his great Stalinist dream of a state pornography. The reason given for this refusal was that as it was the *Royal* Mail, allowing it to go by post would in some way taint the Queen – thus risking, so the joke went at the Secretariat, making her subject to a charge of living off immoral earnings. Anyway that was that.

Nick, however, was not going to abandon his prize plan for a civilized solution to the problem of smut. He couldn't stop the porn distributors asking for an '18' certificate for their sex tapes but if the 'R18' certificate were to remain viable he had to make a clear distinction between the two. If circumstances meant that there couldn't be much sex in an 'R18' tape, then there would have to be significantly less in an '18'.

After a few weeks of cutting and snipping away in his private editing room like some mad alchemist, Nick finally came down with one tape cut for 'R18' and the same tape cut for '18'. It was right after watching this presentation that Walter Casey joked that watching an 'R18' porn tape was like watching *Match of the Day* with all the goals removed but that watching an '18' sex tape would be like watching the same match with everything cut out except the throw-ins and the passes back to the goalkeeper.

But Walter was wrong. Nick could never keep things that simple and the reasons why were revealing. Many of his decisions were political and pragmatic – he made compromises because he had to balance the way he was perceived by politicians, the law, the press and the numerous pressure groups, mostly on the right but also on the left. Though he often claimed he was being pragmatic, at the deepest level he hated the idea of being seen as anything less than entirely sincere. Slowly, always,

Nick's pragmatic decisions evolved so that they were no longer based on the kind of compromise inevitable in such a politicized job but instead, mysteriously, became deeply held moral and intellectual convictions.

The problem for me was that while a sex video without any sex in it might be ridiculous (as well as brief) it was perfectly possible. The joke about *Match of the Day* was funny but sadly not accurate. Nick decided that some sex was to be permitted but instead of it being cut to simple rules that served to make the 'R18' viable he had to have an elaborate set of fine distinctions based on principles that were morally, psychologically and even spiritually coherent. It wasn't just that Nick tried to treat *The Texas Chainsaw Massacre* as if it were *Pride and Prejudice*, he tried the same trick with *Debbie Does Dallas* and *Little Me and Marla Strangelove*.

For the next three months, I spent hours watching porn in the company of the three other luckless members of the committee. Every two weeks I would trudge up to Nick's office with my collection of filth samples and Nick would pore over them with gimlet-eyed concentration – approving of this cut to an erect nipple, deciding that another needed to be made because the woman's knees were too far in the air or a man's arse was too energetically thrusting.

On one occasion, I went up while Sadie Boldon was talking to him and she stayed to have a look. When Nick observed that I should have cut an erect nipple, she asked why.

'It suggests real sex,' said Nick affably, 'something quite literally a harder experience – hence it's "R18".'

She wasn't having it, however. 'But nipples go hard for all sorts of reasons. Mine go hard if the temperature drops a few degrees, or if someone brushes up against me. They even get hard if I read something really brilliant. To be honest, I think that taking out erect nipples is just silly.'

With that she left. I am quite sure that I must have been excited at various points during the previous two months of watching endless amounts of pornography but interestingly the only memory I have of being aroused in all that time was during that conversation with Sadie in Nick's office.

So I hope I've given you something of the horror that faced me. It wasn't at all like cutting down a football match to the throw-ins and the passes back to the goalkeeper. What it was really like was cutting out all the crossfield passes where the ball was struck at an angle of more than 25 degrees from the horizontal – but if there were more than three such passes in a two-minute period, then only the longest or the highest should be removed. Square passes of less than ten yards were always permitted and occasional chips, backheads, nutmegs and headers, but, in general, periods of intense activity no longer than two and a half minutes were to be interspersed with aimless backpasses, ineffective free kicks and anything generally sterile and unprogressive. Then began the miserable task of codifying this gobbledygook so that the other examiners could make some practical sense of it. An example or two:

HEAD BOBBING IN FELLATIO

Can be shown at '18' – more acceptable if it is obviously simulated. Cut shots where it is vigorous or levels of noise indicate real rather than simulated.

THRUSTING

Medium shot (waist-up) thrusting acceptable at '18'. Where

bodies are seen more or less in full length, only brief thrusting shots are acceptable. Shots of thrusting where both the woman's legs are stretched up in the air must be cut for '18'.

SOUNDTRACK AND DIALOGUE

During oral sex the sound of 'slurping' is to be cut for '18' as is the sound of 'squelching' during genital intercourse.

You will understand now why watching porn sent our hearts into our boots. Before I was finally discharged from my hellish task I had to spend another month looking at the tapes cut down according to the instructions I had written out. Two things struck me: one, that by and large they managed to follow the ridiculous and horribly complicated rules I'd given them with remarkable consistency; the second was to wonder what on earth the punter who got one of these tapes out would make of it. The term wanker is invariably used with dismissive contempt – but anyone who could get an erection while watching one of my creations, let alone maintain it to the point of orgasm, bordered, in my view, on the truly heroic.

One other thing struck me during my sex sentence: how porn could delineate with strange exactness the difference between cultures. American porn is, well, hardcore and blatant: *Fuck me baby with your big cock in my wet pussy*. In American porn a couple meet, take off their clothes and have sex. They may or may not know each other. All the women look vaguely the same – blonde hair and fake tits. The men are nearly always too old and clapped out to convince you that even the most desperate trailer trash would strip off to have sex with them unless offered money. In English sex films, the fucking may be similarly anonymous but the men are nearly always slightly ridiculous. Somehow you can always hear the sound of a comedy trombone. The dialogue: *I've got a snorkel. Ooh! A big one I hope*.

Both of them reflect the audience's sense of wanting to get on with it – the first deals with guilt by getting into each scene with as much speed as possible so that shame is driven out by excitement; the second approaches the dark heart of desire with a wink, hoping that not even the deepest shame can survive a smirk.

The French, however, typically approach the business of sex just like everything else – they like to talk a lot first and require all the trappings appropriate to the sophisticates they believe themselves to be. The women may look like Catherine Deneuve but there is a plot as routine as that of any Bollywood film about the heroine being kidnapped (with the collusion of her lover who realizes she needs to be initiated into the proper attitude to sex) and taken to a gorgeously appointed château where a sophisticated older man in evening dress drones on and on in detail about why she must be whipped and undergo a huge number of sexual humiliations before she can be liberated back to her beloved. The explanation will go something like: *By the end of your enlightenment you will impetuously insist that you be treated like a trash can to be emptied and then cast aside on the greasy sidewalk of obscenity. Only then will you be free to know true love.*

Was I never excited during the hours I spent watching this stuff? Hardly ever, but sometimes. A few of the examiners, including some of the women, swore by *The Punishment of Anne* (a château fuck-film if you haven't already guessed, though wittier than usual) but for myself I only ever saw one video that I thought stirring and exciting and that was because it understood something, God knows why or how, about the need for limits, for something to be broken down, a line crossed. It was called *Jeremy Jism Does Berkshire*.

First I may need to explain something about a certain kind of not quite upper middle-class Home Counties woman illustrated by an unusual experience I had a few months before Jism and I met professionally.

I had decided to go and pay a cheque into my bank account in Marlow, the centre of which was about two miles from where I lived. It was a beautiful day and I decided to walk the dog rather than drive. This turned out to be a mistake because on the way into town he ran into a stream and emerged soaking wet and covered in mud. When we got to the building society I realized that he was too much of a mess to take inside so I looked for somewhere to leave him safely. The nearest place was a post near the edge of the road. As I tied him up a woman in her late thirties pulled up in an enormous Range Rover and started to try to park just near the dog. Worried that she hadn't seen him and that she might mount the pavement, so unsure did she seem of her parking skills, I smiled and signalled to her. The window slid down and I said in what I hoped was a friendly manner to disguise the fact that I was telling her to be careful: 'Mind my dog, would you?' She looked at me as if slightly puzzled, smiled herself and then said hesitantly, 'Oh. Yes, of course.' With that I left the dog and went to pay in the cheque.

As it happened there was a long queue and there was just one girl behind the counter, who gave the impression that she had only recently learnt to count without using her fingers, so it was a good ten minutes before I re-emerged. You can imagine my astonishment to discover the woman from the Range Rover sitting with the door open and watching the dog while occasionally glancing longingly at the row of shops that began some fifty yards away. Needless to say I was horrified. It was clear that she had completely misunderstood my request to mind the dog, but what was I to do? If I explained that she had mis-understood me it would only make her feel horribly foolish. So I simply thanked her. She smiled at me pleasantly as if it was the most natural thing in the world to inconvenience herself in this way for a total stranger, locked the car and headed towards the shops.

If you keep this strange story in mind as we return to Jeremy Jism you may perhaps understand why his video, alone amongst so many thousands, made such an im-pression on me. The modus operandi of the series, for this was one of many to follow, was that Jeremy, acting the part of a gormless and slightly unsure of himself chancer, would approach women while carrying a video camera on his shoulder and ask them to have sex with him. In all the others of this series the effect was, as you might expect, grubby and rather offensive, though it should be pointed out that all the women he approached were models hired to respond positively to this unlikely request. But in the Berkshire episode something fascinating happened. I hope I won't come across as a snob but the plain fact of the matter is that the women who usually appear in these videos are, to put it bluntly, common. The difference here was that the model he approached in a Berkshire Waitrose car park (Jeremy knew his retail class distinctions) replied to his initial request for the time in a beautifully cadenced Home Counties accent and with a helpful smile that precisely echoed that of my woman in the Range Rover. Everything about her was just right – the flat shoes, the Hermès scarf around her neck, and the navy blue pleated skirt falling just below her knees. Jeremy, with his hair cut like a B&Q toilet brush and a face like a boiled potato, was suitably abashed at meeting a woman so clearly his social superior. Nevertheless, awkward and bumbling, he pressed on with non sequitur observations about the weather and the attractiveness of the local countryside, comments to which she replied with courtesy and only slight puzzlement considering he was a complete stranger carrying a video camera on his shoulder. Having helped her with her shopping he then asked her a direct question: 'Um . . . would you mind if I took some pictures of you with my camera?'

An inexperienced viewer of pornography could have been forgiven until now if they were unsure whether she was a real middle-class woman in a Waitrose car park, so brilliantly had the model become her role. Clearly by now even the most helpful of women would have made an excuse and left but so convincingly had the model captured the emotional difficulty a certain kind of well-brought-up woman has about being in any way impolite, especially to one's social inferiors, that disbelief was entirely willingly suspended (given of course that this was a work of fiction starring someone called Jeremy Jism). She had caught, with a method brilliance that would have made Brando weep, the emotional landscape of the woman, and the many like her, who had stayed to watch over my dog.

'Perhaps,' said Jeremy, hesitant himself, 'we could go to your house. Um . . . it would be easier to set up my camera there.'

She registered that he, also, was embarrassed by this request which only made things worse, because now she was responsible for putting him at his ease. The only way possible was to agree.

'Oh.' A pause and an awkward smile. 'Ah. Well. Of course.' Again so cleverly captured was the sense of her reluctance, the agony of not knowing what was the right thing to do in a social situation of this unusual sort, that you were almost convinced by her agreement to go along with this bizarre request. Farraday, my partner for the day, and I were in stitches as she got into the car and opened the door for Jeremy. Yet unlike the usual ghastly comedy of the British sex film this was both wonderfully subtle, genuinely funny, and, above all given its purpose, genuinely arousing. From somewhere they had grasped the idea that sex was not something that just happened between strangers but that it usually required complicated negotiations, that acres of unknown territory had to be crossed, of class and gender, of attractiveness and avail-ability, of the sheer barrier-annihilating and blatant nature of the act of sex. Her awkwardness and deep reluc-tance about agreeing, that she was going along with this in spite of herself were in every way the opposite of the dreary mutual determination to fuck of the participants in virtually every sex film ever made.

In the house itself there was just the right mix of furniture from John Lewis and Laura Ashley, the fawn carpet, the solid silver picture frames, the garden outside exactly as dull as it should have been with its striped lawn and bedding plants. Jeremy finished setting up his camera and the woman sat looking bewildered on the beige sofa (cotton jacquard, loose covers).

'Would you . . . um . . . like to undo the . . . top button of your blouse? Just . . . you know . . .' He gestured meaninglessly at the camera as if it was a requirement he was reluctantly forced to make by virtue of its mere existence in the corner of the room. In the deep yet underplayed struggle that took place in her eyes as a result of this request you could see years of childhood con-ditioning bending her into acceptance: please may I, could I possibly, would you mind terribly, all her adoration of her mummy, the desperate willingness to please. It was both touching and hilarious. Slowly she reached for the top button of her Country Casuals blouse and eased the button free. Meticulously sexless until now, the slight hint of curved breast by contrast made her suddenly riotously delectable.

Her legs were crossed, the left leg curled around so that her left foot tucked itself behind her right ankle. This was a woman who had practised with the discipline of an Olympic athlete how to sit and not give away even the slightest hint of thigh.

'What . . . ah . . . could you just raise your . . . uh?' He moved his hand towards her skirt with such hesitancy, itself a wonderful parody of working-class deference, that she had no choice but to do as he asked, as if he were a tradesman she had hired herself to do something vaguely unpalatable, unblock the loo, say, and she could not now be uncooperative and refuse his reasonable requests. She slowly, and as unprovocatively as it was in her power to do, delicately pinched the hem of her skirt and raised it a few inches along her thigh. She stopped. He gestured, as if reluctantly, that more was required according to some unalterable code over which he had no control. This was something, of course, that she understood all too well. Realizing he was not to blame, that they were comrades of a kind driven by iron laws of behaviour impossible to disobey, and with a grimace of distress that showed itself in her expression only as a flutter of anxiety, she raised the hem a little further. Now the darker hem of the tights around her upper thigh came into view.

And so it went on. Slowly, very slowly, each layer of her expensively frumpy clothes was shed – a kind of delicate time-lapse, first blouse, then skirt raised to her waist as she, still elegantly, sat, then tights removed, then white and maidenly bra, then matching (of course) knickers. Then at his wonderfully humble request she took his erect penis into her mouth and sucked with wide-eyed and dazed innocence as his own eyes began to pop with pleasure and amazed delight at what he was getting away with. Then she was bent over the sofa and penetrated by Jeremy from behind with an expression as if all his birthdays had come at once. Finally, a scene of course we had to cut, he entered her anally. Naturally she winced at this but politely suppressed it, not wanting, of course, to make a fuss.

Instantly he was all concern.

'Am I going too far in?'

'Just a little,' she squeaked uncomplainingly.

Finally the inevitable money shot. But throughout this despite the expressions of uncertainty and bewilderment she demonstrated neither repugnance nor desire. This was the last most brilliant erotic insight of all – it was not possible to tell whether she was merely being taken advantage of or whether at some point she had come to a decision to use this chance to behave like a disgusting slut and put the responsibility for doing so at the door of good manners. In its way it was the most mysterious, unknowable performance that I had ever seen.

A few minutes after it had finished and while I was writing the cuts required before a member of the public would be allowed to see it, Emma and Sadie wandered past and Farraday signalled them to come in. I suppose only he would have had the confidence to try to explain the brilliance of what we had just seen. They didn't get what he was going on about, but they laughed at his description, even as they mockingly reviled him as a pervert. Had I tried to do the same, I don't suppose I could have brought it off, there would have been no amused insults, they would just have found it creepy. But it made an impression on me and there it is.

Enough of that for now. Let me explain myself. A while ago in fiction the unreliable narrator was all the rage. The fixed and to be trusted storyteller of the Victorian novel had been replaced by the dodgy fabulist, con-man, cheat and perjurer. The authorial voice became instead another character, slippery, evasive, as likely to be the hand that struck the blow as any other member of the cast – butler, angry lover, resentful son.

Let me reassure you, you can rely on me, I am no jive turkey fabler, no fabricator of misleading tricks, I'm doing my best to tell it to you straight and only if I do so can there be any hope for me. I am the dead, unjudged, and this is my chance even at this late date to avoid the near and present opening of the jaws of hell that roar and call for me. This is my chance and I have been given a helping hand to put things right. The recording angel has given me access to the facts. When I was alive I only knew the bits and pieces of what took place, fed through things I will not speak of for a while. I was ignorant, both of myself and of others, ignorant of the facts and of the meaning of those facts. Now I must use this gift to get the meaning right, not just for myself but for you. And that's of course the tricky bit: the drift, the significance, the bottom line of what was really going on. And I'm struggling here to select the new known facts they've given me to understand.

But it's scary stuff even if you really really want to tell the truth and get it right, especially if the price of screwing up is torment throughout eternity. So, bear with me, take pity on a wretch (you'll see) and understand why it is I now know things that only the dead would know. Believe that a terrible gift and terror of failure make me conscientious and forgive my fumbling attempts.

C. G. Jung once remarked that whatever is unacknowledged in your character happens to you as fate. I suppose he's right, but I wonder if I hadn't seen my personnel file in Walter Casey's office towards the end of my dreary months working on standards for sex tapes whether things might have been different. The fact that I read the file was certainly my responsibility – there was cause and effect at work here. But to have left the key in the lock was entirely uncharacteristic of Walter whose meticulous nature was a byword at the Secretariat. And if it had not been left there I could not have decided to read it, and if I had not read it then one of the first great links to what happened would not have been forged. I may of course be deluding myself. But what if I'm not? What if but for a highly uncharacteristic slip from Walter the misery that began here might never have happened? The many personal flaws, mine and others', that had nothing to do with this rare act of carelessness would all have still existed but the thing, the arbitrary chance that set them in motion, would not have happened. It makes you think. Though what exactly it is that it makes you think I'm still not sure.

At any rate I was in Walter Casey's office working on the presentation of the sex guidelines when he left to take someone from the Broadcasting Standards Council to lunch. I worked on for about half an hour and when I'd finished went to put some of his files back in the half-open drawer from which he'd taken them. When I tried to close it the drawer wouldn't budge and after a few shoves I tried a trick from my Civil Service days that often worked on clapped-out filing cabinets. The drawer above was locked but the key was still in it. Unlocking it I pulled the drawer fully open and sure enough the lower drawer slid home easily. But as I went to close and relock the upper drawer I recognized one of the names on the files in the drawer, and then another. These were the personnel files for every one of the examiners. Mine included, of course. I was a cautious man by nature and I had written enough confidential reports in my time to realize that it was entirely likely that were any given individual to read a file about themselves they had better be prepared for a few things that might upset them. But it's like an unread review, isn't it? To read it might humiliate you or it might make you feel like a god, and a vindicated god at that. It's a gamble, this kind of thing, but what tempted me was that it seemed like one worth taking. I had won through an Everest of a selection procedure and I was part of an elite – I was, in this place, literally one in a thousand. Why not take this gamble? This was, unusually, I think I've already said, a place where praise was not uncommon and when it came was rarely accompanied by some back-hander just in case you got too big for your boots. So I checked that the office outside was deserted, which being lunchtime it was, and then I removed the file and opened it.

It was disappointing. There wasn't much in it and the first few pages were just forms I'd filled in myself: my original application, and various other official documents. Then there was an envelope, but the slight rush I felt on opening it was stilled by the fact that I recognized the handwriting inside: it was the twenty or so pages of the essays – or whatever you want to call them – on the three films we had had to view as part of the selection process (in case you're interested, *I Spit on Your Grave*, a rape-and-revenge film; *Turkish Delight*, a controversial art film starring Rutger Hauer and directed by Paul Verhoeven – both to go on to better and worse things – and finally

The Texas Chainsaw Massacre). Anyway, it was with a mixture of disappointment and a certain relief that I started to put the essays back in their envelope. It was then that I noticed a memo slip inside. I took it out. It was from Walter Casey to Nick and dated about two weeks after our final interviews. It read as follows.

Nick

I realize you're a bit put out that Melanie Cohn turned us down and then so did our first reserve – though both refusals seem pretty odd given all they had to go through. But to be honest I think it may be no bad thing that we've been given a chance to think again about the intellectual and character mix of the seven. Much as I'm genuinely excited about the arrival of such an interesting group of people, I have reservations (stick-in-the-mud as I am) about choosing just the dynamos – too much intellectual energy brings its problems. The more I think about it, the more I'm convinced that we need a bit more ballast. I think we should offer the spare job to Duncan Purcell – we need a water-carrier who's got the temperament to cover the important but boring ground that makes up so much of what we do. Let's hear it for bland and uninspired competence – it's always worked for me!

Walter

I read it again carefully, then put it back in the envelope, the envelope into the file and the file in the drawer. I closed it and locked it.

That, I suppose, was that.

Struck by Lightning

Love is ever a matter of comedies, and now and then of tragedies; but in life it doth much mischief; sometimes like a siren, sometimes like a fury. Love can find entrance, not only into an open heart, but also into a heart well fortified, if watch be not well kept.

Francis Bacon, *Of Love*

THE AFFAIR BETWEEN SADIE and Farraday started at a Secretariat Christmas dinner. Farraday was single. Sadie had been married for four years to a lawyer she met when she was doing her first degree somewhere in Wales.

They shouldn't have been sitting together at all. Considerable effort had gone into placing each examiner next to assorted members of the great and the good whose presence around organizations like the British Film Secretariat seems to be as inevitable as that of rats in a barn.

Sadie had been specially selected by Nick to sit next to Sir Robert Mathias, a former Home Office Minister, still with much influence, who was renowned for his taste in beautiful young women. Sir Robert, however, was at death's door in the Royal Free having suffered a heart attack, according to press reports, while engaged in his onerous duties as Chairman of one of the major London ballet companies. He had, in fact, suffered the heart attack not while exerting himself over the finer print of a contract to build a magnificent new theatre but while in bed with a dancer from the chorus whose unusual flexibility had put too much strain on a constitution that had laboured too long at the trough of publicly funded largesse.

Farraday was not supposed to be there at all, having cried off because of some long-standing engagement with a Lord Fauntleroy pal of his. But this had been cancelled and he'd been slotted in simply by giving him Mathias's place.

Sadie was pleased to see him. 'Hello, Sir Robert. You know it's a funny thing but you're the spitting image of someone I work with. I suppose it's all the inbreeding that makes it impossible to tell you apart.'

'Look, Sadie, don't take it out on me because you missed your opportunity.'

'What opportunity?'

'Sir Robert got his decree absolute about three months ago. I hear he's on the lookout for some good peasant stock to be the next Lady Mathias.'

'Why?'

'Like you said – inbreeding. We always try to re-invigorate the old bloodline – keeps the chins from receding too far . . . reduces the imbecile count.'

She laughed. 'The fact that I'm black wouldn't be a problem?'

Farraday looked at her as if seeing her for the first time. A mock puzzlement crossed his handsome face. 'You never told me you were black,' he said, as if slightly hurt by her lack of candour.

'I suppose I thought the colour of my skin was a bit of a giveaway.'

Farraday looked thoughtful. 'To be honest I always thought you were a dwarf with an unusually deep tan.'

She burst into outraged laughter and hit him on the shoulder. 'You monster!'

'Serves you right for calling me inbred.'

'It's not my fault I'm so small.'

He looked at her appreciatively. 'Small, perhaps . . . but perfectly formed.'

He had not meant to say it quite the way it came out. He was trying to ease away from the friendly insults and say something gracious. But it came out wrong. The easy compliment sounded like something else: it sounded like desire.

And until he said it he didn't, genuinely, realize that Sadie's magic had been working on him all this time.

He could see instantly on her face that she had felt it too. She drew back as if repelled by a magnetic force and her face fell, her eyes reflecting only distaste and shock. And then she turned away and started talking to the woman on her left, a noisy agony aunt Nick had invited onto an advisory group of fifty worthies. He gathered them every couple of months or so, fed, watered, and flattered them. And paid absolutely no attention to anything they said.

Farraday, meanwhile, the wind taken out of his habitually unruffled sails, felt both foolish for having appeared to make a play for a married colleague and shocked at his realization of what he really felt about her.

'I can't believe it.'

'What did you actually say?'

Farraday sighed. 'She said she was small and I said she was small but perfectly formed.'

McCarthy laughed.

'That bad?' said Farraday miserably.

'It's not your fault, Tom,' said McCarthy with obvious pleasure. 'It's your background – all that time in Harrow washing each other's back in the shower. You just don't know how to deal with women.'

'Fuck off! I'm fine with women. I've never had a problem talking to them and I was at Winchester. Big difference.'

McCarthy looked thoughtful. 'As it happens, I agree. In fact, if anything, I'd describe you as a bit glib.'

'That's what I think, too. I've always prided myself on being shamefully slick when it came to –' he paused and did a self-mocking Terry-Thomas style leer '– the fair sex.'

They both laughed.

'I still can't believe I said it.'

'Have you spoken to her since?'

'I tried to say hello just before morning prayers.'

'And?'

'She looked at me as if I were about to steal her purse. Then she rushed downstairs.'

McCarthy looked thoughtful. 'Did you mean it?'

'It just came out. One minute I was teasing her and then I was being a crappy chat-up artist. But I *did* mean it.'

'And you didn't realize before?'

'No. I mean if you'd asked me I'd have said she was beautiful. I mean she is beautiful, right?'

'Everybody thinks Sadie's beautiful.'

'But you don't . . .' Farraday's voice trailed away.

'What?'

'Find her desirable.'

McCarthy shrugged. 'Look, if Sadie came to my door

with the top button of her blouse undone and asked to borrow a cup of sugar – well I'd be only too happy. But that's not what we're talking about is it?'

Farraday looked miserable. 'No,' he said at last, 'it isn't.'

Tom Farraday came from an old Northamptonshire family who could trace their origins back to a sheep farmer in the fifteenth century. The first family fortune had been made from sugar plantations in the West Indies; the second in the cotton factories of the Industrial Revolution. After that the entrepreneurial spirit, indeed any spirit at all to speak of, went into decline and so did the fortune. To some extent this was restored in the late 1970s when Central TV began renting part of the run-down estate for a new soap opera set in a fictional village they built on the site. The soap opera was a much greater success than Central had expected and the fake village had grown and, along with it, the rental to Farraday's family who quickly realized that they had the programme makers over a barrel. To rebuild the sets elsewhere would have cost a fortune and so the Farradays were able to charge well above any market rate.

Farraday's relationship with his parents was odd, even by the peculiar standards of most members of the rural gentry. Farraday had been sent to boarding school at the age of six. On his infrequent visits home his mother and father seemed mildly pleased to see him, but also some-what surprised as if they had forgotten they had a son at all. They were in no way cold towards him but their attitude, Farraday came to feel, was rather as if he were a youthful acquaintance who had taken too literally the invitation to drop by whenever he was passing.

Given this eccentric introduction to human intimacy it was surprising how well balanced he was emotionally. He had an extraordinarily easy way with people no matter what their background or sex (or gender as Emma Saward always disapprovingly corrected him). Strikingly handsome, six foot one, blond hair and blue eyes, he looked, according to McCarthy, like something made up over the telephone by two gay Nazis. His charm lay in something deeper than a pleasant manner; everyone sensed and appreciated how much at ease he was with himself and his capacity to include anyone he was speaking to in that ease. You enjoyed being with Tom Farraday.

But since the Christmas dinner with Sadie, for the first time in his life, his confidence in himself was shaken. He was miserable. The sudden realization of his feelings for Sadie and the alarming sensation for the first time in his life of not being in control of himself left him bewildered as if someone had spiked his drink with a poisonous substance that was now eating away at every nerve in his body.

She was on his mind not just when he was awake but in his dreams. Every time he saw her at work it was not his heart that surged and battered him but every part of his body from stomach to brain. How was it possible to feel like this? He'd had no idea that this depth of emotion and misery existed. All his life he had been in relaxed control of himself and, it would be fair to say, of others too. He had ridden the amiable indifference of his parents and the emotional and physical deprivations of an expensive English education with apparent ease. In a world of shallow emotions and philistine cruelties he had emerged a clever and, though one usually only uses it of women, a captivating human being. It should be granted, though, that this came at the price of a certain complacency and a tendency to expect others to give him what he wanted without his having to take too much trouble to get it. But now this. It didn't make sense. Some hoax or voodoo must have been responsible because this was not Thomas Farraday.

Every time he saw Sadie she seemed more achingly beautiful: the turn of her throat, the way she looked whenever she disagreed with someone, the eyes opening wide with interested dissent. The way she walked – always away from him because avoiding his presence was clearly uppermost in her mind; the sight of her in the wide-necked jumpers she often wore that revealed the terrifying curve of her shoulders, the torment of her collar bone, and the curse of her soft brown skin. And all the time he could feel how repelled she was by him. What to anyone listening at the Secretariat dinner would have seemed a pleasantly mocking compliment between two people who were comfortable with one another began to assume in his mind the proportions of some vilely crude remark in appalling bad taste. Every time he played the moment over it came out as leering, a coarsely leering sexual innuendo, primitive, rude, boorish, brutal, vulgar, wild.

He would have to take deep breaths to calm himself. But it didn't work.

It was an agonizing three weeks before the inevitable happened. Late as always, Farraday rushed up to the notice board for the most important moment of the day and its big question – was it going to be manure or something to look forward to?

A good start: a film in the theatre, *Stand By Me*, Rob Reiner, usually pretty good. Then a video: *Risky Business*, seen on film in 1983 so pretty straightforward. Then they were to meet up with four others to watch something ominously titled *Nappy Love*. Grimacing, he then looked to see who he was working with. It was Sadie.

* * *

138

Now flush with money from overcharging the video distributors, Nick had started a major refurbishment of his empire. From the single seedy floor of a few years before he had now taken over the entire building. It was said of Augustus that he found Rome made of brick and left it made of marble. Nick's ambitions tended in very much the same marmoreal direction. I did not understand the high regard that some people had for the importance of architecture until Nick started to renovate (not really an adequate description) No. 8 Golden Square. By the time he was finished three years later I had to change my view. The Secretariat had become a man's soul made flesh in plaster and stone and glass and high end fittings. But this full incarnation was still some way off and the result of all the building work was that the various small cinemas used by the film industry in Soho were often used by the Secretariat.

So it was that with chest heaving and a heart filled with dread as well as terrified longing, Farraday made his way over to Mr Wu's viewing theatre on D'Arblay Street.

Most of these viewing theatres were simply smaller versions of ordinary cinemas but, fortunately for Farraday, Mr Wu's had a console desk at the back with dim reading lights and an intercom patched into the projection booth. It was fortunate because it meant they had no choice but to sit together whereas normally he would have had the appalling freedom to sit anywhere in the cinema and whether he sat near or far it would have screamed out his awkwardness, his shame and guilt.

The wintry trace of a smile she gave him as she looked up shattered any hope that perhaps he had been imagining she'd been avoiding him. Instantly she went back to writing something in her log book that seemed to require Herculean concentration – the equation that finally solved the creation of the universe perhaps, or the paragraph that finally unravelled the meaning of life.

Not looking at her he sat down and took out the thick red log book in which he would novelize the entire film as he watched it, noting down the action scene by scene. He opened it at a clean page, wrote out the title and director and his partner's initials – especially painful – and then waited. The problem was that one of them would have to speak first to tell the projectionist to start. Neither of them said anything. The excruciating silence expanded, as physically real as if the air pressure in the room had been pumped up by several atmospheres. Still the silence went on, an ecstasy of awfulness.

BUZZZZ!

Both of them started, nervous as cats. Instantly they both reached for the intercom and touched hands.

Once, when he was in a chemistry class, one of his teachers had demonstrated the effect of burning sulphur on the human nasal passage by sticking a fuming lump of it on a spatula under his nose. To this day he could remember the explosive and completely involuntary reaction as his head jerked back so violently that his neck was stiff for days.

That was pretty much her reaction on touching his hand.

'Could you start the film please,' he said into the microphone, his voice full of irritation.

'Keep your hair on, squire,' came the unruffled reply through the squawkbox.

The lights dimmed; or rather the dark began to fill the room, the magic precursor to the strange cocoon of light and shadow that gives, to all of us, surely all, such a premonition of delight. Amaze us, says each and every one of us as the dark comes up at the flickering beginning of a film. And though we are nearly always disappointed, that spellbound moment of anticipation always comes. But not for Farraday. Today the clatter and uproar of his emotions deafened him to everything.

The result was that while *Stand By Me* turned out to be a little masterpiece, one he was privileged to see virtually before anyone else, a great pleasure of his job was entirely lost to him that day. Indeed for ever afterwards he could not bring himself to watch it again.

In general (with some eccentric exceptions, of which more later), Nick completely rejected the idea of a check-list with hard and fast rules. But when it came to *the* sexual expletive, the F word, there was only one option. One use of the word 'fuck' and it was a '15'. There were no exceptions. Under normal circumstances Farraday would have regarded it as a crying shame to prevent children from seeing one of the best films about childhood ever made. But there were a number of 'fucks' during the films – the most spectacular being a question from the young hero to the teenage villain asking him, 'Why don't you go home and fuck your mother some more?' So that was that. Nick's fiat on the use of the word held sway and it was hard to argue that the public he served would have taken a different view.

When the lights went up there was a pause. Neither of them looked at each other.

' "15" for the fucks?' he said at last.

'I suppose so. A pity.'

He picked up the yellow form, filled in a few details and scrawled 'Pass 15 uncut' in a large box. He handed it to her to sign. And that was that.

A minute later they were out in the street.

'Look, Sadie . . .'

'I have to get a few things,' she said. 'I'll see you back at work in five minutes.' And with that she walked off. He watched her leave, his heart attacking him, a pitiless and cruel traitor.

Ten minutes later they were in one of the video rooms at the Secretariat watching *Risky Business*. When they finished, the decision to confirm the same category on video as on film was a formality that required little discussion. Nor did it get any.

It was lunchtime. 'I'll be back at two thirty,' she said, and was gone.

For a good ten minutes he sat where he was. He was appalled at himself as he realized that he was close to tears.

'What's the matter with me?' he groaned to McCarthy. 'I'm twenty-nine years of age. My insides feel like . . .' he desperately searched for what they felt like '. . . I feel like some hysterical sixteen-year-old girl. What the fuck is going on?'

McCarthy looked at him. 'Desire is a terrifying leveller.'

Farraday looked back at him – he sounded as if he knew what he was talking about. 'Have you ever felt like this?'

'No, I haven't,' he said softly. 'To be honest, a bit of me envies you.'

'What?'

'I mean it. It must be quite something to be able to feel that way about a woman.'

'It's humiliating. I feel fucking horrible. This just isn't me.'

'Obviously it is.'

'What am I going to do?'

'It'll pass.'

'If you've never felt like this how do you know it'll pass.'

'OK . . . I don't *know* but it's what I think will

142

happen.' There was a silence. 'Do you want it to pass?'

Farraday stood up and began pacing back and forth across the room.

'If I can't—' he stopped pacing, '– have her is the wrong word. But you know what I mean?'

McCarthy nodded.

'If I can't, then I want it to stop. It hurts, it physically hurts.' He started pacing again.

'What if you can?'

'Not very likely. She can't bear to be anywhere near me. And she's married.'

'Would that stop you?'

'I'm ashamed to say that I wouldn't give it a moment's thought. Terrible, isn't it?' He smiled grimly. 'All's fair in love and war.'

Preoccupied with his own thoughts, he didn't notice McCarthy's odd reaction to what he'd said. McCarthy, slightly pale now, stood up. 'I'm going to get some lunch. Want something?'

'Not hungry.'

'I've got to go over to the Fox Theatre in Soho Square to see *Howard the Duck*. See you later.'

When McCarthy arrived at Fox for the afternoon stint, Emma Saward was waiting for him. Both had spent the morning working on their own going through the formalities of giving 'U' certificates to *Fraggle Rock* and a Charlie Chaplin compilation.

Unusually, Dave the projectionist was late and Emma was writing a report.

'Hi.'

'Hello.'

McCarthy sat down and started to open his Boots sandwich. He took a bite and grimaced. 'They keep these

143

things so damned cold they don't really taste of anything.'

She nodded but did not reply, making it clear simply by the way she moved her head that food hygiene regulations were of absolutely no interest to her and what on earth made him think that they were. She carried on writing.

'So,' he said, gesturing at her report, 'what's that a chilling indictment of?'

She sighed and looked at him. 'It's my report on *The Accused*.'

'Oh. So, what did you think?'

'Not bad.'

'I hear a couple of people want to cut back the actual rape.'

'Well,' said with an air of complete finality, 'they're wrong. It's unpleasant but why shouldn't it be? Rape's a violation and as long as it's not trying for a turn-on then I'm all for it being as violent as the real thing. Have you seen it?'

'A couple of days ago. Six of us including Nick –' he paused '– and Sadie.' He smiled. 'You heard what he said to her afterwards?'

For the first time she showed some interest in the conversation – the curious relationship between Sadie and Nick being a source of general curiosity.

'No, I took a couple of days off.'

'Go anywhere interesting?' He was not at all interested, as she well knew, in where she'd been.

'No. So what did he say?'

'After the discussion – apparently he didn't say much – he took Sadie aside and apologized.'

'Really?' said Emma, intrigued. 'What for?'

McCarthy took a thoughtful bite of his sandwich. 'Apparently he said the film made him ashamed to be a man.'

'Why?'

'He said the film made him realize for the first time that there was a profound relationship between the way that men looked at women and the possessive abuse of power relations that was at the root of all rapes. Some claptrap like that anyway.'

She looked thoughtful, but it wasn't clear to McCarthy what she really felt about what Nick had said and he wasn't going to leave it there. 'So, what do you think?'

'Of what?' she said, innocently.

'Of Nick's apology.'

She looked at him directly, and said coolly, 'Seems fair enough.'

'Why?'

'Rape is the means by which all men keep all women in a state of subjugation all of the time.' Her tone was unassertive, as if she were merely stating an uncontroversial truth universally acknowledged.

'One of yours?' said McCarthy.

'Susan Brownmiller.' She looked at him with pretend surprise. 'You don't agree?'

He smiled. 'So you'd like an apology from me, too?'

'If you want to say something to me, Rob, I'm very willing to listen.'

He laughed. 'You don't seriously think that all men are rapists.'

'Are you telling me or asking me?'

He looked at her reproachfully. 'Emma, I wouldn't dream of *telling* you anything, I wouldn't dare. I'm terrified of you.' He smiled. 'Which seems to indicate that I'm the one in a state of subjugation.'

'It's because men are afraid of women that they need to use their physical strength to keep them under control.'

She looked at him, again directly in the eyes. 'Your fear of me as a woman *is* the problem.'

'Come on, Emma, you're not seriously saying that as we're having this disagreement one of the factors, something that's banging around here between us now, is that you're having to overcome a fear of being raped just because I disagree with you?'

She sighed as if she were a teacher dealing with a slightly dim pupil who repeatedly kept not getting the point of the lesson. 'Don't be literal, Rob. It's wrong to say that all women are imminently under threat of rape by any man they happen to be talking to. Rape is a symbolic act; it's not about sex at all. It's about power, an assertion of power based on fear of women, of the feminine.' She smiled. 'Your attempt to provoke me could be construed as a piece of amicable teasing. On the other hand, some might see it as an act of dominance. You want to belittle the intellectual position I hold as a feminist to make it seem extreme or self-evidently unreasonable. Slightly mad.' She looked at him again and said sweetly, 'You don't think it's possible?'

His feelings for her then were by no means charitable and some unpleasant words were repressed. But he replied brightly. 'You mean a kind of word-rape?'

'That's one way of putting it.'

'But Emma, I'm the one who's been defeated by your words. What does that make you?'

The intercom buzzed. It was Dave the projectionist.

'Sorry I'm late. Some stupid cow at the surgery mixed up my appointment. Shall we crack on?'

He did not wait for a reply. The lights dimmed and the screen burst into bright life.

146

The Recipe for Shit

MEANWHILE IN VIEWING ROOM three at Golden Square a group of six examiners were watching *Nappy Love*. So far they had seen an overweight, middle-aged man being stripped by a woman of similar age. She had washed him on a rubber blanket on a dining table while he watched, all the while sucking a dummy. She'd dried him carefully, pausing only to tell him in strict but affectionate terms to stop struggling and be a good boy while Mummy finished changing him. She had then powdered his bottom and pinned him, with some considerable difficulty, into an enormous nappy.

During the previous three years the censors in the room had seen between them some twenty thousand videos. A few had been enthralling, some admirable, some simply enjoyable, some ordinary, some dull, some bad, some worse. During the most hideous they had experienced almost every kind of depravity and mayhem, the loathsome, the brutal, the downright disgusting, the malicious, the simply cruel. But they had never seen anything like *Nappy Love*; more to the point they had never felt such a strange mixture of disbelief, astonishment, disgust, pity and general bewilderment. Things were about to get worse.

Up to the ten-minute point there had been no edits in the video – *Nappy Love* observed the classical unities of time and space. Then suddenly the baby was sitting in the corner playing with a rattle and with a dummy still firmly in place in his enormous gob. Then at once it fell from his lips and he began to bawl. His mother came back into the room.

'Oh dear, baby,' she said, 'I expect you need changing.'

There was a groan of appalled anticipation from the watching censors. Another edit. Now baby was back on the rubber mat. Mother duly undid the pins, folded the nappy back and with considerable help from baby himself raised his legs into the air.

There was a spontaneous cry of disgust from everyone present.

Baby's bum was covered in shit. For the remaining ten minutes Mother wiped and cleaned and sponged and swabbed. Then she smoothed on cream for his rash and talc to keep him dry. And then she wrapped him again. All the time baby cooed and gurgled happily.

Then it was over. For a while no one said anything. It was Rhys who spoke first. 'Fucking hell!'

The others followed with assorted groans, grimaces, 'Dear God!' and a number of shudders.

The door opened and Nick came in carrying the file. He was smiling.

'So,' he said, 'what did you think?'

Again more groans and shudders. He laughed and opened the file. 'Just a little test of the law for you. There's an important legal problem to get out of the way here.' He looked around amiably. 'Anyone?' He looked at me, smiling. 'Duncan, you're usually the one who knows this kind of thing.'

I was being nakedly condescended to. Now that I'd seen the letter in my file I'd revised every compliment I had received at the Secretariat and felt a burning shame that I had not seen it for what it was. I could barely answer.

'I don't remember the exact words,' I said, 'but the Obscene Publications Act makes specific reference to images involving something like "human excretory functions".'

Nick looked at the others. 'Take your example from Duncan Purcell. The complete censor. He's quite right.'

'That's it,' I thought to myself, 'just keep on talking down to me, you fuck.'

'Why?' said Sadie.

I felt a surge of hatred for her as if my guts were being cruelly scalded by some cackling devil. Almost immediately I realized she was not questioning my abilities but merely querying the law with regard to acts of defecation. I was astonished by my own reaction. Where had it come from, this squall of hate?

'What do you mean?' said Nick.

'Why would you have a law specifically banning shit in videos? It's such a bizarre thing to worry about. I mean, you've been a censor for nearly fifteen years – how often have you seen "excretory functions" before this?'

'Only once,' he said. 'Pasolini's Salo, 120 days of Sodom.'

'So why do we need to have a law specifically forbidding it?'

'Perhaps they're worried it'll catch on,' said Molly Tydeman. 'I mean you can see the attraction.'

The laughter was as much of relief as amusement. It acted like water and soap.

'Notwithstanding Sadie's objections, the law is the law. So what do we do?'

'Surely,' said Molly, 'it must be relevant whether it's real or not . . . the shit, I mean. What did you do about the shit in Salo?'

149

'Indeed it is . . . in my view at any rate. I wrote to Pasolini and not only did he assure me that the shit in *Salo* was not real – it was hardly likely to be after all – but he even gave me the recipe.' He looked around the room, pausing for effect. 'Cocoa, marmalade and the crumbs from digestive biscuits.'

'So that was OK then, you didn't cut?' said Sadie.

'I'm afraid that's a long story and the film was tricky in all sorts of other ways. I'll get the file sent down later and you can have a look. But then, of course, it was Pasolini. *Nappy Love* isn't.'

'Is that relevant?'

'I don't know,' said Nick. 'Is it?'

'Did you ask the *Nappy Love* people if it was real?'

'Indeed we did.'

'And?'

'Apparently not.'

'Thank God for that,' said Rhys.

'So what was it?'

'What was what?'

'Their recipe for shit.'

'Jelly and HP sauce.'

There was another general shudder.

'I don't see that it really gets us off the hook. I mean *Salo* ran into a lot of trouble legally, didn't it?'

'Absolutely. But as I said that was for other reasons. The Vice Squad seized a copy of the film but as far as I know they were worried about other things than the shit-eating. Though having said that, it wasn't easy to get anything very clear out of them. Basically it came down to the fact that they were genuinely disgusted by the film. What that implies is that they might very easily seize this. I imagine the average copper would be pretty disgusted by *Nappy Love*. I have to say that I'm having a pretty hard time with it myself.'

'Me, too,' said Rhys. 'Let's face it, this is about as abject as human sexuality gets.'

For a moment no one said anything.

'But it wasn't made for us. It's a special tape for people who have a special relationship with this kind of thing.' It was the first time Farraday had said anything.

'I don't understand what that's got to do with it,' said Rhys, irritated.

'Me neither,' said Nick.

'I don't think it's meant for an audience at all, at least not in the usual sense.'

RHYS

How can it not be meant for an audience? Obviously it is.

FARRADAY

I said, in the usual sense. The thing is that we *think* we're capable of understanding everything we see. Some of us like horror films and violent movies – we're not supposed to be above this material in some Olympian way . . . we're supposed to understand it, not just judge it. Even if some of us don't like horror films they're still rooted in conventions that are so common, so inherently human if you like, that they're a long way from being incomprehensible. When Sadie wrote her piece on horror . . .

He'd said her name before he realized what he'd done. Her eyes opened wide in shock. He could only keep going.

FARRADAY (cont)

. . . some of us who didn't care for it began to understand what the pleasures of such films might be. Not to put too fine a point on it – she educated us. But only in the sense that she reshaped our views by making us more aware of pleasures we take in other kinds of films and making it clear that

151

similar pleasures existed in horror films. But I defy her or anyone to do the same for *Nappy Love*. The pleasures here are . . . untranslatable if you like. We're never going to understand this in the way you understand the pleasure of watching a voluptuous woman being stripped of her clothes by a bunch of hooligans. No matter how much part of you might be revolted, another part of you – I'm speaking of the men here obviously – can understand the pleasures of watching something like that.

But our disgust at the sexualized rape is quite different from the disgust we feel looking at a 200-pound man having his shitty bottom wiped – even if it is made from custard powder and HP sauce.

MOLLY TYDEMAN

Jelly and HP sauce.

FARRADAY

I stand corrected.

RHYS

You were probably confusing it with your favourite pudding at Eton.

There was much laughter at this, not least from Farraday who then turned to Rhys bristling with mock hauteur.

FARRADAY

Actually I was at *Winchester* – and there my favourite pudding was a first-former served arse upwards on a bed of lukewarm tapioca.

The laughter was even greater at this. It wasn't easy to come out on top in an exchange with Farraday.

MOLLY TYDEMAN

I've got a problem about what you're saying, Tom. I disagree

152

that you have to share a pleasure to understand it. I certainly don't feel a dodgy thrill when I see a sexualized rape but I'm perfectly able to understand what's going on – nudity has an obvious sexual pleasure attached to it, and so does watching the taboos being broken that stop men from having sex with a woman unless she agrees.

NICK

You've lost me here, Molly. Are you saying you can understand the pleasures of *Nappy Love*?

MOLLY

God, no. And I don't want to. To be honest I wish I hadn't seen it. I don't want the image of that man in my head.

NICK

But why, that's the question?

MOLLY

It clashes with everything I am, I suppose – how I feel about babies and adult men, and, I suppose, shit.

NICK

But it's our job. This is what we're paid to do.

FARRADAY

It doesn't matter how much it's our job. What I'm saying is that you can't understand what you can't understand.

NICK

How are we going to categorize it if we don't understand it?

FARRADAY

What's wrong with owning up to the fact that our way of putting a grid over the world of human experience just falls apart at certain points? After all why shouldn't it? I mean the thing that people usually accuse censors of is that we're morally vain – that we think we're better than other people, made from morally stronger stuff and so we can take the depravity that would corrupt ordinary people not as morally upright as we are. But in fact our vanity is exactly the opposite – we all think that we are, at least in part, as bad as the audience – at least the corruptible audience because we know that most people are not depraved by what they see. It's our old friend the vulnerable minority we're really dealing with and we think we can be like them. We think we can look into the corruption of our own souls and recognize the illegitimate desires festering there so we know what to cut out and what to leave in.

He looked at Nick and smiled.

FARRADAY (cont)

When you apologized to Sadie the other day about *The Accused*, Nick, it was a kind of boast, wasn't it? What you were really saying – a vanity I freely admit we're all guilty of – was that you are a morally upright, responsible, civilized man but you also recognize your job is to boldly go into the dark recesses of your inner hooligan, the beast inside, and interrogate him, at whatever risk to yourself, so that right may be done. A noble sacrifice.

Everyone was laughing now, except for Nick. It would be difficult to put your finger on his response. It was nothing as crude as anger at having had his motives questioned. But what was that odd smile? It looked like someone who knew he was still in the right but who also knew that others would not understand his explanation because they lacked his self-knowledge. He had taken the jibe with a mixture of good humour and condescension – a kind of 'you laugh at me now but one day you'll understand'. Nick could be a forgiving god. Farraday wasn't thinking at all about Nick, however, his heart had exploded and contracted simultaneously because when he had finished Sadie was laughing, too. He was too delighted to do more than merely register that she was also turning him into an idiot being suffocated by a deranged obsession.

'Thank you for that, Tom,' said Nick drily. 'Illuminating even if insulting. Although the one thing it didn't illuminate was what we should do about this tape. Suggestions anyone?'

'Make it "R18",' said Rhys.

'Not really possible.'

'Why not?'

'The few licensed sex shops there are are owned by two companies. This is highly specialized material and there's not much profit to be made by the producers of *Nappy Love*. They found it hard enough to raise the fee to certificate it. They'd make a loss if they tried to sell it through the sex shops because they'd want a huge cut to distribute it. The only way it can reach its very rarefied market is if it goes out at "18". Then they can advertise in a few selected magazines and send it through the post. They've no idea what the size of the market is for material about adult babies.'

'What are you going to do?'

'Think about it. I can't say I'm altogether happy about the idea of men having shit wiped off their bottoms being out in the public domain.' He laughed. 'God knows what the *Daily Mail* would say if it found out – and there's plenty of trouble ahead there in any case. My feeling that things have been going too well turns out to be right. A couple of days ago I was summoned to appear before a Parliamentary Select Committee. My information is that they're going to be extremely hostile. Frankly, I need *Nappy Love* like I need a hole in the head.' He stood up. 'Anyway, let me have your reports and I'll come up with something at the next Examiners meeting.'

When he'd gone, Molly looked thoughtful. 'That's odd,' she said.

'What?' replied Sadie.

'I've never heard him refer to it as the Examiners meeting. Before it always used to be the Secretariat meeting.'

'A slip of the tongue?'

'Of course,' said Molly, 'why would anyone be paranoid about what Nick is up to?' She raised her voice to catch Farraday's attention. 'So, Tom, you seem to have been deeply touched by *Nappy Love*. Is there anything you want to share with us?'

Tom smiled. 'There's no way that I could be an adult baby, attractive though the idea is in so many ways.'

'Why's that?'

'I don't like jelly and I'm allergic to the anchovies in HP sauce.'

'Whatever you say, I felt a real empathy when you were talking.'

'Quite right – it was what Allan said about this representing human sexual desire at its most abject.' He looked at Rhys. 'Sorry, but at the risk of sounding like a limp-wristed liberal, I think that's pretty harsh.'

'Don't be sorry,' said Rhys, clearly irritated. 'It was meant to be harsh. Though I wouldn't accuse you of being liberal – how about pious?'

Farraday laughed. 'Touché. I suppose I deserved that.'

'Don't tell me that if you knew someone who dressed themselves up in a nappy and got someone to wipe their bottom, you wouldn't be revolted . . . because I wouldn't believe you.'

Farraday's smile had changed – he'd tried being charming but now it was going to be a fight. Molly was interested, even excited, as she saw the two men squaring up. She turned to Sadie.

'I think it's going to be behind the bike sheds after school, don't you?'

But Sadie was clearly uneasy, looking at Farraday with her wide eyes.

'The thing is, Allan, you don't know what I think. I'll admit that if I came into the room and saw you with your arse in the air and some woman wiping it with Johnson's Baby Oil I might find it difficult to see you in the same way.'

Rhys said nothing.

'The thing is,' continued Farraday, 'that what occurred to me while watching the tape is that while dressing up in leather or wanting to be tied up and beaten might be pretty unusual, it's still something, even if leather and bondage weren't to your taste, that you could pretty easily understand. I mean suppose after watching all the weird stuff we see in this place you were to discover that it turned you on, probably no one here would be that bothered if they knew you were into rubber or bondage or whatever—'

'Speak for yourself,' said Molly. 'I'd be appalled if people knew I couldn't have an orgasm unless I have a rubber truncheon in my bottom.' She fluttered her eyelids as if daring those present to disbelieve her.

'Well, even so,' continued Farraday, 'I don't see that there could be any element of choice here about the adult babies. Leather and bondage and practically every other activity that used to be regarded as perversions are being absorbed into mainstream culture – these images are everywhere: adverts, pop videos. But that's never going to happen with this stuff. Maybe I'm wrong, maybe the adult babies are quite happy with their obsession but I don't think so. I think this is a terrible, arbitrary visitation and that it could have happened to anyone. Because you couldn't choose this. I agree with you, Allan, after all – it *is* abject. Perhaps you're right, you probably are – I couldn't be anything but disgusted if I knew someone was doing this. But it wouldn't be a choice – how could it be? You couldn't *blame* someone for wanting this because I just don't believe anyone could choose it. It would . . . it could only be visited on you – a terrible, horribly undignified affliction that if other people knew about they could only be revolted by. But I just think it could, with a lot of bad luck, easily be you or me.' He paused and smiled. 'So, be sickened all you like Allan, just thank God it didn't happen to you.'

Rhys shrugged. 'Thanks for the sermon.' Then he picked up his stuff and walked out.

In the awkward silence that followed Farraday realized that Sadie was looking at him directly for the first time in weeks. For a moment his eyes locked on hers. Then she turned away, picked up her log book and also left.

When she'd gone, Molly started chattering on but he wasn't listening. He was thinking about the look that Sadie had given him and that he had absolutely no idea what it meant.

Without ever really thinking about it carefully I realize that I had always thought of the pivotal moments in one's life as being *obviously* pivotal: the marriage proposal, the birth of a child, someone asking you at knifepoint to hand over your wallet, you *know* that these are the experiences that count. So I want to tell you now about something that at the time I regarded as simply an odd thing that happened but which now I realize was a key moment in my life, a central one at which the points on my rail lines shifted and took me in a direction very far from the one I had in mind not just *for* myself but *as* myself. Now I know what it meant but not then.

I'd been working solo on a fresh print of *Spartacus*. A newly discovered sequence had been inserted of Olivier and the beautifully youthful Tony Curtis in the bathhouse, for which the original soundtrack had been lost. The dialogue had been recreated from the screenplay, with Anthony Hopkins impersonating the late Olivier as he was being washed by his new body servant while he engaged the young man in a magnificently camp discussion about oysters. Throughout the exchange Curtis is obliged to soap Olivier in what can only be described as a lascivious manner while the latter curls his lips and rolls his eyes as suggestively as a Soho transvestite.

MARCUS LICINIUS CRASSUS: Do you eat oysters?

ANTONINUS: When I can get them, master.

MARCUS LICINIUS CRASSUS: Do you eat snails?

ANTONINUS: No, master.

MARCUS LICINIUS CRASSUS: Do you consider the eating of oysters to be moral and the eating of snails to be immoral?

ANTONINUS: No, master.

MARCUS LICINIUS CRASSUS: Of course not. It is all a matter of taste, isn't it?

ANTONINUS: Yes, master.

MARCUS LICINIUS CRASSUS: And taste is not the same as appetite, and therefore not a question of morals.

ANTONINUS: It could be argued so, master.

MARCUS LICINIUS CRASSUS: My robe, Antoninus. My taste includes both snails and oysters.

Odd, I thought, how discussions of taste and morality always seem to come with a hidden life of their own.

I paid for this treat with the remainder of the day being spent watching cartoons. Despite the caution instigated by the infamous discovery of numerous obscene titles in the background of the Rupert Bear cartoon I got fed up, especially as it was an unseasonably hot day and the air conditioning wasn't working, and fast-forwarded through three hours of this sherbet dip. Then I decided to go and hide on the roof – not as daring as it sounds because it was completely flat and could be easily accessed by a door in the upstairs kitchen. But on getting out on the roof and turning a corner so I couldn't be seen, I came across Sadie sunbathing on a white towel. She was not enticingly naked, nor was she even topless. She had hiked her long, pale blue summer skirt to the top of her thighs and she had taken off her blouse. Nevertheless, the bra she was wearing was almost as old-fashioned as the ones my mother used to wear in the fifties, and the amount of leg she was showing was no more than if she had been wearing a bikini. But it was a dazzling sight even so. She was the most modest of dressers, nice enough clothes but never tight or revealing, except for her shoulders.

'Sorry,' I said and turned my back.

'Oh, don't worry,' she replied – a little flustered but she certainly didn't make much of being found like this – after all she was as covered up as if she had been wearing a bikini on the beach. But context in these matters is everything, I suppose. 'I'm decent,' she said and I turned back. For about ten minutes we chatted idly and then she left.

During the time we had been talking and for some time after I thought – though that's not the right word – about the brief moment I had seen her so modestly undressed. Everyone recognized that Sadie was beautiful – it was a fact just like the fact that she was tiny. But seeing her like this, however briefly, was astonishing. She didn't look at all the way I had vaguely expected – a skinny model's body to go with her model's face. How someone barely more than five foot could be described as statuesque seems impossible but that's what she was. I don't think I've ever seen a more womanly body on someone barely taller than the average thirteen-year-old. Her calves were beautifully curved with just the seam of her muscles to give them a streamlined elegance. Her thighs seemed endless – though they weren't – smooth and taut and creamy brown. Her stomach was flat with a perfect covering of subcutaneous fat over the strong muscles. And her breasts seemed both large for such a small woman and yet entirely in proportion while the upper half gently shook as she reacted suddenly to my arrival. Without clothes – although of course she wasn't – she seemed both like Sadie and an entirely other person.

I now realize that something in me failed after I saw her like that, the way a weak bridge fails in a high wind. It was hope that collapsed, I think. Because I saw something entirely beautiful up there and if any woman were ever to be given as evidence for the assertion that the human body is the best picture of the human soul, that woman was Sadie with her wonderfully womanly body and her wonderfully beautiful mind. And what I realized but could not acknowledge up on the roof was a terrible despair that this was something I could never be touched by. No one this beautiful or this extraordinary would ever look at me in the way that you would want to be looked at by such a creature. It would, *could* never happen. Never. And that loss was a terrible, a fatal blow to the heart and soul. I had seen loveliness and grasped something closely of what it was, but only enough to realize that this was it. I wasn't good enough for it. Not worthy of it. Horrible, horrible, most horrible.

You will think that the root of all the misery you are about to see unfold is because I coveted her – that I decided I would destroy her because I desired her and she would never desire me. But it wasn't that, I swear it was not sexual jealousy, it was beauty envy. There was no lust

Watching the Detectives

A WEEK BEFORE THE next Secretariat meeting a tract appeared on the examiners' notice board. This in itself was not unusual; the examiners were always writing down bits and pieces of general interest that they wanted to bring to the attention of their colleagues: polemics about this or that, rape in films, use of weapons, drug use, and replies to them usually expressing disagreement. People would often pin up another examiner's report they'd read in a file and thought others should see. What was odd on this occasion was that the short essay came from the Deputy Director Walter Casey, and the tone was rather different from anything that had gone up on the notice board before.

The last few years since the passing of the Video Recordings Act have been stimulating and often challenging. Perhaps in some ways too challenging in that one way of looking at what we do increasingly predominates and does so at the expense of more instinctive reactions to what we watch – the now much derided 'gut reaction'. The most vigorous opponents of this more intuitive approach are of course two examiners (mostly) affectionately

163

known as Lord Snooty and his pal, Gnasher, otherwise Tom Farraday and Rob McCarthy. In pursuit of what they see as a more rigorous and closely argued approach to the work we do here they have, in my humble opinion, marginalized something that I am convinced, and I know others agree, is central to our arriving at decisions: not just what we think but how we *feel* about what we are watching. It is not always possible for some people to clearly articulate why they feel, perhaps, deeply disturbed about a particular film that they feel crosses the line into the destructive and malign. Because of the McCarthy/Farraday steamroller such inarticulate doubts are dismissed immediately and even, on occasions, derided in an examining culture which now favours only the intellect. Yet human beings are more than intellects and human judgements more than intellectual. The work we view, and specifically the problematic work, mostly comes from the irrational and murky depth of the psyche and makes its appeal there also. Certainly the public on whose behalf we do our work would be, I think it is fair to say, pretty hostile to the mandarin intellectual approach which has increasingly become a kind of blasphemy to question.

Walter Casey

Having watched, back-to-back, The Big Easy (wonderful) and Can You Keep It Up for a Week? (beyond belief) Rob McCarthy was bursting and headed straight for the loos. Both cubicles were locked but this was not a problem because there was another much larger one across the aisle which had been expensively designed for wheelchair access. For those of you who feel strongly about the misuse of such facilities it should be pointed out in McCarthy's defence that not only weren't there any disabled people at the Secretariat but they wouldn't have

164

been able to use this facility in any case because the toilets had been built halfway up a staircase. Desperate to relieve himself by now he pushed the door with greater strength than would normally have been the case. Whoever had bolted the door had barely allowed the bolt to touch the lock and after holding momentarily it flew open with a crash.

There was a cry of astonishment from a good-looking Japanese woman but not because she had been caught on the loo. In fact she was bent low over the large basin. She started back in alarm, a tell-tale white smudge dusting her upper lip.

'God, Katie, I'm so—' McCarthy's apology was stilled by the two lines of coke laid out neatly on the Italian lime-stone surface (only the swankiest for Nick).

'Christ, Rob, you nearly gave me a heart attack,' Katie said, clearly relieved. 'You won't say anything?' It was not a plea but rather a taken-for-granted bit of reassurance.

Agumi Ohashi – always known by her middle name, Katie – was the daughter of a Japanese father and a Scottish mother who had come to England when she was eight, soon after her parents had divorced. She had been hired by Nick to translate the videos expected to arrive from distributors renting to the twenty thousand or so Japanese resident in the UK, as well as the visiting tourists. It was some time before it was generally realized that Katie's strange behaviour had nothing to do with her being Japanese and therefore something that could be explained by cultural misunderstanding, but was because she was both thick and, as it later turned out, frequently high on drugs.

The Japanese videos she had been hired to translate never materialized. This was just as well because her grasp of Japanese was, after all these years, pretty ropey. Nick

165

had taken a liking to her, oddly inspired by the fact that she was regarded as careless and incompetent by her colleagues. His approval of her was not, of course, because of this but more that he was inclined to believe that the examiners were against her because she was not like them. The examiners were aggravated by Katie because she was incapable of writing anything clearly and her judgements were wildly unpredictable. Nick defended her on the grounds that she was instinctive and emotional and had a wisdom beyond the self-important rationality so typical of most of his employees. In short, she was a half-wit. Nevertheless with the occasional flash of low cunning of which even a dunce is capable she knew when not to disagree with Nick and, more importantly, when to disagree with the mass of examiners about Nick's right to make arbitrary decisions – or as he put it, his right to manage.

The more the examiners complained about her for trying to cut or ban films for no clearly articulated reason, the more Nick defended her instincts as a necessary balance. Nevertheless, despite Nick's enthusiasm for her emotional sincerity, Walter was always careful to put her with an examiner he regarded as a safe pair of hands and who would be sure to stop her from doing anything daft. Her already erratic judgement was not helped by her increasing dependency on a bizarre range of experimental drugs, a habit she could afford to indulge because of the hefty salary she now earned as an examiner, a wage, given her talents, well beyond anything she had earned before or was likely to earn anywhere else.

Katie nodded towards the lines of coke next to the basin.

'You're a sweetie, Rob. Do you want some?'

'No thanks,' replied McCarthy, hearing a cubicle across the way being unlocked, 'not while I'm censoring. I find

166

it tends to bring out the chattering classes liberal in me.'

A few minutes later he wandered back to his room and on the way met Molly Tydeman. 'Watching anything interesting?' he asked.

'*Animal Farm*.'

'The cartoon? I haven't seen that since I was a kid.'

Her face wrinkled. 'Nothing to do with Orwell. It's the one where the women have sex with animals in a farmyard.'

'Oh dear,' replied McCarthy sympathetically. He sighed. 'Poor old Boxer.'

But something else was on her mind.

'Have you seen the notice board upstairs since this morning?'

'No.'

'Walter has had a go at you and Tom.'

At the meeting a week later Nick was unusually silent until the agenda had been dealt with and it was time for Any Other Business.

'I'd like to say something,' said Nick quietly, 'and I would like you to wait until I've finished before you respond.'

Then he denounced us. Have you ever been denounced? Probably not. We tend to associate that kind of thing with communist regimes and the odd dictator. (In general, fascists seem to prefer the visit in the night and the mysterious disappearance. I wonder why the left likes to wag a public finger before it puts a bullet in your head.)

At any rate for the next twenty minutes we were, all of us, denounced. We had turned away, he said, from an honest, emotional response to the growing violence in videos and towards an intellectual, overly analytical approach that was far removed from either the public whose servants we were or the ethos of the Secretariat itself.

He did not raise his voice but it was the calm of the profoundly stirred. He had, he went on, worked for many years to balance the rights of those who took pleasure in extreme material even if he disapproved of it, against the rights of the wider public to be protected from the potential that such material had for harm. He accepted that this line was a difficult one to tread but it was essential, it was fundamental that the desire to protect the public from the thug, the bully, the abuser, the rapist should be uppermost not in our minds but in our instincts. 'It is time to make a stand against gang violence in particular. And I have to say that we need to be careful not to trivialize violence by using such terms as "splatter violence" to undermine our emotional responses to mutilation on film and video. However impressive Sadie's defence of horror films may have been I can't allow such terms to disguise that what we are seeing here is a person being brutalized for entertainment.'

At this point Sadie spoke up. 'Look, Nick—' she said, furious. But Nick wasn't to be stopped.

'I made it clear when I began that I wanted to finish before there were any comments.'

'Your remarks about my paper', she replied, 'are a travesty of what I wrote. I want to register a complaint now and I want it to be minuted.'

Nick was livid. 'I'm sick and tired of being interrupted – this kind of thing happens far too often. I expect to finish what I have to say. Is that understood?'

He glared around the room. The atmosphere was a mixture of the astonished and the sullen. Then he continued the attack.

It was the censor's obligation to defend the weak from

the malign. But we, by which he meant the examiners, had gone too far. We had deserted those instincts in favour of an increasingly cerebral approach which lacked a simple fundamental that we should care deeply for the victims of violence and abuse. ' "The supreme triumph of reason", ' he quoted softly, ' "is to realize its limitations." I cannot allow the examiners to undermine the true work of the Secretariat.'

Having finished he leant back with the iron look of a man who *knows* he is right but expects to be howled down by his utterly misguided opponents.

You will have gathered by now that the examiners were certainly familiar with Nick's capacity to take sudden and inexplicable positions on any number of matters. But this time they were as mystified as when he had claimed that they had not been fired but given a contract. Even those who were furious at being condemned in such terms were utterly bemused. What on earth was he talking about? He had given no specific examples; the consistent grumbling in the *Daily Mail* and *Express* had been no worse than it always was. What did he mean?

With unfazed righteousness, Nick produced a newspaper clipping and began to read:

New Yorkers are still reeling with horror after last week's attack by a group of twelve or so Harlem teenagers on a woman jogger in Central Park during a 'wilding'. The term was unknown to New York detectives until this attack but it meant going out in wolf packs and assaulting anyone, especially women, they could find.

The attackers, all boys between the ages of thirteen and fourteen, chased down the 110lb investment banker and dragged her 200 yards to a secluded section of the park where they fractured her skull with four-foot lead pipes and some large rocks. The boys ripped her clothes off, tied her hands behind her back, gagged her and then took turns beating, raping and stomping on her, all the time singing a version of 'Wild Things', the song from which 'wilding' takes its name. Although the woman survived she was so badly beaten, losing 75 per cent of her blood, that initially she was declared 'dead on arrival'.

Almost as shocking to Americans is that after being arrested the young attackers spent the night in jail joking to their guards about the rape, singing songs and making obscene jokes to policewomen. In a written confession one of the boys said, 'It was fun.'

Nick finished and sat back defiantly. Walter Casey and Beth Ackroyd sat on either side of him, faces impassive.

There was silence for a moment. The first person to speak was McCarthy. 'Look, Nick, what you've just read out is pretty unpleasant . . . no one is going to disagree. But I have to confess that I don't understand what it's got to do with us.'

There was a general murmur of puzzled agreement.

'The fact that you don't see what I'm driving at may be the problem, don't you think?'

'I don't think we know what to think, Nick,' said Molly Tydeman.

Before he could reply, a clearly furious Emma Saward interrupted. 'Are you seriously saying that the women examiners don't take violence against women seriously? Would you like to give us some examples so we know what the hell you're talking about?'

For the first time, Nick looked uncertain; a slight hint of caution hedged his reply. 'I don't mean that everyone, all the time, is . . .' he paused, searching '. . . letting their head rule their emotional response to violence, but that this is a growing tendency and it's something we at the Secretariat all have to take on board. Our discussions are too academic, too stuck on some abstract notion of rights and not enough on the fact that we live in the real world – a world where the kind of people who commit attacks like this exist. I want you to stop and think about violence and ask yourself next time you want to commit your often wonderfully well worked out and clever arguments for passing it . . . to ask yourself if you really want people like this –' he tapped the newspaper cutting '– if you want them to watch it. These people exist,' he declared, 'and I want you to take that on board, to remember that part of your job, perhaps the most important part, is not to come up with lots of theories about films but to protect the public from people like this.'

And with that he stood up and walked out.

For many years it was believed that Trobriand Island had no word for 'because'. In their world view there was no cause and effect: for them things just happened. As it later turned out this theory was based on a misunder-standing – the Trobriands were just like the rest of us: they knew perfectly well that there was an explanation for the things that happened to them but hardly ever understood what it was. The trouble is, I find, that most people's explanations for the things that happen to them, or any-body else, are rubbish. I include myself in this dismissal. Especially.

For a group who prided themselves on their under-standing of complexity, the Seven's attempt at an explanation for their denunciation was less than im-pressive, to the point of being feeble, in fact.

If I were being generous I might say that the three women were furious at being blamed for their in-difference to the abuse of women. This had opened an old

Lord Snooty's Pal

YOU MIGHT WELL TAKE the view that Nick's censure of his employees and Walter Casey's criticism of Farraday and McCarthy the week before had been part of a planned attack on the emerging power of the examiners. Strangely enough I don't think this was true – it wasn't really in Casey's temperament to be calculated in that way. I think it was simply coincidence that they had both become uneasy about what was happening at the same time. And given that what they feared actually was taking place perhaps it wasn't really much of a coincidence at all. At any rate Casey's piece wasn't going to go unanswered. Ten days after it went up and three days after the meeting, Rob McCarthy pinned his reply (to both Walter and Nick) to the notice board.

In a recent tape about zombies in Wolverhampton one of the characters claims: 'Part of my Id is missing'. After Walter Casey's roasting on the Noticeboard of Truth I was beginning to wonder if I had much the same problem. It is an ardent, sincere and deeply felt criticism but it's also a caricature. 'It's the supreme triumph of reason,' said Nick at the meeting quoting someone or other, 'to realize its own limitations.' Amen to that – but the argument is not that reason doesn't have its limitations but that any other way of approaching what we do here is far worse. You can at least reason with reason but you can't do the same with someone's gut reaction. It is what it is and there's no point in telling someone they don't feel what they patently do. If you want to change their mind all you have is reason; asserting your own gut reaction will clearly get you nowhere. I can readily admit that your gut reaction might be more honest and even just plain more right than my attempts at providing a clear account of what I feel and think – but gut reaction is a dead end, there's no arguing with it. Rationality is the one means human beings have of mediating between their intuitions and emotions, of trying to clarify and explain them. Walter's implied alternative feels wrong in my gut as it happens.

Only a couple of years ago we had the assorted shrinks from the Farber Clinic come here with their deranged tales of satanic ritual abuse, not only failing to provide evidence but deeply dismissive of the idea that they should do so. They left the BFS with a flea in their ear precisely because of our commitment to the rationality Walter is now wringing his hands about. As I write this there are more than seventy investigations into such abuse around the country involving foetal sacrifice, dismemberment, massive sexual abuse of children, the skinning of babies and so on. Almost two hundred children have been taken away in dawn raids and placed in care without a shred of solid evidence to back up these claims. And while we saw the small beginnings of these witch-hunts in this very building Walter wants to argue that we should bow down to instinct and gut reaction in Nietzsche's phrase 'like stupefied peasants'. I don't know what the parents of these seized children would have felt about mandarin intellectuals before they were so grotesquely accused, but I'm prepared to bet that many of them would have agreed with Walter. What connects us so closely with them is that the BFS owes its current power and wealth to the same worry about what is being done to children. Not all of this alarm is irrational, any more than concern about the sexual abuse of children is irrational, but the intellectual steamroller disdained by Walter (not all the product of two people by any means) has meant that whatever our faults as an organization our reaction to these fears for children has been reasonably balanced and reasonably sane. That these same concerns can lead to what is happening in Rochdale and the Orkneys shows how thin the line really is between madness and civilization, and what can happen when those with power are in the grip of instinct rather than reason. I don't think those now accused of black magic and cannibalism would feel quite as enthusiastic about the exercise of the law by intuition and intensity of feeling as Walter Casey and Nick Berg. When it comes to the exercise of institutional power I'd rather take my chances with the mandarin Lord Snooty and his pals than the head of Rochdale social services any day.

Rob McCarthy

He was a strange character, McCarthy, not least because for a long time until his past came out I thought he seemed the most well-balanced of us all. Except, that is, for myself – the stripping of my own delusions on that score were still a way off. He was amiable, very intelligent, almost as smart, in his own way, as Farraday. He seemed to epitomize the notion that what you see is what you get. Annie Byers, one of the examiners who had come to the Secretariat about five years before the Seven and who had just finished training as a psychoanalyst, said of McCarthy, 'He knows who he is.' Perhaps, though in a way she certainly didn't intend, she was right.

As a civil servant I had always regarded myself as a good organizer but McCarthy had a natural ability for seeing how offices worked. He once spent an hour during some ghastly cartoon explaining how the Secretariat could be made to function more efficiently. Certainly I was aware of the clumsy way it worked: it didn't take a genius to see that no one had ever sat down to simplify the ludicrously complicated paperwork, or work out a way to give people feedback on mistakes they had made. The thing that impressed me about McCarthy's solutions were that they were often very simple – but you could see how effective they would be. I encouraged him to approach Walter Casey with his ideas, but Walter was evasive to the point of being dismissive. One of his suggested reforms, however, had been seized on with real enthusiasm by the examiners. Walter Casey and Beth Ackroyd had tried to argue it was unnecessary, yet oddly, it turned out, Nick was keen. That was because he didn't understand what it meant.

McCarthy was arguing for the creation of something he called the Review Committee. The RC, as it was always referred to from then on, would meet once a week. There would be three examiners and one member of the management team. They would look at any tape referred to it by either group on the grounds that if it threw up an issue of general importance then it ought to be examined in detail. The Committee would then report back to the monthly Secretariat meeting. If this seems rather dry and technical you should know that the remit was pretty tough and threatening. The RC had the right to criticize anyone it felt had failed to justify a particular decision in sufficient depth or clarity. It would act as an informal court: establishing good practice and accusing bad. A kind of Internal Affairs department for policing the policemen.

What was surprising, and I would say admirable, was that any group should volunteer to subject themselves to such a potentially unpleasant scrutiny. But I was particularly puzzled by Nick's agreement. Why had he given power, however unofficially, to the examiners to hold him to account? And particularly as he had only recently told them to stop getting above themselves. As it turned out, his enthusiasm for the Review Committee was based on an assumption he made that beggared belief.

One of the first reforms instituted by the RC was the creation of a written set of guidelines for the decisions we made. There was hostility to this from some examiners: censorship should not be governed by hard and fast rules. It was Farraday who got everyone onside by making the point that the rules didn't need to be hard and fast – the rules could be soft and conditional.

In less than two months Farraday looked through all the most important decisions made on everything from shooting up heroin to smashing in people's heads with baseball bats. What emerged was a surprisingly clear picture of what we actually did with scenes that defined each category. From all these he produced what he called a presumptive rule. A presumptive rule stated clearly that, for example, if you had a scene where you saw someone shooting up heroin in close-shot then the assumption was that such a scene would be '18'. But it was not a rule to be obeyed without question. All he asked was that you acknowledged in the report you wrote that this was what we generally did with such scenes. If you wanted to pass it at a lower category than the usual '18' then you had to argue in detail why this should be an exception.

It seems straightforward enough and I suppose it is. But I think I was more impressed by Farraday's creation of the presumptive rule than I was by anything else I came across at the Secretariat. It was brilliant and simple, combining clarity with flexibility. It prevented examiners or anyone else from making arbitrary decisions based on their own peculiarities or prejudices. But it didn't prevent change or development. And because such changes had to go through the Review Committee who would bring them back to the Secretariat meetings and oblige everyone to think about what was being changed, it made sure that the fifteen or so examiners acted coherently without being rigid. It seemed to me then, and now, that there was no complex situation about which decisions had to be made by a wide range of people that couldn't be immeasurably improved by Farraday's way of constructing supple rules. And yet it's been forgotten, gone with the wind, this great and simple idea, like the dodo.

I was a bureaucrat by training but McCarthy and Farraday were naturals. You will realize that this is not an insult. It gets on my nerves when people rant on about there being too many managers and pen-pushers, too much red-tape, as if the world didn't have to be run, organized, codified, shaped, put together and ordered. Anything more complicated than shovelling shit needs to be administered. And even then: where does the shovel come from? What kind of shit shovel should it be? How do we stop the shit-shovellers from shovelling shit in the wrong place? How do you prevent them from being corrupt and lazy? You get the point.

Nick thought he got the point but he didn't. Although he didn't know it, McCarthy and Farraday were plotting his soul-death, were draining away the very life of Nick. Nick was a helmsman, he was courageous, he defied (those to the right and those to the left), he saved (women from bad men, children from corruption, and men from themselves); he led, he found new worlds to conquer, new truths to reveal. But above all he wanted to inspire, to make others thrill with admiration for his visionary wisdom.

If this seems like lunacy then I hope that by the end of this I may persuade you that madness is as much a part of all of us as legs or eyes. The ineradicable Bedlam in the human soul is usually smothered, I grant you, by fear, lack of imagination, lack of power, a bit of sense. But make the circumstances right, stew them for long enough and there is barely anyone who can't be driven, or drive themselves, to a bit of carpet-biting lunacy.

Nick's sense of himself as demi-god was softened under layers of intelligence, of restraint, of good humour, and charm and generosity too (remember the adult mentally impaired whose lives were much improved by Nick). But I swear that he was as convinced as Alexander, underneath it all, of his divinity. And now he sensed that the very group that he had given life to (just like any god), his sons and daughters, were planning to steal his throne.

The trouble with Nick was that from the very beginning when he decided on creating this Round Table of excellence he also thought, without consciously thinking it, he profoundly *assumed*, that they would be his acolytes. Why wouldn't they? He was right. He knew he was right. He understood and *saw* things others did not see. They would support and honour him as he deserved. But now they were devising committees, they were creating rules. They were dispensing with inspiration, abolishing vision; these were atheists replacing the need for a divinity who shaped their ends, replacing it with laws, ideas, protocols – things that tied and bound.

179

Nick was not made for this – the Secretariat was his, made in his image, and now the angels he had created to praise him were getting up a committee to make him merely important. If this seems bonkers, think of it as jealousy. And remember he didn't know that he was feeling it. This was the explanation for the indictment at the meeting. And because no one, for all their supposed intelligence, had any idea, not Nick and not his employees, about what was really going on, this was where the inevitable end began.

But like a lot of wars it had a phoney element. After the scolding reprimand, nothing happened. Things calmed down, the fuss was buried in the practical demands of the everyday working world of depravity.

'There's nothing much to tell you today,' said Walter at the morning prayers, 'except for those of you who want to know what happened to *Nappy Love*.' There was a groan from the assembled examiners. Walter smiled. 'Nick talked to the producer who, incidentally, also directed and took the lead part, and he has to have an "18". Nick arranged to send him a cuts list of about five minutes to all the brown sauce stuff and make it safe to go through Her Majesty's postal service. Oh, and by the way, the mother in the video was played by his wife. That's it.'

Slowly the examiners dispersed to the viewing rooms, stopping to chat in the corridors – sometimes for as long as half an hour if the day's viewing was particularly dull. Molly was talking with Sadie about George Sluizer's *The Vanishing*, a film that had attracted unusual critical admiration as well as bewilderment at its certificate.

'I don't know what Emma and Walter were on when they passed it "PG". I had nightmares for a week. I was absolutely terrified.'

'I really want to see it,' said Sadie. 'I can go on Thursday. I don't suppose you'd like to see it again?'

'No thanks. It was a great film but people being buried alive really freaks me out.'

It was then that Farraday, driven by an impulse that he cursed even as it drove him forward, interrupted. 'I'd like to see it, too. I'll go with you. All right?'

Sadie looked at him in dismay. 'Oh . . . um . . . of course.'

He turned, appalled and embarrassed, and walked down to viewing room three for a day of *The Unbearable Lightness of Being*, *Nudists of Portugal No. 3*, and two episodes of *Catweazel*.

His partner for the first two was McCarthy.

'I asked her to go with me to see *The Vanishing*.'

'A particularly fine date movie in my opinion. Did she say yes?'

Farraday looked glum. 'I think to describe it as a yes would be putting it a bit strongly. I don't think she quite knew how to refuse given the circumstances.'

'Don't get your hopes up. Once she's had time to think about it she'll come up with some excuse – they always do.'

'To you, maybe.'

McCarthy, unfazed, looked at him. 'You're not making it easy to be sympathetic – you realize that?'

'Are you? I mean, don't you think I'm just behaving stupidly, as well as immorally?'

'I feel sorry for you because I can see you've got it bad. The trouble is that I've never felt that way about a woman. It must be . . . . intense.'

'And you've never felt that?'

'Not about a woman.'

'What then?'

181

McCarthy looked at him and smiled. 'I was thinking about what Walter was saying about *Nappy Love* this morning.'

Farraday wrinkled his nose in disgust. 'I can honestly say that until that day I'd never watched anything that I truly wished I hadn't seen. I don't think I'll ever get the sight of that bloke's huge hairy arse having that shit wiped off it out of my head.'

'That's one way of looking at it – I mean the question not his arse.'

'And there's another?'

'Absolutely. It's the woman who did the wiping who interests me.'

'His wife? Yeah, that *is* strange.'

'I mean what greater act of devotion could there be? The thing is that she didn't just do something appalling out of love for him. The really amazing thing is that she clearly hasn't lost respect. How many people, how many deeply loving wives, faced with a need like that could just accept it and carry on feeling the same way about the man they loved? Hardly any, I'd say.'

'How do you know she did ... she does?' asked Farraday.

'Because she's a part of it. And anyway I could see it in her face. She was taking it in her stride. An amazing woman. In my opinion, Mr Hairy Arse is a very lucky man.'

I have tried to give you a grasp of where my weakness lay. But I'm not a mediocrity, I will not abuse myself. I have my talents and they are pretty hard to find. But while I was not outstanding in the way that Sadie was outstanding, or Farraday, my problem was that I was fairly talented, certainly enough to keep up with them if not to dazzle the way they could. But the thing is, my success in getting the job of censor in the face of so much competition had been a kind of vindication against all those – teachers, colleagues, employers – who regarded me as highly but merely competent. But I didn't want that, I wanted to shine and be seen to do so. Only I didn't really realize how badly I wanted it, how poisonous to me was a reputation, entirely deserved as it happens, for being a safe pair of hands. Most people never get even to that summit: how many have the gift of talented competence? There was no reason I should not have been satisfied with that, except for the fact that I wasn't satisfied, and that I was dissatisfied to a depth, to a horribly poisonous depth, that you would find hard to credit – except that it drove me to such terrible extremes. And it was all the worse because for a moment I felt what it was like to be a star. That was what did for me – the belief that I was, for a few months, what I truly desired to be, followed by the horrible discovery that I was not. It was a bitter blow to the heart I can tell you.

Have you heard of the Mohs test? It's a way of measuring the hardness of minerals by testing their resistance to abrasion. The discovery that in Nick's eyes I was an also-ran in the Seven and therefore less than magnificent had filed away the first layer of whatever it was that protected my sense of myself. When I stole a look at the report on me by Walter Casey identifying me as the water-carrier to my colleagues it had scraped away the next protecting coat. But it was what happened one lunchtime in the Conference Room that did for all of us. Without it, everything would have been all right. I think so. Or maybe not.

One lunchtime I came into the boardroom with my sandwiches. Emma Saward and Rhys were there already. And Sadie, quietly reading a book next to McCarthy who was reading what was clearly a long film report.

183

He looked at me and smiled, nodding at the report in his hands. 'This is your piece on *The Cage*. I have to say, Duncan old son, it's absolutely brilliant. I don't think I've come across anything this clear about the way that modern action violence works – Fucking A. Everybody else who's read it thinks so, too.'

The others looked at me, impressed. Praise like that from McCarthy was worth something. Sadie, however, looked down at the table to hide her reaction to this commendation of me, as if though unwilling to let it show publicly out of kindness, nevertheless her intellect could not prevent her true opinion from leaking out. I could see her mouth turn down in an impossible to suppress expression of amused disdain for my abilities, inadequately disguised, only just I grant you, by condescending kindness for me personally. Oh, that look, how it struck a knife into my heart, such a killing blow and yet delivered with barely any thought.

Why did you have to do it, Sadie? Why? In the turn of her mouth and the terrible dancing laughter in her eyes, I had been weighed and dismissed as a nonentity worthy only of common or garden thoughtfulness.

And it pierced me. Whatever the final layer that protected me from my most abject flaw it was pretty tough, I think. It would have defied the Mohs test, have refused to be ground away or filed. But that look of hers was like a magic blade and I could only stare in horror as it pierced my heart.

Had I not known that I was someone who only got the job because others had turned it down, had I not read Walter Casey's admiring assessment of my limitations – perhaps I would have confronted her later, asked why she had been so cruel. But I *had* read it and the knowledge that I had done so had weakened me so that I simply couldn't bear to have it out with her.

And so I never got to the bottom of that terrible look. But now I know precisely and exactly why she looked at me like that. Since time and knowledge of so many of the facts are no problem to me now, I'll take you back to a couple of minutes before I entered the Conference Room with my sandwiches from Boots. Here's the score. Everyone was there except for Sadie. When she came through the door McCarthy, who was working with her that day, looked up and smiled.

'How did it go?' he said.

Everyone looked at her, mildly nosy as to what she'd been doing.

'It hurt like hell,' she said. 'It was an abscess right under the root at the front.'

Her reply was barely comprehensible because half of her face was completely numb from the injection to deaden the pain of the treatment.

'Can't talk,' she said and, taking out her book, sat down, smiling at McCarthy. But her face was frozen on one side and so the smile she gave him looked like a sneer. But of course he knew. And I didn't. But then if I'd been McCarthy I would have had the carelessness to ask. That was the problem, that was what was really the thing that caused it all: my poor eroded soul. That, and a two per cent solution of lidocaine. It had started when I found Sadie sunbathing on the roof but this was the moment when my soul collapsed.

Dachau Story

LATE ONE AFTERNOON I had gone to Nick's imposing office overlooking Golden Square to find him drinking with Farraday and McCarthy, who had just come back from Pinewood Studios where they'd been to look at an early cut of the latest James Bond movie (*Licence to Kill*, if I remember). They'd finished whatever they had to say about the film and I was offered a drink and we continued talking.

I don't remember how the conversation turned to the subject but Nick began telling us about an article he had written for the *Sunday Express* in 1960 (he'd been a journalist for a few years) on the fifteenth anniversary of the liberation of Dachau by the Americans. He went there a couple of weeks before the ceremony to get some background and talk to the survivors who'd decided to return. On his way through Berlin he'd met up with an interpreter, a woman who'd been hired by the paper. She was in her mid-thirties, a few years older than him, he said, and was the most beautiful woman he'd ever met. She was clever and funny and spoke perfect English with the very slightest Geordie accent because she'd learnt from an English teacher who'd been born in Newcastle. Nick smiled as he remembered this detail and you could see she was one of those, I don't know, living memories that people have where the way they closed their eyes or brushed back their hair can recall an entire person, and the deepest feeling. 'When she got excited, and she used to get excited by even small things, she used to talk about "wor dad" or "wor bed". It took me', he said, 'about two days to fall in love with her.'

She felt the same, he told us, and within a week they were talking about her coming to live with him in London.

Then they got to Dachau.

'The town,' he said, 'is rather a charming place. Most of it's seventeenth-century. In the nineteenth century it was famous as an artists' colony – a bit like Brighton, I suppose. Anyway, the next day she was supposed to go with me to the camp but she said she was feeling ill – and she looked it, too. It didn't really matter because the Americans had brought in translators for the press in any case.

'So, off I went. The odd thing is you'd imagine that a place like that would be hidden away in the countryside somewhere. But it wasn't. It's in the outskirts, not much more than a mile from the town centre.

'There were lots of photographs in the camp, blown-up, exhibition-type things of the piles of emaciated bodies and the mass graves. But you didn't need them, not really. The place reeked of evil. When the Americans arrived there, they were so disgusted with what they found they executed nearly four hundred German guards. It's hard to blame them even though most of the Germans they shot turned out to have arrived there only a week before.'

He took a long drink, paused, remembering.

'Anyway, when I got back she seemed a little distracted but much better and she was also naked.'

I looked at the others as he said this. They, like me, were getting ready to squirm. 'She was an amazing sight. I'd never had sex like it.'

The squirming started. But thank God that was it.

'Later she seemed to have calmed down a bit and she said she had something to tell me. Two things actually. One that she loved me. And second that she hadn't been entirely honest with me. It turned out she'd lived there in Dachau during the war. She'd been born there. She was fifteen when the war started and she was there the whole time all that was going on. She said that they didn't know what was happening in the camp. They'd heard rumours but they heard rumours about all sorts of things. But when the Americans came they made the people from the town go and look at the piles of dead bodies, the graves, the train wagons piled with more dead. She was in tears at the memory. Her mother was repeatedly sick. And she had nightmares for years afterwards.'

He paused and took another drink.

'And you know . . . she was angry. Angry at the Americans for making her go through that. It was nothing to do with her, she was a young girl when it started – but they made her and her family feel as if they were responsible. And it was nothing to do with them.'

Nick looked out of the window, rehearsing his bad memory.

'So I looked at her, so beautiful and sexy and pale. And I told her to get out.' He finished the last of his drink. 'I never saw her again.'

The response to this from the three of us was one of amazed silence. Nick took this to mean that we understood and were deeply affected by his pain, his loss and his integrity.

We left together soon afterwards and it was McCarthy,

shaking his head, who spoke first. 'It's nice to know six million Jews didn't die in vain.'

And he was right. Somehow, Nick had managed to turn the holocaust into a personal event. Perhaps this seems harsh to you. After all Nick was a Jew and it must have been a terrible day. That he might have been angry that her response had been about the deep injustice done to her and her family rather than feeling the rather deeper injustice done to the many thousands who had been murdered there – that would have been easy to understand. It would have been right. Fair enough, I agree. But he claimed to love this woman and to be loved by her. She was not some nameless German trying to avoid a general responsibility for the events of the Second World War. She was a young girl when it started and nineteen when it ended. The American soldiers made her personally responsible, they made her stand over the piles of rotting bodies in their thousands and said, 'You did this.'

I don't blame the Americans for doing it. I don't blame Nick for being angry with her. But you can't fail to understand why she was angry too. If he'd loved her he would have stormed out. Then he would have come back and explained what was wrong with her crying foul. And then maybe she would have understood. And then, perhaps, he might have understood what it was to be accused of being responsible for such a dreadful thing when there was nothing she could possibly have done.

But to be fair, and I'm trying so hard to be scrupulous here, I can still understand why he threw her out. Because you can see why a Jew having stood in that place all day had felt the murdered dead all around him. You could see how you might strike out, especially at someone you loved, someone who had lived and played and ate and

189

slept while all this was going on just up the road. It might be too much for anyone.

Going even further, I believe this is what he truly felt when it happened. But in telling us about it now, all these years later, there was something about the way he did so that made it clear that this was very far from the first time, so measured were the cadences of the often told story: the evocation of intense passion, the deferred information for greater astonishment, the shocking frankness, the unanswerable seriousness of the time and place of these events, and the tragic regret and strength of mind. The thing about the story that repelled us all was that whatever he had once genuinely felt had gone through a terrible reverse refinement in which everything pure had been burnt off and only the dross remained. Now it was a boast, an invitation to look into the far reaches of his soul. It was like looking into a deep and muddy pond where if you stared for long enough you might glimpse his vanity moving effortlessly along the bottom like the dim shadow of a grey carp.

And yet. And yet I remember his memorial and the surprise I felt on hearing of his dedication to the ageing mentally impaired. Why, if I am right in arguing the corrupt depth of his pride, why didn't he mention them? Everything that I understood about him dictated that he should have told us. But he never did.

So what am I supposed to do now, desperate to tell the truth so that I might save myself? How do I explain this? I have to try to get things scrupulously right. Yet Nick keeps getting in the way of my attempts to get the story straight. And maybe it's the story that's the problem. The trouble with people in books is that they make sense. And when they don't, when things are arbitrary or don't add up, critics and audiences alike they get their noses put out of joint. A lack of skill or laziness is blamed. But the arbitrary twist is always happening in life – the action that's out of character happens all the time. The devoted husband with a lovely wife who needs to fuck an ageing tart in urined alleyways. The yummy mum, one who isn't mad or desperate, needs once a month to steal a loaf of bread, a bottle of shampoo. It's not because there is no cause, that sometimes things just happen, but that the flaw is out of reach, or intermittent, like the grinding noise in the gearbox that purrs whenever you take it to the man to fix. I've heard it said that, the way the universe is built, it may not be stranger than we know but stranger than we can know. We don't have the kind of mind to master more than a bit of what is going on. Why should our wives or friends or fellow workers be any easier to grasp? I can't explain why Nick told us about the girl so that we would listen and admire but declined to mention his charity towards the backward elderly. Perhaps I'm just not sufficiently well read but nothing I've ever come across shows me the hero or the heroine who struts their stuff without the nod that by the end you'll get to grips with what they did and why. And I want a guide here from the eminent dead. I have a need to know.

People are probably not *like* anything but if they are, then landscapes seem to me a good comparison. There are paths in the landscape of the human heart, good and useful thoroughfares. But some of these helpful paths, they slowly peter out or simply stop. Sometimes a marsh gets in the way, a mountain or a gulch. And so a useful and a truthful path just ends. It doesn't *go* anywhere. That's what happens in books, in stories: you *arrive*. But it's not what happens in life. In books there's always a hidden trail up through the mountains that only *seem* to block your way. There's always a magic word to open up the doorway into the enchanted halls. But that's not the way it is in life. It's filled with dead ends without an exit for the plucky lad out to make his fortune. The bullet meant for someone else strikes down the hero just as he's about to save the world. The capricious, the wayward and the wilful are just as much a part of us as pattern, causation and character-as-fate.

Don't get me wrong. I'm not saying we never really know another human being, because I think we do. I *know* that Nick was vain and falsely proud of his great moral worth. His Dachau story shows you that. But this hidden generosity to the frail of mind is also true. Most people's grasp of human contradiction is nothing of the kind. The killer who loves his ageing mum is easy to explain. That Hitler was nice to children and was a flirt is nothing much to lie awake at night about. But the problem that I have with Nick, and now with everyone, is rather like the one you would encounter on discovering that Hitler's secret bank account revealed he had, throughout the war, been sending money to a charity for Jewish refugees.

Impossible? But people do this kind of thing pretty much all the time. I refer you to the cruising husband. There's nothing to say he doesn't really still desire his wife. I saw a porn film just the other day in which a woman was taking it from three men – arse, vagina, mouth. After a few minutes back and forth I noticed she was wearing a golden crucifix and wedding ring. Almost certainly these symbols of piety and fidelity had become merely things to wear, empty of religion or romantic love. But what if she goes to church on Sabbath days? What if her spouse is deeply loved? Tell me it isn't possible, in your experience. But don't tell me it's a contradiction. It's more than that.

Do you remember, Reader, Mrs Beamish, wife to Alan of the nappy and the hairy bum? I think perhaps that she has something to tell us here, maybe more than Jesus, Tolstoy or Sigmund Freud. Anne Beamish must want the same things that any woman wants from any man: love, kindness, a strong pair of arms, someone to respect, a rock. And just suppose her husband is all that. Why not? It's only impossible if you connect this up. In your mind and in mine, in Shakespeare's and in Tolstoy's too, we'd make a narrative of this, a path that leads from admiration to pity or disgust. For everyone but Mrs Beamish. No man, no Bond or Darcy, no Indiana Jones or Romeo gets to survive the recipe for shit because for everyone but her we have to take a view, we have to connect, to sum up, to come to a conclusion in the end. But Alan Beamish doesn't need to hide himself from Anne. She won't solve, make sense of you. She'll just look and let it lie. Everyone is all all right with Mrs B. But how does she do it? I think we should be told. I know that people are not like something else (not like stories, not like houses, not like foreign countries), but what *are* they like? I'm confounded. What I'm driving at here is not something about the complexity of the heart, that it has its secrets and its paradoxes, everyone knows *that*. I'm not even saying that it's incoherent – after all there are plenty of puzzles about people that we work out satisfactorily. But the idea that if only you had enough facts, enough backstory and enough good sense you'd work the whole thing out: it isn't true. Our metaphors and similes are just not up to it. And they're not the only things. The task they've given me, to write this story down, nothing extenuate nor set down aught in malice, may turn out not to be a task at all. Maybe it's my punishment. I don't remember reading that anyone told Sisyphus it was impossible to roll the stone up to the top of the mountain. Why would he bother if they had? Tantalus keeps trying to eat and drink because

Blind Date

For there was never proud man thought so absurdly well of himself, as the lover doth of the person loved; and therefore it was well said, That it is impossible to love, and to be wise. For whosoever esteemeth too much of amorous affection, quitteth both riches and wisdom.

Francis Bacon, *Of Love*

THOMAS FARRADAY'S ATTEMPTS TO take Sadie out started badly. He pretended to be just passing the room she was working in and put his head around the door. 'We should leave in about half an hour if we're going to make the six-thirty showing.'

He had never actually seen a rabbit caught in a car's headlights. But he imagined it must be something very similar to the trapped, bewildered fear he was witnessing as she looked at him. She was going to back out but she couldn't speak. Despite the fact that his heart was pounding he had enough composure to say, 'See you in half an hour.'

He turned and fled.

He went up onto the top floor and hid from her in one of the rooms used for stacking furniture. He tried to calm down. *Why are you doing this to yourself?* he thought. *This is stupid and pointless and humiliating.*

It was perfectly clear that she wanted nothing to do with him. He felt a flash of irritation at her. She was turning him into some pathetic stalker. She was making him weak and this was a most unfamiliar and unwelcome sensation.

I should just leave and never speak to her. Just look down at her and make her feel the real deep disdain—

He realized that he was starting to rant. The noisy lover stalking the chambers of his heart was losing it. *Calm down*, he told himself.

But he couldn't, not really. If only her eyes weren't so brown and deep it would be all right. He could have borne it pretty well. But for her eyes and her skin of course. And the turn of her throat. But for them he would have been safe. And her shoulder blades. The swell of her breast under her loose jumper when she reached for her log book on the top shelf. But for them none of this would have happened.

At six twenty-five he walked down to her room with as much dread as he had ever felt. She would be gone. But she wasn't. She looked at him with all the enthusiasm of a condemned prisoner on seeing the preacher come to prepare her for the short walk, and not to a gurney and an injection either. It was the look of someone who expected a noose and a none-too-skilful executioner.

'Oh, right,' she said and stood up.

He kept the door open for her and followed her out.

God this is awful, he thought. But he couldn't stop himself. He had no hope. He knew that not only was he not going to get this girl but that she regarded him as a pest. But he couldn't stop. He could see it unfolding in front of him like some terrible train crash where the driver could see the stalled car on the line but the momentum was too great for any brake.

Slowly the condemned couple marched down the road

towards the Panton Street Odeon. Farraday had not been out of control in a seduction zone since he was fifteen and had persuaded the prettiest girl at the local girls' school to go out with him solely because he had a ticket to see David Bowie at the Oxford Town Hall. The nearly eighteen-year-old Melissa Wanstead was way out of his league and greeted every attempt by him to act as a suitor with a mixture of contempt and incredulity. However, it was not long before Farraday became the catch in any date. He was never unkind in the way of the Melissas of this world. He was above treating people who desired him – and there were many – with that kind of supercilious hauteur. But his thoughtfulness towards the unsuccessful girls who yearned for him was very much the politeness of kings. He was in charge, no matter how sweet he was about it. Have some sympathy then for his current wretchedness.

They talked hardly at all and he had plenty of time to consider how wrong in every way George Sluizer's *The Vanishing* was as a means of seduction. For those of you who don't know it the film's plot is terrifyingly simple: a young couple, Rex and Saskia, are on holiday and pull into a service station. Saskia disappears without trace. Rex spends the next three years unsuccessfully looking for her. Only then is he contacted by her abductor, Lemorne, an ordinary middle-aged man whose only distinction is that he once risked his life to save a young girl from drowning. Lemorne offers to reveal what happened to Saskia only on condition that Rex allows himself to be chloroformed. Horrified but driven to know the truth Rex agrees. The film ends with Rex waking up and discovering not only Saskia's fate but also his own: Rex has been buried alive.

Thrillers are probably the only art form where the arbitrary gets much of a look-in. And it's no accident that it is not a form that has much status. For artists and critics alike, fate is the product of character, of qualities present or absent in the protagonist. Things that just happen are considered cheap. So it's left to the thriller to point out that there's something foolish about high-minded stuff like this. In Hitchcock, for example, how often is an amiable, ordinary man the victim of a coincidence, a dumb mistake. An act of chance, a trivial error of identity plunges our hero into a world completely alien to the one he knows. The one he knows is always safe, the accidental world is always deadly. And all it takes, the thriller rightly says, to ruin everything that you hold dear is for you to bend down to tie your shoe at the wrong time, or to pick up the coat that's almost identical to yours.

When they emerged it was dark and she seemed to have added being spooked by the film to the doleful state of mind she had taken into the cinema. But it was still only 8.30 p.m. and, to his surprise, she allowed him to steer her into a café on Frith Street.

It was one of those Italian restaurants which now are under threat like pandas or the Sussex liverwort. The Artexed niches were full of bottles with raffia on the base. There were horrible murals of bilious green mountains lowering onto lakes coloured a blue you would normally encounter only in the skin of newborn infants starved of oxygen. It was nearly empty though. She sat down on a banquette which curved around so that she could not be seen by anyone except Farraday. The coffees were brought, half a cup of pallid froth sitting in a saucer wet with grey water. They drank in silence for a moment and then he noticed she was shaking.

'Are you cold?' he said. 'Have my coat.'

She looked at him directly for the first time in weeks.

'I'm not cold,' she said. 'I'm afraid.'

'Why?' His heart seemed to swell and throb in his chest.

She looked down at the cup and said miserably, 'Because I love you. And it's killing me.'

Answered Prayers

Speaking in a perpetual hyperbole is comely in nothing but in love.

Francis Bacon, *Of Love*

I DON'T KNOW IF you've ever felt pure joy. Imagine wanting something so badly that it filled every waking and sleeping moment of your life, a desire so great that the knowledge, no the *certainty*, that it could not be yours was sure to poison every day until your death, years soured with terrible longing and regret. And then suddenly it was given you.

'Because I love you.'

Can the heart truly leap, the blood really surge? That was how it felt to Farraday, as if he had taken a hit from one of those famed drugs so powerful that once taken you could never quit. Indescribable joy. Because I love you. Because I love you. Because I love you.

And then he began to shake as well. It's not in our nature to move from misery to happiness without some kind of toll. He wondered if he was going to be sick. They just stared at each other for a long time. Then he moved to sit next to her on the padded bench so that now neither of them could be seen. And then he kissed her.

Is there any sensation, I wonder, like the soft lips and sweet breath of the first kiss of someone you adore and who adores you in return? I wouldn't know, myself.

Watching them as we are, my own reaction now is hardly to the point. But you? What do you feel? Do you envy them or find them ridiculous? If so perhaps it's my effort to give a sense of what these two are feeling that's at fault. With just a simple kiss, the earth moves for them, the stars are falling from the sky. Heaven is in her touch.

Nearly two hours later after an ecstasy of mutual adoration he walks her to the tube at Leicester Square. One final kiss and she is gone, leaving him standing in the under-vault – shattered, amazed and born again.

All that night and through the next day he was restless and overjoyed. What kind of love it was I find it hard to say. Was it rare? I don't know but I suspect it was. I don't think it felt quite right to me. My experience of them both was that they were intelligent and sensible enough. They seemed well balanced but not in this. I felt the heat of what they felt and it seemed to me, then and later, that there was something deranged about the two of them in each other's company.

All through the next day he walked in a stunned frenzy and all through the following night. Then on the third day after their, what, tryst? I can't, off-hand, think of a better word – it needs something peculiar to describe the sheer depth of their fascination for each other. On the third day they were back at work together.

Assembled at morning prayers he looked around for her as Walter fired a shot across their collective bows: 'There are suggestions', he said thoughtfully, 'that some examiners have been fast-forwarding cartoons.' He leant forward as if considering an entirely theoretical question of some weight that hadn't been asked. 'I'm not sure if this constitutes a sacking offence.'

It was then that she came in, hair wet from the rain, her deep brown eyes shaded by a faint puffiness. She had not been sleeping much.

'Ah, Ms Boldon,' said Walter, 'good of you to come.' It was a tease and not a rebuke. Like everyone else (except for me) he had a soft spot for Sadie. But she did not smile.

'Sorry, the trains.'

Farraday gazed ('looked' would be inadequate). But though she caught his eyes, immediately she turned away. In his hyper-aroused and barmy state he felt a stab of fear. He moved forward, trying to talk to her, but in the crush she was able to collect her box and get away with her partner for the day.

He stood and watched her leave and felt as he had nearly a quarter of a century before when as a six-year-old he watched his parents drive away from him on his first day at boarding school. He was bereft.

Later and throughout the day he made several un-necessary trips past the room where she was working with Molly Tydeman. But whether viewing or report writing Molly was always there. He checked on her again at five and she was head down, writing with Molly still alongside her. He returned at six and she was gone. He panicked and began to search the building. It took nearly fifteen minutes to find her: she was on the admin floor, now deserted because everyone in admin had gone home. No one ever wrote there.

'Hi,' he said.

She looked at him, smiling pleasantly as if he were a neighbour with whom she was on reasonably friendly terms, but no more. 'Hello.'

'I thought we could go for a drink.'

She grimaced in a way that suggested this would be a mildly pleasant idea – though no more than that – but that something prevented her. 'I have to finish these,' she said, nodding at the reports.

'I'll wait.'

She looked at him. But whatever the message was, Farraday refused to take it in.

'I'll be a long time.'

He smiled. 'That's OK.' He took out a book from his briefcase, *The Satanic Verses*, and began reading.

Seven o'clock came. Then seven thirty. Throughout this time she kept writing and he kept reading. Several times people wandered past looking bemused – why was Sadie writing there and why was Farraday sitting near her reading a book?

By eight she realized that he was not going to budge so, with a sigh, she packed up her reports and signalled she was ready.

Together they went down to the examiners' floor where she left the reports and then they headed out into the cold night air and over to a bar in the corner of Golden Square that had opened only a few weeks before.

He bought a glass bottle of Beck's for himself and a Bowmore single malt whisky for Sadie.

'What were you reading?'

'*The Satanic Verses*.'

'Enjoying it?'

'Not really my kind of thing. I was curious to see what the fuss was about.'

A discussion of contemporary fiction was not something he wanted to encourage.

A long silence followed.

'I can't do this,' she said at last.

The shock of this was as physically intense as the joy of

just a few days before. He could barely reply. 'Don't say that.'

'I'm married. I can't.'

'Don't. Just please don't. I couldn't bear it.'

She looked at him and she felt at once what he meant. Had he been articulate, had he tried to argue, perhaps she would have been able to hold to a decision to end things there and then. But he was so clearly touched by her and so deeply that no words were necessary, even if he had been able to come up with anything. How, after all, do you persuade a married woman that it is in some way rational to betray her husband? But Sadie could see that she had robbed him of everything, that his love for her had erased his character in some way – and such a strong character, so bright and tough and subtle. So very strong. And she had made it disappear. What in the end could be more eloquent to any woman? I am not myself in your presence, you have utterly conquered me.

She reached out and took his hand. 'I won't let you go,' she said. 'It will be all right. I won't let you go.' She smiled. 'Until you don't want me any more.'

He looked at her, a terrible relief rushing through him because he was certain, without any doubt, that she meant it.

'That will never happen,' he said.

De Sade in Birmingham

Dearest T   *Tues*
How was it possible to have passed today without you? I am
beside myself with amazement and thankfulness. Have you
any idea what it means, what you have done? What you do?
You sweet, sweet man.
I could almost love you.

Sadie x

IS THERE A DREARIER place in all the world than the centre of Birmingham? Not even the square of one thousand socialist martyrs in Magnitogorsk, or the heart of Knoxville, Tennessee has quite this absence of the human in its architecture. With its concrete walkways, Escherian road network, its grey malls, its pavements the colour of bones bleached by a salt wind, it feels like a place devised by no human mind, nor no satanic one either. Nothing that lives, natural or supernatural, thought up this dump.

But it is to the Black Country that McCarthy and Emma Saward have come, along with lovebirds Farraday and Sadie.

They are here to attend a conference on censorship and

pornography where Nick is to give a speech on a platform that includes Catherine MacKinnon and Andrea Dworkin. Perhaps these names are now only distantly familiar to you, if at all. But in the late eighties these two were cold war warriors of feminism, the Stalin and Beria of the fight for the equality of women.

In the early eighties they had persuaded the Minneapolis City Council to let them draft an ordinance allowing women to sue the producers and distributors of pornographic works on the grounds that pornography was a form of sex discrimination. They defined pornography as the sexually explicit subordination of women, graphically depicted either in words or pictures, that included one or more of nine elements: women presented as dehumanized, as sexual objects, things or commodities, sexual objects who enjoy pain or humiliation, sexual objects who experience pleasure in being raped, presented as sexual objects tied up or cut up or mutilated or physically hurt, where women's body parts are exhibited such that women are reduced to those parts, women presented as whores by nature, presented being penetrated by objects or animals, presented in scenarios of degradation, injury, abusement, torture in a context that makes their condition sexual.

When MacKinnon spoke to the audience of some three hundred women and a handful of men, she crisply and cogently pointed out that the ordinance was a new kind of model for dealing with pornography. It was, she said, no longer based on moral arguments that threatened to align them with the right who were, in all other respects, deeply hostile to the Women's Movement, but based on human rights arguments. Then she lowered her voice and spoke to her listeners, less as an audience than as a group of friends. 'Liberal males who argue against us need not

206

detain us at all. As for liberal feminists—' she paused and smiled as if sharing an exasperated joke. 'I want them to stop their lies and misrepresentation of our position. I want them to do something about their thundering ignorance of the way women are treated by the pimps of the sex industry – these women are mostly beaten and coerced into what they do, they are not exercising a lifestyle choice. I also really want them on our side but failing that I want these liberals to stop claiming that their liberalism, with its elitism, has anything in common with feminism.'

There was a huge burst of applause which she allowed to die.

'These liberal feminists who refuse to see that in a context of a world where women are silenced by men, even sexual intercourse itself becomes an issue of forced sex. No matter who their sexual partners may be – lover, husband or rapist – at its root it involves penile invasion of the vagina. It is an issue of forced sex.'

Some of the audience, and not just the few men, seemed a little startled at this. As a result the applause for this was rather more scattered. But MacKinnon was unperturbed.

'Most liberal feminists are house niggers' – with a gasp from the audience at the N word – 'who side with the masters.'

It was hard not to admire her absolute refusal to tread carefully on her audience's finer feelings – suspecting as she clearly did that there were liberal tendencies at work even in this uncompromising setting.

'The Black movement', she continued, as pitiless to softies as a witch-finder to a coven, 'has its Uncle Toms. The Labour movement has its scabs. The Women's Movement has liberal feminists.'

She sat down to a burst of applause that had no small

element of fear rippling through it as if some of those harbouring weaker tendencies suspected insufficient enthusiasm might cause them to be dragged away and be disappeared into some gulag or chain-gang.

Next it was Andrea Dworkin's turn. She was a big woman with an abundance of long dark hair. Even before she spoke, what was striking about her was that she seemed to have a nearly visible aura of misery and pain. She began to recount a litany of abuses against women as photographed for male pleasure in the countless porno-graphic books she had read, listing them like an Old Testament prophet setting out the lineage of Solomon.

'There are nipples being torn off by wrenches, there are labia being nailed to tables, heated wires are applied to buttocks, toenails are torn out, electrodes applied to breasts and genitals, there are bound women whose anuses are being invaded by eels and by the penises of donkeys, there are razors being used to slice off nipples, women being hung by their breasts from meat hooks . . .'

When I say it was a litany of atrocities I mean this precisely. She did not speak in varied tones of shock or horror, she did not incite the women listening in rapt and appalled attention. She intoned in a carefully rhythmic monotone – a fearful Gregorian chant of atrocity that went on for more than five minutes. Then she paused and looked out over the audience who were now held in something like a hypnotic trance.

'I want to tell you of a practice that many admire as if it was an accomplishment for a woman, like painting water-colours or playing the pianoforte. It's the practice known as deep-throating.'

She looked miserably around the room.

'The so-called liberated women who joke about this might just as well be light-hearted about the torture of

208

women with electrodes to the genitals, or women who have red-hot metal vibrators inserted in their rectums.'

Again she looked around balefully.

'It is not possible to perform this act safely: it is a dangerous act that can only be done under hypnosis. The emergency rooms of hospitals in America are filled with the women victims of throat rape.' She paused. 'Not to mention the ones who didn't make it to hospital and died in the act.'

McCarthy leaned across and whispered into Emma's ear. 'You are feeling very sleepy.'

You might consider this a risky thing to do considering that Emma was no liberal in these matters, as McCarthy well knew. But the strange intimacy forced upon them by years of watching the deeply private, as well as the deeply bizarre manifestations of human desire had bred a peculiar shared sensibility. In matters of taboo, the censors of Golden Square allowed themselves a give-and-take that could not be permitted elsewhere. Words that would shock and offend or horrify their husbands and wives were freely spoken between them.

At any rate, all Emma did was look at him, roll her eyes and tell him to grow up.

By now it was Nick's turn to speak to the assembly. It would be unfair to say the reception was hostile, chilly would be more like it. Fortunately MacKinnon's list of nine factors that would lead to the prosecution of pornographic works provided Nick with ample opportunity not just to express sympathy for their cause but to crow about the way he was putting it into practice.

At one level, Nick's boasting was fair enough. He would certainly not have permitted the horrors abstractly defined by MacKinnon and graphically denounced by Dworkin to have passed through the Secretariat. Indeed, not even the mildest implications of violence to women were permitted. He had even, somewhat bemusedly, banned an entire series of tapes where women were loosely tied up and tickled. To be fair, their cries and screams as this was done to them were remarkably similar to the cries and screams of tapes where women were the victims of rape, and it was felt, not without some doubtful headshaking, that it was a kind of trick: a way of getting bound women to scream and cry while not falling foul of the law. The possible loss of rights to possibly entirely innocent tickling fetishists was balanced against the possibly much less innocent desires of those turned on by surrogate rapes. Unsurprisingly, concerns about the dangers of the latter won over a desire not to tread on the rights of the former. After all, aggrieved ticklers were unlikely to complain, nor to be listened to if they did.

So Nick was able to thunder sonorously against violence to women in pornographic tapes and to state without the slightest equivocation that he would never permit these terrible images to pass through his hands.

He made nothing at all of the fact that they hardly ever did pass through his hands because no one ever submitted them – or hardly ever. In this way, Nick was able to imbue even something as straightforward as an absolute ban on images of violence to women with a certain dishonesty. He implied, or more subtly, allowed it to be inferred that there was a tidal wave of such stuff waiting to flood the country and that he, Nick Berg, was standing alone in his determination to prevent it. They could rely on him never to bend one iota to the libertarians on these matters.

The tapes existed, of course; images of the kind described by Dworkin were real enough. But in comparison with the repetitive mass humping of the overwhelming majority of sex tapes, the tidal wave was, in reality, no more than a trickle.

Nick sat down to a considerably warmer response than when he had stood up. He was followed by a speaker who denied that to be against pornography was to be against a free sexual life, that such opposition was not inevitably bound up with a repressive Puritanism. However, she spoiled this rarely argued position somewhat by an attempt to set out what a *good* pornography might look like. It would be mutual, not propaganda for fucking, but for love and conjoining. She tried to describe how this could be easily regulated by having the right understanding of the principle of mutual conjoining but frankly it made Nick's deranged distinctions about heavy thrusting, soft and hardened nipples, quality of lighting, the angle of upraised legs and so on look staggeringly straightforward. No wonder the cops at the Vice Squad wanted something simple: if it's erect we confiscate it. It might be absurd but – unlike Nick's or this woman's solution – it was at least absurd and clear.

That night a dinner had been organized by the sponsors of the conference in the private room of a local Chinese restaurant. Nick arrived at the same time as his four examiners. While they were taking their soaking coats off – they had been drenched by the curious mixture of sleet and drizzle unique to the city – he pulled McCarthy and Farraday aside.

'Remember,' he said mildly, 'you're representing the Secretariat.'

'Meaning?' said McCarthy.

'Meaning – behave yourselves. I know you two of old. I want these people on my side. All right?'

'Yes, miss,' said McCarthy.

211

As it happened, Nick's concerns were entirely justified, it was just that he could never quite shake free of the belief that women were sugar and spice to the slugs and snails of the male psyche. It was Sadie who was going to behave badly.

During the first course MacKinnon held court with no one daring to contribute much as she fiercely gave her opinion that the feminism in which they all believed was coming into its own. 'I'm convinced that we have made a crucial move in the emancipation of women by using human rights and not morality as the basis of our attack on patriarchy.'

There was much head-nodding from the diners at this, as if they too had sensed the change.

'Actually,' said Sadie, 'I don't really understand the difference between moral arguments and human rights arguments. The view that we all have innate rights is itself a moral assertion.' She looked at MacKinnon sweetly. 'Don't you think?'

MacKinnon didn't react badly to this. She looked more awkward than angry. She looked, in fact, as if she knew exactly what Sadie was saying. Her reply was almost conciliatory.

'That's fair enough. But it is vital that we don't allow ourselves to be drawn onto the same terrain as the right.'

Sadie, however, was not really interested in being accommodating. 'But you *are* on the same ground for much of the time. When you were talking today, and the others too, I could have been listening to my dad. All men are ravening beasts who only need the merest opportunity to slake their lusts on innocent women with their hugely powerful penetrating penises. Don't get me wrong – it is not that I don't agree that inside every man is a hairy wild animal – it's just that in my experience it tends to be a gerbil.'

There was a roar of laughter at this from McCarthy and

Farraday – and even a couple of the women smiled. Nick started to look uneasy but failed to catch Sadie's eye. MacKinnon however was Victorian in her lack of amusement.

'I understand from Mr Berg that you at the . . .' she hesitated.

'The British Film Secretariat.'

'You're an official there?'

'Yes.'

'Well I understood from him that there was unanimous agreement about removing images that show the subjugation of women.'

'Yes, pretty much. I'm no liberal feminist. But that doesn't mean I want to go along with your view of men as attack dogs who can't help being full of hatred and aggression towards women.'

MacKinnon bridled at this. 'Perhaps you'd like to tell that to the half of all women who even by conservative definitions are raped at least once in their lives.'

'And these absurd figures come from where?' replied Sadie, gasping with contempt.

'Established experts in the field.'

'I can show you a dozen analyses of the incidence of rape in America that put the figure much lower than that. At most, not more than ten per cent. Bad enough, but your figures are grotesque.'

MacKinnon seemed caught between fury and astonishment. But it was Dworkin who spoke next.

'I know the kind of studies you're talking about. I don't waste my time with outdated and irrelevant data and investigations. The figures Catherine quoted are solid.' Her voice dropped an octave. 'And denying the validity of such high-quality work is not professional. It is not objective – it is incompetent.'

213

Sadie just laughed. 'The pair of you go on and on about patriarchy silencing women's voices. But, goodness me, you can give it a run for its money.'

In the stunned silence that followed, McCarthy turned and whispered quietly into Farraday's ear that they needed to leave by ten if he was to drop him off at Aylesbury station in time for the last train to London.

MacKinnon watched them coldly, assuming they were smirking at this catfight, and then turned back to Sadie. 'I imagine they must be delighted that they've got a woman stooge who's ready to deny that pornography is central in creating and maintaining sex as a basis for discrimination.'

It was meant as a deadly insult, but Sadie just laughed again. 'I suppose if I took you seriously,' she said, still smiling, 'I might be offended. But the reason I don't is that the idea that pornography is as important as you so shrilly claim it to be is just foolish. There are any number of more important things involved when it comes to perpetuating sexism. Pornography may be soulless and sometimes nasty but you can't blame misogynistic sex images of women for creating the English common-law tradition of treating women as chattel property. It's lack of day-care not beaver shots that damages the lives of women; that men don't do enough to look after their kids or enough housework to stop their wives from becoming drudges, that's the problem – not because they're looking at mucky pictures. In the end the pair of you are just prudes who think that men are beasts and women are pallid little angels who are inevitably devastated even by one contact with that nasty, thrusting, all-powerful purple-headed monster. Purity campaigns are as old as the hills and you're just another in a long line of prigs.'

At this the horrified organizer of the conference, seeing that her guests of honour were getting ready to storm out, stood up and asked Sadie to leave. Smiling, Sadie nodded at MacKinnon and walked out followed by Farraday, and then a reluctant McCarthy who hadn't eaten all day and in the excitement had barely had a chance to eat anything at the meal. As he left he stopped next to Emma Saward who looked very much in two minds about what she was going to do.

'Sorry, Emma, but if you want a lift back you'd better come with us.'

Outside in the corridor Farraday looked back to see he was alone with Sadie. He touched her shoulder and she turned, relieved to see him. She was not smiling now but shaking and a little pale. With another look back to see they were still alone, he kissed her.

'My God, it's a lion I've fallen in love with.'

'Lioness,' she corrected him, smiling though she was still shaking.

At that point McCarthy came into the corridor followed by Emma. McCarthy came close to Sadie and took her hand. 'If I had a hat I'd take it off to you. You were brilliant.'

'I think I went too far.'

'Don't be such a big girl's blouse,' said McCarthy. 'I'm telling you it was worth missing dinner to see that. Talking of which, why don't we go and get something to eat?'

A multi-cultural Britain is, I suppose, always likely to contain the odd juxtapositions involved in their eventually deciding to eat at the Delhi Durbar on Clive Avenue, a road named after one of colonial India's most unscrupulous exploiters. While they were waiting for the first course, McCarthy explained why he had missed lunch. He had been fascinated to discover that the speaker who had been advocating making illegal all sexual images that did

215

not promote an acceptable approach to women's bodies, also belonged to a pressure group called Women Against Censorship. He was delighted, if baffled, by the idea that someone could be profoundly in favour of something they were deeply against and so had sought out the woman, a Catherine Itzen, and tried to get to the bottom of this strange paradox.

For all his careful politeness, Itzen had regarded his enquiry with some suspicion, showing that she was not entirely without good sense. Nevertheless she consented to explain. 'Pornography silences women,' she said, defiant but wary.

McCarthy nodded sympathetically. 'Right.'

Still cautious she proceeded. 'To silence someone is to censor them.'

'Ah, yes.'

'So pornography is a form of censorship of women and we are against such censorship.'

'I see, right. But aren't you worried that people are going to get confused? I mean I have to be honest and say that I certainly was.'

'We need to make it clear to liberals that, while they're always obsessed with censorship as an act and not an idea, pornography in reality is not an idea but an act. Pornography *is* the oppression of women not just talk about oppression. It acts against women twice. First when it's made and women are coerced into taking part. Then all women are degraded by the men who view it and recreate their little porn film in their head when they have sex with women.'

'The thing is, what I think,' McCarthy said between mouthfuls of chicken jalfrezi, 'is that while most of the people here are mad, prudish, mean-spirited and humourless, they've put their finger on something I can't help agreeing with.'

'Which is?' said Farraday, worried in case McCarthy might trample on his beloved, who was now increasingly ill at ease that the argument with MacKinnon had got out of hand.

'Well, remember I told you I was at a party a couple of months ago when I was buttonholed by one of the guests – that tosser Mark Carmody?'

There was a universal growl of derision.

'First of all he started up by asking me who gave me the right to decide what he could and couldn't see. So I said Parliament. Well, that didn't stop him for long and then he started on about how censors think that they're not corrupted by what they see so why should anyone else be.'

'What did you say?' asked Emma.

'I told him I had been deeply corrupted by what I've seen.'

'And how did he take that?'

'Well, it shut him up for a bit. But after a few moments he said, "How has it corrupted you, then?"'

At that, McCarthy took another mouthful of jalfrezi, spinning out the moment for full dramatic impact.

It was Emma who broke and, smiling, said, 'All right, so what did you say?'

'I said it was none of his fucking business, that he was a witless bag of shit and that if he didn't clear off I'd take him outside and rip his lungs out. Then I told him I was just kidding, and walked off.'

The disdain for Carmody went back at least as far as an appeal to the Video Consultative Committee against the Secretariat's rejection of *Last House on the Left*.

It's Only a Movie

AS THE GHOST OF a censor, how am I to be fair to a film that I despised, how to keep my revenant's fingers out of the till, my phantom thumb off the scales? Perhaps, if I let an admirer tell the story, we can if not get it straight at least look at the matter in the round. So here is some of the film translated, I grant you, into mere words by a fan, who is neither a half-wit nor blind to the film's weaknesses.

First, a brief synopsis from the witness: Two teenage girls are kidnapped by a sadistic group of hoodlums. After repeatedly raping the girls the hoodlums disembowel one and shoot the other. By coincidence the villains end up staying at the house of their victims' parents who, realizing what has happened, slaughter them gruesomely.

Now to Mr David James Nock:

The most infamous (and most censored) part of *Last House* is the scene where the two kidnapped girls, Phyllis and Mari, are dragged off into the wood. Showing his full sadistic nature, Krug asks Phyllis to 'piss her pants'. Phyllis is disgusted by his request, but when Krug cuts Mari and threatens to kill her, Phyllis relents, and a wet spot appears on her trousers. With much sickness, the criminals find this incredibly amusing, while an equally disgusted Junior watches with discomfort. The whole process is very difficult to watch, and this part of the film has lost none of its power to shock. Krug then gets Phyllis to remove her trousers, and beat up Mari. An increasingly alarmed Junior tries to distract his father by suggesting they should force the girls to 'make out with each other' instead. Delighted with this idea Krug stops the violence.

It is here that we get a very strong sense of that exploitative sleaze that inhabited Craven's first screenplay draft. The gang force Phyllis and Mari to strip. Whichever version of *Last House* you own, there will be various cuts to the shots of Mari and Phyllis performing sexual acts upon each other, spurred on by the cruel and sadistic torments of Krug and his posse.

After this cruel exhibition has ended, Krug states that he is returning to the car, in order to get something 'that'll cut fire wood' leaving Weasel in charge of watching the girls. Phyllis whispers to Mari that she is going to make a run for it. Grasping her opportunity, Phyllis bounds off into the forest. Weasel and Sadie chase after her. Junior is left guarding the scared Mari.

We follow Phyllis as she continues to run through the woodland. Then she spots the road and salvation, Krug jumps out from behind a bush, wielding a machete . . . There is no escape.

Phyllis is then surrounded by the gang and Weasel stabs her in the back. She drops to the ground, and blood oozes from the cut etched at the base of her spine. With much brutality, the criminals repeatedly stab her to death.

The end of Phyllis's murder ends with her disembowelment – a segment of the scene which has appeared heavily cut in every released version of the film. The despicable Sadie reels out the poor girl's intestines. Many fans of the film have been trying to uncover the full footage for this scene for many years. However, some of it is feared to be lost.

The gang return to Mari and Junior. Asking if Phyllis got away, Mari is answered as her friend's severed hand is flung onto the floor. Continuing the assault of brutality, Krug carves his name into Mari's chest, blood flowing everywhere. This is yet another one of those segments which is usually cut heavily. A close-up shot of this atrocity only lasts for a few seconds on most versions of the film, or is absent in others.

Craven really tries to make you feel disgusted by these criminals. The vile Krug then proceeds to rape Mari – the most difficult to watch segment of the film. He then shoots her.

For a brief moment, they show signs of a conscience at their actions. What it achieves, however, is the fact that these heartless thugs are indeed human, but it doesn't make us feel sorry for them at all.

There is, I think it's fair to say, a curious innocence about this description. Mr Nock is an almost perfect example of a horror fan in that he is clearly not a leering, woman-hating rapist drooling over the appalling sight of two teenagers being raped and disembowelled. He's obviously perfectly aware of the film's extreme nature and is appalled and shocked by what he sees and in no sense (one of the greatest clichés of the accusatory censor) does he share the point of view of the perpetrator. He seems, Mr Nock, a likeable chap, an enthusiast, a bit of a geek perhaps. But it never occurs to him, in any way, not ever, that words and images are real. The clever selling point for the film was that you must keep telling yourself it is only a movie. For the fan and the extreme libertarian no image or word really exists, they point to nothing that is anything but a shadow: words and images are ghosts, mists, reflections, smoke. For the committed censor words are sticks and stones, an image of anything is a copy of the world itself. For them, nothing is ever 'only' anything.

Listen to Mark Carmody berating McCarthy at his party as he desperately tries to get away and find a drink and some food. Imagine, if you can, Carmody talking to Andrea Dworkin.

However, the only person he could get to talk to was McCarthy. The exchange that McCarthy told them about in Birmingham had not, in fact, ended with the satisfying put-down that had finished his story – does it ever? McCarthy had indeed walked off, but a few minutes later as he was engaged in a promising encounter with a tall brunette from the Features Section at *The Times* he was buttonholed again by Carmody.

'Your decision to ban *Last House* because of its' – he made an inverted commas sign with both hands – '*sexual violence* leaves horror fans, once again, in the wilderness.'

McCarthy groaned inwardly as *The Times* girl slipped away. He looked at Carmody. 'A wilderness, I hope, inhabited by inbred mountain men intent on buggery and cannibalism.'

'You may think it's all right to make glib jokes but this is about people's freedom. Though of course as long as it's *"art"* ' – the inverted-comma fingers again – 'then it's all right, you'll defend that stuff. So it's OK if it's in *Salo*, where naked young men and women are whipped and buggered and forced to eat human excrement . . . but of course it's Pasolini so that's all right. But Wes Craven is a good director.'

'I agree, as it happens.'

Carmody wasn't going to be mollified into shutting up

221

and going away. 'I don't give a fuck if you agree. *The Last House* was inspired by Bergman's *The Virgin Spring* – it's widely acclaimed as a milestone genre movie. It's his strangest and purest movie. But it's clear that it's the kind of purity that remains unappreciated on these pathologically censorious shores. I have to say it makes me ashamed to be British.'

And at that he stared defiantly at McCarthy, daring him to contradict. McCarthy looked at him carefully as if considering something, something quickly dismissed. He sighed, and then said quietly, 'Look, Carmody, if it makes you ashamed to be British because you can't express the' – and he gestured inverted commas with his left hand – '*purity* of watching a teenager being made to piss her pants before being disembowelled then . . . um . . . I don't know, perhaps you should surrender your passport. Or failing that you could try looking up the word "shame" in a dictionary. Excuse me.'

And with that McCarthy walked away for the second time. A few moments later one of the guests at the party who knew Carmody slightly came up to him.

'Hello, Mark,' he said.

Carmody looked at him.

'Dave Webster,' he prompted.

'Oh, right, sorry. Kathleen Hammond's boyfriend.'

'That's right.' He paused. 'That was very brave of you.'

'What, that prick from the Film Secretariat? He's lucky I didn't give him a thick ear.'

'To be honest, Mark, I don't think that would have been very wise. You don't know about Robert McCarthy, do you? I mean who he really is.'

smoke had been filtered into Robert McCarthy's Citroën BX during the return journey from Birmingham, what strange vortices and currents, underflows and spates would it have revealed, what eddies and coils?

Farraday had managed to ease himself into the back seat with Sadie by claiming to the two women that if he let them sit together they'd spend the whole journey talking about boys and make-up. Our enchanted smoke would have revealed a mixture of amusement from both women and under that a surge of alarm from Sadie lest the others guess from Farraday's insistence that something was going on; there was a tug of miff from Emma that Farraday clearly preferred to sit with Sadie (but it was only slight, nothing approaching jealousy, merely an awareness that someone who liked her liked someone else more). But Farraday's heart was surging as he sat beside his love, surging with desire and adoration, longing and gratitude that for the next three hours he would actually be sitting next to her. And mixed though separate, though also blurring into them, the smoke reveals his astonishment at her performance earlier: her courage, her cleverness, her wit, her reckless defiance, her stunning confidence in herself – love and wonder were coiling around each other here. But the smoke curls and eddies deeper still, wrapping its tongues around Sadie's under-character. There is nothing, let me say, of a veneer about this courage and this confidence. But they are not made up in the same way as those qualities that ran as well so deep in Farraday. Consider that our smoke has the power to reveal the political as well as the personal; those ugly abstractions class and gender get to make their presence felt in the back seat of McCarthy's Citroën. There is a simplicity about the weft and warp of Farraday's self-belief: he does not realize how easily aplomb and poise come to you when natural

224

brains are supported by wealth and status, education, a solid place in the scheme of things. He took all of this for granted (how could he not have?) as much as he took for granted his first breath of air.

But how very different for Sadie Boldon. Her first breath was mongrel stuff, polluted, tainted and impure. Her parents had barely a fingerhold in the country into which she'd been born. She was poor, she was black and she was a girl. She sucked in some bad history when she first drew breath. And so her confidence and courage, naturally as great or greater than her lover's, was fatefully admixed by all the things that come with poverty and prejudice.

But, of course, there is no such smoke and no one could have seen these things. Only life itself can reveal them – and the trouble with life is that it's nothing like smoke at all. Life is hard.

'You know what I think?' said McCarthy.

'I bet you're going to tell us,' said Emma.

'I think that Carmody and Dworkin are just different sides of the same coin.'

'Because?'

'The thing about Carmody is that to him the world divides neatly and tidily into the symbolic world and the real world. For Dworkin things are even tidier: there *is* no distinction. So what makes us superior to them both – not to put too fine a point on it – is that to varying degrees we see these distinctions for what they are.' He paused.

'And?'

'I'm glad you asked me that, Emma – there is no line between the real and the symbolic, just a permanently shifting, foggy liminal . . .'

'What's a liminal?' asked Emma.

'A threshold – the space that links one space with another – like a no man's land or a doorway. Films and images and words on a page are places where things are real and unreal at the same time. Which is why I say Carmody and Dworkin are pretty much the same – they want things to be totally unambiguous.'

'Maybe', said Emma, 'it doesn't make us superior, maybe it just makes us feeble, fence-sitting liberals.'

'But we're censors,' said Farraday, who was really only half-listening as he enjoyed the touch of Sadie's hand on his in the dark. 'How can we be liberals?'

'That's the irreducibly ambiguous for you,' said McCarthy.

For a few miles there was silence, again broken by McCarthy. 'What about a game?'

'What sort of game?'

'A competition with a prize. The prize being that who-ever wins buys the coffee at the next services.'

'I don't like games.'

'You'll like this. I've been thinking about Women Against Censorship being a pressure group that's actually in favour of stopping people from seeing things, and I really love the idea – so the competition is to see who can come up with the most unlikely pressure group – you know: Nazis Against Anti-Semitism or Vegetarians for a Woman's Right to Choose.'

There was a short squabble between McCarthy and Emma because Emma was both a vegan and a member of the Abortion Access Project. But McCarthy wanted to get on with his game and, laughing, withdrew his pressure group on the grounds that he now agreed it was only too likely. The suggestions then started in earnest. 'Hedgehogs for More Trunk Roads' (Farraday).

'The Burglars' Coalition Against Petty Larceny' (Sadie) was ruled out on the grounds that the pressure group should be unlikely but not impossible. She then responded with 'Sado-Masochists for Peace and Reconciliation'. Emma protested against that as well, but was overruled. Finally getting into the spirit of the game Emma took the lead with the 'Drug Dealers' Baby Milk Action Group' only to be topped shortly after by McCarthy's 'The Gentlewomen's League Against Buggery'. For some reason this had them all in hysterics for several minutes. However they all agreed that Farraday's last contribution was the winner: 'Concerned Parents for Pornography *and* Family Values'.

By the next morning their mood was considerably less jovial. As soon as Sadie arrived she was taken aside by Walter Casey and told to go to Nick's office. It was clear from his demeanour, usually almost avuncular but now disapproving and hostile, that this was something serious. Sadie paled beneath her golden brown skin and looked over at her lover who watched her leave to go to the second floor with all the anxiety of a parent watching a child go off for their first day at school.

First she had to pass by Nick's new PA who glared at her. Then she approached the half-open door of Nick's office. She knocked.

'Come in.' The request was soothingly pleasant and welcoming. But as soon as Berg saw her, his face blackened.

'Sit down.'

'I'd prefer to stand.'

'Sit down.'

She did so. Nick stared at her for a moment and then sat down himself.

'I'm extremely angry with you.'

'Why?'

There was a strong note of defiance here. As an adult

227

Sadie had had little experience of severely displeasing others in authority. Unmitigated admiration was more her thing and her question had something of an adolescent's 'don't care' about the way it was asked.

'You know damn well why.'

He was shouting now. She felt it almost like a blow, her face reddening with fear. But she tried to cover her alarm by becoming angry herself. 'No, I don't, Nick. And I don't like being shouted at.'

This only infuriated him more. 'Well, if you behave like you did last night you'd better get used to it.'

'Perhaps you'd like to stop threatening me and tell me what it is that's made you so angry.'

'What's made me angry is that I thought you had more sense. I told the other two to mind their manners because the kind of grandstanding you went in for yesterday is more their style.'

'I wasn't grandstanding, I was disagreeing with them. I thought this place was about intellectual debate.'

He gasped with irritation. 'We weren't in *this* place. Outside of here, as you obviously haven't noticed, people don't go in for debate. The pressure groups and the newspapers who are always on my back don't believe in "on the one hand this, on the other hand that" – what they believe in is their own ideas and nothing else. People don't change their minds in the real world, Sadie. They don't listen to evidence or weigh up the complexities of their own or someone else's position. People know they're right – haven't you got that through your skull yet?'

Again the blood drained from her face at this assault. No one, let alone with such vehemence, had ever questioned her intelligence. She was stunned because it was impossible.

'So, you're saying I'm not supposed to disagree with

people outside the Secretariat, no matter how fanatical they are?'

Another snort of disdain from Nick. 'Most people don't really give a damn about us. But the ones who care are pretty much all fanatics – if only because they just won't think about what we do.'

'And I'm supposed to go along with that?'

'You're supposed to have enough sense to realize that it's hardly ever, in anything, that it's about thinking. People outside this place don't care about how clever you are, Sadie, they only care about one thing: do you agree with them.'

'So what's the point of all the debating and writing and talking we do here?'

'That stuff is for *my* benefit. It's not about persuading people outside – you can't persuade them. There's only one thing you can do when it comes to the outside world and that's to reassure it – if it's a part of the outside world that can cause us grief.'

'And if it isn't?'

'Then we ignore it until it can.'

She did not reply. Nick took in a deep breath. 'The point about Dworkin and MacKinnon is that though it's true they're too extreme to have any influence on the people who can really cause me problems, they do have a constituency in the mainstream.'

'Really?' she said dismissively. 'Who, *Guardian* readers?'

'Yes, *Guardian* readers. The point is that we're vulnerable to almost everyone. Nobody loves a censor. If we make a mistake no one is going to spring to our defence – and more to the point if we make a mistake in one area and there are people out there with a voice who are annoyed with us, then it creates a sense that the Secretariat isn't on top of things. It doesn't have to be fair or even justified in any way. But if the *Mail* attacks us for being too lax because we've hit trouble over *Rambo* or video violence then I don't need the *Guardian* taking advantage and having a go at us as well because we haven't mollified them when we had the chance.' He stopped and looked at her.

'Do you get it now? What's making me angry? I had MacKinnon and Dworkin eating out of my hand and at no cost to me or the Secretariat. We've always taken the view that sexual violence is unacceptable. So have you, I might add. The result of that is that I can get a pair of fairly powerful fanatics off my back and even praising us to their supporters – and all for nothing. And you ruined it.' He looked at her. 'So I think you owe me an apology.'

She swallowed hard and stared at him. She had never been in a position like this before. It was as much a lack of familiarity with what to do under such circumstances that led to her response. Certainly there was pride and vanity but at least half of her reply arose out of simple confusion. 'I don't think I have anything to apologize for.'

Nick stood up, red in the face. For a moment she thought he was going to come around the desk and strike her. 'Then you'd better get out.'

By lunchtime the examiners' floor was buzzing with resentment. Something of a crowd gathered as people came out of viewing to express solidarity or get up to date on Nick's infamy. Soon it turned into a meeting although, as McCarthy later put it, it was a meeting touched with something of the lynch mob. The mood was all for sorting Nick out there and then and there was no doubting who was holding the noose. Thomas Farraday was beside himself with rage and this fuelled a willingness to take a stick to the Director that made it all too clear how relations had deteriorated in the last few years. There had been too many attacks and condemnation from both sides, far too many opportunities for shin-kicking – an arbitrary decision from Nick on this or that, a willingness to turn the knife over something trivial enough from the examiners. Irritation became bickering, then animosity, rancour and spite.

There were only two people reluctant to storm up to Nick's office as if it were a Winter Palace or Bastille. One of them was McCarthy, the other Sadie herself.

'Look,' said McCarthy, 'why don't we just come down through the gears on this one. We all know what Nick's like: he wants to see himself as the great strategist who alone can play off the Secretariat's enemies. And be fair, to some extent, it's true.'

'You've been here too long,' said Emma.

'Undoubtedly so, but I still think we should calm down and let it blow over. Why don't we just wait and see what he does and if Sadie's still unhappy by next week we'll bring it up at the next Secretariat meeting?'

'I don't agree,' said Farraday. 'If we do nothing Nick will think he's got away with it. He can't just pick us off singly like this. We need to make it clear that we regard this as an issue for all the examiners, not just something between him and Sadie.'

Sadie was looking increasingly concerned as this went on – on the one hand her heart beat faster as her lover offered to tear down the building in pursuit of the man who had dared to upset her; but on the other she realized that McCarthy had a point.

'Look, thanks everyone for your support but what Rob says makes sense. I'll let things calm down then I'll go and see Nick in a couple of days and we'll see what he has to say. Perhaps we can just agree to disagree.'

International Guerrillas

I inform all zealous Muslims of the world that the author of the book entitled *The Satanic Verses* – which has been compiled, printed and published in opposition to Islam, the Prophet, and the Qu'ran – and all those involved in its publication who were aware of its content, are sentenced to death. I call on all zealous Muslims to execute them quickly, wherever they may be found, so that no one else will dare to insult the Muslim sanctities. God willing, whoever is called on this path is a martyr.

Ayatollah Khomeini, February 1989

IT IS NOW PRETTY well known that the largest film industry in the world in terms of production is in the Indian sub-continent. What is true now was also true then and a sizeable part of the throughput of the Secretariat were videos of films made in Hindi and Urdu – and there was a huge backlog. There were, of course, other racial minorities within the film industries whose output, though considerably less, also required certificating by the Secretariat, most notably Greek and Arab. However, the Greek video importers, and most of the Arab importers too, regarded the hefty charges made by the

Secretariat as simply too expensive. Theirs was a restricted market and the charges made by the Secretariat made the business uneconomic. They solved this problem by the simple expedient of ignoring it.

Nick was appalled that someone could just ignore the law and he expected something to be done. So he scooted off to the Trading Standards Officers and wailed loudly about the moral dangers of unregulated videos, followed by a calculation of the revenue lost to the Secretariat, and demanded they act. It was not that there was little sympathy from Trading Standards, there was none at all. They said they had more important things to do. And to Nick's bewildered frustration, that was pretty much that.

Fortunately for the Secretariat's finances, Indian and Pakistani distributors were punctilious about submitting everything. According to Shahnaz Mai, head of the Ethnic Video Department at the Secretariat, this was because Indians were culturally used to having money extorted from them in the guise of meaningless 'taxes' charged for spurious services.

There were two more examiners under Shahnaz, Maya Gurinder and Ela Buchar. All wrote impeccable English, had lived here for years, had English husbands and a bewildering number of degrees. They weren't confined to Indian videos either. They regularly watched with the other examiners and in general were completely integrated into the Secretariat. While the native British examiners were entirely content with this in principle there was one problem that existed like a stone in the shoe of this multi-cultural utopia: they loathed watching Hindi videos. Each one was more than three hours long. The stories had, to the British eyes at any rate, a monotonous similarity about them that went something as follows: Two men, one a policeman, one a criminal, come into conflict. They have lots of very badly choreographed fights. There is a song. Then another fight. Another song. Halfway through a villain strangles the policeman's saintly mother. Then it's revealed that the criminal and the cop are really brothers separated at birth by the machinations of the evil villain. There is a song. Then there is more fighting of a kind which would make the average playground pretend martial arts game look highly polished. Then another song. The brothers fall in love with two sisters. The sisters are kidnapped. There is a song. They are rescued. The villain is beaten to a pulp. There is a song.

To the British-born examiners these videos were silly, predictable, garish, sentimental, incompetently made and interminable. After six and a half hours of this stuff in one day even the most piously multi-racial of them began to feel a numbing sensation in their limbs of the kind normally consistent with the early signs of failure in the central nervous system.

Speaking for myself, I loathed watching them just as much as everyone else. The ethnic examiners were impressively tolerant of this disdain. Indeed the only examiners who irritated them were the ones who pretended to enjoy them. The thing that struck me at the time was that there was something encouraging about the impossibility of our understanding their films. The curious thing was that while the ethnic examiners were sophisticated readers of western films and enjoyed, were bored by or stimulated by them in exactly the same way as we were, they nevertheless took huge pleasure in watching the same Indian and Pakistani videos we couldn't bear.

It's a commonplace of the global culture, no doubt mostly true, that slowly everywhere is becoming like everywhere else. The motto of McDonald's is that you can expect the same from a Big Mac in Boise as you can in Phuket. MTV, Hollywood, cable, the internet: everything is merging into a multicoloured uniformity.

To me, Hindi videos are a ghastly but heartening denial of this. If you were Indian or Pakistani you got them, and if you weren't you didn't. Everything cannot be assimilated and blurred and softened for the universal palate. It has become a sin to think of other cultures as genuinely other. It smacks of fear and hate. And so it may. But I liked the fact that I loathed these videos. Long live the difference. Raise your glasses to not understanding, not absorbing, not adapting. Here's to the unbridgeable gaps that lie between us.

On the other hand, unbridgeable gaps can be pretty dangerous and the arrival that day of a video from Pakistan called *International Guerrillas* brought us a strange and complicated example. It also brought a kind of prophecy in all its weird and hallucinatory barminess – a prophecy of the next century, an augur of the shape of things to come, the death of thousands and a murderous war.

INTERNATIONAL GUERRILLAS: SYNOPSIS – *Shahnaz Mai*

Sinister anti-Islamic international villain, Salman Rushdie, plots against Islam while living on a luxurious island protected by Muslim-hating thugs. Meanwhile, in Pakistan, police officer Mustafa is appalled when he is ordered to open fire on a protest march against the publication of Salman Rushdie's *The Satanic Verses*. He resigns in protest and instead goes to address the protestors using the standard passion-rousing gimmicks of religious rhetoric (used in every war confrontation and political crisis in Pakistan).

He urges, along with others, that Rushdie must die. The police do indeed open fire though unprovoked. (A snipe at the Pakistani authorities who opened fire and killed a number of people during early rioting against Rushdie's book.) Mustafa's son and daughter are both shot and martyred to the cause. Teaming up with his estranged criminal brother, Mustafa learns that Salman Rushdie has hatched a plot to destroy the entire Muslim world. The newly formed International Guerrillas vow to prevent him whatever the cost . . .

INTERNATIONAL GUERRILLAS: SYNOPSIS – *Rob McCarthy*
. . . following this momentous decision we have a song that has no relevance to anything that precedes or follows. It involves some wet saris and a mass dance in what appears to be the local municipal park. Meanwhile Salman, in a fetching pastel safari suit, defiles some underaged Muslim girls and strangles their grannies. Finally the heroic brothers trap Rushdie and he is, and at inordinate length, bashed, thumped, crushed, mangled, kicked and beaten to death. Celebrations all round that the hairy great Satan is dead. But not so fast! They are shocked to discover that Rushdie is alive and well and that the previous Salman was a doppelganger, designed to fool our heroes. Time for a song . . .

INTERNATIONAL GUERRILLAS: SYNOPSIS – *Shahnaz Mai*
. . . the brothers learn more of Rushdie's attempt to destroy the Muslim world in such a way as to forget the name of the Ka'aba, the holiest place of pilgrimage and one which devout Muslims live and die to visit. They also encounter his demonic cunning in his use of

mask-wearing lackeys made up to look like him, brilliantly conceived lures and decoy trails (much like the villain in western adventure yarns – from Rider Haggard to James Bond). Finally he is cornered by the brothers, but he is not to be killed by bullets but by the divine wrath of God, who strikes him down with a fearsome series of lightning bolts.

INTERNATIONAL GUERRILLAS: SYNOPSIS – *Rob McCarthy*

. . . after disposing of the honours of several more Muslim women and a few more granny stranglings, our heroes again catch up with our villain with predictably painful and unpleasant consequences for Sal. But (apologies to Tom Stoppard) while the fighting style of the guerrillas may be elephantine, the same can't be said for their memories. The now hamburgered blasphemer begging (fruitlessly) for mercy like the vile and craven apostate that he is turns out to be another fake, and so on until the real Rushdie manages to kidnap the guerrillas' saintly grandmother who is subjected to a suffering far worse than dishonour or asphyxiation: Salman reads to her from his novel until her ears bleed.

Finally the guerrillas run the true Rushdie to ground but before they can deliver the retribution he so justly deserves a flying copy of the Koran swoops out of the heavens and blasts him with a thunderbolt.

It might be useful to say that the Secretariat divided into three parts on *Guerrillas* – the scoffers, the sanctimonious, and the finger-waggers.

The scoffers' position was that the video was drivel that no one could possibly take seriously and that to do so would give it an importance it blatantly didn't deserve and that banning it would do far more harm than good.

Shahnaz Mai was caught in a bind in responding to this. On the one hand she was clear that she didn't much care for the cultural implications of the ridicule aimed at the film by the scoffers. So they got a stiff rebuke:

> Although to the uninitiated this film may appear to be an unconvincing farce, it speaks to an informed Pakistani or Indian viewer in a familiar language of exaggerated symbols, meaningless to westerners, laden with significance to us. Within generic terms it is no more exaggerated than Greek drama, for example. Any number of people who would find *International Guerrillas* laughable and ridiculously childish, would happily pay fifty pounds to sit reverently through an opera full of monsters, flying Rhinemaidens and overweight middle-aged divas pretending to be innocent virgins.

This clever stuff, however, gave ammunition to the finger-waggers, me included, who argued that if *Guerrillas* would be taken seriously by its intended audience, then the argument that its patent absurdity should allow us to pass it out must fail. Salman Rushdie, the waggers' argument went, was a real person now under sentence of death. That this should be taken literally was clear from the fact that two of the translators of the book had been stabbed, one of them fatally. The Secretariat, as a matter of course, routinely cut many videos on the grounds of general harm; those disposed, for example, to sexual violence might be triggered to act out their fantasies by watching an erotically charged rape. Here an individual under threat of death is grotesquely labelled as a violent paedophile and murderer, and his death is urged by all the heroic characters in the film. If it is our obligation to protect society in general, how can it not be our obligation to protect a particular individual presently in hiding for fear of his life?

Shahnaz was not particularly happy with the waggers either. While a liberal Muslim herself, and an admirer of Rushdie's work, she feared that banning the video would send out a message that British Muslims were universally fanatical and that they were capable of being enraged enough by religious concerns to take the law into their own hands. By implication the book-burnings in Bradford of *The Satanic Verses* and a number of threats from hotheads would become something identified with Muslims as a whole. A tricky problem, then, and Nick did what his instincts always told him to do with tricky problems, real or imagined: sit on a decision for as long as possible in the hope that it would go away.

The Scarlet Letter

EXTRACT FROM 'THIS WEEK'S letters to the BFS':

'You fucking wankers,' begins a letter that arrived on Monday from a Mr Schofield of Chingford who wrote to tell us how offended he was by the language in "Beverly Hills Cop" and obviously wishes us to share something of his outrage. Continuing on this note a couple of days later we had another letter, this time from Mr and Mrs Brown of Shenfield, who begin their letter even more offensively than the one from Chingford: 'Why not,' they write, 'abolish the British Film Secretariat altogether?'

Their concluding paragraph hurtfully puts the case:

'We do not believe that you can defend your activities by claiming that were it not for you, more overt and illiberal intervention by the State and the courts might occur. If the self-important who wish to assuage their own insecurities by intrusion into other people's sexual morality, be they high court judge, religious bigot or latter day Mary Whitehouse calling herself a feminist, wish to tell us what is good for us, let them do it in the open. We hope they lose the ensuing fight as they did over "Lady Chatterley".

Even if they do not, the battle lines are clear. Your function preempts an open application of the law and thereby protects its arrogant presumptions from public exposure.'

Nick will, apparently, be answering this one himself but I'm sure any contributions will be gratefully received.

Molly Tydeman

It was while we were watching *Misadventures at Megaboob Manor* that Emma Saward observed to me in passing that we lived in an age where we had all been irrevocably changed by the theories of Sigmund Freud. This is wrong on two counts. The first is that hardly anyone, even well-educated people, could give you an account of Freud's theories beyond the idea that we have some large but vague creature at the back of the mind called the Unconscious that sometimes directs our actions without our being aware of it. Like you, probably, I have certainly heard of the ego and the id but I couldn't explain what they were in any reasonably precise way. How then can his ideas (good or bad) have had much influence on us? She was wrong for a second reason as well: even if we were as well drilled in his analysis of the human mind as we all once were in our times tables, it still wouldn't make any difference. Nick Berg had a degree in psychology along with at least five other members of the Secretariat and despite the fact that all were entirely familiar with his theories about the dark and inaccessible part of our personality it never made the slightest difference in the way that they allowed their hidden resentments, malice and capacity for self-destruction to dictate many of their actions.

The truth of this alone explains why it was that some three days after the row in the office with Sadie she received an official letter from Nick warning her as to her future conduct and informing her that the occasion for a second such letter could be used in a dismissal procedure. You may think this either disgraceful or entirely justified according to your views on how she'd behaved, but the reason it was almost insanely self-destructive was that it was delivered on the morning of the Secretariat's monthly board meeting. This ensured that everyone would know about it instantly and gave them the hour-long examiners-only meeting that took place prior to the general meeting to work themselves up into a fury – plenty of time to plan a response and then spend the rest of the day venting their collective fury on Nick.

It might seem strange to you that the chief executive of any organization would tolerate even ten minutes of the kind of pasting that Nick knew he was going to have to endure for an entire day. But you must remember the strange constitution of this place and the strange constitution of Nick's character of which it was such a weird reflection, or more an incarnation. Every contradiction, desire, lust, vice, intellectual and moral virtue, every delusion, every bit of good sense, every ounce of wisdom and foolishness he possessed had made itself felt in everything from his choice of personnel to an insanely plush reception area designed to impress all who entered the Secretariat. His desire to share in the glamour and status of film as an artistic medium showed itself in an unnecessarily large cinema with luxurious seats and fabric-lined walls at £50 a square metre. His resentment of the examiners, and the low status of video, revealed itself in viewing rooms that he almost never entered and which were some of them so small that it was difficult for two people to sit side by side. A stranger visiting the Secretariat would have been of the opinion that these were naughty rooms for the workers' disruptive children or certainly rooms where nothing of very much significance for the organization took place. Instead they were, as you will by now have realized, the central reason for the Secretariat's existence as well as by some distance the greatest source of its power and revenue.

Nick did not take such huge amounts of crap from the people he employed around the boardroom table because he was weak, but because he was locked in a strange psychological embrace with them, rather in the way that some fathers are locked in an embrace with their dysfunctional family. Everyone who worked there was carefully chosen by Nick through a process he had personally devised and which was as apparently rational as was humanly possible – but the noisy spirit deep in his heart was lonely perhaps and wanted to rouse his fellow poltergeists dormant around the table.

This is true, you'll no doubt say, to some degree in every place of work – but what prevents the strange ecstasies and hatred of the Secretariat from happening everywhere is repression. There is no office where this stuff is absent – the hatreds, resentments, loves, the friendship and the rage – but much of the time it's held in check by fear, some discipline, a bit of self-restraint, a decent boss and common sense.

Shahnaz Mai once said to me that the difference between soap operas and real life was that in soap operas families were allowed to express emotions to each other on a daily basis that would tear any ordinary family apart. The fascination that they held for people was that they simply acknowledged, in a manner that was safe, the seething enmities common to even the most loving family.

The Secretariat then was Nick's family, one that had

244

begun in harmony but where now the gloves were off. And it was Nick who undid the strings, something in him that slipped the horseshoes into his children's fists and demanded that they strike. A fish rots, say the Italians, from the head down. So does a family. So does a place of work.

It was McCarthy's turn to take the chair of the examiners-only meeting and, having read out Nick's letter to Sadie, he pushed it to the top of the agenda. The initial reaction of the meeting was more one of astonishment than anger. Sadie was Nick's favourite, everyone knew that, and for him to have turned his anger on her so abruptly and in such an official manner was completely unexpected. I do not except myself from this general surprise. Though, of course, unlike everyone else around the table I was both surprised and delighted. Despite her being Nick's favourite, no one else shared, even in a small way, my pleasure, because Sadie was everyone else's favourite, too. She was beautiful and clever but good-natured and rather innocent about her own abilities. She admired herself, no question, but it was a frank and generous admiration that she also shone upon her colleagues: no one was quicker to praise than Sadie. Everyone, except me, thought she was sweet. I knew, or thought I knew, that she was not. If only because of my own inadequacy and her unfortunate trip to the dentist.

So it was support all round and pass the umbrage to the left; when Nick came down for the full meeting, his grim expression of defiance made it clear that he knew exactly what was coming. He was not disappointed.

What followed was like a row at a particularly large familial gathering, a christening or a wedding. Along with the clearly significant issue of Sadie's official warning, there lurked years of old feuds and resentment which got an airing, not necessarily masquerading as concern for Sadie but certainly hitching a ride. Nick, in turn, used his justification of his official rebuke to launch a shoal of sly and not so sly attacks on the attitudes of his examiners. But one thing you should be clear about: there was nothing of the Machiavellian about this spat. A cooler, more cynical leader than Nick might well have taken the opportunity to blow a misdemeanour like Sadie's out of proportion in order to have an excuse to provoke a reaction and clean out the Augean stables of insubordination that had begun to smother the Secretariat. But Nick was not capable of this – not because he was a good man but because he was too morally vain to behave with such overt malice. Nick had to believe in the immediacy, in the truth and justice and righteousness of his cause. That was why he was always provoking fights.

So both parties slugged it out for at least two hours (God knows how) until Nick finally brought the meeting to an end by suddenly claiming he had to make a phone call to the Home Secretary. With Nick gone there was a bewildered pause rather as if one of the heavyweights in the seventh round of a world title fight had stormed out of the ring muttering that he would return at some unspecified round in the future. In fact he did not return until after five thirty. The row flared up again but as the meeting ended at six it was, by Secretariat standards, a fairly truncated affair.

Only three people said nothing: Sadie herself, Rob McCarthy, who was chairing the meeting, and, after a fashion, me. Please understand that I wasn't foolish enough not to speak (my colleagues and friends would have taken such a lack of solidarity badly) but I was careful to give my opinion in a way that offered nothing to either side, while sounding thoughtful about this plight in which we found ourselves. After the meeting McCarthy called me aside and it was clear he had taken my evasive vacuities as statesman-like.

'It was a stroke of luck,' he said to me quietly, 'that I was chairman today. I thought you were right to keep things neutral. I think it would be a good idea to let Nick calm down overnight and then I'll go and have a word tomorrow.'

I wasn't entirely sure if he was asking my opinion but I decided to treat it as if he had.

'Yes, a good idea.' I paused as if a thought had struck me. 'But I wonder, on the other hand . . .' I tried to put as much thoughtful uncertainty into this as I could, modest thinking-aloud stuff. 'I mean Nick knows you're close to Sadie and Tom. I mean Tom was very –' I oiled the word '– aggressive to Nick. Perhaps it would be better coming from me?'

More quizzical self-questioning modesty. In fact I had every intention of pouring poison into Nick's ear at the next available opportunity, but if I could head off McCarthy's intervention it would be no bad thing. Nick's relationship with McCarthy was unusual. For some reason it was never so personal, probably because McCarthy didn't seem to reflect much of Nick's personality. They were not opposites – there were plenty of opposites to Nick in the building – they just seemed psychologically to pass each other by, with the result that they never rubbed each other up. The only other person who seemed to reflect nothing of Nick was me.

Unfortunately, if not disastrously for my plans, McCarthy was unpersuaded. 'Perhaps we should both talk to him. Separately I mean. The thing is I was at the row with Dworkin and MacKinnon so . . . well . . . Nick and me we get on OK.'

247

'But of course,' I said, smiling agreeably. *Fuck you, you fucking fucker*. 'Good idea.'

This left me with one problem: whether to go and poke around in Nick's wounds while they were still fresh or wait until after he'd been possibly mollified by McCarthy then try to stir things up again. On balance I thought it best to wait. So McCarthy and I found the others in The Three Greyhounds on Greek Street and while they whined about what a shit Nick was, I considered who could be wound up further over this and in what way.

It wasn't until after work the next day that McCarthy had the time to go and see Nick. His door was half open as usual – the examiners used in the past to drop in on him all the time. But now, rarely.

'Come in.'

McCarthy entered and Nick looked up, surprised at first and then wary.

'Could I have a word Nick?' McCarthy was smiling, casual. Nick's wariness eased.

'Sit down.'

He did so, crossing his legs and trying to look relaxed.

'That was quite a day yesterday.'

'Management has a right to manage,' replied Nick stiffly. He was prone under pressure to come out with stuff like that. What McCarthy wanted to reply was that it was management's *obligation* to manage.

'Look, Nick, I honestly don't want to get in the middle of all this,' he said dishonestly. 'It's just that there seems to me, legally, to be a problem perhaps you hadn't foreseen.' He paused. 'Maybe you have.'

As intended, this unsettled Nick.

'I've talked to the Secretariat lawyers. I'm perfectly within my rights.'

'Well, I'm not a lawyer obviously, but I would have thought that there would be a problem, I mean, legally speaking, about the fact that you warned Tom and me to be very careful what we said at dinner, but as far as I know you didn't say anything to Sadie.' He paused and looked at Nick with quizzical and entirely feigned innocence. 'Or is that wrong?'

It was not wrong and the implications were immediately apparent to Nick. He paused for shocked thought.

'I haven't spoken to the others about this,' said McCarthy, which was true enough. 'I thought perhaps I'd speak to you first and that maybe it would be possible to sort this out without making things worse.'

'I'll have to speak to the lawyers,' said Nick, cold now.

'Fine,' replied McCarthy affably and stood up, his smile implying that in some way he was doing Nick a favour but it was all the same to him if he declined. 'Talk to you later, perhaps.' And without waiting for a reply he left.

As soon as McCarthy had gone, Nick flicked the intercom to his PA. 'Get me Richard Konchesky at Erskine Chambers.' Nick liked to employ the most expensive lawyers the Secretariat could afford.

When he put the phone down some ten minutes later Nick's mood was grim. It was clear that his mild, almost affable comment to McCarthy and Farraday had cost him dear. Richard Konchesky's judgement was simple. 'Sorry, Nick, but if you directed the other two examiners to be careful but not Miss Boldon, well, you don't have a leg to stand on. You'll have to withdraw the warning.'

An hour later his PA came in with a fax from the United States. As Nick began to read his mood, already foul, grew fouler. When he had finished he stared at the document for a moment. Then he tore it up and threw it in the bin. How different might everything have been if the fax had arrived even only a day or two later. But then, perhaps not. The tragic view of life is one where things happen inevitably: the ghastly death can only be the result of fatal flaws alone responsible for the necessary unhappy end. Sorry, but this just isn't so. Lots of fatal flaws lead only to a minor grief. Luck nearly always has a part to play in dreadful ends or the near miss. Getting out by the skin of your teeth is always possible. If the lookouts on the *Titanic* had spotted the iceberg a mere two minutes later the ship would have hit it head-on and so would not have sunk. A piece of shrapnel higher to the left or right and Hitler would have died in 1916. Character and necessary fate is just for books. The theory of complexity has put a crimp in tragedy for good.

At any rate it was two days before Nick could bear to call Sadie to his office. As she sat in front of him the atmosphere was polar in its frostiness.

'I have to tell you,' said Nick, 'that because of a legal technicality, and for no other reason, the Secretariat has decided to withdraw the official warning sent to you on the seventh of this month.'

She tried to hide her surprise and her relief by sitting up straight. 'Do you mind if I ask what this technicality was?'

'It's immaterial. But let me be clear – if there is ever a repeat of your behaviour you can be sure that I will take serious steps. And next time there won't be any technicality to come to your rescue.'

A surge of anger shot through Sadie – but she knew a victory when she saw one, however partial and dangerous it might be.

'Is that all?'

He looked at her for a moment – their eyes meeting for the first time. 'Is there anything you want to say?'

She was surprised, even shocked, by his question but

she knew immediately what he wanted. He wanted her to say that she was sorry that things had got out of hand. And if she had, then in my opinion, the American fax would have somehow found its way out of the bin and things would have turned out differently. But she couldn't. Not in a thousand years. It was tragic.

It had taken years for this peculiar cross between a polygamous marriage and an adopted family to come to this. Early honeymoon rows had been put to the back of the mind, and they had been followed by many ups and even highs – but gradually things had gone downhill in fits and starts until it had reached a point where I felt confident that I was in a position to get up to no good with considerable hope of success.

I think it was in *Magnum Force* that Harry Callaghan pointed out it was important for a man to know his limitations. And I knew mine. No doubt, there were Cruyffs and Pelés of organizational dissension, people with a genius for setting their colleagues at each other's throats. I wasn't one of them, I knew. Nevertheless I could see that in the row over Sadie, Nick had made two mistakes that had cost him, as it were, his majority. From this point the Noes had it. First he had tried to make an example of someone who was the favourite of nearly everyone (including, of course, Nick himself) and secondly he had attacked the love of Thomas Farraday's life. The thing is that he had failed to realize Farraday was of huge importance to him and the balance of power at the Secretariat. While Farraday was often critical of Nick, their disagreements lacked the animus that had come to infect Nick's relationship with most of the other examiners. On the other hand Farraday refused to side with his colleagues when he thought they were merely spoiling for a fight. Because he carried weight by virtue of his general popularity and his intellect he had on numerous occasions, unknown to Nick, throttled attempts by others to start a row. But now Nick had made a deadly enemy because he had been horrible to the one Farraday loved.

My opportunity to make mischief had come not because I was more perceptive than the others about Sadie and Farraday, but because I had seen them kissing in the corridor when they thought no one was looking. What a very costly kiss that was – again how different things might have been if they had shown a little more resistance or if bad luck had not meant that having gone through the door ahead of them I'd turned back to fetch a forgotten book and just (and I mean only just) caught them as they parted and turned from each other. The point is that never again at any time did I see anything else that would have given them away.

If you're surprised that Farraday had not confronted Nick himself, he had indeed threatened to 'disembowel that fucking cunt'. (By his own admission his time as an examiner had seriously affected his use of bad language.) He had only said this in front of McCarthy who, somewhat surprised at his passionate stance it has to be said, persuaded him to back off and let him go and talk to Nick instead. This is why I was only the second examiner to approach Nick about Sadie. By now we all knew that he'd had to back down and as a result he greeted my arrival in his office with as much sour touchiness as I'd ever seen in a human being.

'Yes?'

'If it's a bad time I can come back later.'

'What do you want?'

'I . . . uh . . . I just wanted to say that . . .'. My hesitation was not feigned – he didn't look like someone who was ready to be flattered. '. . . I happen to think that you were right – you know, about the business in Birmingham.'

He looked down at his papers and started writing. 'Is that all?' he said, still looking down.

Clearly I'd miscalculated, although I wasn't sure why. It wasn't as if I'd underestimated Nick: he may have been slightly deranged, or even very, but I had never made the mistake of thinking that he was a dope. But now it seemed he saw straight through me, that despite the fact that everyone else was against him he despised my expression of sympathy and chose not to make an ally of me. I stood there, shocked and humiliated.

'Yes,' I said and left.

Outside my shame quickly turned into anger. How dare he look at me that way, how dare he despise me. I did something then that I'd never done before. I behaved recklessly, without fear or calculation.

I launched myself back into his office with such energy that he looked up at me with near astonishment. Before he could speak I let him have it.

'Look, Nick, I came here to support you in all this at some real risk to my relations with the other examiners. I really have no intention of being dismissed by you in this way just because you're in a bad mood.'

He was still looking at me, lips apart in surprise. I thought I'd just tone it down.

'Surely all this is too important? I don't think it's fair of you or good for the Secretariat to treat me—' That seemed wrong, too self-centred. I corrected myself. '– my ideas for how to deal with this situation in such a dismissive way. I'm sorry but that's how I feel.'

That was a good point to stop. Nick liked feelings. He was unusual in this: in my experience at any rate intelligent people usually gave priority to their intellect.

Nick was very bright but his intelligence was only a kind of tool at the service of a deeply emotional way of responding to, as it turned out, almost everything. He trusted his emotions in the way that normally only foolish people trusted them. That, I think, was what made him so very odd.

That was why he had an immediate change of heart. He could see how strongly I felt and it was this that overwhelmed not only his anger but also his good judgement. Because, of course, until this moment of recklessness he'd basically despised me as nothing more than a dull man without a soul – a void. But in a moment he'd changed his mind. And all because he failed to see what sounded like passionate integrity for what it really was: pique. It never occurred to Nick that even a dead soul is capable of feeling affront.

After that it wasn't too much different to being the interlocutor of a put-upon wife, whining about her ungrateful husband/sons/daughters. Excuse me if I seem to keep shifting my familial metaphors but I can only tell you that it seems to me to be fair enough – these roles do shift themselves around in families, haven't you found? Sooner or later anyway.

So things came out pretty well for me all told, and if only McCarthy hadn't stuck his big nose into things they might have fallen apart there and then. Still Nick had marked my card about McCarthy that afternoon by telling me what he'd done and it was clear that sooner or later there would be another brawl. Had I but known, the cause of it was festering in the torn-up fax at the bottom of Nick's waste-paper bin. I'm glad I didn't know, to be honest, because waiting for it to come to light – which of course it might never have done – would have given me many anxious nights, for it was to take quite a while and a hefty coincidence for it to do so.

* * *

At any rate, the next day the hostilities had to be toned down because a special meeting had been called to discuss what the Secretariat was going to do about Salman Rushdie and *International Guerrillas*. Fortunately for Nick its sheer unprecedented oddness as a problem was a distraction – the Secretariat was an organization that only considered made-up harms to made-up people. Now it was faced with the opposite. As a result it blind-sided the conventional relationships in the Secretariat and exposed some of the cracks. Instead of rowing with Nick the examiners started to squabble with each other.

People changed their minds at the Secretariat more often than most. Is this to be admired? Not that much, in my view, and for two reasons: firstly, thinking about other people's opinions was what they were paid to do and, secondly, they only altered their views as the result of a careful consideration of the arguments of others once in a blue moon (as opposed to never, which I take to be the case with the population in general).

The debate over Salman Rushdie therefore was as much a rehash of the opinions I've already reported to you as you might expect. I return to them briefly, not to deal with issues of free speech but to give you some idea of the fault lines, ideological and personal, that existed between the examiners themselves. And when I say 'fault lines' I mean, of course, bile and hatred.

'Surely, as sophisticated a man as Salman Rushdie would laugh at the overblown portrait of himself in this film,' said A.

'Right up to the point at which someone cuts his throat,' said B.

'Look at the satirical forms in the Anglo-Saxon tradition where the demonization of out-of-reach people is entirely familiar. Look at the folk-devils made of Thatcher or Scargill,' said C.

'Why don't we get the distributors to add a caption stating there is no relationship between the anti-Islamic murderer named Salman Rushdie in the film and the real British writer of the same name?' offered D.

Bursts of scornful laughter from E and F.

'I know for a fact that the Salman Rushdie affair has legitimized racism,' said G.

'Instead of worrying about racism in general, why isn't it plain to everyone that here is a man in fear of his life and being guarded twenty-four hours a day?' replied H. 'If he's killed after we pass this I don't see how we can argue we don't have blood on our hands.'

'People', replied I, 'don't get their morality from films; they bring their morality to it.'

'A brilliant argument for not being a censor,' said J. 'Can we expect your resignation in the morning?'

'It will do more harm than good in my opinion to ban this film. There's a robustness in British society that will take criticism of icons like Rushdie, however distorted. And there is little doubt,' added K, 'that Rushdie has shifted from being simply a writer to being a representative and a symbol. It may not be of his own making, but it must be recognized.'

'I don't like Salman Rushdie – or his work – but I have to say that not only is that the most specious argument I've ever heard, it's also the most fucking heartless.' It was Farraday who had let rip and it was a furious Allan Rhys who only barely flinched at what he said. But I could see the hatred flowing down his arms into his fingers and tainting the very table he was touching.

So Nick was left with a tricky decision. The point was that he had not in fact ever watched an Indian or Pakistani video all the way through before. Whatever the arguments about respect for other cultures, ones that he deeply agreed with in principle, he found these films incomprehensible and boring in practice. His instinct, therefore, was to simply pass it out as not worth taking seriously. This was certainly an attitude reflected in the Secretariat's President Lord Joyce, who fell asleep halfway through a viewing and, much to the delight of the examiners who were with him, did not wake up until it was over, doing so with a loud snort and an astonished look around him that made it clear that for at least five seconds he had no idea where he was.

On the other hand, Nick was genuinely worried about Rushdie and the remark about blood on our hands struck home. How would it look if someone got to Rushdie after we passed it? He knew for certain that the current enthusiasm in the press for releasing it, sight unseen of course, would evaporate if Rushdie was murdered. The least risky thing to do was refuse it a certificate. So, full of the deepest misgivings, that's what he did.

The distributors, realizing that the huge publicity generated by Nick's decision could make them a fortune, immediately appealed to the Video Review Panel, a committee comprised of impartial citizens of experience and integrity. The examiners claimed that the VRP actually stood for Venal Raving Pushovers – based on the odd behaviour of some of its members and the tendency of its judgements to reflect what Nick wanted – something that was hardly surprising given that Nick had appointed them in the first place.

On the matter of *International Guerrillas*, however, they ruled against him and ordered it to be given a certificate. This was neither because of the excellence of the arguments presented for doing so by the distributors' lawyers, nor because of a sudden fit of independence. Oddly enough it was because of Salman Rushdie himself. Still unable to appear in public because of the threats to his life, he wrote a letter to the VRP:

> The film *International Guerrillas* has been refused a
> certificate by the Film and Video Secretariat because it
> correctly sees the film as extremely defamatory. However
> I find myself in the extraordinary position of having to
> write to you and waive my legal rights to sue either the
> distributors of this ridiculous film or the Secretariat
> itself. I do not want to be defended by an act of
> censorship.

So that was that. At least in public. Some of the examiners, particularly McCarthy, argued that it shouldn't be down to Rushdie to decide the issue because it had much wider significance and: 'There's a pretty big distinction in law between attacking someone's ideas and attacking an individual.' But Nick spoke pretty much for everyone by pointing out that the Secretariat would look distinctly foolish trying to protect someone who said they didn't want to be protected. This piece of obvious good sense was somewhat diminished by his bizarre claim that the VRP's verdict 'was exactly what I wanted'.

'How the bloody hell', said a still grumpy McCarthy, 'can you claim that a verdict overruling your decision was exactly what you wanted?'

Nick's reply was, it has to be said, not easy to follow but he finished his explanation with a smile which made it perfectly clear that he himself was entirely satisfied with it.

With a sigh McCarthy gave up and all that remained was for Rhys to rub in what he clearly regarded as a crushing victory over Farraday. 'The decision of the Video

Review Panel', he said with triumphant piety, 'has to be considered as a serious censure of our judgement.'

With the pleasure and conceit of a conjurer pulling an entire warren of rabbits out of a hat, he produced a copy of the previous day's editorial in *The Times* which he described lovingly as 'a harsh reprimand' and began reading out its conclusion with unfettered delight: ' "It would have been much better for the censor to err on the side of freedom of speech and allow Mr Rushdie to look to his own defence." '

Rhys looked around the room seeing only the heads nodding in agreement, and not the eyes rolling in disdain. 'This was, and should remain,' he said, more in gleeful sorrow than anger, 'a salutary experience for us all.' He sat back, bathing himself in victory and vindication. 'There is,' he intoned glaring at McCarthy and Farraday meaningfully, 'a thing called hubris.'

'What a prick!' Farraday said to McCarthy, who was delighted with Rhys's performance and was laughing silently to himself. But it was not in Farraday's nature to let such an attack go unremarked.

'Frankly,' he said aloud, 'I've heard and said enough about Salman Rushdie to make my own ears bleed. So I won't add much to this except to say that in general none of Allan Rhys's views, in my opinion, hold water – though they most certainly contain bile.'

There was an affronted look from Rhys and a thrill of delight through the room rather as if at the promise of a playground fight.

'As for *The Times*, it hardly needs to be pointed out that what the editorial has to say has got bugger all to do with free speech and everything to do with the fact that whoever wrote it would be happy to see some fanatic blow Salman Rushdie's brains out.'

* * *

A few months afterwards Salman Rushdie pointed out that his intervention had demonstrated that his lifelong held position on censorship was correct because if the video had been banned many thousands would have been illegally copied and it would have become glamorous as an object. He went on to say with relish that because it was given a certificate it had lost this allure and as a result hardly anyone bothered with it. 'It just goes to show that actually if you do let people make up their own minds they can tell the difference between rubbish and what is not rubbish. In the end the thing turned into a rather shapely parable of the free speech position.'

But as it happened there was a weakness in Rushdie's interpretation of why no one subsequently watched the video: it was completely wrong. In a subsequent and very much off-the-record conversation that Nick had with a member of the Indian Video Retailers Association, Nick had quoted Rushdie on *International Guerrillas'* lack of commercial success.

'Oh, that had nothing to do with it, Mr Berg.'

'Really?' said Nick, surprised as to his absolute certainty. 'Why not?'

'Strictly between you and me, my colleagues and I took the view that this bloody video was a bloody nuisance, stirring up trouble like that. We're a law-abiding community, Mr Berg. At any rate the distributor received an anonymous phone call in which he was informed that if he released this *Guerrilla* film of his, all his video shops would have petrol bombs thrown through their windows. He knew they meant bloody business. Of course,' he added, 'we strongly disapprove of people taking the law into their own hands.' He smiled with pleasure at Nick's astonishment. 'You tell that to bloody Salman

Rushdie and his bloody shapely parable of free speech.'

A storm in a teacup, then, given that *International Guerrillas* vanished without trace? It depends, I suppose, on whether you believe in the change in the earth's magnetic field that some claim alerts certain animals to a coming earthquake. Nobody took Islam seriously then, not even the people who knew it well. There was one report, a few lines really, that seemed to say it all. It was written by an examiner who specialized in Arab videos, who had been born in Cairo and spent most of her life there. She was always deeply respectful of the Muslim world but this was what she had to say about taking expressions of Islamic rage with a pinch of salt.

> Coming as I do from a majority made up of Muslims, one is accustomed to hearing the voice of the Imam of the Mosque booming from the loudspeakers and the radios using similar language as that used in the film. It usually includes fierce denunciation and proclamations about achieving martyrdom by ridding Islam of its enemies, the Imam inciting his congregation into religious fervour in the style of Christian Evangelists. It puts the fear of God into you but falls on stony ground, very rarely taken seriously, the cry for 'holy warriors' to take action is not new.

How then did even those with so much sympathetic insight get it wrong? I think, now, that it comes down to play. Playfulness has become the West's thing – gregarious, it likes to get about. Playfulness will play with anyone. *The Satanic Verses* is a riot of the fanciful. Year after year the Secretariat bore witness to the fact that in the West nothing was sacred any more. The West was ready to play with everything: rape and murder, plaster Christs in piss, wonderful gangsters shooting from the hip and human flesh in all its many tangibles, stroked and ripped and thumped and fucked. Harry have you met Darth? Sneezy do you know Jesus? Bart do you know Ché? Barbie, this is Adolf.

Consider this, all this endless fun, in the light of what Ayatollah Khomeini had to say on his return to Iran: 'There is no room for play in Islam. It is deadly serious about everything.'

No Turning Back

Dear T
I wonder how my stomach is going to stop aching when I
know that only your touch will soothe it, your breath on my
skin the only way I could sleep, and as for dreaming . . .
Tomorrow more pining for you I guess and then Monday
which I am already waiting for with far far far too much
longing than is dignified. Think of me. Love me. Want me. Be
crazy about me the way I am crazy about you. Nothing less
will do.

PS These letters are a source of release to me when I sit alone
late at night finding my thoughts naturally turning to you. All
this emotional stuff and guilt and turbulence is all well and
good but allow me to tell you, sir, that the way you leant back
against the wall and allowed your neck to rest gently against
the wall drove me out of my mind.

Sx

EXTRACT FROM ROB MCCARTHY'S report on *Thrash 'n' Burn*
posted on the notice board by Molly Tydeman.

Since 1977, and, ironically, almost solely because of Nick Berg, the test of illegality for films being based on their indecency and offensiveness has been specifically ruled out and replaced by the much tougher test as to whether or not it depraves or corrupts. And yet we're still invoking indecency and offensiveness as grounds for cutting videos. Consider Molly Tydeman's decision to pass a video of the Macc Lads in concert at '18' without cuts. These charmers, a rock group from Macclesfield, sing lines like 'Dig up your dead granny and fuck her up the arse'. Walter Casey's comment on Molly's decision was: 'Doesn't sound terribly suitable for viewing in the home – but what can we do?' as if cutting for indecency and offensiveness were beyond our scope. Yet we happily take out scenes from John Water's *Pink Flamingos* (of poodle shit eating fame) on grounds of offensiveness. 'Excess rather than legal reasons would seem the reason for cutting here,' says Allan Rhys, for instance, of the shot of a castrated man's dead body in *Pink Flamingos*, with an obvious sense of reluctant obligation. A free dog turd to anyone who can explain to me on what basis we judge that the public might find someone singing 'Dig up your dead granny and fuck her up the arse' less offensive than a not very detailed shot of a castrated man in a deliberately bad taste comedy.

Rob McCarthy

It was about three weeks later that Farraday and a nervous Sadie approached the door of his flat near the Kennington Oval. He opened the door and signalled her through, pretty nervous himself because this was the first time she had agreed to come. She didn't move. Her eyes widened as she looked at him and she swallowed hard.

'I can't,' she said.

'Nothing's going to happen.'

'You want to make love to me.'

She often caught him off-balance with this sudden directness of hers.

'You make me feel like a cad.'

She smiled, though he could see she was shaking. He felt shaky himself.

'You are a cad, aren't you? A ladies' man?' But already the smile had gone to be replaced by something that almost seemed by the tone of her voice to be an accusation.

'I don't know what to say.'

'You could answer my question.'

'OK,' he said, 'I'm not a ladies' man.'

'I don't mean that,' she replied. 'Do you want to make love to me?'

'Of course,' he said quietly.

She looked away down the street for some time, and back at him.

'I'm married.'

'I know.'

She looked as if she were about to cry.

'Just come inside and have a cup of tea.' He smiled, 'You don't even have to take your coat off if you don't want.'

She smiled back. 'I wouldn't get the benefit of it when I went out.'

He held out his hand to her and without hesitation she took it.

Several hours later they lay in bed looking at each other with their heads on separate pillows. He was stroking her side with the back of his hand, barely touching her as he moved from just below her shoulder to the curve of her hip bone.

'You're very gentle,' she said calmly.

'You expected me to be a brute as well as a cad?'

She laughed. 'I suppose I thought that it wouldn't be your fault, if you didn't have a soft touch – you know, all that rugby and cold showers. But your touch, it's like a girl's.'

He laughed, surprised. 'I'm not sure about that one.'

'Ooh, have I threatened your masculinity?'

'It's a fragile thing, you need to be careful.' He leant forward and kissed her though not so gently. After some time she pulled back.

'I'll remember.'

After she had finally agreed to come in off the street it was as if she had crossed some bridge, burning it as she went. Even though he was trying to be tactful and went to make tea as soon as he had sat her down, she followed him into the kitchen and kissed him with so much passion and intensity that it left him clear she had made up her mind.

Making love to her had been quite the most astonishing experience of his life. Before Sadie, everything else had just been fucking – this was like nothing he had ever felt or even imagined feeling. It was as if they had thought up what they were doing entirely for themselves, as if no one had even kissed a breast or held an erect cock. It was as if being inside her was something terrifyingly original, like the discovery of a place you'd never imagined. It was, he thought later – and he could not think straight for many days after – so *un*pornographic.

And this was despite the fact that after her almost tearful fear of being alone in his flat she had devoured him. It was like being eaten by someone starved of you – lips, chest, erection – she swallowed him up in a way that shocked and amazed. She'd hooked him up and that was it.

'How are you?' he said after a silence of nearly twenty minutes. She didn't reply at first, but he could tell she was thinking about what to say.

'In love,' she said, at last.

How well it sounded to him, as if everything he had ever wanted, even unknown things, had been given to him. This is bliss, he thought. It *is* possible.

'I ought to feel ashamed,' she added, 'and I will soon I know, but I don't feel it now.'

'I don't want you to feel ashamed.'

She let out a sigh. 'It's not something you can really do anything about. Anyway, let's not talk about it.' She looked at him thoughtfully for a moment. 'Did you like it?' she asked.

He laughed.

'Don't laugh at me.'

'I can't help it. You're so strange sometimes.'

She wrinkled her nose. 'Don't say that, I don't want to be strange.'

He stroked her cheek. 'It's just that you're so direct sometimes, just like, just like a clever nine-year-old.'

She took a deep breath as if considering what he said carefully. 'I think perhaps I am a bit like that. When it comes to men that's about how old I feel. I mean I don't know much about them. I'm not like you, a cad and a ladies' man.'

'I'm not a cad or a ladies' man, I told you.'

She cleared her throat. 'But you would say that, wouldn't you, if you were. You're right, I'm very ignorant about sex.'

'But you're an old married woman.' He knew what he was doing saying this – he realized that there was no point in trying to pretend her husband didn't exist, comforting though the idea was.

267

'I met David' – he felt a jab in the heart at the mention of his rival's name – 'when I was eighteen. I'd only kissed a couple of boys before that. My dad was very strict. Even then I was a virgin until I was twenty. I've never been with anyone else.'

He felt a childish rush of anxiety and, though he felt its clumsiness even as he was saying it, he couldn't stop himself. 'Until now.'

She turned inside his arms and faced him. 'I was unfaithful to David a long time ago – with you, I mean. That night at the dinner. I was unfaithful in my heart. That's what counts, isn't it?' She smiled. 'But I suppose it's the sex that's the thing for you.'

'I see . . . this is you're so deep and I'm so shallow.'

'Not at all – I'm the one who's shallow, a shallow slut who's having an affair and who's not feeling guilty.'

'I'm very glad about that.'

'But I will do . . . soon.' She looked at his face, scanning it with her large brown eyes. 'You didn't answer my question – was it all right for you?'

He looked at her, holding her face in his hands. 'I've never felt anything like it.'

She closed her eyes and settled into his chest. 'That's nice,' she said, and after a silent few minutes she fell asleep.

In the nineteenth century literature and life were pretty much in agreement: adultery was something that would end in disaster. In both, as the century wore on, there were mitigating factors. But even in the greatest and most sympathetic of all novels of adultery, the woman ends up throwing herself under a train. In legal terms to have seduced another man's wife was to have engaged in criminal conversation.

All that changed in the century that followed: art and life grew apart, but in a complicated way. In fiction, to sleep outside the marriage bed became an act of authenticity, a daring expression of the self. Stable marriages in twentieth-century works of art always seem to be tainted with a lack of imagination: in *Brief Encounter* the husband has no face, being represented only by the sight of his pipe and slippers. But in twentieth-century life not even the easiness of divorce stopped the recognition of the pain and treachery involved, the hurt and lies and the bewildered kids; no-pain hasn't followed from no-fault. Novels about middle-class divorces are regarded as a joke, but nobody thinks divorce itself is much to laugh about.

Thomas Farraday's thoughts about the man he had wronged were strangely simple for such a sophisticated and decent man (how oddly that sentence would have sat in, say, *Pride and Prejudice* or even *Middlemarch*). Farraday had met David Boldon on two occasions: a Secretariat function and a dinner at another examiner's house. He had never warmed to him. There was no obvious reason why this should be so: he was a pleasant and witty enough man, intelligent. Farraday had even voiced his vague sense of dislike to McCarthy who expressed only mystification. 'He seems a perfectly nice guy to me.'

Now, of course, Farraday saw things in a different light: his shadowy antipathy hardened into a deep sense of distaste which he did not question. Love as intense as his, I suppose, makes you simple.

Sadie, on the other hand, with the odd psycho-pathology of the married cheat, grew more affectionate towards her husband – she felt a deepening goodwill and smiled at and touched him more often. The intensity of the love and desire she felt for Thomas Farraday acted like a bright light that often obliterated all the shade of conscience and regret. For now, she managed a greater tenderness towards her husband alongside an ability to tell him she would be late home again because of a sudden increase in submission of new videos that would have left even the most conscienceless psychopath grinding his teeth with jealousy.

At work, Farraday's euphoria made itself felt everywhere: nothing could diminish his ebullience. After viewing a nature film with Emma Saward she had written in her report:

> This is an eloquent documentary devoted to a single task: observing insects. Beginning with a sweeping pan of an immense sky accompanied by a glorious classical score, the camera slowly inches closer and closer to earth finally focusing on an ordinary meadow on a single summer day from dawn to dusk, following the comings and goings of a micro-metropolis of the tiny insects who cohabit the planet with us.

Farraday's report was rather different in tone.

> Bugs fucking to Mozart. Pass U uncut.

At lunchtime, McCarthy came down into the theatre.
'Fancy a walk?'
'Yeah.'
It was a habit of theirs to take a break by walking round and round the pavement that encircled the small park that made up the centre of Golden Square.
'You seem very cheerful,' said McCarthy.
'I am.'
They walked on in amiable silence.

'What were you watching this morning?' asked Farraday as they both looked with interest at an attractive woman bemusedly trying to bite into a baguette so large that she was having difficulty finding a purchase on it with her teeth.

'Um, a comedy. Can't remember what it was called.'

'Any good?'

McCarthy looked thoughtful for a moment. 'It would have been better with a scriptwriter not under the impression that "there hasn't been a famous carpenter since Noah"'.

There was a brief pause as Farraday considered this for a moment and then burst into laughter.

'How's Sadie?' said McCarthy, smiling.

'Why don't you ask her?' replied Farraday, amiably.

'Because I'm asking you.'

'Pretty amazing as it happens.'

'Well, I'm glad. You were beginning to look permanently as if somebody had stolen your rabbit and sold the hutch.'

Farraday laughed. 'Is that a quaint working-class saying?'

'It is, actually. My mother always trotted it out whenever I was glum. She used to drive me up the wall, especially when she used to say, "I know you of old" – I had absolutely no idea what that meant.'

The square was filling up now, particularly as the sprinklers were on in one corner, forcing the lunching office workers and tourists to bunch up to avoid getting wet.

'Did your mother', asked Farraday, slyly, 'ever tell you things would end in tears?'

'All the time.'

'Is that what you're trying to say?'

McCarthy seemed almost shocked. 'I wouldn't stick my nose in that far.'

'But it's what you think?'

'I don't know. Perhaps, I suppose . . . obviously it could. It depends how bad you've both got it.'

'Speaking for myself, I'd say pretty bad.'

'Yeah, I thought so.'

They walked on in silence.

'Got any advice?'

McCarthy laughed. 'No, I don't. I envy you to be honest. I can imagine that it would be quite something to be loved by Sadie.'

'You liked her husband, if I remember.'

'He seemed like a nice fellow.'

'I harbour', said Farraday, 'ungenerous thoughts towards him.'

'Yes, I suppose so.'

'But I don't want to think about the future. I'm too ecstatic, just amazed and bowled over.'

They walked on past three down-and-outs, two men and a woman, who had occupied a bench since their last lap and who were sharing a six-pack of Carling and chatting amiably while enjoying the sun.

'Actually, I've been thinking about the future,' said McCarthy. 'Mine, I mean.'

'In what way?'

'It's time to think about going. I think I've had enough of telling other people what they can't see.'

'You mean you're going to leave now, immediately?'

'Nothing so rash,' replied McCarthy, smiling. 'I was talking about later rather than sooner. But it's time to start looking for a way out.'

'Any ideas?'

'I do have a notion. I'd like to write a book.'

'A novel?'

'God, no! I was thinking a biography.'

'Of?'

'Louis Bris.'

'Right.' Farraday looked dubious. 'Is that wise? I mean didn't he slap a writ on some guy who was doing a book on him?'

'He's got lawyers coming out of his arse. He's sued at least eight newspapers around the world.'

'A good reason to leave him alone, then.'

'I suppose. But I was thinking of approaching him directly. Making it an official biography. Get him to co-operate.'

'So you'll let him have the final say?'

'Not exactly. See, I'm not interested in writing an indictment of his business practices or his abuse of his money and power, or who he's fucked. I don't really care about what makes him tick. I just want to see how that kind of power actually works in practice. I don't want to make any judgements about him, how bad or good he is. He's a bizarre character but he's smart, thoughtful in his strange way. I just want to look at how all that stuff works. Do you know who Rosalind Franklin was?'

'Remind me.'

'She was one of the scientists who broke the structure of DNA. She said something that really stuck in my mind – that as a scientist she didn't want to touch anything, she just wanted to look. That's the kind of book I want to write.'

'Have you tried approaching him?'

'No idea how to. If I write out of the blue, I mean, why should he trust me?'

Farraday considered for a moment. 'I know someone who's a friend of his.'

'I was forgetting, you and your upper-class mafia – the Cosy Nostra.'

'Fuck off, motherfucker! Do you want my help or not?'

'OK, all right.'

'Don't do me any favours.'

By this time they were once more approaching the three down-and-outs on the corner bench. Their mood had changed and one of the men was arguing with the woman. It was no squabble, the man's voice was heavy with rage. The woman's reply, hard to make out, was truculent but afraid.

Without really thinking, Farraday moved to intervene. But McCarthy took him by the arm.

'You'll make things worse for her.'

Reluctantly Farraday moved on, but turned his head to keep an eye on the couple. The moment he turned to face forward there was a loud cry from the woman and a soft *Thwack!*

Both McCarthy and Farraday turned instantly, McCarthy softly groaning as he did so. Farraday rushed between the woman and the man as he raised his hand again.

'That's enough.'

The man looked at him, unfocused, mystified. 'Fuck off Jew!'

'I will. Just don't hit her again.'

The man pulled away, much stronger than Farraday expected for someone who looked in his sixties but could have been twenty years younger. Seeing that the man was trying to get the room to lash out at him, Farraday moved with him, holding his left shoulder and right wrist.

Part of Farraday realized that he was now in a real fight, part of him was shocked that his friend was standing by as if afraid. But then the drunk pushed angrily forward, almost knocking him down. Scrabbling for purchase on the dusty pavement Farraday was pushed back towards the railings, almost tripping on the kerb and falling. Then he found some grip and pushed back, keeping hold of the drunk's right arm as he tried to pull free so he could hit him. He felt a hefty blow on his back.

'Fucking leave him!' screamed the woman as she hit him again, a painful blow on his right ear.

Then he felt the drunk's arm being held and someone talking to him. For a moment the struggle went on. Another blow to his back from the woman.

'Fucking leave off, Maggie.' It was the voice of his attacker. He was being held by the other male down-and-out, who was talking softly to him. The fight was over. Warily, Farraday let go and moved back. The woman, who'd done as she was told, glared at him resentfully.

Then the second man picked up what was left of the six-pack, two cans, and keeping himself between Farraday and his attacker, led his fellow-drunk away. Keeping an eye on Farraday the woman followed. Within a few seconds they were out of the park and gone.

Farraday looked at McCarthy who in turn was looking back at him.

'I'd better get going,' said McCarthy casually, as if nothing had happened. 'I'm working with Allan and he wanted to start early.' And with that he turned and started back towards the Secretariat.

At half-past five that day McCarthy was writing his reports when the door opened and Farraday came in, face black as a rain cloud.

'Hi, there,' said McCarthy, mockingly agreeable.

'Why didn't you help me today?'

McCarthy could feel his friend's sense of angry loss so

275

intensely it almost broke his resolve. 'Oh, you mean your dashing rescue?'

'I don't see that it's anything to sneer at.'

'I wasn't sneering,' replied McCarthy gently. 'Well, perhaps a little bit.'

'Look, I want to know why you didn't help me.'

'To be fair, I did try to persuade you to stay out of it.'

'He hit her. What was I supposed to do?'

'I think, as it happens, that you behaved very . . .' McCarthy chose the word carefully '. . . properly. You did the right thing. Definitely.'

Farraday looked at him, confused now as well as deeply offended. 'Then why didn't you help?'

McCarthy opened his eyes wider, as if surprised. 'What makes you think I didn't?'

'Don't piss about. What do you mean? You stood by and did nothing.'

'No, you just think that's what I did.'

Farraday stared at him, unwilling to be strung along in the dark. McCarthy felt he had pushed his friend far enough.

'When you went to stop the guy who was hitting the woman, I can't imagine why but I thought you could probably cope with a clapped-out drunk. So I kept an eye on his pal who, as it happens, had his hand in his pocket reaching for something and was starting to move to get you from behind. I don't know for certain that he was reaching for a blade, but unless he was going to offer you a sandwich I'm pretty sure that's what it was.' He smiled, enjoying Farraday's growing discomfort.

'So I took a twenty-pound note out of my wallet, held his arm at the end of which he may or may not have had a knife, and showed him the money. That's why he stopped the fight. So I'd say that you owe me twenty quid and an apology.'

Farraday looked at his triumphant friend and said nothing for a full twenty seconds. 'Why didn't you tell me this at the time?'

'Because I'm a cunt,' replied McCarthy cheerfully. 'And because I thought you needed to be taught a lesson.'

'What do you mean?'

'What you did was really stupid. I don't mean that you wanted to help a woman in trouble. What was stupid was that you rushed into a fight with one man when you were clearly in a fight with two of them. And, as it unsurprisingly turned out, all three. You had no idea where the second guy was once you grabbed the first. And just as dumb, you assumed they were too fucked up to hurt you. And you were wrong, weren't you?'

There was a short pause from Farraday.

'Yes.'

'So,' said McCarthy, smiling, 'are you happy now?'

Farraday reached into his wallet and passed over a twenty-pound note.

'You're right, of course,' he said, as McCarthy took the money. 'You *are* a cunt.'

The Exorcist

Dear Tom

. . . when I said I wouldn't call you I was just playing, responding to your 'I don't want to dominate your life' nonsense – of course you dominate my life, why else would I be in this position? You said to me before that you never stop loving me even when we quarrel. Well I lashed out at you tonight about Friday because of all the most obvious reasons. I don't think (tell me if I'm wrong) that you'd prefer me to want you less, expect less from what we have. Because my feeling is that you have infiltrated every corner of my heart (I know hearts don't have corners – look what you've done to my brain). I honestly don't know how to expect everything but also not mind when it's not there – but, I suppose, this is exactly what's demanded of us. I could force myself to pretend to be cool if you want, if it makes you feel less burdened, but I doubt if I'd be very successful and think you'd be offended. I only have to say playfully that I'm not calling you on Thursday because I have so much to do and immediately your pride is hurt. Believe me, on balance, I think, you're happier to feel I am obsessed with you.

I shall have to be away soon, never an entirely happy thought because, as you know (don't deny it), the most interesting landscape is yours. But perhaps with me away you might even be a little jealous to know that I am in someone else's bed – not because I want you to suffer but because it might make you understand how it often is for me. I know how you like women and love to charm them – and I know that you are a ladies' man whatever you say. I admit I feel great stabs of jealousy. So there it is and hence my sometimes uncontrollable feelings. Doesn't it bother you that I'm with someone or is it that you are so simply and correctly confident in my love and desire for you that you can afford to be magnanimous? Or is it some class thing – having a mistress who's married is just something to be philosophical about? Which is it? Too many words, now, and not sharp enough.

The thing is, you and I have, for me, a unique relationship – uniquely full, thorough and truthful. It brings meaning to life. I know these are big words but what you are to me is big. It is huge and yes it dominates my life and affects everything I do.

I am, as ever, your imperfect, deeply uncool lover but from now on I intend to stare you in the eye and not flinch.

Sadie x

EXCERPT FROM THOMAS FARRADAY'S report on *The Exorcist*:

. . . now we learn, almost by accident, that as well as *The Exorcist* Nick is also holding back the video of *Reservoir Dogs* with cuts to Tarantino's film being strongly considered in the light of the 'suitability for viewing in the home test' in the Video Recordings Act which he repeatedly claims demands that we treat video more restrictively than film. So I went back and re-read the Act to which many of us owe our jobs. What struck me having looked at it again after so long and after so many years as a censor is what an astonishingly bad and spineless piece of legislation it is.

It's almost impossible to find anywhere a declaration of its purpose – some identification of the public wrong the Act seeks to rectify. Surely the minimum you can expect of any law is that it tells you what it's a law against. Not here – the first four pages identify who is exempted from the scope of the Act but provide no hint as to what they're exempted from. The solitary clue as to what this law is actually about comes in a statement that the designated authority must determine whether video works are 'suitable for classification certificates'. In other words the body that classifies videos must decide whether a video is suitable for them to classify. Is there another law on the statute books more spectacularly meaningless than this one? This circular gibberish is qualified only by the equally unintelligible 'need' to bear in mind that the said videos will be 'viewed in the home'. Concerning the videos of *Reservoir Dogs* and *The Exorcist* Nick refers to the much more loaded legal 'obligation' for a video to pass the 'suitable for viewing in the home' test – but this phrase and this 'test' exists nowhere in the legislation.

This is a classic case of what Ted Lowi calls 'The gift of sovereignty to private satrapies', the increasing tendency for the government to hand over huge powers to nearly autonomous non-governmental organizations like the BFS. The Video Recordings Act doesn't constrain us much at all, on the contrary it's pretty much a licence for us to interpret it as we want. But this gift does come at a price: it comes packaged not with a legal threat but a political one. If you cause any trouble by sticking your neck out you won't be getting a writ from the courts but you will be fired – what the government designates the government can de-designate. If ever there was a charter for climbing into bed with the police, the Video Recordings Act is it.

Thomas Farraday

During the early 1990s the Secretariat settled into the kind of pattern familiar to any endemically grumpy family wearied by years of strife, the combatants drifting into a spiteful truce where neither side had the appetite for all-out war, nor the goodwill to make things right. This is not to say that there weren't fraternizations, jokes, the office equivalent of the football match in no man's land. But there were plenty of rumbles to keep things simmering. The most significant of these running furuncles was *The Exorcist*.

I had seen it at the Regal in Abingdon when it came out in 1973. I remember it for two reasons: brought up on campy Hammer flicks it was the first truly frightening film I'd ever seen. The second reason why I have such vivid memories had to do with the girl I took to see it.

This was not then the ridiculous idea it seems now because I had already, on more than a few occasions, found that the merely spooky would bring a teenage girl close enough to allow an easy passage of an arm around her shoulders. How was I to know, I ask you, that it was to be a revolution in the possibilities of what could happen to you in the public dark of the picture palace? When I say this I mean that *The Exorcist* demolished all prior sense of the real and the imagined. An exaggeration you may think, but I know different because the girl I took to see it, no nervous nelly, no sensitive plant, was sick in my lap.

1973 was a watershed year for the flicks in other respects: a number of films not so much breached as annihilated the boundaries of what you could see for forty pence, to whit buggery, rape and ultra-violence manifesting themselves as *Last Tango in Paris*, *Straw Dogs* and *A Clockwork Orange*. Their arrival might now be seen as the sign of a wider change in the social mores of the West. To some it was the beginning of the dissolution of restraint, decorum and a sense of privacy; to others it was a triumph of a new openness, the turning point where whether cinema was art or not became a question only for the philistine. But there were other things at work besides big issues.

It's no surprise that Nick had his fixations, who doesn't? But his relationship with *The Exorcist* was particularly idiosyncratic. When the Video Recordings Act was passed in 1984 there was, of course, a backlog of tapes that were already on the market. *The Exorcist* was available to buy in WH Smith. Because of the way the regulations worked the distributors were not obliged to submit it until the end of 1988, by which time it had to have a Secretariat certificate or be taken off the shelves. It was Sadie who noticed early in the next year that this was indeed what had happened: copies of *The Exorcist* once available everywhere had now vanished. She brought the matter up at the monthly meeting and Nick said that the distributors had not submitted the film. There was consternation – a widely admired and hugely popular film was now unavailable. Surely Nick could talk to the distributors? He did not exactly say, though he implied it, that alas the Secretariat had no powers to oblige them to submit a film, however important it was.

It was a particular talent of Nick's to be able to tell barefaced lies while, strictly speaking, telling the truth. It was certainly the case that the distributors had not submitted *The Exorcist* for certification. The reason was simple: Nick had told them not to. When he had first mooted this to the company, the head of distribution had rung up Nick with an indignant refusal.

'This is an important film, and we have an obligation to our customers. Besides, we're talking the revenues from more than eighty thousand units a year.'

For Nick, dealing with such outbursts of integrity and commercial interest was like shooting fish in a barrel. By the time he had finished detailing all the problems associated with *The Exorcist* – 'seizures, police, satanic abuse, prosecution, depraved and corrupt, suitability for viewing in the home, vulnerable youngsters, common-law precedent, public outcry, court appearances, not the right time, leave it to me' – well, after half an hour of this stuff, the Head of Distribution at Warner got off the phone truly convinced that only Nick Berg stood between him and a cavity search at Wormwood Scrubs. It's an odd reflection on the British that for all that stuff about never being slaves they don't really seem to care much about freedom of expression. The only people who ever seriously challenged Nick's right to do whatever he wanted were pornographers, the *Daily Mail* and his own examiners. A point made, not infrequently, by an exasperated Nick himself: an unchallenged emperor whose authority was questioned only by a nagging wife and cheeky kids.

Needless to say when the examiners found out about this there was hell to pay and over the following years it took its turn along with a growing inventory of ructions, spats, set-tos and squabbles. He was as confident as ever in his assertion, his *indignant* assertion, that he had not lied about the submission of *The Exorcist*.

'You lied.'

'I did not lie. The company didn't submit it.'

'Because you told them not to.'

'I have no powers to prevent a submission. It's the company's decision.'

'But you made it clear you'd refuse a certificate.'

'I couldn't possibly have refused a certificate until they'd submitted it.'

'But you told them not to.'

'I have no power to prevent a submission.'

And so on, and so on. Nick was like Geoffrey Boycott under this kind of cross-examination. He would stay at the wicket all day. The Chairman of a Commons Select Committee had once wearily asked him after a particularly fruitless attempt to pin him down: 'Mr Berg, if we asked you shorter questions would there be any chance of you giving shorter answers?'

What was really odd was his reasons for regarding *The Exorcist* as a problem: they were spectacularly feeble, easily the most hopeless set of arguments he had ever come up with about anything. He blathered about reports of severe emotional disturbances among a small but worrying number of adults . . . newspaper reports . . . letters in our files indicate the very real and serious disturbances . . . uneasy being a party to this sort of damage . . . reasons to be cautious at a time when charges of satanic abuse appear regularly in the press and alleged instances have been reported.

Despite repeated requests he never produced any evidence of these youngsters driven mad by viewing the video. The regular reporting in the press turned out to be mostly from the *Daily Mail*, a paper he ordinarily vilified about as much as it vilified him. And we had all met the fanatics who claimed that there were satanic conspiracies infecting all levels of society. Puzzling about Nick's desperate response, McCarthy came up with a theory that came to be widely accepted. By now Nick had delivered a similar performance – that is, a uniquely poor one – about *Straw Dogs*, and admitted he would have done the same with *A Clockwork Orange* but for the fact that Stanley Kubrick had withdrawn the film in the UK and, for once, had genuinely refused to submit it on video.

'What', asked McCarthy, 'do they all have in common?'

'They were all released in the cinema about the same time.'

'Exactly.'

'And,' said Emma, 'they caused a huge fuss.'

'More than that. They brought the Secretariat to the brink of collapse. And more to the point, they got his predecessor fired.'

'I thought he resigned.'

'He resigned because otherwise he would have been fired. And because these films destroyed his predecessor they've always had this huge significance for Nick. This is about his fear of losing control, certainly, but he was hired *because* of these films, to repair the damage. And he did. I mean, let's be fair, he did a brilliant job. But if he just passes these films then he's pissing on his own legend. Nick saved the Secretariat from these films. And we just want to pass them as if they don't have the same power any more. Which they don't – and he can't bear it. That's why his reasons are such rubbish. If films like this can just go out on video a decade or so later without anyone making a fuss, then what's the point? The significance of censorship is temporary. Give it twenty years and every censor's decision looks laughable. I'll bet you ten to one, as soon as Nick has retired it won't be five years before most of the films he's banned will be uncut on the shelves. And no one will care. All his great stands against *The Story of O*, and *I Spit on Your Grave* and *The Texas Chainsaw Massacre* will have come to nothing – gone with the wind. The fact is that he knows somewhere inside that if he passed *The Exorcist* now, no one would notice. And he can't bear it.'

Deputy Director Walter Casey once tried to lighten the mood during one of these wrangles by telling the meeting that a friend of his who ran a cinema in Norwich used to screen *The Exorcist* once a year at Halloween. But in the end he'd stopped because the screenings were always followed by an infestation of rats. There was much amusement at this. Walter had a dry way with a joke. But perhaps the joke was on us all, given the pestilence of bad feeling raised whenever it was discussed.

Despite being the person responsible for bringing the subject up in the first place, Sadie was growing uneasy about the deterioration in her relationship not only with Nick but also with Walter Casey. Her disquiet had its origin in her lack of familiarity with being disliked. Too independent of mind and forthright ever to have been a teacher's pet she was nevertheless used to being admired. Her demand for attention and her occasional excesses were always allowed for because she was, after all, a golden girl, beautiful and so clever and in so many ways rather sweet. She was also ambitious and Nick had more than once spoken glowingly of the future. 'You could be the Secretariat's first woman director,' Nick had said to her in the privacy of his office. 'And its youngest.'

Although even then deeply wary of any of Nick's promises, she was still flattered, and besides she had been favoured with many of the best professional perks that Nick had to offer, where others were given talks at Leicester Poly or a sixth form college in Gants Hill. It was usually Sadie who went to Oxford or spoke at the Commonwealth Institute. All of these had dried up since the Dworkin incident.

Sensing that Walter was trying to make some kind of effort to lighten the mood between Nick and the examiners, the following day she knocked on Walter's door holding a note he had left pinned for her on the message board on the examiners' floor. To her relief when he looked up to see it was her he was smiling.

'Sadie, what can I do for you?' he asked, looking at the note in her hand.

She smiled fetchingly back.

'I was wondering how many places of work there are in the world where it's usual for a memo between colleagues to contain the words "cunt" and "arsehole"'.

He laughed, clearly pleased to be at ease with her.

'It's just that I can't read your handwriting. This word here.'

She passed it over to him. He examined his scrawl carefully for a moment then put on his glasses. There was a pause and then he handed it back to her.

'Orifice,' he said.

Child's Play

Sunday night
All weekend filled with thoughts of you. Catching myself in
this ridiculous behaviour I could kick myself. I really think I
need to rethink how to survive. To have and have not. Is this
it? The builder has been and says that the house may need
underpinning and I keep thinking I'm going to disappear into
a hole in the garden while I'm having my bath. I don't think I
had truly understood what want means. Sheer want. Oh well,
tonight I shall practise closing my heart again and read The
Independent or something . . .

Sadie x

BECAUSE THE WORLD OF images and what they have done to
me is much on my mind I have been considering how
recent the world of images really is. If you were to walk
into your bathroom and were to find a walrus taking its
ease among the bars of soap and hair conditioner you
would undoubtedly be shocked and bewildered. But even
if you had never seen a walrus you would know what it
was because you will have seen a picture of one. It is
probable that in real life you have never seen a kangaroo,

a submarine, a pyramid, New York, a couple having sex, a dead body, or David Beckham.

I bought an amusing gift for my wife for her birthday just before things got out of hand for me. It was a collection of the one hundred most important images of the twentieth century. Each page was blank except for a short description:

The Destruction of the Hindenberg
Albert Einstein
Marilyn Monroe in a White Dress
The Assassination of John F. Kennedy
Neil Armstrong about to set foot on the moon

And so on for one hundred empty pages. I don't remember exactly, but there were about two that I could not instantly and precisely bring to mind. It is hardly any time at all since such an idea would have been utterly and profoundly incomprehensible. It's difficult to grasp that prior to the middle of the nineteenth century people had hardly seen any images at all – paintings for a few, illustrations for more, a cartoon or woodcut for the rest. And infrequently at that. The book of one hundred unphotographs reveals how much our minds are supersaturated with images of absolutely everything. There are barely any words like this, few shared phrases and sentences like the image of Lee Harvey Oswald wincing as he's shot, skeletal Jews staring out from behind a barbed wire fence, the flag of the United States.

One image, though, has set me back, it can't quite seem to find a place – flat, banal, uniconic, dull. The width of pavement and the shopping bags indicate some sort of mall; it's hard to tell, so featureless and blurred is it. Someone, probably a male, is holding the hand of a child who could be any sex. Out of focus they have their backs to us. Here the explanation really needs to come in words. This is the last photograph of James Bulger, nearly three, being led away to his death by one of his killers, Jon Venables, barely ten, who'd called the toddler to him while his mother was buying chops. 'Come on baby,' he said. The security video captured them at 3.47 p.m.: the ordinary and the unique walk hand in hand.

There were witnesses as the three of them made their way through the city – thirty-eight in all: sometimes the boy was laughing, swinging between the other two, sometimes crying, a toddler with his brothers whingeing because he could not get his way. One man saw them kick the boy, a 'persuading kick' he later said. But it was rush hour and he was in his car, hard to stop and kids are always squabbling only to make up. An older woman, seeing he was cut around the face, approached the boys who told her that they had only just found him at the bottom of the hill. She told them to take him to the police station on Walton Lane. But they walked off and turned in the opposite direction. Puzzled, she was about to act, until another woman said that earlier she had seen the toddler laughing with the boys. Later, another woman suspicious of what was going on decided to take James from the boys and walk him to the police station. But she couldn't find anyone to mind her little girl and so on it went until they wandered onto the embankment leading to the railway line.

The attack started at around 5.45 p.m. It began with one of the boys flinging paint on James's face. They threw stones at him, then kicked him, then beat him with bricks. They pulled off his shoes and trousers and possibly sexually assaulted him, though both the boys indignantly denied that this was so. Then they hit him with an iron bar. When they thought he was dead they left his body on the tracks, covering his head with bricks. Then they went home.

The trial was covered everywhere, the verdict leading the news even in America.

The reaction here, you might say, divided along familiar lines. One thing for me, besides the shock, stood out. Many in the press and on the television referred to James as little Jamie. A pet name none of his family had ever used. Why would you need to wring more pity out of such a fate? At any rate, there was blame and there were explanations: pure evil, emotional deprivation, the parents, the children themselves, an act of bullying that tragically got out of control.

There was talk of the death of innocence and childhood and there was talk of the need to avoid moral panic. And inevitably there was talk of the British Film Secretariat.

CHILD'S PLAY 3: EXAMINER'S REPORT   Rob McCarthy
Synopsis:
Child's Play 3 is yet greater proof of the law of increasing infirmity as it applies to film sequels: the first was lively, the second lame and this one's dead-on-arrival. The conceit is as before: Chucky is a doll animated by the soul of a murderous lunatic, now intent on taking revenge on the young boy, Andy, who has bested him in the two earlier films. Andy has now been sent to military school and the vengeful Chucky follows him there. Once he's arrived on campus, Chucky decides to transfer his malign soul into pint-sized Tyrone, and the rest of the film is taken up with Chucky slaughtering everyone who gets in the way of his planned transmigration. It ends up in an amusement park with Chucky being spectacularly sliced in the blades of a ventilation fan.

Comments:
While the general level of (feebly) comic violence would put this no higher than the '15' awarded to the two previous *Child's Play* videos (note comic violence at 6 mins 20, 15 mins 30 and 64 mins) it's really the final amount of gore when Chucky, with no doubt un-intentional irony, hits the fan and is blended into the next world (82 mins onward) that just about takes it into '18'. I can't say that it's a decision made with much conviction, but the recent fuss about violence in teenage films and the effects of horror, in particular on the young, mean that some sort of craven gesture towards current anxieties (i.e. the *Daily Mail*) seems the right course. We should keep our powder dry in case a decent teenage horror film comes along.

Pass 18 UNCUT.

It was this report that Nick had in front of him as the just summoned McCarthy sat warily facing him. Nick handed him a copy of the report. 'Remember this?'

McCarthy scanned it for some time, nervous although he didn't show it. Problems with reports rarely came up to Nick himself. Finally, McCarthy put it back on Nick's desk.

'Is there something wrong?'

Nick looked thoughtful. 'The judge in the James Bulger case has put some of the blame on the collection of, and I quote, "violent videos" owned by the father of one of the boys, which the boys had probably watched while they were playing truant.'

Nick handed over a copy of the *Sun*. McCarthy closed his eyes and sighed as he saw the front page: it was entirely given over to a menacing picture of Chucky, smiling sadistically and holding a knife dripping with blood.

'Any thoughts?' said Nick.

'Other than that it's all bloody nonsense, you mean?'

'Are you sure?'

McCarthy started to look through the paper. He said nothing for a minute or two, then looked up. 'There's nothing here about how *Child's Play 3* would inspire two children to murder a toddler. The story doesn't bear any similarity in any way to what happened to James Bulger.'

'You're clear about that?' said Nick, non-committal rather than sharp.

'Have you seen it?' asked McCarthy.

Nick sighed, irritated. 'The tape's gone missing from the archive. I sent someone from technical to go to Virgin and buy a copy but it's not in stock. I'm getting the distributors to bike over a copy.' He looked at McCarthy thoughtfully. 'I just wanted to see if in the light of the trial you thought there was anything in this.'

'Not even in hindsight,' replied McCarthy. 'As it says in the report, I was being pretty timid passing it "18".'

Nick paused. 'Well, no one could call your defence timid at least.'

'I'd like to see it again,' said McCarthy.

Nick smiled. 'I'll put it on for you tomorrow morning. I'll watch it myself tonight.'

Later on in The Black Horse having a drink with Farraday and Sadie, McCarthy was less sure of himself. 'The thing is I don't think it was much of a report. It came across as pretty . . . I don't know, flippant really – considering.'

'Considering what?' asked Sadie, softly dismissive.

'Considering that it's now connected to the murder of a small boy.'

Farraday refused to be impressed. 'I've been following the case and I've heard what you said about the tape – and

293

despite the fact that I've often complained to Sadie about your frivolity and your tendency to act the giddy goat, it's obvious this is all bollocks.' He looked down at the copy of the *Sun* that McCarthy had brought. 'I mean, I notice they don't actually have anything you might call evidence that the father had rented the tape, nor that the two kids had seen it. Besides, you passed it "18", not "PG". I'd say that pretty much covered you.'

'I'm not worrying about being covered,' replied McCarthy irritably. There was a shocked silence. 'Sorry,' said McCarthy. 'That was incredibly self-righteous.'

Sadie touched McCarthy's hand.

'You know,' said Farraday admiringly, 'it's not everyone who can be flippant *and* self-righteous.'

And so it was an uneasy McCarthy who made his way to viewing room four the next day, only to feel worse when he realized his co-examiner was going to be Allan Rhys. But as the video progressed his disquiet began to ebb. It was a mediocre ghost story for teenagers; nowhere was the malign talent visible that could connect it with the baffling horror that led to the murder of a small boy on an urban railway line.

Rhys unusually said nothing for a while, and McCarthy had no intention of defending himself to the Welshman, so there was a long silence. Rhys was thinking complicated thoughts; insofar as he had a straightforward belief in anything it was in the wrongness, or more accurately, the pointlessness of preventing anyone from seeing anything. It was not that he had an excess of tolerance – it would be fair to say that he felt disdain for anyone who disagreed with him, rising to pathological hatred if his opponent managed to make him feel that in the eyes of others he had lost the argument. His ill will towards

McCarthy was exceeded only by his loathing for Farraday. I often had the sense that when he smiled at something funny that one of his colleagues said it was with a slight uneasiness, like an adolescent pretending to understand an adult conversation that was slightly beyond him.

His dilemma for the moment was this: how to reconcile his deeply held view that *Child's Play 3* could not possibly have a causal connection with the crime it was accused of inspiring, with his desire to take advantage of a rare opportunity to get McCarthy into trouble. At the very least he wanted to make it look as if McCarthy lacked his understanding of the values, fears and indignations of society. Rhys, of course, felt only condescension towards these values, fears and indignations but nevertheless believed he understood them completely. He cursed the fact that McCarthy had passed it '18' because it was uncharacteristically conservative of him to do so – it was plain (and I also took the same view when I saw it myself) that this was a pretty straightforward film for teenagers that genuinely should have been passed '15'. And Rhys was right, that's exactly what McCarthy would normally have done. If he had only done so, thought Rhys to himself, he would have been able to criticize McCarthy's lack of awareness of public concern.

Particularly during the periods of bad relations with his examiners, Nick was frequently heard to lament the failure of his employees to take public concern with sufficient seriousness. Curiously in doing this he frequently echoed, though rather more elegantly, the accusations that were continually being levelled at him by the *Daily Mail*: namely that he was an out-of-touch liberal with a complete disdain for the convictions and moral standards of ordinary people (which is to say readers of the *Daily Mail*). Had McCarthy only given *Child's Play 3* the '15' it so richly deserved Rhys could have given his second most hated rival a nasty kick in the shins by making it clear that he would not have made such an egregious error given the sensitivity of the wider public to questions of mutilation and horror being purveyed to impressionable young minds. The fact that McCarthy had not done so and that it was pointless to repine didn't stop Rhys from fantasizing about the shit-stirring opportunity that had so closely passed him by. He had to content himself with a milder version of the same strategy.

'Of course,' said Rhys sympathetically, 'I entirely agree that "18" was the correct decision.' He sighed. It was an exhalation that implied much: personal sympathy, professional fellow feeling, the wisdom of a more thoughtful man, condescension, hatred and loathing.

'The problem is that people at the moment are very –' he paused, '– concerned about this kind of thing. Of course, it's the papers that stir it up, playing on people's fears.' He smiled, regretfully. 'But we have to recognize it as a fact of life.' He started to muse. 'I've been thinking that this kind of thing has been coming for some time. Only the other day I referred a tape straight up to Nick that a year ago I would have been happy to sign out directly.' He paused. 'I wonder,' he said, regretfully, 'if I shouldn't have made it even clearer in the report I wrote that we needed to discuss the way things are changing out there. It might have been of some help to you.'

Despite himself, McCarthy was really rather impressed by Rhys's performance. He felt able to be relaxed about such a naked attempt to condescend to him not just because he felt such disdain for Rhys, nor even because he took a certain pleasure in watching him perform his complicated personality stunts, but mostly because his own anxieties about *Child's Play 3* had been considerably eased by watching it again.

He phoned Nick to tell him he'd finished the viewing.

'I'll see you now if that's all right.'

'Do you want Allan Rhys to come as well?'

'No.'

McCarthy put the phone down. Rhys looked at him expectantly.

'Does he want me to come?'

'No.'

Rhys nodded and smiled as if this was entirely in line with what he expected and, more, something he had actually planned.

How very odd it must be to be you, thought McCarthy as he looked at Rhys. 'See you at around two,' he said and went upstairs.

The Conversation

'SO, WHAT DID YOU think?' asked McCarthy as he sat down in front of Nick.

Nick wrinkled his nose. 'If I'd been watching with you on the day I would have strongly disagreed with you.'

There was a silence.

'You mean you would have passed it "15"?' said McCarthy.

Nick smiled. 'Exactly.'

'Then it's lucky you have me to save you from yourself.'

Nick laughed. 'To be honest, I enjoyed it more than you – there were a few good one-liners – but if anything was meant for teenagers this was it. I thought the violence at the end was more Tom and Jerry than anything else.' He shrugged.

'So what now?'

'I had a word with Homes at the Obscene Publications Squad. He knew the police officer who ran the investigation and gave me his number. He rang me back an hour ago.' Nick looked down at a piece of paper on his desk. 'They just faxed me their official response,' he said, picking it up and starting to read: ' "Blah, blah, blah . . . we have carefully collated all the videos found at the family homes of Jon Venables and Robert Thompson and there were no copies of *Child's Play 3* nor any other similar video among them. Neither had this tape been rented from any of the video stores that the families belonged to." ' Nick looked up at McCarthy. 'He had an unofficial response as well, though he only gave it to me on the phone. He said, and I quote, "It's total bollocks." '

Nick got up and walked over to the uncharacteristically naff walnut laminated fridge in the corner of the room. 'Would you like a glass of wine?'

'I wouldn't mind a glass of white.'

Nick had already opened the door and taken out a bottle of Pouilly Fumé. He did not stint himself when someone else was paying. The size of his salary was often commented on darkly by the press during his periods of unpopularity. What they were not aware of was that this generous amount was more than doubled by the considerable number of often hard to understand perks: a pension the size of the GDP of a small African country, free theatre tickets, heavily subsidized air travel and, most curiously, a twenty-four-hour chauffeur-driven car.

He handed a brimming glass to McCarthy who, while not knowledgeable about wine, realized from the first musky, smoky mouthful that it was several steps up from the stuff he was used to drinking.

'Oddly enough he also told me that during their investigations it turned out there was one video that Venables used to play over and over again.'

'Really?'

'*Teenage Mutant Ninja Turtles* – a film, I seem to

remember, all about the duty of the strong to protect the weak against the power of evil.'

They sat in silence for a moment, McCarthy in particular enjoying the wine as he contemplated, entirely wrongly as it turned out, that he was now off the hook in practical as well as moral terms.

'What now?'

Nick drew in a deep breath as if readying himself for the weighty task ahead. 'I'll prepare a press release based on what the police have sent me – not that the tabloids will let mere facts get in the way – but the broadsheets will probably buy it. Most of them anyway. But I've got forensic psychologist Professor Stephen Dole coming in this afternoon to take a look. Between the two of them we should be able to put out a pretty solid case without looking too defensive. Probably by tomorrow.'

Unusually for a man who usually liked to explain things in relentless depth, Nick Berg preferred to keep his press releases brief and generalized. There would be an expression of concern, a more-in-sorrow-than-in-anger lamentation of the mischievous constructions too readily placed on the Secretariat's professionalism, followed by an assertion that many outside opinions had been canvassed in either coming to a decision in the first place or, as with *Child's Play 3*, reviewing the decision it had already made. The press release went on to point out that all of the Secretariat's examiners had now seen the video as well as a leading QC and, of course, an eminent forensic psychologist whose judgement about the dangers of children seeing the film had been reflected in the Secretariat's decision to confirm it as suitable only for adult audiences. Finally, Nick emphasized there was no evidence whatsoever that either of the boys had seen *Child's Play 3*.

The *Sun* ignored the press release. The broadsheets did much as Nick predicted. The *Daily Mail*, however, decided that it was time Nick Berg got the fate he so justly deserved. The headlines aimed at Nick that followed included:

BAN THIS EVIL HORROR VIDEO
CENSOR SAYS YES TO DEPRAVED VIDEO
CHILD'S PLAY HORROR GO-AHEAD MAY SINK CENSORS

and finally:

DOES ANYTHING APPAL THIS MAN?

But it was not only Nick who was on the receiving end of the *Mail*'s wrath. They may not have known what a forensic psychologist was, nor have any sense of the detail of what Professor Stephen Dole actually said to Nick about *Child's Play 3*. But they were in no doubt that he was wrong.

'All of Professor Dole's psycho-babble', a leader thundered, 'cannot refute the simple fact this video is sick. It should not be shown.'

For the next two days the *Mail* enthusiastically rubbished Professor Dole's career and credentials and claimed that his peers regarded him with a lack of esteem that bordered on ridicule.

The following day Professor Dole issued a statement pointing out that he had not supported the passing of *Child's Play 3*, even for adults. He had made it clear to Mr Berg that he supported a complete ban. The *Daily Mail* immediately promoted him to 'a leading clinical and forensic psychologist who is highly regarded by

301

colleagues' and condemned the BFS roundly for not taking his advice.

In passing you might want to note that Nick had given a completely misleading impression of the Professor's views without saying anything that wasn't, strictly speaking, true. To remind you: 'The BFS has consulted an eminent forensic psychologist whose judgement about the dangers of children seeing the film has been reflected in the Secretariat's decision to confirm it as suitable only for adult audiences.' Not bad, I think you'll have to agree.

As for the killers themselves they had brought about something rare in a world with an endless supply of grim news: everyone pretty much everywhere had stopped to think about what this death meant.

'What does it feel like now, you little bastards!' someone had screamed from the gallery in the court after they had been sentenced. Perhaps you could say it was a cry that stood for the depth of anger and disgust and enraged bewilderment felt by many. Others took the view that these emotions were an ugly echo of the crime. 'Here,' said the *Guardian*, 'we see an anger which is consonant with the act itself. It reflected the feelings of those who were disgusted themselves that the accused should have to face such fury, the adult majesty of the law when they were only ten. The solution it seems', continued the editorial, 'has the same nature as the crime.'

At about this time I was curious to note that something started to change in me: it became less and less important to me to have an opinion. About anything. Perhaps it had something to do with being obliged to have so many over the last few years; I'd grown sick and tired of taking a view. Whatever it is you need in order to have convictions now seemed to be in short supply.

You might think this would have made my job difficult

but just the memory of old habits of feeling was sufficient. Besides there were plenty of other opinions about to latch on to if I felt particularly indifferent to some burning issue. Though even here I detected an echo in my fellow examiners of what I was feeling – or, to be precise, not feeling. There was a predictability about their attitudes even when they expressed themselves most passionately. There was a good deal of intensity there but something was not quite right about it these days; it had gone off, I thought, in some way, its fervour rising from something shrill rather than something deeply felt.

Now I think of this view as unfair, unfair because what was happening to them was that they were suffering from an industrial injury, like a lung disease to a miner, or a crippling repetitive strain injury to a secretary. They were suffering from too much stuff, too much image stuff, too much story stuff, too many histrionics on too many screens. It wasn't the blood and guts and sex that were corroding their hearts and souls and characters. In the age before everyone could get access to a thousand channels in the home for thirty quid a month, the examiners at the Secretariat were suffering the fall-out from the tragedy of too much.

And now everybody has it, and they don't realize they breathe it in like gas, that radon stuff, that hangs about in every house and gives a thousand people cancer every year. Cancel your package, don't renew, it's choice that's threatening to do you in. Never mind how good it is, or bad, you weren't designed to watch and gawp and take in so much stuff. It's not crisps and burgers, beer and chips that are piling on the weight, you're getting fat on images, story obesity is putting a strain upon your heart. You need to stop devouring comedies, the murder mystery and the panel game. Stop gorging on the evening procedural, the documentary, and the challenging drama from the BBC. Cut back on sport, the proms, the news and talent shows. Take drugs instead, heroin or crack, drink alcohol until you puke, use patches or iron will but don't watch so much stuff where people laugh or cry or punch, have sex, and run and kick, report on more disasters in the Middle East, or fall in love. And stay off the internet. Don't get me started there.

Sorry, I was talking about not taking a view and there I go. Tricky isn't it, generally? At any rate I want to say something about the death of James Bulger. Some time after the two boys had been sentenced, Nick Berg met someone who was a colleague of someone who had treated one of them, Jon Venables. The boy had dreamt that he was pregnant, growing a new James Bulger inside himself.

Have you ever heard of the psychiatrist Ernst Jentsch? Me neither. I know about him because I read Sadie Boldon's report on *Child's Play 3*. She could be an education, Sadie. Insofar as anyone remembers Jentsch at all, it's because Freud disagreed with him about a paper he had written called *The Psychology of the Uncanny*. Jentsch defined the uncanny as the uncertainty created in a reader as to whether or not an apparently animate being, a wooden golem or a devil doll, was really alive or not. Chucky, the children's doll inhabited by the soul of a maniac, is merely an updating of this old idea. But to me the uncanny refers to a much deeper question, a question I have been asking about myself and the real source of the horror and revulsion at the two young killers of James Bulger: we know they are alive, just as we know every terrorist is alive, every serial rapist; but we don't know in what way. That's what's uncanny about them, they're living but not in a way you can understand. You are capable of wickedness too, but just as we (for now that I think about it I am to be reckoned with the uncanny) are not alive in the same way as you, you cannot be wicked in the same way as us. It is only given to a chosen few to plant a bomb where the innocent are bound to die, always to be on the lookout for a chance to rape, to strip a three-year-old and smash his head in with a brick. Understand that the terrorist, the rapist and the killers of toddlers are no more dead to feeling than anyone else. I feel things. But we are not the same as you. Don't expect me to tell you how. If I could tell you I would let you know. All I can do is to ask you what it means, the ten-year-old with the encouraging kick and the brick in his hand dreaming of giving birth to a baby boy. If his internal life was capable of such rich remorse how could he have beaten him to death less than a year before?

This is the censors' delusion, not that they are better than the rest of you, but that they think they are just as bad only set about with more restraint than the evil-doer, a sense of right to go along with their universal capacity for wrong. We thought we could read the rapist constructed by the torn blouse and the voluptuous breast by comparing him with our darkest thoughts. But the censors, unless they happen to become like me, are just deluding themselves. Goethe once said he'd never heard of a crime he couldn't imagine committing. So don't feel bad, my fellow censors, better minds than yours have made the same mistake.

And as for my crime (nothing of course to do with rape or bombs or bricks): before you make your judgement about who was to blame for what happened, you'll have to take into account how Nick dealt with the business over Robert McCarthy.

In the offices of the *Daily Mail* on Kensington High Street, the paper pursues its firebombing of the BFS (SACK THIS

305

FEEBLE CENSOR NOW). There is a meeting in the editor's office. It is 11 a.m. and his view of the issues of the day is beginning to coalesce. His most significant underling, the news editor, sits facing him in the lone chair. A prodigious stretch of pale carpet separates them from the lesser executives perched like nervous buzzards on two sofas in an L-shape. They wait for their master's voice.

'Who are these bloody people at the BFS?' he says at last.

'Sorry?'

'Who are these examiners that bastard Berg keeps going on about?'

'No idea. He keeps them away from pretty much everyone – no interviews with the press or TV.'

'What's wrong with them, then?'

The news editor laughed. 'For a start, they don't take the *Mail*.'

'I'll bet they don't. Find out what you can.'

The news editor put up his hand to signify the strident block of a headline. 'Exposed: Secret Censors who Refused to ban Bulger Murder Tape. That the sort of thing?'

'You can mock all you like but I think we need to know about the people who are making decisions about what the nation's children are watching. If they're anything like Berg I'll bet you they're a right bloody shower.'

Three days later the news editor returned with a slim folder and sat down. 'Right, the BFS examiners. Pretty much what you'd expect. Mostly public-sector parasites, social workers, natch, teachers, probation officers, academics, fucking *Guardian* readers to a man I shouldn't wonder. No surprises that Berg keeps a lid on that lot.'

'Is there a story?'

'Only if we do another piece on Berg – mention them in passing.' He smiled, producing several sheets of paper.

'There's only one who doesn't fit here – Robert McCarthy. He's a former soldier, lots of history, Northern Ireland – and he was a marksman with the Irish Fusiliers in the Falklands.'

'What the fuck is someone like that doing amongst that bunch of wankers?'

'Seems he's not quite your conventional squaddie. While he was doing his stint in Belfast, he started an Open University course in uh . . . European Thought and Literature.'

'Christ, no wonder we can't defeat the fucking IRA.'

'He was honourably discharged after the Falklands – then was a mature student at Birkbeck . . .' He looked down at his paper again. 'Philosophy since 1750. Has an overdue master's thesis on Thomas Hobbes.'

The editor shook his head in disbelief. 'Well, we're not going to get anywhere with that. It'll make Berg look good if we let it out that he's hired one of our boys – even if he has got a pointy head.'

The news editor smiled. 'It's better than that. But this is tricky, though, given he is one of our boys. It turns out our Mr McCarthy has been up to no good.'

For about ten minutes the news editor went through what he'd found. When he finished there was a thoughtful pause from his boss.

'Write it up. Make McCarthy come across as an outsider. I don't want our readers to think we're attacking our victory in the Falklands or the ordinary squaddie.' There was no cynicism here. To the editor of the *Daily Mail* it was a duty to bring down Nick Berg. As well as a pleasure.

Three days later the *Mail* published an article on Robert McCarthy under the headline: CHILD'S PLAY CENSOR QUESTIONED OVER FALKLANDS ATROCITY.

Though it was by no means a short article, its spine was simple enough: the former Corporal McCarthy had been a sniper with the Irish Fusiliers. While in action and operating alone he had encountered three Argentinian soldiers and during the resultant fight, some of it hand-to-hand, had succeeded in killing all of them. At first he had been recommended for a medal by his superior officers. But suspicions were aroused when the bodies were examined: one of them had been shot in the back and the other two each had a left ear missing. McCarthy's account of the engagement was confused and unconvincing particularly in his account of how he came to shoot the Argentinian soldier in the back. The unlikeliness of one man being able to overcome three Argentinian soldiers also added to a general disbelief in the truthfulness of his accounts. He claimed to know nothing about the dismemberment of the bodies. However, there were no witnesses and, as McCarthy's account could not be disproved, no action was taken. The recommendation for a medal, however, was withdrawn. In addition, no record of McCarthy's single-handed defeat of three enemy soldiers was entered into the regiment's records – an omission that unofficially declared belief in his guilt. He saw no further action in the Falklands war and was discharged as soon as the regiment returned to England.

When McCarthy arrived slightly late for morning prayers, Walter Casey was giving out the day's instructions, which meant that, fortunately for everyone, his colleagues could only nod at his arrival. But he could sense the shock: only Farraday, who was on holiday, knew that he had been in the army. It was hardly surprising that they were bewildered by the accusation that he had murdered three people in cold blood and cut the ears off two of them as a memento. When Casey had finished he walked over to McCarthy.

'Hi, Nick would like to see you.'

'I thought he might.'

Casey smiled awkwardly and, as curious as the rest, watched him leave.

'Sit down, Rob,' said Nick, as McCarthy knocked and put his head round the open door. He did so, noticing there was a copy of the *Mail* open on the desk.

'This must have been quite a shock for you,' said Nick. 'When did you find out?'

'Last night. A reporter rang me from the *Mail* telling me that they were going to print it and did I have any comment.'

'Do you mind if I ask you what you said?'

'No.' There was a short pause of misunderstanding. 'I mean, no I didn't make any comment.'

'Good.' Nick seemed genuinely pleased.

'Because?'

'These . . . allegations, for want of a better word, don't seem to me to add up to much: some unsubstantiated rumours about an unofficial investigation and a few . . . anomalies.' He chose the word carefully and smiled. 'This was all done during the middle of a battle after all . . . the fog of war . . . your distinguished service record . . .'

'I think distinguished would be going it a bit.'

'All right.' He paused. 'Unblemished?'

'A bit of a hostage to fortune, wouldn't you say?'

'Commendable?'

A pause.

'That would do. But what would it do for? Where's all this going?'

Nick sat back and looked at McCarthy carefully. 'We need to do a press release.'

'I thought you might be going to ask me to resign.'

309

There was a long pause from Nick.

'No.'

'I see.' He said nothing for a moment. 'Or at least ask me if it was true.'

'No.'

'Right.'

Nick continued, matter of fact: 'I suggest strongly that we stress your service record, that your superiors investigated a confused report and that no evidence of wrongdoing was uncovered and that—' He stopped. 'You were honourably discharged, weren't you?'

'Yes.'

'And you decided to leave the army after five years because you wished to pursue your academic studies having obtained a first-class degree from the Open University while still in the armed forces. Something like that. Are you agreeable?'

In truth, McCarthy was taken aback by all this. 'Uh . . . yes.'

'Good. I'll have a copy of the press release sent down to you later. Let me know if there's anything you want to discuss. Then we'll send it to our lawyers.'

The meeting was over. McCarthy stood up. 'Thanks.'

Nick nodded but said nothing.

Still bewildered by Nick's response McCarthy made his way down to the first floor to check on his day's work. At the very least he had expected Nick to distance himself and McCarthy would not have found such a response unreasonable. By now the first floor was clear of everyone except for a couple of temps. He looked at the day sheet and was relieved to find that he was on his own for the morning watching tapes that on another day would have made him feel that working at the BFS was one of the world's most wonderful jobs: *Now Voyager* and three episodes of *Yes, Minister*. It was a pity that for the afternoon he was working with Emma Saward.

When McCarthy came into examining room three, Emma was doing the paperwork. Without looking up she said, 'I've zeroed the first tape.' The tone of her voice was surprisingly soft given the stiff and awkward way she was sitting. He sat down, opened his log book, wrote down the title and, still without looking at him, Emma pressed play. For fifteen minutes they watched as an assortment of middle-aged women took off their clothes, writhing seductively on their immaculately hoovered carpets with a gambolling enthusiasm, for all the world as if they belonged to an amateur dramatic society that had decided to make porn films rather than *The Winslow Boy* or *Annie Get Your Gun*. For the first time the numbness that had afflicted McCarthy since the phone call from the journalist the previous night began to blur. The horrible past and the bizarre present: the soldier squirming under him repeating 'Please, please' over and over in English as McCarthy held the knife deep under his ribs; and the woman in front of him on the screen pouting and squeezing together her tiny breasts. He felt as if some weird dissolution was taking place, everything in him bleeding into everything else.

Then the tape switched off. Emma was looking at him, holding the remote.

'Is it true?' He didn't say anything. 'I had to ask. I'm sorry.'

For a moment he was angry with her. Then it drained away and he just felt sick. Emma didn't look too well herself. She was shaking and close to tears.

'I know you killed them, but you didn't just . . . you know. It was a fair fight?'

Despite himself, he laughed. Of all people it was hardest to credit that she believed in such a notion. He was rather touched that she had dredged so deeply not to think badly of him. 'No,' he said. 'It was anything but fair.' Then he reached over and taking the remote from her started the tape again.

'Wouldn't you like to kiss my nipples?' said the woman lying lasciviously on a rug. 'I know you would.'

Guess Who's Coming to Dinner

And most of all would I flee from the cruel madness of love,
The honey of poison-flowers and all the measureless ill.

Alfred Tennyson, *Maud*

'INTERESTING,' SAID FARRADAY, WHEN he returned from holiday two days later. 'I mean it's rather sweet of Emma asking if it was a fair fight – considering that she'd normally take it for granted that even being a member of Her Majesty's Forces made you a psychopath. By her standards she was practically bending over backwards.'

'I'm not stupid. I'm perfectly well aware of that.'

'Anybody else mention it?'

'No. Except Sadie.'

'Really? What did she have to say?'

'She touched me on the arm and asked me if I wanted to talk.'

'And?'

'I said: no thank you.'

'Nicely?'

McCarthy laughed. 'And if I didn't are you going to ask me to step outside?'

'Not now that I know you can kill me with a rolled-up copy of the *Guardian*.'

McCarthy snorted. 'I wouldn't need a rolled-up copy of the *Guardian*. A damp paper towel, perhaps, or a wet dishcloth.'

Farraday laughed and pulled over a passing waiter. 'Another bottle please.' Then he turned back to McCarthy. 'So what did Nick have to say?'

'When he called me up I thought he might take a high moral line and suspend me. I even thought he might have the nerve to ask me if it was true.' It took a few moments before Farraday realized he was being warned. 'Nick was completely stand up. He took a few details about my record and the status of the investigation and wrote a really rather brilliant press release – it gave the impression that the BFS was completely behind me and strongly refuted these allegations, but without saying anything remotely specific.'

'So if they find out you did it he can completely disassociate himself from you.'

'But that's fair enough.'

'Absolutely.' Farraday took a heavy drag on his cigarette and blew out a long stream as if deep in contemplation. 'Just when you've got Berg nailed as a complete cunt he goes and does something impressive.'

The waiter arrived with their second bottle and they waited until he'd gone.

'You all right?' asked Farraday.

'I feel a bit strange – obviously things are going to be different.'

'You're not worried?'

'About an investigation? No. There were no witnesses. There's nothing to investigate.'

'You could always sue.'

'Don't be stupid. There isn't any proof one way or the other. Just one or two unpleasant facts. Frankly it would be a risk – financially I mean. Anyway, fuck 'em.'

So they talked on. When they finished Farraday walked McCarthy to the tube.

'See you tomorrow,' said Farraday, shaking his hand.

McCarthy smiled at the gesture. Then he turned down the stairs into the station.

Farraday walked on up Shaftesbury Avenue, postponing the taxi he was going to take.

McCarthy had told him that he'd been a soldier as soon as they had become friends. Sadie had phoned him while he was on holiday to tell him about the *Mail* and he was certainly surprised, even shocked. He had never known someone who had actually killed people. He certainly did not disapprove, but it was still a shocking thing that Rob McCarthy had actually killed three men single-handed. It was a little scary – but he was also impressed. Something, however, about the evening had unsettled him. Something was not quite right. It began to cross his mind that his friend had done something terrible.

'While I was away,' said Farraday lying naked on top of his bed, 'I realized something about you.'

Sadie was lying under the bedclothes with the sheet pulled up almost to her neck. 'What?' she said, expecting it to be something flattering.

'That one of the things that makes you so very desirable is that when you're not making love to me, you're actually incredibly prudish.'

'What do you mean?' she said indignantly.

'Look at you now. You're completely covered up. I hardly ever see you naked – you know, except when we're having sex.'

'Having sex. Ugh!'

'All right. Making luuurve.'

'You think I'm not sexy enough. Like all your other trollops and sluts?'

'Not at all. You're easily the sexiest woman I've ever known precisely because you're so modest.'

She looked at him suspiciously, wary that a criticism was masquerading as a compliment. 'You said prudish.'

'OK, that's more what I meant. You're a prude until the moment when you just let everything go – like something so powerful that you're doing it against your better nature. It's very sexy.'

She sighed and pulled the sheet up a little further. 'It's because I feel so guilty.'

This shut him up. It was unwelcome and she realized it too.

'I'm sorry,' she said softly. 'I can't help it.' She reached out to touch him, to reassure. He did not so much move away as shrink – but not so imperceptibly that she couldn't feel it. As she was intended to.

'Don't let's argue. I missed you so much.' She moved in closer to him, trying to push his arm so that he would put it around her. He wouldn't. She pushed again, and then again like a pet demanding to be stroked. Eventually he gave way and she pressed herself against him, head on his chest.

'Sorry,' he said at last.

Neither of them spoke for five minutes.

'When do you have to go?'

'Not for another hour.'

He felt a wave of loss and misery like a small boy being deserted. *What is the matter with you?* he thought. 'Rob McCarthy said you asked him if he wanted to talk.'

'Yes, but he didn't.'

316

'How do you feel about it all?'

She sighed. 'It's so strange.' She lifted her head up and looked at him. 'Did you know he was a soldier?'

'Yes.'

'Why didn't he tell the rest of us? Or, to put it another way, why didn't you tell me?'

'Because, and I say this with the deepest respect to my colleagues, most of them have a *Guardian*-reading tosser element to them. They think all soldiers are mindless thugs.' He cleared his throat. 'I didn't tell you because by the time we were together I didn't think about it.'

'That's rubbish.'

'OK, in hindsight I don't think it would have bothered people much. But he didn't know that when he started – and after that it never came up. I mean I don't know what most of them did before they got to the Secretariat.'

She looked doubtful. 'It's made people suspicious – as if he's got something to hide.'

'What do you think?'

'Me?' She was genuinely taken aback. 'Rob would never do a thing like that.' It was his non-reaction that surprised her, as if he were trying to suppress something. 'You don't think he did it?'

'I've run out of cigarettes.'

'Answer me.'

He swung his legs over the side of the bed and rifled through one of the drawers of the bedside table. Finding nothing he lay down again. 'The thought did cross my mind.'

'Why?'

'I don't know. When I was with him yesterday, it just . . . there was something odd. So the thought crossed my mind.'

'He's not capable of it, I'm sure.'

'So am I . . . nearly . . . I feel bad thinking it. But there it is, it crossed my mind.'

'If you don't believe him, who else is going to?'

'You, obviously. I didn't say I didn't believe him. It was just a dishonourable thought that crossed my mind. As they do. Probably it's because I've got too many films going around in my head – you know. It's always the least likely character who did the murder.'

He looked at her. 'It's crossed your mind as well.'

'So what?' she said irritably. 'Sooner or later everything crosses your mind, doesn't it? It's what you do with it that counts.'

'So I'm not supposed to tell you what I'm really think-ing?'

'Don't be stupid.'

'That's what you're saying.'

She pulled the sheet from under him and carefully arranged it around her so that he could see nothing. She grimaced at him as if to say 'so there!'. Then she turned and walked out of the room.

This had taken place on a Friday and their work schedule the following week, usually carefully co-ordinated, was compromised by their other lives so that they would not see each other until the following Wednesday. On the Tuesday he was delighted to find a letter from her in his post box. His heart beating with anticipation (he had stopped being amazed at his own intensity) he opened it and began to read.

Mon 5 p.m.

I know I was angry with you on Friday and so you got angry with me but it's hard all of this in a way you can't understand or don't want to. You are the most important thing that has

318

*ever happened to me and you have simply transformed my life
so that when I die I will know that I have lived completely
once and in all its dimensions and it's because of you. And
that I would always love you and care for you and like you
and, probably, keeping it quietly to myself, always desire you.
But the other day – I'm not saying this to flatter or placate
you – I was alarmed to realize that in the central place was
you and near, but on the outside, David. And for years he was
there, in the middle. I'm married and I made promises that I
meant deeply – I can't just walk away and act as if my
husband is just a mistake. I feel just slippery and horrible. So.
I must try and make something of my marriage and be really
tough on myself. So it means you have to leave the central
place in my heart so there is a space for David to return. On
paper this is a bitter thought but in reality it fills me with
despair. I love you and will not allow you to be in the
humiliating position of being lied to. I don't know if I'm
lying. I can only suggest that you put me out of your life as
best you can. My feelings for you are true. Or, at least, in my
endless self-doubt and faithlessness in myself, I can only say
that I believe they are true. If they're not then I've fooled
myself.*

*When we started I didn't think. I thought a little but not
much. What I thought, I told you next day, was that there could
be nothing but a relationship based on the form of a friendship
(see how badly I write it) – but you were, it was, compelling and
I couldn't fight any of it and it all deepened gradually and daily
until it occupied me completely. But you have to leave me now
and with all my love which feels to me infinite and true even
though it will seem to you to be finite and false.*

*So there you are, a weak woman after all. Or a foolish one,
or both.*

Sadie x

In the public sphere, at any rate, the matter of Rob McCarthy's guilt took an unexpected turn. Max Hastings, veteran journalist of the Falklands war and editor of the *Daily Telegraph*, thundered mightily against the *Mail* for attempting to blacken the reputation of the British soldier. The *Daily Express*, belatedly waking up to an opportunity to do some blackening of its own of its biggest rival, also weighed in, not only behind McCarthy but also behind Nick, praising him for his loyalty to his beleaguered employee. The *Guardian* strolled briefly in the opposite direction, raising the profile of other rumours of atrocities during the war. But it was, after all, a popular war and old news. Without evidence of any serious kind, Max and the *Express* won the day. The editor of the *Mail* needed only the slightest hint from his proprietor to drop the story. Even the campaign against Nick suffered. The *Mail* would have to rein back its attempt to unseat him until memories of their lack of patriotism ceased and Nick presented them with another opportunity.

At the BFS, the reaction of the examiners to Nick's determined defence of McCarthy was divided. Some were ready, even pleased, to give him credit for his courage in championing Rob. Others suspected that he had realized all along what would happen, that it was a sign of his cunning and not his moral valour. People hardly ever give the devil his due, not even quite sophisticated people, reckoning, I suppose, either that he is not really due, or not really a devil.

As for the relationship between McCarthy and his colleagues, there was no doubt that there was a change. It was complicated and it was subterranean but in time McCarthy barely noticed it at all.

For myself I was curious and, besides, I thought that such information as I might find out could well be useful.

I had spent three years working with a fellow civil servant who had gone on to greater things at the Ministry of Defence. He owed me a favour because as his former boss I had covered up for a foolish attempt he had made to inflate his expenses on a trip to Northern Ireland. I telephoned him and we met for lunch. We chatted this way and that and then he came to the point.

'I looked into the business about your friend.'

'And?'

'You won't refer to this?'

'Absolutely not. It's just for my own peace of mind. That's all.' He didn't look as if he believed me. 'I promise. There won't be any repercussions.'

'The report was unofficial. It was written in the middle of a battle for God's sake. There's no question – the evidence wouldn't stand up in court. But –' he paused, thinking perhaps that this was unwelcome news '– everybody knew he did it.'

On the day after Farraday received the letter from Sadie he went to check his pigeonhole at the Secretariat and found another note from her.

Dear T   *Wed Eve*

I think I've missed you. Have you gone? If you find this go to the Italian café. I'll be there until 6:15 OK? I need to speak to you. If you don't make it you can call me until 10 tonight. I really must speak to you this evening.

When he had finished reading it, he put it in his inside jacket pocket and went home.

He was already on his third glass of whisky when the

doorbell rang at about seven thirty. Despite the fact that they were large glasses he was barely affected as he walked down the corridor, so neutralized had the alcohol been by black anger. He opened the door as if what he really wanted to do was tear it from its hinges. It was Sadie. Something inside him at once came to the boil – hope and fear. Hope – that she had come to throw herself abjectly at his feet and, weeping, beg his forgiveness. Fear – that she had come to throw herself abjectly at his feet and, weeping, tell him that she meant everything she had said in the letter. He couldn't bear to look at her (beyond a glare that he hoped made her realize the utter loathing and contempt in which he held her) and turned and walked back into his flat. Was she aware that, despite the silent fury with which he opened the door to her, in dismissing her so completely he had nevertheless left it open for her to follow? She was so distracted in her distress that it's possible she did not. At any rate she entered and closed the door behind her.

When she entered the front room, silently and ashamed, he had his back to her and was staring out of the window. He did not turn round. There was a silence as the blackness of his rage and despair seemed to grow out of his back and deepen the shadows of the dimly lit room. Does this seem to you strange and excessively melodramatic behaviour for such a wry and balanced man? For all the calculation behind the hunch of his shoulders, the backward projected hurt and wrath, there was nothing insincere, no pretence about the way he was feeling. Perhaps it was that he was just not himself when it came to Sadie.

Finally she spoke. 'If the idea of not talking to me today and looking as if you wanted to kill me was to punish me for writing the letter then you'll be pleased to know you've succeeded.' She stopped, hoping that this would prompt him to speak. A less agitated person might have noticed that he had moved his head to one side, a signal quite unconscious, that she should, indeed must, continue. 'You hope I had a lousy time of it and I have. All I feel is wretched for trying to do the right thing. Does that make you happy?'

The appeal for pity and compassion infuriated him and he turned round to face her. 'Yes, it does. Perhaps now you know what it feels like.'

She looked at him, her face a picture of utter misery. And though he loved her this was very satisfying to him.

'You think I've betrayed you,' she said quietly.

'What else would I feel? You tell me . . . you write to me . . . everything about how deeply you love me . . .' He stopped, inarticulate with emotion and humiliation at having believed her. But also there was a sudden shame there, a sudden fear that he might have misread, in some way exaggerated to himself, the depth of her feelings – that she was about to say that she had never meant to give the impression that . . . Along with all the other boiling emotions a new thought struck him: *Am I foolish?* But her reply instantly dispelled this most repugnant of notions.

'I *am* a traitor to you. And a cheat.' She made a sound somewhere between a sigh and a cry of despair, but there was also a bass note of self-mockery. Can one be deeply desperate and ironic at the same time? 'I'm horribly sorry I tried to do the right thing and I want to beg your forgiveness for trying to be a decent human being and keep the promises I made my husband.'

There were tears in her eyes now and this, and the sheer power of her misery, was too much for him. Impossible for him to reply to this – he furiously tried to sweep past her and out of the room but as he went by her she pulled at him and managed to stop him from leaving.

And then she hit him, a blow to the chest.

He looked at her, astonished.

Sadie, if anything, seemed even more shocked than he did by what she had done – but there was also something else in her expression, something at once fearful and defiant. For a moment they just looked at each other. Then he laughed.

'You hit like a girl,' he said.

'But that's what I am,' she replied solemnly, knowing that she had won him round. 'I'm a girl who loves a man who enjoys knowing what kind of hell I'm in.'

'And where do you think I've been for the last two days?'

She looked up at him, seeming even smaller than usual. 'I'm not as mean as you are. I didn't want you to be in hell, I just wanted not to betray my husband.' She sighed again and placed her hand on his chest where she had struck him. 'But I can't give you up. And that's all there is to it.'

She squeezed her nails into the skin of his chest beneath his shirt, like a cat with claws extended demanding its absolute right to attention.

'If you don't put your hand on me,' she said, 'I shall most surely rot to death.'

Corruption

They made him an offer he couldn't refuse.
The Godfather

As it happened, I soon realized that I could have saved myself the trouble and expense of taking my former colleague out to lunch. The information was useful as it later turned out, but I could just as easily have made it up myself. The trick when spreading lies is in making sure that whatever the nature of the fib it is impossible to prove one way or the other. McCarthy may or may not have been a murderer but no one could prove it.

Buoyed by his success over the *Daily Mail* and enjoying the credit for supporting McCarthy he'd gained from some of the examiners, Nick now decided to improve communications between himself and his employees. This might not have seemed difficult when there were relatively few people involved in the decision-making process but you must understand that Nick saw himself in imperial terms and he needed the trappings of an imperium to go along with it. The result was that to administer fourteen or so examiners there were no less than three tiers of management. Nick, his deputy and an assistant deputy. That is to say, one manager for every five people. The trouble was that the deputy and the assistant deputy took their management style from Nick and except for a few minutes in the morning they hardly ever went near the examiners. A more successful recipe for creating misunderstanding and resentment, and failing to alleviate it, would be hard to imagine. But Nick Berg managed it. If three managers couldn't successfully manage fourteen people then clearly what was required was another manager. And so Nick decided to create the post of Deputy Assistant Director, instantly acronymed by the examiners as DAD.

To be appointed from the examiners' body itself, the DAD was to promote the flow of information throughout the building and play a major part in easing the tensions that had so damaged the atmosphere in the Secretariat. As it happened, there were only two applicants but so enthused was Nick by his plan that by the time he had finished interviewing them both he'd decided that if one DAD was a good thing, then two would be even better. So it was that in one stroke the ratio of examiners to managers fell from slightly over four and a half to slightly under two and a half. One of the new deputy assistant directors was Allan Rhys: the other was me.

You need hardly be told that because the problem between Nick and the examiners had nothing whatsoever to do with the number of managers these appointments were a complete waste of time. Indeed, given that Rhys had an eye only on further advancement and that I was bent only on mischief, here was fertile ground for yet more discontent. Even had we been less woeful choices we could have done no good. All that happened was that from then on we hardly had anything to do with the examiners either.

The Friday after our accession the two of us were invited to Nick's office for a celebratory drink. He welcomed us into the management team (which had become a reasonable description given there were now enough of us to enter a five-a-side or basketball tournament) and praised our qualities as candidates. Then he said something typical of Nick, not malicious I'm quite sure of that, but weirdly artless in a man of his age and political nous.

'I asked Sadie and Thomas Farraday if they would apply for the posts. But they didn't,' he said with a kind of cheerful ruefulness. 'Farraday is such a clever guy and Sadie such a wonderful writer – easily the best at the Secretariat.'

Then he waffled on but I had stopped listening. Rhys looked as if he had swallowed a weasel and I had no very generous feelings towards Nick or the two lovers.

I'm not sure what it was that caused me to seek Sadie out at lunchtime the following Monday. I suppose it was like sticking your tongue in a decaying tooth – sometimes you can't stop yourself. For once she was on her own (loverboy was usually hanging round like some yearning calf or puppy).

As always she offered to share her lunch with me: something that at the time (you can tell in what bad shape I was in) I regarded as an insulting affectation – a pretence of generosity. I declined (I had my pride). But we talked for a while. She congratulated me (again) on my new job.

'You didn't think of applying? I'm sure Nick would have liked you to.'

She looked uneasy. I'd given her the opportunity to be straight with me but all I got was an evasive smile. 'I wouldn't be any good at all that stuff. Organizing things is more your style.'

'A good bureaucrat,' I said, smiling back.

'Not at all,' she said, a little too quickly. She shook her head. 'What I mean is that the world needs all the good bureaucrats it can get.'

I'd had enough. My ill will towards her was vindicated which was, I suppose, why I had come to talk to her in the first place. I was both satisfied by this and resentful at being condescended to. Hatred is exhausting work.

It also benefits from time to weed and water it and I had plenty of that. Unsurprisingly, it turned out there wasn't enough work for one of us let alone two. The reason that Nick was able to be so careless of the cost of running the BFS was that he had skilfully ensured from the start that the film and video companies would be lavishly over-charged for the Secretariat's services. Who, after all, was to say that it wouldn't cost what Nick said it would cost? How could anyone know? There were no competitors and, once legally established, no alternatives. In 1984 when the price of viewing a tape was established at eight pounds a minute, the industry was both fragmented and terrified. Its tapes were going to be stripped from the shelves, shades of the prison house were upon this growing boy and Nick was offering to sort it out. No one had had such a sweet deal since the Tudor monopolies and Nick was pitiless in squeez-ing his compulsory customers for as much as he could get.

Despite his high salary and generous perks, let me be clear that this was not done in the interests of personal gain. It was in the interests of a strong and independent BFS and its prestige that it should be as lavishly appointed as a successful advertising agency.

The only reason that there weren't huge surpluses of cash at the end of the year was that Nick made damn sure he spent it all on the building and its luxurious appoint-ment. Another couple of (I'm grateful to say) highly paid managers looked convincing on the balance sheet and managed to soak up enough money to justify their existence whether or not they actually did anything useful. None of this was conscious on Nick's part – it just happened to work out that way. But you should not take from this that he was corrupt in any personal sense. Something that took place in his office a few months after my appointment illustrated that, along with his capacity for ruthlessness, he could be as innocent as an unusually chaste schoolgirl.

I was present at the meeting with Nick, Walter Casey and the two owners of a newly formed video company, although I was there merely to gain experience of 'the industry'. The owners were worried. It turned out that for a knock-down price they had bought the UK video distribution rights of an American children's film shortly before it had become an unexpected runaway success. Anxious to exploit their good judgement they had taken the opportunity to duplicate more than two hundred and fifty thousand copies before the video, which required a separate certificate from the film, had been submitted. They had reasoned that because the cinema release had been a straightforward 'PG' then the video would be the same. This was certainly a risky strategy but in due course the video was indeed passed 'PG'. But this was not the problem. The examiners had noted that there was a trailer for another video on the front of the one they were watching. The trailer had already been passed '18' for the cinema and for video. It was, of course, present on every single copy. Because, logically enough, the whole tape had to take the category of the highest feature on a submission, including trailers, the distributors were in possession of two hundred and fifty thousand children's videos now classified as only suitable for those over the age of eighteen.

'Look, Mr Berg,' said one of the distributors desperately. 'It'll cost us a quarter of a million to have the video re-copied.'

'I know we made a stupid mistake. But that's all it was,' said the other. 'It won't happen again.'

Berg looked at them, his face all concern and sympathy. 'I can see that it's going to be expensive to put it right but I can't ignore the fact that the trailer is both violent and sexually explicit. Parents who bought or hired the video for their children would be appalled. And for good reason. Besides, I don't have any discretion. The law states clearly that a tape has to take the highest category of any feature on that tape, including trailers.'

'But we'll go out of business.'

'You should have read the regulations governing submissions. Of course I want the video industry to be successful but, well, I don't mean to rebuff you with a cliché but my hands are well and truly tied.'

The two video distributors misunderstood the lack of genuine sympathy in Nick's tone of voice. He was quite right to take the view that it was a ludicrous request. But they interpreted this as something much more dubious.

'Perhaps,' said one of them after a quick exchange of glances, 'we could pay a fine.'

Nick looked at them, puzzled. 'The BFS doesn't exact fines.'

'It could be an unofficial fine.'

'Say, ten thousand pounds.'

'And we'd undertake, in writing if you like, never to do it again.'

I looked at Walter: he was clearly as astonished as I was at hearing such a naked attempt to offer a bribe. Both of us looked at Nick, who seemed to be registering only con-descension. The two distributors were looking at him expectantly.

'I obviously haven't explained myself very well.' He then went on to repeat what he had said before, only more elaborately. Taking out a booklet from his desk while he did so, he went on to read them the relevant statute from The Video Recordings Act. He concluded with what he clearly meant as an air of finality, but the video distributors merely interpreted this as a subtle way of asking for more money.

'What if it were to be fifteen thousand?' ventured one of them. Before Nick could reply, the other quickly interrupted.

'Look, I can see that we really made a big mistake. I think twenty, or even twenty-five thousand would be very fair.'

Both Walter and I were staring at them, wide-eyed by now. But Nick simply sighed and explained the rules all over again. Fortunately by the time he finished Walter had recovered his usual calm and immediately stood up.

'I'm sorry, gentlemen, but we have another meeting and we're already late. If you wouldn't mind?'

'But—'

'Our decision', said Walter, menacingly, 'is absolutely final. Now please.' He gestured towards the door. Miserable and with their hopes dashed just as they thought victory was in their grasp the two men allowed themselves to be shown to the door. Walter closed it heavily behind them to see Nick looking at him faintly bemused. Walter sighed.

'Don't you realize they were offering you a bribe?'

Nick's face fell with astonishment. 'What?' he said and then stopped. He was clearly playing their responses over in his mind. 'Are you sure?' he said at last.

'Completely sure,' said Walter.

Nick looked at me.

'I'm afraid he's right.'

How could he have missed it? I put it down to two things: morality and vanity. He was not attuned to the offer because his weaknesses as a human being did not extend to the taking of backhanders. It was not a temptation he had ever felt and so, in a way, there was no space for suspicion of what they were up to. But there was also, I believe, something you might find hard to understand. He did not see himself as a guardian of the nation's morality but as a guardian of the nation. Before a rapist could rape there had to be a becoming, a process had to be undergone whereby a man had to divest himself of his humanity to a degree sufficient to allow him to act. And so for the murderer and so for the bully and the yob. Before the blouse was ripped, the kick delivered in the playground, the knife driven in below the ribs, something had dissolved their humanity. He was not foolish enough to believe that the images that flowed through this building, his building, were solely responsible for these dissolutions of human sympathy. But that there were women unraped, children sleeping unbullied, men and women alive because of what he did, of this Nick Berg had no doubt. You could not buy the power of such self-belief. This is the kind of conviction, as I hope you will see, that burns.

At any rate, both Walter and I enjoyed mocking Nick at the time for his naivety – but not as successfully as Thomas Farraday, who listened entranced at the next Secretariat meeting as Walter told the story to the examiners in front of our smiling Director. It was Farraday who reduced the entire meeting to delighted laughter when he remarked that the distributors had made Nick an offer he couldn't understand.

The Power and the Glory

BUTLER: Excuse me, sir, but I'm concerned about the wedding gifts.

DRUMMOND: It's quite all right, Tenny, the detective is watching them.

BUTLER: Yes, sir, but who is watching the detective?

Bulldog Drummond's Peril, 1938

Dear T   *Thurs p.m.*
*Last night after I saw you my cheeks stayed flushed until I got
home and I had to douse my face with cold water. I am so
touched by how gentle you are. Who would have thought it?
(Don't think I'm idolizing you because I know what an ill-
tempered bastard you can be.)*

*It's just as well you can't come here because I would tie you
to the furniture and not let you leave like some deranged
Stephen King character. I'm going to train myself not to spend
all my time pining away for you. What would all my feminist
colleagues think if they knew the things I say to you? I am a
desperate and total traitor to my sex – a failure on all counts.
I should be denounced before the central committee. My
hunger for you is absurd. Don't ever stop loving me.*

I feel like a pot of boiling water pushing against the lid. Why

can't you be beside me now and all night long we can talk about
nothing in particular? I should snap out of this. You must be
terrified by how much I want you, how irresistible I find you,
and you must understand how I would hate you a little for
having so much power over me so that I lose all restraint, con-
trol, and any ability to have a cool head or a cool body. And I
love you for making me dizzy and I hate you for it.
   When I see you alone next I'll show you all that I mean.
   Sadie x

NOW I WAS IN a position of authority, the next question
concerned the best way in which to misuse it. The trouble
was, however, that I didn't actually have much in the way
of authority; the sheer pointlessness of our new jobs was
never better revealed in that we had no power to do anything – no access to the really important meetings nor
even to the powerful and sometimes interesting people
who came through the Secretariat. Nick was as possessive
of these things as a pack leader of his females.

So for the moment there was only one obvious source
of mischief: the personnel files in Walter's office. All I
needed to do was wait until Walter was away and find an
excuse to work there. My chance came about a month
later. Walter was off to speak at some media conference or
other in Edinburgh. I asked if he minded my using his
office while he was away, a request he clearly didn't find
difficult to understand as Rhys and I had been parked in a
bloody awful cubicle with barely enough room for one.
So far, so easy. Having installed myself on the first morning of Walter's two-day absence I felt it would be too risky
to remove Sadie's file and read it there and then – too
many people popping in and out. I decided instead to
remove it at the end of the day and take it home so I'd
have plenty of time to read it and photocopy anything

worthwhile on my way to work the following morning. All of this was, of course, based on the assumption that the filing cabinet with the files inside was unlocked. I checked first thing – it was indeed open.

I waited until six thirty and, having checked the floor was deserted, it took only a few seconds to get out Sadie's file and slip it into my briefcase. I was surprised to find that my heart was beating fiercely and I felt a strange surge of blood in my cheeks. My unease lasted until I got home and went into the small bedroom I used as my study, telling my wife I had a few hours' work to do. By now I had calmed down, not least because I had persuaded myself that there was no reason to think there would be any great revelation in the file, which I now noted was disappointingly thin.

The first few pages were straightforward: references and so forth. Then something of interest, if no great significance: the withdrawn official warning over the row in Birmingham with Andrea Dworkin. Attached to the back of it was a photocopy of a fax. It was striking because the original had clearly been torn into pieces and then sellotaped together before being copied.

When I finished reading it I was so thrilled, I felt so blessed with the discovery, that I wanted desperately to thank a supernatural power, so much did it feel like an intervention by some ministering Beelzebub or Asmodeus. The fax came from a Professor Janet Bergeron, Head of Faculty of Feminist Literary and Film Studies at Princeton. It came addressed care of Nicholas Berg of the British Film Secretariat but (and you should keep this in mind) was addressed directly to Sadie herself.

Dear Sadie Boldon,
A colleague of mine was present during the discussion

between you and Andrea Dworkin and Catherine MacKinnon over the question of censorship. The faculty here at Princeton is organizing a four-day Colloquium on feminism and censorship running from 14-18 of July this year. Having heard of your spirited opposition to them both I was intrigued enough to look you up. Fortunately there was a copy of your thesis on Women in Film available on the US University Interloan library service. I was very impressed and would like to invite you to be a speaker at the Colloquium. It would also be great if you could take some of the plenary sessions. It will be the biggest event of its kind for some years and we have many prestigious speakers, but I think that you have a fresh voice that we all could benefit from hearing. We will, of course, pay all your expenses.

Best wishes,

Janet Bergeron

Beneath was a contact number and fax number.

For a few hours I was very nearly euphoric – my enemy had been delivered into my hands. But as I lay awake that night I began to realize that I had a real problem: how could I possibly let her know about the fax without incriminating myself? And as I was to discover the next morning, I had in truth more than the one problem to deal with.

I arrived at work that day, slightly late having stopped off to make a copy of the fax, only to find that my guiding demon (in the way of all devils, I suppose) had a treacherous shock in store: Walter was sitting at his desk.

'Are you all right?' he asked. I suppose that because I felt as if I was going to have a stroke something of this must have shown on my face. It was an unpleasant discovery this, that while I had lost all sympathy or care for my fellow human beings – and one of them in particular – this had not in any way diminished my sympathy for myself nor its attendants: fear and self-pity.

'Yes,' I said. 'Just surprised to see you. Something wrong?'

'Bloody conference centre – they think the air-conditioning system is contaminated with Legionnaire's disease. Why they had to wait until yesterday to discover it – all that damn way for nothing.'

Back in my cubicle my panic only increased. Should I dump the file? Destroy it? Do it now? Or wait until the end of the day? What if they searched me? Why would they do that?

Slowly, I began to calm down. I'd work until late and then put the file back. I spoke harshly to myself – *If you're going to try and destroy Sadie you'd better grow a backbone.*

Despite the fact that it was a Friday night Walter did not go home on time. By seven thirty I felt I was likely to cause suspicion by remaining – why, after all, would someone who barely had anything to do during the week need to work late on a Friday night? It would have to wait until Monday. I spent an uneasy Saturday but by the next day I had begun to recover my nerve and on returning to work I felt much calmer. Not even the fact that Walter worked late that day too and that again I was forced to take Sadie's file home could return me to the alarming state of Friday.

The next morning Walter called Rhys and me into his office. He looked worried.

'Last night, Nick came down to look for a personnel file. It's missing.' He looked at the two of us (accusation? suspicion?). 'Nick is pretty angry. I don't suppose either of you saw anything around my office on Thursday? Someone who shouldn't have been there?'

'You were here all day weren't you, Duncan?' Rhys had

turned to look at me and it seemed to me that he moved himself back in his seat as if to sidestep any suspicion and deflect it towards me.

'Yes, I was. I didn't see anyone.'

'Did you go out for lunch?'

'Yes, I was out for a bit more than an hour – an hour and fifteen minutes perhaps.' There was a silence. 'Was the filing cabinet locked?'

Walter looked deflated. 'No.'

'Ah.' I let that hang in the air for a moment. 'Well, I definitely didn't see anything. But with more than an hour to come in and get a file . . . is it just one file?'

'As far as we know.'

'Presumably, then, they knew what they were looking for. It wouldn't have taken a minute and secretaries and managers and technical, they do drop in, don't they?'

Walter nodded wearily. 'Nick is very unhappy about this. Frankly I got a bollocking for leaving the cabinet unsecured and from now on the office will have to be locked when I'm not using it.'

This was going to be a bloody nuisance for everyone – for me it was fucking tragic. I couldn't believe my luck. What were the odds of Nick deciding he wanted to look through Sadie's file?

'Are we allowed to know whose file has gone missing?'

'Uh . . . no, I think the less said on that the better. It goes without saying that you're not to talk about this with anyone else.'

For nearly a week I decided to abandon my plans for revenge. I was, I admit, in a blue funk. But the thing is, fear like that only stays with you when you believe you have something to lose. Within those few days I realized that I didn't. All I possessed was my hatred of Sadie and without it I just felt numb. As things stood, the now discovered misappropriation of the file compounded the problem of how I could get Sadie to learn of the contents of the fax without implicating myself when the inevitable row erupted. Nick would want to know how she found out and if I was the one who told her, I'd have to depend on Sadie to keep her mouth shut. Even if she did, she'd almost certainly tell that prick Farraday. Would he keep it from McCarthy? I didn't rate my chances. And once there was even a sniff that I was involved, it wouldn't take Nick two seconds to realize where the information about the fax had come from and how I obtained it. If that didn't count as gross misconduct and instant dismissal I don't know what would.

At any rate it seemed clear to me that I had to find a way of ensuring the missing file turned up and in such a way that its disappearance seemed innocent. Then I had to work out how to get Sadie to discover the truth without telling her myself. It was all very frustrating – I had Sadie in the palm of my hand but no way to deliver her to evil without serious risk of bringing myself down in the process.

At first I was determined to craft some ingenious method of placing the missing file somewhere plausible where it would seem likely that it had been mislaid rather than stolen. My hope was that if I thought carefully enough I might hit on a plan so cunning that it would also, somehow, ensure by the file's discovery that Sadie was also certain to be informed of its content. I'm afraid, in the end, I had to accept my limitations here as in so much else. I was getting to the point where I was considering dropping it behind the personnel filing cabinet and hoping for the best but I managed to avoid this shamefully feeble contrivance by coming up with an idea while mowing the lawn. If by no means brilliant it went some way to restoring confidence in my abilities as a fink. Not that I thought of it in such terms at the time: to myself I was the wounded party hideously done down and unjustly dismissed as a nonentity. In my anger I felt huge, blown into a kind of giant of resolve and wrath. I found myself surprised that people did not stare at me, were not afraid when I entered the room with my stern and vengeful soul, iron and flint in its unbending power. That they could not see how great the change was in me was something that fed my rage and caused me to despise them even further. How does this square with my blue funk over the replacement of the file? Why should it, I ask you?

My plan, and one quickly executed, was to put Sadie Boldon's file in the cabinet in Walter's office where he kept the billings records of all the video distributors. I decided, just in case he had checked the Bs, to place it under S for Sadie. It was a plausible explanation given that some of the smaller distributors were called by personal names: Fiona Smith Videos, for example, a soft porn video company (Fiona, however, was strictly fictional; Ms Smith's videos were really made by someone called Trevor Hat). The double misfiling could easily be explained by the error of some half-wit temp often employed to do the job. As to how Sadie's file got mixed up with the files for the video companies in the first place, well these things happen. With luck, Walter or even Nick might blame their own carelessness.

A couple of weeks later it was found by Nick's secretary. Both she and Walter, I'm pleased to say, jumped to pretty much the conclusion I had hoped for, helped by the fact that they had both had bad experiences with temps in the previous six months. Nick was less easy to convince. He still saw some conspiracy. The bloody lunatic even decided to have the file fingerprinted to find out if anyone not authorized to touch it had left behind clues to their identity. Fortunately, Walter just about persuaded him that he was being ridiculous. No doubt Nick's scepticism and fear were bred from an uneasy conscience. The question is, why, having initially torn up the fax, did he choose to piece it back together and then put it in her file? There couldn't have been a good reason, but then it's a mistake to think that people make many rational decisions, particularly when they're in an emotional state (and people, don't you find, are so very often in an emotional state most of the time). And, of course, as you will now have gathered, the Secretariat like all rotting places of work had become a great sounding board, a living amplifier of the bedlam that inhabits the soul. Every human being is like one of those pleasant English suburbs with a prison for the criminally insane at its edge.

Next came the problem of how to get the fax to Sadie. I even considered not using it at all. It would have been ideal if I could have, in some way, arranged a kind of chance meeting between them – powerful academics like Professor Janet Bergeron went abroad to conferences all the time. Given their mutual interests it was not beyond the bounds of possibility that they might meet. If I'd had any power, even a little, to send an examiner here or there for plausible reasons this might have been engineered. But I didn't – so in the end I just sent her a copy with a note:

I think you should know about this.

However banal, I was still pleased with this. The advantage of my solution to the file was that the video companies' billing documents were in constant use by the secretarial staff – any one of them with a grudge against

341

A Letter from America

The heart is a small thing, but desireth great matters. It is not sufficient for a kite's dinner, yet the whole world is not sufficient for it.

Francis Quarles, *Hugo de Anima*

Sadie Boldon
118 Walm Lane
London NW2 4QY
19th May 1994

Walter Casey
Deputy Director
British Film Secretariat
8 Golden Square
London
W1F 9HT

Dear Walter,
Following my conversation with you yesterday I have written
as follows a brief explanation of the background to a serious
grievance that can only be dealt with through the formal
grievance procedure between the BFS and my union,
MSF.

On Monday 9th May I received an anonymous letter containing a fax addressed to me that had been received by the Secretariat more than three years ago. The fax contained an invitation from Professor Janet Bergeron, Head of Feminist Literacy and Film Studies at Princeton, inviting me to speak, at their expense, at a conference and conduct several seminars.

On the 13th May I arranged a meeting with Nicholas Berg and he offered me the following information: the fax had indeed been received by the Secretariat but at that time he did not believe that I was sufficiently trustworthy to represent the BFS at such a high profile conference. It was for this reason that, despite the fax being addressed to me, he had taken it and failed to inform me of its contents or even its existence.

My grievance relates to the following:

1) by intercepting and keeping secret a fax addressed to an employee for whom he has some responsibility, the Director has, I believe, involved himself in a clear case of professional misconduct.
2) Nicholas Berg's stated reasons for withholding the fax have serious consequences for me as an employee. In effect, my career was being seriously damaged without any proceeding, formal or informal, having taken place.

This was clearly a singular opportunity for me to advance professionally but not only was I to be deprived of it, I was not even to be made aware that I was being disciplined. In addition, my failure to respond to such a prestigious invitation will have caused my reputation untold damage in the academic world.

I would therefore be grateful if you would institute the agreed stages of the grievance procedure as soon as possible. I

344

should make it clear that I deeply regret having to do this but under the circumstances it seems to me unavoidable.

Yours respectfully,
  Sadie Boldon

BRITISH FILM SECRETARIAT
8 GOLDEN SQUARE, LONDON, W1F 9HT

Sadie Boldon   23 May 1994
118 Walm Lane
London NW2 4QY

Dear Sadie
<u>GRIEVANCE PROCEDURE</u>
I write to confirm our verbal agreement to meet on
Wednesday at 12.30 p.m.
Yours,
Walter Casey

Sadie Boldon
118 Walm Lane
London NW2 4QY
27th May 1994

Walter Casey
Deputy Director
British Film Secretariat
8 Golden Square
London
W1F 9HT

Dear Walter,

Thank you for the calm and reasonable meeting on Wednesday. I have been giving serious consideration to your offer of a meeting with the Director, in your presence as a neutral chair. It is no reflection of any lack of personal trust in you that I would only agree to this if there were no chair and if Emma Saward is present in her capacity as union representative.

I would also have to insist, as this meeting is an informal attempt to reach an equitable in-house resolution, that should I be dissatisfied with the result of it then the grievance procedure should be automatically returned to stage 3.

Please let me know if the above conditions are acceptable.

Yours sincerely,
Sadie Boldon

30 May 1994

Sadie Boldon
118 Walm Lane
London NW2 4QY

Dear Sadie,

Thank you for your letter of 27 May and for your kind personal remarks. Before we proceed further I thought it worth responding to your two points.

First, we are discussing a meeting where the chief executive of an organization might have to be questioned and judged by an employee or their representative both considerably junior to him. I think you will see that this is untenable without my performing the role of disinterested chair, seeking to maintain a calm and reasonable atmosphere. It is my own personal view, born of long experience, that an unchaired meeting is unlikely to produce this.

To answer your second point, if you are dissatisfied with the proceedings of this informal meeting you, of course, have the right to return to the Official Grievance Procedure.

As you note in your letter, we are all anxious to reach a resolution as quickly and painlessly as possible and I would urge you to reconsider my original offer to chair this meeting. If you would care to discuss this I would gladly make the time available.

Yours sincerely,
  Walter Casey

Sadie Boldon
118 Walm Lane
London NW2 4QY
2nd June 1994

Walter Casey
Deputy Director
British Film Secretariat
8 Golden Square
London
W1F 9HT

Dear Walter,

Thank you for your letter of 30th May and the subsequent meeting in the presence of the union representative the following day, at which your offer of yourself as chair and conciliator was again discussed.

Whilst appreciating that you have repeated this offer for what you feel to be the best reasons, I believe that in the interests of keeping your involvement in this procedure as uninvidious as possible, I again have to refuse your offer. My reasons remain as stated in my letter of 27th May. These still stand and I have to express some personal regret that I had to reiterate them to you at our meeting yesterday.

I have accepted in all good faith the offer of a meeting with Nick Berg to resolve this matter with as little fuss as possible, and I hope that this sadly unacceptable condition which you have laid down for this meeting will not stand in the way of an acceptable informal resolution of my grievance.

Finally, thank you for your confirmation that the official grievance procedure will be returned to if the informal meeting, which I hope will go ahead, fails to produce an acceptable outcome. It is, of course, my sincere hope that this will not be the case.

Yours sincerely,
  Sadie Boldon

Sadie Boldon
118 Walm Lane
London NW2 4QY
3rd June 1994

Walter Casey
Deputy Director
British Film Secretariat
8 Golden Square
London
W1F 9HT

Dear Walter,
Thank you for your letter concerning the informal meeting
with the Director in which you kindly accept that there need
be no chair. I have discussed this both with the union rep and
the Regional Officer of the MSF, and we find the conditions
acceptable.

Yours sincerely,
   Sadie Boldon

All this epistolary rancour was, of course, like a fine wine
and, dear Reader, I drank deeply of its sub-texts of
animosity, churlishness, sourness and ill will. Choler, do
you know gall? Huff, have you met miff? Rage, do you
know pique? Is there anything better than a spite satisfied?
I think not. It's true that ideally I should have been a direct
witness to much of this, which I was not – though it has
to be said that there was a wonderful pleasure in the long
and gentle swirling of each and every sentence to smell
the aroma of what lay behind each carefully constructed
circumlocution. Nevertheless, even in this one regret I was
not to be unsatisfied.

Nick had insisted that minutes should be taken. As
someone who had performed this task in an official

capacity as a civil servant, they had mutually agreed that it should be me. There was no Iago, no Machiavelli so subtle and with such tactical nous who could begin to carry out such devastation on his foes as Sadie and Nick were blithely devising all on their own.

The Meeting

'My sentence is for open war.'
Moloch, in *Paradise Lost*

THE FIVE OF US sat in Nick's plush office as awkwardly as
you might expect with Nick Berg and Andrew Taylor, the
Secretariat's administrative manager (and someone we
rarely had much to do with) on one side of the room and
Sadie and Emma Saward opposite. I sat at Nick's desk, the
easier to write the minutes. I was there to provide a verbatim
copy of what was about to be said because I was trained in
Pitman's shorthand, a skill now as forgotten, I suppose, as
wheelwrighting or bodging. For some reason both parties
were uneasy about a straight sound recording.

Nick spoke first. I had expected at least a certain coldness but his tone was almost shy like a nervous lover
trying to make things up.

NICK

Thank you for agreeing to this. I realize it's stepping outside
the procedure. I think it would be better if you began and
said what you'd like to come from this meeting. And I, uh,
can meet the points you make.

351

I expected Sadie to be made cautious by this soft-spoken opening – conciliatory, sad – but her reply was implacable.

SADIE

I'd prefer it the other way around actually, Nick. I talked a lot at the last meeting with Walter. I think because this is a [pause] concession from me setting aside the grievance procedure, I think it's incumbent on you to talk at this point.

Whether he was genuinely saddened by this early resistance or too fly to have his hand forced by this whippersnapper was a question that crossed my mind even as my hand raced indecipherably over the paper.

NICK

As . . . as the whole thing really turns on whether or not I've demonstrated a lack of trust in you, I think that for the most part I've regularly given demonstrations of my trust in you. And it was only for one moment in the heat of a very bad time at the Secretariat that I, uh, thought this was not the moment for you to do something on behalf of the Secretariat. Had the request come before that unfortunate . . . uh . . . time I would certainly have trusted you to go.

SADIE

You're talking as if it's self-evident that I did something wrong at the conference in Birmingham.

NICK

No. No, I accept that it was my mistake for not making it clear to you what was unacceptable. I think I made a very serious error.

Not bad, I thought to myself, to keep apologizing for

not having realized how seriously lacking in judgement she was.

> ### NICK
>
> At the last meeting that lunchtime between me and the examiners concerning what happened between you and Andrea Dworkin, there was a clear lack of trust between the two groups. Things were hostile. It was that lack of trust which led to my action in retaining the fax. When I came upstairs, it was at that precise moment that the fax arrived from America. My reaction was really very simple when I saw it: it was 'Oh, Christ, that's all we need.' That was not the moment to send you abroad as an ambassador for the Secretariat – something I'd never done with any other examiner. I thought it would be difficult, remembering the anger at the meeting that day, for us to speak together at all. I thought tempers needed to cool and that was my only motivation.

He stressed the word *only* in such a heartfelt way that one could almost forget he had torn the fax into pieces and had to stick it together again with sellotape – though for what reason I still can't fathom.

> ### NICK (cont)
>
> Now . . .

He paused.

> ### NICK (cont)
>
> . . . with hindsight, yes I could have called you up and told you about it. But I have to say I thought when I came upstairs that you would be so upset about the disagreement over the dinner in Birmingham that it seemed to me to add

insult to injury to tell you: 'Sadie, you've had an invitation to speak at a prestigious conference in America but I'm not going to let you go.'

It seemed an unnecessarily cruel thing to do. Now you may say that you'd rather have known. Perhaps, as I said with hindsight, I should have known that with hindsight you would like to have known. I didn't discuss it with my colleagues. I wish I had . . .

I loved the emphasis on *wish* – so suggestive – but of what precisely?

NICK (cont)

. . . at the time. But I didn't. All I can say is that I didn't. I'm sorry. There's nothing I can do about it. I can't . . . I can't go back and rewrite history. That's what happened.

She had done well, I thought, very well to let him keep talking, to allow him to weave his reconstruction in detail.

NICK (cont)

You did say, it's minuted at the last meeting, you considered it a malicious act on my part. It certainly wasn't malice and I'm pleased that afterwards you withdrew that because it certainly wasn't – it was thoughtless on my part not to talk to you . . .

He paused. Was an apology coming? Not quite. Or at all.

NICK (cont)

. . . Perhaps I should have done.

Perhaps? And what would he have said? I was full of admiration here: his tone so conciliatory, his rueful sadness – and yet he circled and bobbed around her. Was he fearful of a trap, wanting to make it up, or was he waiting for a chance to land a blow? Or was he probing, seeing that she had won the opening move by forcing him to speak first? Such a clever and determined girl, I had to hand it to her – and also that she seemed herself, watchful and uncommitted in her body language, to be alive to everything he said. I began to sense that there was something epic here; some Stalingrad or Waterloo, something that far exceeded my (it has to be said, alas) petty-minded nastiness was taking shape in front of me. Nick had finally stopped talking. Sadie waited a little longer than would normally have been considered, I don't know, polite? appropriate? She looked at him with an expression of something like courteous hostility, if you can imagine such a thing.

SADIE

That – is that what you wanted to say?

NICK

I don't see that there's anything else that I *can* say.

SADIE

Is that right?

Again this wonderfully odd, non-committal tone. Where was she going with this? I had never seen Nick quite so ill at ease, battle-hardened as he was through years of fighting off the minister of this and the editor of that. He could sense the danger here because he was no clearer than I was (I began to see) about what Sadie was feeling. He needed to get her to reveal at least something. He tried giving her a light prod with a sharpened stick.

355

NICK

In my mind those are the facts.

SADIE

I see.

NICK

And certainly not your summary in your written documents.
I mean you're perfectly entitled to draw those conclusions –
but those are your conclusions.

Throughout this Sadie had certainly reacted to almost everything he said, but it still wasn't clear to me what these reactions meant. She began to nod and murmur, not in agreement, but as if she were suddenly clearer about the meaning of what he was saying. It unnerved Nick at any rate because he started repeating himself, and not as part of his usual tactic of swaddling his opponent in explanations but out of nervousness.

NICK (cont)

Uh . . . I certainly didn't say that I held you to be insufficiently trustworthy to represent the Secretariat in America.

Now she had stopped nodding or reacting at all. This really threw him.

NICK (cont)

No. It was simply that I thought, Oh Christ! this was no moment to send you abroad on behalf of the Secretariat when we don't trust each other.

Anyone else at the BFS would have pointed out that what Nick had just said was that the reason he'd decided not to allow her to go to America was not because he

356

didn't trust her, it was, on the contrary, because he didn't trust her. Normally that's what she too would have done and Nick would have welcomed it: sarcasm, disdain would have brought her out from the ropes of the non-committal.

And then I realized the reason, perhaps, that Nick was so unlike himself. I don't know why I hadn't thought about it before but we were almost hermetically sealed away from the outside world in much of our working lives. The various committees who technically oversaw the Secretariat were handled so smoothly by Nick and he kept them so far apart from every other mechanism that theoretically checked and balanced him, that he had forgotten that he ruled here as an Emperor not by law but only in practice, because he was able to keep his notional overseers weak through a mixture of flattery, their idleness and their ignorance of the arcane and complicated nature of censorship. But what Sadie had done was to run a bus through this – she had started a legal procedure inside the Secretariat that he could not control. He was already having to dance to her tune when she came into the room. It was obvious that this informal departure was an attempt to bring her and the procedure itself to heel by the very act of making it informal. What he'd clearly expected was that once she was in his office he could flatter and flannel and explain his way out of this disagreeable controlling device. He was nervous now because it wasn't working. The trouble was that the ripping up of the fax, then not telling anyone about it, looked so bad to everyone – and Sadie was so strangely implacable with her weird coolness and anger. There was only one thing he could do to stop this from moving on to humiliation. And he was beginning to see what it was. I felt a little gasp of shock in my throat as I, too, began to see what was unravelling here. Oh Christ! indeed.

SADIE

Right.

Sadie drew the word out softly, and to twice its normal length.

SADIE (cont)

I appreciate you going through this in [pause] some detail.

She sucked her perfect little white teeth. But meaning what? Reflection? Well-mannered disdain?

SADIE (cont)

Like you I really don't want to bring up the whole Andrea Dworkin thing. Like you I feel all that's history – though it's history that is very much attached to me personally. But this is not just a personal thing. It's a professional thing as well. And this . . . this is why I've gone down this route with the grievance procedure. Because I don't think it is a matter of . . . of . . . hurt feelings or protecting people from their own feelings – something you felt you had to do as a senior employee of the Secretariat.

Clever I thought that, the 'employee' bit.

SADIE (cont)

. . . I think the problem that arises out of your action with this fax hasn't been addressed by what you've just said to me. What you just said to me explains why it is that I, in your opinion, was not the right person to go to the conference in America—

NICK
(interrupting)

That's not what I sai—

SADIE

(interrupting)

I accept that—

NICK

I didn't say you were not the right person, I said that it was not the right *moment*.

Her eyes dulled over with wearily amused acceptance.

SADIE

Well, let's say then that I wasn't the right person at that moment to send.

Her breath in was one of clearing this away and let's get down to it.

SADIE (cont)

Now I think that's debatable – at best that's debatable. I can tell you now that had I gone to the conference in America . . . um . . . despite my chagrin and upset over Birmingham, I would have behaved professionally.

No one disputes that it's your right as the Director of the BFS to send or not send your staff here or there. But if it comes to the point where your staff are receiving faxes in their own name, faxes addressed to them, and then you consider it fitting that you have sufficient power and control over your staff that you can [pause] hide faxes such as this one, conceal an invitation that would have, self-evidently, huge implications for my future, well, I have to say, I con-sider that to be a legitimate professional grievance.

NICK

It . . . if . . . Look, the fax is a machine owned by the Secretariat. It used Secretariat paper – it's Secretariat paper. I . . . uh . . . it's never happened before or since. No other examiner has ever been invited to speak at a conference. And no other examiner has ever been given permission.

SADIE

Right. But I didn't even know I was being invited so that – that remains the problem. That's what's wrong here.

NICK

I told you what happened. I can't change it. It was an impulsive decision on the day.

SADIE

I can understand an impulsive decision on the day. We can all understand that. But not telling me – that's something you've continued not to do for the three years since it arrived. I don't understand how that can be impulsive. You see my problem.

She stopped and let Nick dangle on this uncomfortable observation. There was something about her strength of utter and deliberate purpose that I just couldn't put my finger on. Nick simply stared at her.

SADIE (cont)

You're appealing now to a kind of superhuman magnanimousness from me as an employee: I have to see that you have the right to do this very ... uh ... very, as I see it, underhanded thing because I represented a threat at that point to the Secretariat if I had gone to America. That's what it boils down to. No matter how you choose to describe it, that boils down to a professional accusation.

Sadie had slowly moved forward in her seat as she had been speaking, as if physically pressing home her attack. Now she sat back like some general waiting for the smoke of a bombardment to clear and reveal the damage done.

NICK

I . . . uh . . . well. I'm sorry you feel like this, Sadie. Obviously
I'm not quite sure what you wanted from this meeting.

But it was pretty clear what Nick wanted and even
expected. He'd do a routine where his tone carried a sense
of the deepest, the most heartfelt regret. There would be
expressions of sorrow but while it might – if you were
willing to go along and let the matter go – be enough so
you could convince yourself he had conceded bad
behaviour on his part, there would be nothing if you read
back what he said that amounted to an apology or even anything close. Despite the strange quality in Sadie that I
couldn't pin down, she showed the ten years of experience
of listening to Nick in her absolute refusal to be placated by
non-apologetic apologizing. We should have a word, I think,
for that (maybe we do) – for expressions of remorse that are
infused with deniability: 'I'm *sorry*,' he unapologized. '*I'm
sorry, too*,' she replied, deregretfully.

NICK (cont)

All I can tell you is that that is the atmosphere in which the
decision was made. I've told you it was an impulsive
decision. I don't think it constituted professional misconduct
because I think the fax belongs to the Secretariat, it doesn't
belong to you.

SADIE

You are not the Secretariat, Nick. You're an employee as
well. It doesn't belong to you either.

There was a faint gasp at this from Nick's neutral
observer, Andrew Taylor. Call Augustus an employee, call
Charlemagne a hireling. Emma Saward's silence was the
result of an unexpected self-discipline. She must have

361

been aching to intervene. Sadie's tenacious violence was simply beyond not only Taylor's experience but his imagination. Her last words had cut deeply and when Nick replied it was with a cold note in his voice I had never heard before.

NICK

I'm not quite sure what you want from this, Sadie.

Despite the angry tension that vibrated from Sadie as something that you could feel on the skin, even she was taken aback by his tone. For the first time there was a note of hesitancy from her.

SADIE

Well I . . . uh . . . I think . . .

NICK

If you'll tell me what you wanted from this meeting . . .

For the first time there was aggression from Nick as he felt the mood in the room shift. Had Sadie realized suddenly the enormity of what she was doing? Was she going to pull back?

SADIE

I'll . . .

[pause]

I'll cool this down a bit . . .

[pause]

What I . . . what I wanted from this was . . . this grievance to be solved in-house. I expected . . . um . . . I think, for you not just to offer an explanation for why you did this and expect me to see it from your point of view.

[pause]

362

I'm sorry. But I don't see it from *your* point of view. This isn't a matter of sorting out differences between us, this is a professional grievance.

As truces go, this was pretty short. The other neutrals, it took no mind-reader to see, were thinking the same.

SADIE (cont)

If you feel you did something wrong, Nick, then you should say that – but I'm not sure from the things you've just said to me that you believe you have. Because it appears to me that there's a residual belief there in your mind that what you did here was absolutely right. But I don't believe in any way that you were right to do what you did.

[pause]

What I want from this meeting. I don't know. I don't know what I want from this meeting. You called this meeting, not me.

NICK

I didn't.

For the first time, Andrew Taylor spoke.

TAYLOR

No . . . uh . . . Walter and I suggested it.

NICK

I . . . Walter said to me that he thought both parties should sit round a table and sort this out. I said yes, so here we are. I didn't call this meeting. I'm responding to what I was asked to do.

TAYLOR

We need to find an answer at this meeting because otherwise you have to go outside the Secretariat, and, with the best will in the world, I'm not sure how this would finish.

Bravo, I thought; Taylor was clearly not as lacklustre as I'd imagined. What a wonderfully disguised threat.

TAYLOR (cont)

So if we can solve it, we should do it.

This sparked off an odd, and considering all that had gone before in the way of fury, even bizarre set of head-noddings and murmurs of assent from both Nick and Sadie. Now suddenly they were acting as if this was a dreadful misunderstanding but they were willing, only too willing, to clear it up. But how utterly meaningless this was emerged in Nick's next words.

NICK

I just don't know what I can say beyond what I've said, now I've told you [pause] the truth. I'm sorry, it doesn't sound like the truth.

It was obvious to Sadie that what this amounted to was another apologetic-sounding unapology.

SADIE

I'm not here to have rows in your office about anything.

(she said rowingly.)

SADIE (cont)

There have to be professional ways, when things like this happen, of dealing with them.

NICK

Yes, of course.

SADIE

I'm not here to throw tantrums. I'm also not here to be

absolutely understanding about the fax. The invitation to America was an extraordinary opportunity for me and not only was it denied me, I wasn't even to be told that it had been denied me.

NICK

We had . . . we had a serious difference. I don't see how we can resolve it . . . uh . . . I mean, I don't quite know what you want from this.

She leant back and breathed in, the fine nostrils on that so beautiful face flaring, like some delicate but powerful mare. Did she know what she wanted? Or was she, despite her relentlessness, afraid to make her demand clear, for after this it could be nothing less, surely? Or was she going to shy away, realizing that the answer, one way or another, would decide something of epic significance?

SADIE

Well, can *you* see any way of resolving it? You appear to say to me that the only way of resolving this is for you to stand by your explanation for ripping up the fax that you've given twice before – that just by repeating yourself somehow I'll see that you couldn't have acted otherwise. If that's your idea of resolving this . . . ?

NICK

I said—

SADIE

Then if that's your idea of resolving this, it can't be resolved—

NICK

I said . . . I said I can't take it back – it happened and I'm sorry.

SADIE

Ah. That's the first time you've said you're sorry.

365

Nick hesitated. There was a watchfulness now from the three observers. Had we come to it? After all this, had we come to it?

NICK

I said I'm sorry before at the last meeting.

We looked at her as she seemed to lengthen that very long neck as if raising her head to look down on him.

SADIE

You didn't say you were sorry. What you said to the examiners at the meeting was: 'I suppose I could have told Sadie at the time but it seemed pointless because she didn't know about it.'

With the exception of Taylor we had all been at the meeting and this was indeed what he'd said. It also clearly did not constitute an apology in the way Nick had claimed or anything remotely like it. He looked awkward and shifted in his seat with a gasp of exasperated, awkward laughter.

NICK

Uh . . . obviously I'm sorry it happened, Sadie. But I can't take back something that was done impulsively. It was not premeditated. It was not an act of malice. In the atmosphere at the time, which was very bad between you and me and the examiners as a whole – I still feel it was the right decision at the time.

At this point, even Taylor had become exasperated at how Nick was always dancing away from the central issue, not realizing, I thought, that this was not a failure of grasp, but a tactic.

TAYLOR

But the point at issue is whether—

NICK

Yes, I realize, whether I should have called her in and told
her about the fax. Yes.

TAYLOR

Yes, that's what it boils down to.

But Nick wasn't a boil down type of guy. He was a
fermenter, he increased and enlarged and suffocated by
proliferation: he used words on you the way snow
avalanches onto Swiss hamlets.

NICK

I'm sure I would in future . . . I would consider it. But at the
time I never even thought about the fax.

SADIE

You'd consider what?

NICK

I . . .

SADIE

You'd consider letting a fax addressed to someone get to the
person it was actually addressed to?

NICK

No . . . I, uh . . . I will always be aware of the issues of the uh
. . . fax arriving and the person knowing about it. I . . . uh . . .
I will never allow that to happen again. It didn't occur to me
at the time, because all I thought at the time was 'Oh Christ,
this is not the time'. That's as far as it went. I didn't think
about destroying the fax, keeping it secret. I just disregarded
it. And I disregarded telling you about it.

I confess that I wanted to have a good chuckle at that
lot. This man was a hoot.

NICK (cont)

I wanted to put the whole thing behind me. It was an appalling week – and it's not a week I'm enjoying reliving. I don't . . . I don't know quite what you want me to say. I can't say any more than that.

SADIE

You *can* say more than that. You seem to have this idea that because tearing up the fax was an impulsive act, as an unthought act—

She gasped in disbelief.

SADIE (cont)

. . . It doesn't change the ethicality of it. I think it's quite a bizarre thing to offer as a reason. I mean, if someone said 'I didn't plan to hit my wife, it was just a sudden impulse,' you wouldn't accept that. It just makes it wrong in a different way.

NICK

I don't think the comparison—

SADIE

It's not a comparison! Look . . .

She sighed again with frustration.

SADIE (cont)

I don't want to be unreasonable about this. I think that an injustice has been done here and I thought this meeting was a way of . . . giving you an opportunity to offer me a form of redress.

Nick looked at her and he was genuinely – and let me stress how deeply genuinely – surprised.

But I've addressed all your grievances.

SADIE

No, you haven't. You've just endlessly repeated your emotional state when you did these things. That's all. You haven't addressed anything.

He dealt with this by pretending, apparently, that he hadn't heard. He gestured at the grievance letter.

NICK

I don't think it's relevant at all what you say in point two – that employees at the BFS can't feel secure the Director will deal with them honestly. I can't think of any other occasion on which there's been any reason to think that.

He looked at Sadie, sadly, artlessly. I could see Emma, eyes wide in astonishment. She did a man's job resisting her clear desire to list his various infamies, chapter and verse. But the thing is that he meant it. This was a man who hadn't fired us but only given us a contract that ended earlier than had been anticipated. The moral high ground was the only terrain he knew. It was then that I realized that in one form or another I was witnessing a fight to the death. Behind Sadie's odd and, mostly, calm tone there was an indignation that was, as my children used to say to express their idea of the unimaginably huge, as big as the road. Nick was fighting for his belief in himself as a decent man, more, a deeply moral man – his life and work depended on this: morality was the beginning and end of what he was. He would never accept Sadie's view of what he'd done. How could he and survive?

SADIE

So, you don't accept the implications—

NICK

I don't think you can generalize – the circumstances were so extraordinary. It's a moment that I [pause] very much regret in the Secretariat's history.

How can I put it across to you? The tone in which he said this, Russian novels of explication would be required to catch the so delicate way in which he wafted the entire blame for this entirely in the direction of Sadie. But it was not Machiavellian, not planned, he was above and below that kind of thing.

NICK (cont)

It certainly won't happen again.

SADIE

We're just going round in circles.

EMMA

I think this is the point of all this – it's about the . . . uh . . . non-showing of the fax. Something that had seriously damaging effects on Sadie's professional reputation.

SADIE

Have you apologized to Professor Bergeron?

NICK

I've told Professor Bergeron that you had no blame in . . . uh . . . not replying.

EMMA

That addresses a very important concern.

SADIE

Yes it does. That's extremely welcome.

EMMA

I think the other difficulty is . . . um . . . some kind of written response about your having not told Sadie about the fax.

370

Taylor sensed that somehow the fog had cleared, that suddenly there was a chance to finish things.

> TAYLOR
> I think what you've said, Nick, is that you did it on the spur of the moment – and so forth. And that you probably wouldn't have done the same thing a week later.
> NICK
> I'm sure I wouldn't. Yes.

This all looked too rosy for my liking. My former faith in the irreconcilable nature of this conflict had suddenly been shaken. Surely they weren't going to patch things up after all this?

> NICK (cont)
> My colleagues would have been cooler at that moment. And as you know, I was not cool.

If one can inwardly groan and scream at the same time, then that's what I was doing. But then suddenly everyone seemed to be becoming if not reasonable then weary perhaps, willing to bodge a way out and let it go.

> TAYLOR
> I'm sorry Sadie, if you feel this was premeditated. Like you, I've heard only recently about the fax. I'm convinced it wasn't a premeditated 'I shall tear it up'. Perhaps I'm biased, I don't know, but I think that's the truth of the matter.

Nick was slightly put out by the implications of this, but aware of its potential for conciliating Sadie, and watchful of her response.

SADIE

The question of premeditation doesn't really arise. What I'm saying is that it was an extreme action to take.

Then it was as if she suddenly saw what was being done to her, what she was colluding in.

SADIE (cont)

Well, later on, now three years later, do you think it was an extreme action to take?

Such a wonderful, polite iciness, all the evasiveness of woolly compromise blasted away. Nick took a deep breath.

NICK

I still think to have told you would have been adding insult to injury.

SADIE

So taking the fax and not telling me was justified to some extent—

NICK

No . . . I . . . uh . . . don't think it was an *extreme* act. A misjudged act . . .

SADIE

Justified to some extent?

NICK

It would have been another blow to you. Relations between us were bad enough then.

Excellent, I thought, *keep telling her that you did it for her sake*.

SADIE

I have to tell you, Nick, that relations are pretty bad now, discovering it three years afterwards.

NICK

All I can do, Sadie, is tell you what happened, tell you the truth. What else can I do? You say now that you would have preferred to know about the fax at the time. But then I didn't believe you would prefer that, I thought it would simply have worked you up again. It was a judgement, perhaps the wrong judgement.

SADIE

I think you're abandoning any kind of ethical judgement on your own actions which is . . . I think, it's quite surprising, Nick, you know. If you can now say to me that under no circumstances was it right to destroy a fax of such importance, personally addressed to me, that you were wrong to do that, then I'd take that as an apology and that would be that. But you're not, you're telling me that you're sorry it happened, not that you were wrong to do it.

NICK

I have to say at the time I never thought of the fax as merely a personal correspondence. It came, the invitation, out of your role as an examiner with the Secretariat. The fax machine is an official piece . . . of Secretariat communication machinery. It came to the Secretariat concerning one of the examiners and through their role as examiner. It wasn't personal correspondence. That was the view I took at the time.

SADIE

Look, I think you now have to see this from my point of view about where this grievance has come from.

NICK

I see it from your point of view now, I didn't then. All I can say is that I'm sorry it happened.

SADIE

If this apology you've given me now is in good faith, if this apology means that you now agree that withholding the fax was entirely wrong, something insupportable even in the, I admit, very difficult circumstances that were happening around it over my conversation with Andrea Dworkin – then I accept that apology. If you write it down and give it to me in a letter and distribute that as a finding of this grievance procedure to all my colleagues I will accept that, and the grievance procedure will be over.

NICK

What do you want me to say?

His reply was more bewildered than aghast, as if he must have misheard.

SADIE

I want you to say that destroying the fax was wrong, that it was unethical behaviour and that it will not happen again. And . . . and unconditionally.

Now he was aghast. Or perhaps it was shock. Certainly his reply was odd.

NICK

I . . . um . . . will certainly say it won't happen again. I'm not going to say I think it was unethical. At the time I didn't think it was.

SADIE

Forget about at the time. What about now?

NICK

Um . . . in retrospect one might think it was the wrong thing to do. But I'm not going to dramatize it into unethical behaviour because . . . because I don't think it is. I really think you're blowing something up into a major thing that isn't a major thing.

[pause]

I think, essentially, it was a very trivial thing.

It was said with deep anger. Oh, how deeply had Sadie's conditions bitten into his soul.

SADIE

Trivial?

They looked at each other. It was as if everyone in the room had stopped breathing.

SADIE (cont)

What I want is an unconditional, brief apology not hedged about with explanations about ... um ... impulsive behaviour and about how, at the time, you felt it was the right thing to do. That would be the one ... the only thing I would find acceptable in these circumstances. I'm sorry you think I've blown this out of all proportion but I haven't. And none of my colleagues I've spoken to think it either. So if you still think this is trivial, then taking out this grievance procedure hasn't actually achieved anything.

Nick said nothing – the longest silence since the meeting began. It was Taylor who spoke and very softly, halfway between a hopeful question and a weary statement.

TAYLOR

But it hasn't concluded.

SADIE

No, it hasn't concluded.

So, since you asked me what I wanted so wearily as if the answer was utterly mysterious – well, now it's clear: an unconditional written apology for hiding the fax.

Nick stared at her, but I couldn't be sure what was in his expression, in his eyes – a deep and burning resentment that I couldn't put my finger on.

TAYLOR

We'll . . . uh . . . have to think about it, of course.

It was then, for the first time, Nick looked at me directly.

NICK

When will you be able to provide us with the minutes of this meeting?

'I could give it to you verbatim the day after tomorrow,' I said.

'Yes,' replied Nick, as flatly as you like. 'That would be best.'

'Could I have a copy?' asked Sadie, but surprisingly not in the tone of the incensed and resolute, but of a nervous girl. Nick just looked at her. It was Taylor who replied, 'We'll get you a copy as soon as it's done.' He looked at me, smiling wearily. 'Is that all right?' I nodded.

Sadie and Emma stood up. There was an excruciating moment of silence. 'Thank you,' she said. It was as weirdly inappropriate as the thank-you we used to be obliged to offer at my school when the headmaster had beaten us. That's just what it sounded like only much odder because it was Sadie who had been handing out the punishment.

Then she turned and left, Emma following. When they

were gone, Nick didn't say anything. He stared at the door and then started looking at his papers.

'I'll get on with this,' I said. He did not look at me, just gave a slight nod.

As I left his office, Taylor called out politely: 'Would you mind closing the door?'

I pulled it behind me and, my head swimming, I made my way back to my cubicle.

Rage

THE FOLLOWING TWO DAYS spent writing out my Pitman's shorthand account of the meeting were, quite possibly, the happiest of my life. All those moments where at the time I was terrified that agreement might, in the face of everything, be reached, I could now enjoy as a child approaches the scenes on video that on first viewing were most terrifying to him, content in the knowledge that everything will be wonderfully all right.

I had it back to Nick as promised. Within hours he had written his letter to Sadie and by the next morning it was making Sadie choke on her cornflakes. By the end of the day all the examiners had read it too and there was a firestorm brewing. You will have got Nick's style down yourselves by now: ... *the decision not to give you the fax was a management decision ... sorry you have been led to feel ... Nothing leads me to believe ... wrong at that time ... job of management to manage ... sleeping dogs lie ... not to exacerbate the tension between us.*

The heart of it was this, however:

I am unreservedly sorry that these events should have led

to a sense of grievance but I do not accept this was
due to any unethical conduct on my part.
   I shall await your reply.
   Nicholas Berg
   Director

I was particularly delighted, I have to say, that in reply
to Sadie's demand that he apologize unreservedly Nick
had written that he was unreservedly sorry that Sadie felt
he had something to apologize for. But there was better to
come. In the same envelope Nick also included his letter
to Professor Bergeron, a letter he had promised would
explain Sadie's failure to reply to her most generous offer.
The letter opened with an explanation of who he was
and then a lengthy encomium of praise to her recently
published book, *The Seeing I – Woman and the Male Gaze*.
He hoped that if she were ever to visit England they would
have a chance to meet and discuss matters of mutual
interest and added that he and the Secretariat were particularly eager to take on board feminist perspectives. Only
after two fulsome pages of this stuff did we get to the sting.

Some three years ago you sent an invitation, via my
office, to one of my staff. At the time it arrived certain
difficulties had arisen at the Secretariat which led me to
conclude that it would be better not to pass the invitation
on to her. Those difficulties have since been resolved and
I'm very sorry if you were in any way inconvenienced by
them, but I felt it right you should know that no blame
should attach to Sadie Boldon for not replying.
   I hope, once again, that we have a chance to meet and
discuss our mutual interests.
Yours sincerely,
   Nicholas Berg
   Director

At 6.30 p.m. on the same day, Sadie, Tom, Rob McCarthy and Emma Saward were having a drink in Quo Vadis on Dean Street and discussing the two letters. Sadie Boldon was seething and you must think of this literally as if her soul was spitting with anger. She had already had two brandies and her eyes were slightly glazed.

'Did he really imagine,' Emma was saying, 'that this would do, that just by using the words "unreservedly apologize" in a sentence, that we'd somehow think he'd done as he was asked?'

'What do you want to do?' Farraday was speaking softly to Sadie, his tone more worried than angry.

She looked at him, puzzled. 'I'm going back to the grievance procedure. Not only has that bastard not apologized, the letter to Professor Bergeron makes me look as if he couldn't bring himself to tell her what villainy I'd been up to. That was deliberate.'

For a moment there was silence. Finally it was an unusually hesitant McCarthy who spoke up. 'Emma was telling me that Andrew Taylor was saying that once the grievance procedure went to the next stage it would go outside the Secretariat for the first time, and that there was no telling where it would lead from there.'

'He was just trying, in his creepy I'm-just-an-administrator-and-quite-objective way to frighten me.'

'Possibly,' said McCarthy. 'Probably.'

'Certainly,' said Emma.

'OK, but that doesn't stop him from being right.'

'Are you saying I should let it go at this?' Sadie shook the letters at McCarthy with all the aggression of a poke in the chest.

'I know you're not going to do that,' replied McCarthy softly.

'But you think I should?'

'What I think is that Nick has behaved incredibly badly. I think you're in the right. The question is whether or not you accept he's never going to give you the kind of apology you want.'

'So you are saying I should give in?'

'No, what I'm doing, what I'm proposing depends on whether you'll accept something more than that.' He nodded at the letters. 'But less than you asked for.'

'No,' she said.

Farraday shifted awkwardly in his seat. 'It won't do any harm to listen.'

She stared at her lover, cold and angry. McCarthy took the chance.

'Nick and I have always got on reasonably well. I was on holiday when the examiners signed the letter calling on him to apologize.'

'Are you saying you wouldn't have signed it if you'd been here?' asked Emma.

'No. I'm not saying that. And I don't want to keep repeating that Nick's in the wrong here. What I am saying is that it might be possible to get him to write something more like a real apology – a compromise obviously.' He turned to Sadie. 'If that's something you'd be prepared to consider.'

Sadie's mood had changed, something cold had entered her eyes. 'I don't know whether you mean well, Rob, or you're just being glib and patronizing as if I'm some stroppy girl having a hissy fit and you're going to rescue me from myself. But I tried to find a compromise and there wasn't one. Nick didn't change his approach at any time. He was rather brilliant really. It was exactly the same at the start as it was at the end. The only way he can be made to put this right is to be *made* to. Forced. So I either give in or see it out to the end. But you have no right to condescend to me. Do you understand?'

'Look, Sadie . . .' It was an awkward Farraday who tried to intervene on behalf of his friend.

'Don't.' It was so fierce, so uncompromising that Farraday was silenced, as much by shock as by fear. And fear had been growing in his heart steadily, day by day. She looked back at McCarthy. 'Do you understand?'

McCarthy stood up. 'Absolutely.' He put his chair under the table and nodded at Farraday. 'I'll talk to you tomorrow.'

'Not about me,' said Sadie.

McCarthy leant forward. 'I wouldn't dare.' Then he walked out.

The two of them did indeed meet the next day although they did not obey Sadie's demand.

'You know something?' said Farraday, as they ate lunch in Lisle Street Poons. 'I lied to her about meeting you. I said I had to meet a cousin of mine.'

'Did she believe you?'

'This is crazy. You know what I feel like? One of those women who's terrified they're going to be beaten up by their husbands if they're in a bad mood. Me?' he said, incredulous. 'I'm ashamed to say that part of me is afraid of her. You wouldn't believe such a little body could contain so much rage.'

'I think I could actually.'

'You see, I can't talk to her about it. It's as if she's certain I'm . . . I don't believe in what she's doing.'

'And do you?'

'Yes. Absolutely. I think that cunt Berg has behaved like a cunt. But I'm afraid about what's going to happen. But it's like she's certain I don't . . . She thinks I don't believe in her. That this is a test of how much I love her. But I'm failing, no matter what I say, I'm failing this test of hers.

And all it's really about is fear. I'm afraid for what will happen to her and now I'm afraid about what will happen to me. You see it really is like these battered women. I can't believe it, if I protest I know she'll stop loving me. And I just can't bear that. Is that pathetic or what?'

'I've never loved anyone that much, so I wouldn't know.'

'All last night she was silently daring me to say something in defence of you. And I didn't. I didn't have the courage to tell her that you had a point worth making – even if I didn't agree.'

McCarthy looked at him, shocked. 'Hold on, are you saying you love Sadie more than you love me?'

'Ah, manly humour,' replied Farraday ruefully. 'You know what, I've been unmanned. But apparently I'll put up with it. The thing is I thought I knew her. But obviously I don't, because I don't understand what's going on and I can't get her to talk about it.' He laughed, but not happily. 'I've turned into a girl.'

Torment

Sadie Boldon & Emma Saward
British Film Secretariat
8 Golden Square
London
W1F 9HT
10th June 1994

The Director
British Film Secretariat
8 Golden Square
London
W1F 9HT

Dear Nick,

GRIEVANCE PROCEDURE

Thank you for your letter of 8th June.

Unfortunately the primary reason the grievance procedure was activated has not been addressed. You have clearly not seen the necessity for making the simple unqualified apology for withholding the fax and keeping it a secret for three years that we offered as a solution.

As a result, the next phase of the grievance procedure, Stage 5, will now have to be instituted.

Yours sincerely,

Emma Saward   Sadie Boldon
MSF Representative   Examiner

384

At the end of the same day as he'd had his confessional lunch with McCarthy, Farraday had gone looking for Sadie. She was in none of the places he would usually expect to find her in what, for all the modernizations imposed by Nick, was still a warren of a building. He was beginning to think that she had gone home and his poor heart felt the full wretchedness of a lover seeing a great passion leaking through his fingers and no way of stopping it. Finally, he searched the old, still unmodified top floor and there she was in a small room filled with broken chairs. She looked up as he came in, her eyes wide as if filled with innocence, and smiling. It was not her usual smile, not least because it froze his heart, as did the wide-eyed innocence of her general expression. It froze it with terror. Someone who did not know her, who did not know that this look had never before appeared on her beautiful face, would have found it pleasing. It reminded him when he thought about it many years later of the expression on the face of the Mona Lisa. It is not generally thought that an expression of intense hatred could be enigmatic but Farraday, from that moment, knew better.

'Do you have time for a drink?' He could hear the fearful politeness in his voice. A tone he had never heard before, at least not from himself.

'I have to get back early today.' Although this sounded like an excuse to be away from him, he knew it to be true. She was going on a short business trip with her husband until the end of the following week. He would not see her again until next Friday.

Part of him wanted to shout at her, to wound as he felt himself to be wounded. Part of him wanted to get on his knees and whine, to beg her to love him again. Be sympathetic to the wretched state in which he found himself. Any love has its rhythms, its periods of greater and lesser intensity, and everyone has rows, sometimes of the burning and blazing kind. Everyone has felt a flush of hatred, if only momentary, for someone they love. Rages between lovers of even the most intense kind can be over after a few minutes of petting and making up and being sorry; and the love between them can be the stronger for it. But whatever was going on in Sadie was nothing of that kind and Farraday could sense its strangeness and its horrible intensity.

'Why are you so angry with me?' he asked.

The same frightening look of ungraspable emotion returned to her face. The slightly too wide eyes and the terrible smile.

'I don't know what you mean.' The coldness of it; like falling into an arctic swell. She stared at him and the smile widened as if he was someone for whom she felt only the deepest disdain, as if having finally seen through him all that remained was an amused disgust.

But I haven't done anything, he thought, if thoughts can scream. But he said nothing and turned and left the room. As for Sadie, she watched the door close with the same look on her face and then turned back to her work, her heart and soul rioting with confusion, fear and hatred.

The following Friday, Farraday arrived early at the Secretariat hoping that she would do the same. But she arrived last of all to morning prayers and hung at the back, disappearing to the appointed viewing room as soon as the meeting finished.

She was never out of his thoughts. Who knows what censorial improprieties slipped past him over the next few days as a result of his distracted state of mind, particularly if he was working with some of his more careless colleagues? But forgive him, dear Reader, if you can. What is a profanity here, the sight of an errant nipple there, to a man living in hell itself?

Curiously enough, it was during one of the few moments when he was not directly thinking about Sadie that he encountered her and I use the word carefully. He was looking for somewhere to write his reports so he could avoid the maddening blather of an even more than usually loquacious Katie Ohashi, high, no doubt, on some whiz or bang or whatever it was she so frequently hoovered up her nose (horse stimulant probably or something used to lighten the mood of depressed elephants). Opening the door of the little-used viewing room 12, unpopular because it had no windows and the air-conditioning, for some never resolved reason, frequently dumped all the stale air from the rest of the building into its already foetid atmosphere. To his shock he was faced with three people: Emma, Jaan Mohammed, the union executive, and Sadie. The first two looked at him merely irritated at the interruption, Sadie as if hardly taking him in. But for the first time in weeks he at least recognized the expression on her face: straightforward, human, exhausted disappointment.

'Sorry,' he said, and backed out of the room.

Of course from my point of view all this was simmering along in a manner I could only regard as exceptional. I had always had to work hard for success at anything I'd ever done. There was always a clear relationship between the small victories of my life and the amount of effort I put into them; so much so that it never really occurred to me that this might not be the case. But already with the business over Sadie and the fax I had experienced the pleasure of discovering what it was like for things just to fall into place. And now, in the most unexpected way, I was to feel this even more intensely.

My wife had come into town for something to do with her work and we had met up at seven and gone for dinner at The Red Fort.

She was a pleasant woman, my wife, and I realized that I had almost certainly loved her once. Now I didn't feel anything about her nor about my children, neither like nor dislike. Such feelings as I had were entirely wrapped up in my involvement with Sadie's downfall.

'How's all that going?' she asked me over her chicken korma.

'Pretty badly. You can cut the atmosphere with a knife these days.'

'I can't imagine what she thinks she's going to get out of it. She needs a good shake, in my opinion.'

This was said with a look of mild defiance. She had conceived a dislike of Sadie based upon all of five minutes' worth of conversation. I have to say that I can't for the life of me see why. I was present during the entire exchange in which Sadie had been as charming and open as she always was, or used to be. I suspect that my wife imagined that I had some sort of crush on Sadie. Nothing else could explain her hostility. At any rate, I drew in a deep breath as if considering what she'd said.

'Perhaps – but if your boss had torn up a letter addressed to you offering you the chance of a lifetime would you be so sanguine?'

'Probably not. But I wouldn't bring an official grievance against him. Where on earth did she think that was going to go?'

'Quite so. Where indeed?'

Leaving the restaurant we cut across Soho heading for Oxford Circus. By now it was just after nine. That was when I saw him as he crossed over in front of us about twenty yards away. He hadn't seen us because he wasn't looking in our direction but walking with a great sense of purpose towards some distant objective. Then he turned suddenly, or rather darted, into a grubby doorway, open as so many on-street doors in Soho were for easy public access.

Despite my astonishment at seeing Nick Berg vanish into such a place, I said nothing to my wife. But all the way home I marvelled at how life was effortlessly flowing towards me.

Needless to say on my way to work the next morning I revisited the scene to satisfy more than just my curiosity. The hall and stairs were dark and greasy; things crunched lightly underfoot. The locked doors on the first two floors gave nothing away. On the third was a bucket shop and a seamstress shop that presumably served the nearby fashion houses. On the fourth, again there was nothing but the anonymous peeling doors in a horrible catarrh colour; but on the top floor there was a small card outside one of them, printed and incongruously elegant with a finely drawn whip curled around the letters:

MISTRESS TORMENT
SWEET SUFFERING

I don't deny that during my walk to the Secretariat I felt a twinge of disapproval, not of Nick Berg, but of myself. I was wondering, of course, how all this might be useful and because of that feeling rather sordid. Nevertheless, I could hardly ignore what power my discovery had placed in my hands and by the time I got to work my thoughts were only for how I might possibly get a picture of him entering the building at night without using a flashbulb.

Within a few days it was not my conscience that was

making me reconsider doing anything about Nick's nocturnal visit so much as the practicalities. I owned a fairly good camera and was reasonably good with it, but I doubted my ability to take a photograph of him without being seen. After all I had ceased to bear a grudge against Nick Berg because it was now definitely in my interests for him to stay at the Secretariat. He trusted me. The chances were I'd never need to use such a photograph. So why risk taking it? I was staring out of the window and brooding about this when who should I see leaving the building at 11 o'clock in the morning but Nick himself. In nearly ten years I had never seen him leave the Secretariat during the day except for important meetings when he would be picked up by his chauffeur-driven car. Once he came in to work at 10.30 a.m. or so that was it: Nick stayed.

I had my camera under my coat. I was down the stairs like a shot. I walked as quickly as I could away from the Secretariat.

And once I was out of sight of the building I ran like hell the length of Beak Street in the hope that he was heading for some sweet pain and finally caught sight of him heading up Poland Street for the hovel in D'Arblay Street. In order to find a place from which to photograph him, an idea that seemed more and more ludicrous every second, I had to race up Berwick Sreet and head him off from the other direction.

Unfortunately I was no longer very fit. By the time I got into position I wasn't so much breathless as half-dead, the air rasping from my throat so loudly that several passers-by looked at me with the alarm only an English face can exhibit at the thought he might be forced to help a sick man in the street. One kinder soul even asked me if I was all right. I nodded because I couldn't speak. Gasping and shaking with the unaccustomed activity I eased my head around the corner. Nick was nowhere to be seen. I moved my head back and tried to get my breath, red-faced and sweaty. I felt bloody awful as well as bloody stupid but again I eased my head around the building. Still no Berg. And then there he was. The same stride as if he were heading purposefully somewhere far distant. I pulled out the camera from my pocket, took aim and kept on pressing as he again turned suddenly and headed into the abyss of the Soho tart's doorway.

Then I knelt down and started retching like a dog.

No Way Out

Sadie Boldon
118 Walm Lane
London NW2 4QY
23rd June 1994

Andrew Taylor
Head of Administration
British Film Secretariat
8 Golden Square
London W1F 9HT

Dear Andrew,

<u>Grievance Procedure</u>

After speaking this afternoon with the MSF Union Representative about my intention to begin the next stage of the Grievance Procedure, I have discovered that, through no fault of anyone concerned, stage 6 cannot take place for another three months.

This procedure has already, and entirely unnecessarily in my view, cost me a great deal of personal unhappiness. The discovery that this will blight at least another three months of my life I find impossible to endure and I wish you to accept this letter as a termination of the Grievance Procedure.

I want to make it clear, however, that I stand by my view

that the Director's behaviour was unethical and that this
whole matter could have been solved by an unreserved
apology.
Yours sincerely,
  Sadie Boldon

BRITISH FILM SECRETARIAT
8 GOLDEN SQUARE, LONDON, W1F 9HT

28 June 1994

Sadie Boldon
118 Walm Lane
London NW2 4QY

Dear Sadie,

I am replying on behalf of the Secretariat to your letter
which was put on my desk at lunchtime today.

It is not ethical nor is it possible for you to unilaterally
withdraw from the Grievance Procedure while apparently
pursuing your grievance by other means. Having made
public a number of accusations against the Director you
have only two choices: either to let the procedure run its
course or agree to withdraw unreservedly all the
allegations made concerning him.

Unless and until you do so, the Secretariat must insist
the procedure continues to stage 6 and if necessary there-
after to legal proceedings in which the Secretariat intends
to be fully legally represented.
Yours sincerely,
  Andrew Taylor
  For and on behalf of the British Film Secretariat

Although I happened to be present at the discussions that led to the composition of this last letter, anyone with enough experience of Nick Berg could have told you that he was its author. The wonderful, one might even say poetic, echoing of the terms 'unreserved apology' and 'unethical' so precisely went to the very epicentre of Nick's profound fury that it could not have been written by anyone else. When Sadie had demanded an unreserved apology admitting his unethical behaviour to the wide world she might as well have asked for his heart on a platter still warm and beating from his breast. But as you can see if he was not going to give an apology for his lack of ethicality, he was very determined to get one. The interesting thing to consider, I thought, as I happily realized that this business was not just going to end at Sadie's say-so, was how far he was ready to go in pursuit of what he wanted.

The following day was what the examiners always referred to as a Secretariat meeting but Nick and his management team with equal consistency now called the Examiners' meeting. For myself, I took the politically important decision to call it by whatever name my interlocutor at the time happened to require.

The mood of the meeting that following day can be easily imagined. I had not myself given much thought to the morality of Nick's actions, but there was much, perfectly righteous, indignation about what Nick had done. You must remember what a favourite Sadie was. No doubt you see her in a different light after this recent business and the strange way in which she had come to regard her blameless lover. In time, everyone came to regard her differently. But then the admiration for her so lightly worn abilities and her good nature was unclouded. With the exception of one or two who avoided the meeting by dint of diplomatic colds, support for her was solid. Of course, all this good stuff was followed by malice towards, resentment of, irritation with, and a desire for revenge on Nick Berg. But the same, of course, was true of Nick. The meeting was orchestrated throughout to the music of old scores being settled.

Nick needed a crisis in order for life to have any flavour. He had rescued the Secretariat from an assault on all sides, from financial collapse, mockery and disdain. You have to understand that he felt himself to be the defender of the rape victim and the abused child. Not for him the weak and piping voice of a bureaucracy, with its rules and checks and balances, its review committees constraining his arm as he attempted to hold back the power of the human imagination at its worst.

But the world was changing: what had seemed so strange only a decade before (a video recorder *in the home*!) was now commonplace. The more rancid of the works that gave society the willies had vanished and no one was making them any more because even the cheapest film cost too much. Nobody wanted exploitation films, cack-handed, unconvincing, inept. The public's growing taste for high production values had crippled the losers who mostly made these films. After the Bulger case, no one blamed videos any more. I'm not sure why. Perhaps it was no more complicated than the fact that everyone got used to it. There were four channels on TV in 1984. By 1992 if you had Rupert Murdoch's Sky you could watch a hundred. That was why Alexander wept when there were no more battles to be fought. Alexander, of course, compensated for this lack by fighting with the people around him.

The meeting began with Emma, as the Union Representative, reading out a response from the examiners to Andrew Taylor's reply to Sadie rejecting her decision to drop the grievance and calling for an unequivocal apology.

' ". . . we unanimously reject the claim in this letter that the Examiners' continuing deep disquiet about the Director's unethical behaviour in this matter constitutes the pursuance of Sadie Boldon's action by other means. Our collective views expressed in the letter sent to you after our last meeting and describing the Director's actions in destroying the fax from Professor Bergeron as unethical are entirely independent of this procedure and are based on the facts relating to these events which are not in dispute." '

There was the 'U' word again, I thought, like a tennis ball flying back and forth across the field of play. For once Nick's reply was abrupt and to the point.

'I've explained my position and I have nothing to add. I am the Director of this organization and I will manage it as I see fit.'

Sadie made two mistakes then; one was in speaking at all. Her colleagues were of one mind, and a bloody mind at that. There would have been many voices raised in her defence. She should have said nothing. But that error was nothing compared to her second mistake. This one was fatal.

'I want to make it quite clear,' she said, intense, pale for all her black skin, 'that the Director of this organization is professionally dishonest, lacks integrity and in destroying the fax was motivated entirely by malice. I, for one, no longer have any trust in him as Chief Executive of the Secretariat even in classification matters.'

That Nick should have been silenced by this was to be expected. But of course it silenced the examiners as well. They were shocked. They had themselves brought knives to the table but now someone had produced a loaded gun.

Nick looked at Walter and then back at the rest of the room.

'This meeting is at an end.'

And with that, he stood up and left, leaving behind an astonished room.

The Odd Couple

You shall find out how salt is the taste of another man's bread, and how hard is the way up and down another man's stairs.

Dante, *The Divine Comedy*, xvii, 58

THE MEETING NICK LEFT behind was almost completely silent bar a few muttered asides that I could not hear, but whose tone was clear enough. Walter Casey stood up, his face black, and with barely disguised fury made an announcement. 'Because the meeting has been cancelled there will be viewings for the rest of the day. They'll be sent down to this room in half an hour.'

Then he too left, and actually slammed the door. I doubted whether the wait for the videos was entirely necessary. I had seen a number of the thick transparent plastic envelopes, in which the day's work always came, hidden clumsily on a table at the back of his office. Of course it would have looked bad if they had been sent down immediately, as if this eventuality had been planned for. Understand me, I don't mean to say that either Nick's or Walter's anger was in any way insincere, only to point out that things had got so bad at the

Secretariat that the chance of the meeting reaching its natural conclusion had not been very high. But it was not the two angry walk-outs that had produced such an unaccustomed hush among the examiners; it was Sadie's outburst. In a few seconds she had, in effect, declared a kind of war: things had well and truly got out of control and it was easy to sense the confusion about whether this had really happened. Some were alarmed (Katie Ohashi had gone white) and there was something new: an exasperation, an irritation with Sadie herself. It was Emma Saward who spoke first. She looked at me and Allan Rhys who was sitting next but one.

'I hope they'll understand,' she said, 'but I think that Duncan and Allan's presence is a problem. Given what's happened, any discussions we have – it puts them and us in an awkward position.'

Allan I could see was positively relieved at being ejected; there would be no chance that Nick would suspect him of sympathizing. I, however, wanted to see as much of the drama I had set in motion as possible, and I was irritated at being excluded from so great an opportunity to bask in the fall-out of such a massive amount of unpleasantness. I looked around the room in a dignified-but-hurt manner and seemed to be assessing the mood of my former colleagues (for that was how I thought of the fractious cunts). I stood up.

'I can see that you all agree. I'm sorry that should be the case.' I pushed my chair back and slowly left, enjoying the little bit of guilt I left behind.

On my way upstairs I comforted myself with the knowledge, from the frightened look on her face, that there was one person who would tell me everything about the meeting I needed to know.

I was pretty sure that Katie would spill about what

happened in the meeting, and so it proved. All it took was some oily reassurance that I would, in complete confidentiality, pass on her support for Nick and I had as full an account of the discussions after I left as you could expect from an airhead addicted to ketamine.

As I've suggested, Katie was not without a certain craftiness and it was clear from her account that the meeting had been an uneasy one. No one had been happy with Sadie's outburst. Whatever their sympathies for her and their anger with Nick, they were alarmed by the way she had escalated the row, already poisonous enough. Ready to support her without much reservation on the business of the fax, it was something else entirely to mount an attack on every aspect of his personality and competence. Sadie had taken this reservation badly and her response was a thinly veiled criticism of those who she apparently implied were using what had happened as an opportunity to back away from supporting her.

Emma had tried her best to smooth over the damage and so had Farraday. He had calmly, considering he must have been in a ferment of fear and worry, attempted to argue that Nick had deliberately tried to provoke Sadie into criticizing him. But still it did him no good; even Katie was surprised at the coldness with which Sadie responded to this. I would have liked, oh so very much, to have an account of her exact words as she cut even deeper into her lover's devoted heart but that would have been too much to expect of Katie. She was already exhausted at the effort involved in putting together so many coherent sentences.

It turned out what was really worrying her was that Emma had succeeded in persuading everyone to sign a letter to Nick. Katie, reasonably enough, had been too scared to be the only one not to put her name to it. What frightened her now was that Nick would be angry with her and withdraw the support she knew was always hers, no matter how often she made a mess of things.

Of course I soothed her, telling her I would make her real feelings known to Nick and explain why she had signed the letter. For a moment it occurred to me not to say anything to Nick about Katie, but I felt ashamed of myself for having such a petty and spiteful thought, ashamed notwithstanding the fact that I despised Katie for her stupidity and incompetence. But I had given my word and so frightened was she by what she had done in signing the letter that I even felt sorry for her: it can't be easy for the foolish and inadequate, living with the terror they must sometimes feel in the face of a world that is always on the brink of finding them out. Besides, telling Nick about her remorse would not only hearten him but create the impression I was a man with his finger on the pulse.

Katie was looking at me in a highly nervous state. She signalled this agitation with a tic I had noticed before: by pulling her tights up. First she rolled up the nylon on the thigh of one leg, then the other, almost but not quite displaying her underwear. Was this an erotic sight? I don't know why but not really – which was odd in that she was rather a pretty girl if you like them small and skinny.

'Thanks, Katie, you've been very helpful.'

With that she left and I was able to consider more carefully the implication of the events of that day. I wondered if Sadie realized how the angry assault she had made on Nick at the meeting had changed things. I was confident she was not only smart enough to see it, but sufficiently paranoid to regard it as a betrayal.

Perhaps you have seen one of those nature programmes about the squid, how when it's threatened it displays an endlessly shifting ripple of colours along its body. If you could have looked at Thomas Farraday's soul perhaps you would have seen something similar as his benighted psyche flashed and undulated with all the colours that our emotions have – green resentment, violet love, red anger, pale blue longing, white fear, purple passion, grey pity, black hatred, all of it moiling and pulsating and all of it tainted by incomprehension (perhaps it's not an emotion, incomprehension, and therefore has no colour but I'm sure you take my point). So it was a spooked and uneasy Farraday who wandered through the building after he had finished four hours' solo viewing of an early Jerry Lewis comedy and eight episodes of *Thundercats*. No matter what feelings dominated, there was always a base note, always the same simple hope that he would come upon her and she would look at him with anxious remorse and tell him, 'It's all a terrible mistake. I've come back to you.'

His considerable intelligence and strength of character, a natural confidence borne up by always being able to succeed at whatever he chose to do – none of it helped, none of it gave him the power to walk away. It was true love, you see.

The only person he met, at least the only one other than Sadie he could bear to talk to, was McCarthy. He was finishing his last report having spent the afternoon watching music videos. The first had been a two-hour concert by Gwar, all elephant-sized dildos and puppeteer buggery, the second by The Dead Kennedys, whose set had opened with the immortal 'Nazi Punks Fuck Off' which had therefore done his work for him and allowed him to devote his attention to that morning's events.

'Hi,' said Farraday.

'Hi.'

Farraday sat down and looked at his friend, at once

402

awkward and expectant, hoping that he would say something that would make the events of the day seem less ominous.

'So, what do you think?' Farraday prompted.

'Honestly?'

'As bad as that?'

'I'm afraid so.'

'Can you blame her for losing her temper?'

McCarthy looked at his friend, sorry at the plain look of misery and loss on his face. 'I don't know about blame, Tom, but she blew everything. You know that as well as I do.'

'Not if we back her completely. If we support her – really get behind her. He can't take on all of us.'

'That's not going to happen. If they—' He paused. 'If we back what she said about not being able to trust his decisions about film and videos, this all moves to a level where it's either Nick who goes or us. Nobody agreed to go that far. Sadie didn't ask anyone. She just went for broke.'

'If we hold our nerve it will work out,' said Farraday. 'We'll find a compromise. Things will calm down.' He did not sound very convinced.

'Perhaps. But Sadie is asking these people to put their working lives on the line. We're talking about a poisonous battle that will last months and that, in my opinion, is inevitably going to end badly for us. The people who decide whether Nick goes or not, they like Nick. They either don't know us or if they do, like the President and Vice President, they can't stand us. You seriously think they're going to fire Nick because a band of stroppy nobodies think they should?'

'It'll look pretty bad for the Secretariat if this gets out.'

'It will make people laugh. Censors on strike! Give me a break. Nobody cares.'

403

'You think it's all right to abandon her?'

'I know that's what Sadie thinks but I'm surprised at you. No matter what you feel about her. She withdrew from the grievance because she couldn't bear it going on for a few more weeks. Now she wants to take Nick down and she doesn't much care apparently if she takes us with her. She had everyone behind her and she threw that away.'

'Not everyone was behind her.'

'I take it you mean me.'

'Isn't it true?'

'OK, it's true. I think it's a bad idea for someone to take their boss through an official procedure to force him to admit he's behaved unethically and to apologize to her in front of all his employees. I mean, what did she expect? That he'd do it? Or that even if he did, it would be possible for her to carry on working here? Couldn't she see that Nick would have to destroy her because he couldn't live with himself if he admitted to something like that?'

'Even if it's true?'

'Especially if it's true. Of course he behaved badly. But she should have told him so and left it at that. That's all the satisfaction she was ever going to get.'

'And of course you knew all along?'

'I had a pretty good idea, yes.' McCarthy sighed and smiled at his friend. 'If you hadn't loved her so much you'd have told her the same.'

'Then it's my fault?'

'She wasn't listening, not even to you.'

He groaned, pained and agitated. 'Especially not to me. And the thing is I have no idea. I just don't understand. She actually hates me. Do you know what that's like, to love someone who used to love you and now they hate you?'

'Look,' said McCarthy. 'She'll come round. She's got so much talent, she'll find a job somewhere else. It's time to get out of here anyway. She needs to get out of this place. If she'll listen, that's the one thing you need to get her to do.'

Farraday looked at him.

'But she won't listen.'

Straw Dogs

BRITISH FILM SECRETARIAT
8 GOLDEN SQUARE, LONDON, W1F 9HT

30 June 1994

Sadie Boldon
118 Walm Lane
London NW2 4QY

Dear Sadie,
Although your right to pursue your grievance is not in question, your comments at yesterday's examiners' meeting were seriously damaging to the Secretariat.

You publicly alleged that the Director of this organization was professionally dishonest, lacking in integrity and motivated by malice. You stated, unequivocally, that you could have no trust in him as the Chief Executive, even in classification matters. In doing so you sought to extend a dispute from which you had officially withdrawn with the clear intention of escalating matters far removed from the scope of your grievance and, furthermore, to involve the entire examining body in this extended and entirely unjustified dispute.

If it is your intention to remain at the Secretariat, we shall expect you to withdraw, without reservation, all these defamatory remarks and to apologize in writing. This written apology must be delivered within one week after which it will be displayed on the examiners' notice board for a period of one month. In this letter you will also undertake to refrain in future from indulging in this kind of conduct. Any future lapse will result in your being summarily dismissed.

While you are considering your position we do not believe you should attend the Secretariat's offices and you are therefore suspended from duty for the next week. A meeting has been arranged for you in my office on the 8th of next month at which time you will either resign or sign a letter which has been drafted for this purpose.

Yours sincerely,

Nicholas Berg
Director

The day after the meeting arranged by Nick at which Sadie had given her decision, I made my way down to the examiners' floor and pinned the following letter from Sadie Boldon on the notice board.

9th July 1994
Nicholas Berg
Director
BFS

Dear Nick,
Following our meeting yesterday in the presence of Walter Casey and Emma Saward I would like to make the following statement:

407

29th of June Examiners' meeting I suggested, in the
   he moment, that certain actions taken by the
   , Nicholas Berg, on which I subsequently based my
   nce Procedure, were motivated by malice. I do not
believe that to be true and on reflection I know that I should
have withdrawn it and had it struck from the minutes. I also,
at that meeting, impugned the Director's integrity and
professionalism by stating that I could have no trust in him,
even in classification matters. I was wrong to make these
statements and I withdraw them completely and without
reservation.

    I apologize for having made such damaging and unjustified
remarks and accept they are completely without foundation. I
also apologize for the damage done to staff relations as a
result of my behaviour.

Yours sincerely,

   Sadie Boldon

The style of this apology, of course, bore no relation to
the way that Sadie wrote, something we had all been
familiar with for the last ten years. In this regard, I particularly liked the use of the word 'impugn'. The sheer
impossibility of her ever using this ludicrous word made
her humiliation all the worse, though it has to be said that
for Nick Berg no other word would have done.

    Beneath it I pinned a second notice.

Examiners

With the delivery and acceptance of the apology above
from Sadie Boldon, her suspension from duty was lifted,
as from today (10 July).

The interesting questions raised by all of this were why
Sadie didn't resign and why Nick didn't just fire her there

and then for gross misconduct. I wasn't quite sure whether at the last moment with his opponent so profoundly defeated he was insufficiently vindictive to deliver a killing blow, or whether the humiliation involved in her staying was evidence of an even deeper malice, revenge being a dish best eaten cold and all that. As for Sadie's disintegration (and how could it be defined as anything else?) I had, I think, a better sense of the paradox involved in the way she had behaved.

You have to remember that Sadie was a self-made woman. Nearly all the examiners, to varying degrees, were middle-class. They had parents who were well educated or at least believed in the importance of education and were prepared to push their children so that they received a good start in life. It varied, of course, but the teachers they came in contact with were sometimes excellent and only rarely less than competent. They had encouragement from all sides, expectations to fulfil and space given to them in which to succeed.

Sadie had almost none of this. Her parents were poor immigrants and did not speak English well. They had ended up in a city where there was no Coptic community that might support them. As a result they were utterly perplexed by how the systems they encountered truly worked. The house they lived in was a damp, decaying wreck along with all the other houses in the area. The school that served it, St Edmund's Primary, was no better: the teachers inadequate, the discipline non-existent. When she was eight Sadie had a stroke of luck: a temporary teacher arrived who was both skilled and intelligent. She instantly recognized Sadie's ability and was appalled to discover that she could not read. Sadie learnt to do so in under four weeks. The teacher left, worn out in less than three months by the relentlessly exhausting effort involved in just getting through the day in a school where the pupils spoke more than fourteen languages between them and where hardly anybody gave a damn. But she left Sadie with this one great gift. Unable to go to the local library outside school hours because her father demanded that she return home where she could be put to work as soon as she came in, Sadie started to skip school to spend her time in the library.

Challenged by the sole librarian as to why she was not at school, Sadie explained in her chatty and charming way that it was impossible to learn anything there. Bemused by the forthright, sweet and articulate little girl, the librarian's conscience was much troubled as to the right thing to do. She knew very well the dreadful reputation of St Edmund's.

On the other hand she was a rather timid woman and very much afraid of getting into trouble. She might have done great good to Sadie just by leaving out books on the subjects she needed to learn. But this required too great an act of courage. Instead she merely guided Sadie to a hidden corner and told her to make her book choices at the beginning of the day and not wander about the place so she would be seen. You can imagine the haphazard nature of Sadie's reading, unguided by the usually competent professionals who taught her subsequent colleagues at the British Film Secretariat.

From then on Sadie would turn up for registration at St Edmund's and then vanish off to the library for the rest of the day, the high turnover of both staff and pupils now working in her favour. Gradually she became aware that there was such a thing as an eleven-plus which would make her eligible for the local Grammar School, a place hitherto untroubled by graduates of St Edmund's Primary. Sadie asked the librarian about the exam and she learned from the fearful bureaucrat that it was decided by an intelligence test and that copies of these could be bought at a bookshop in the centre of town. Realizing that she needed money, and that she had none, Sadie stole ten pounds from her father's wallet and walked all the way, a round trip of eight miles, returning triumphantly with the book of tests.

Her father missed the money almost immediately, flew into a terrible temper and began beating his wife. Sadie arrived home just as he had decided, having given her a fearful thrashing, that she was not the one responsible. When Sadie came into the house she had time to hide the books, heard the dreadful crying and, wide-eyed with fear, came into the kitchen. Something in her expression made Sadie's father suspicious.

'You took my money!' he screamed at the little girl. 'Didn't you?'

Terrified, unable to speak, the little girl nodded at once. He began hitting her, about the face, the legs, the back. Only after several minutes, as Sadie howled in pain and fear, did he demand to know why she had stolen his money.

But Sadie would not tell him. No matter how hard he beat her and despite her cries and screams, she would not speak. Finally he stopped. If the truth were known his temper was played out. He began to feel remorse, both for hitting his entirely innocent wife and for going too far with the now bruised and battered sobbing daughter. And in truth he was also appalled at Sadie, frightened by her determination to say nothing about why she had taken the money, but with a loud and blasphemous curse he stormed out of the house and went for a very long and increasingly guilty and confused walk.

When he returned it was to a broodingly silent house. The matter of the missing ten pounds was not mentioned again until many years later, when, transformed by time and his pride at his daughter's great success in the world, he occasionally made jocular remarks about it.

In due course, Sadie arranged with her timorous librarian protector to take the eleven-plus under her supervision. She, of course, passed easily. When the results came she discovered she had been offered a place at St Mary's Catholic Grammar School for Girls. In those days in Manchester you were either a Catholic or a Protestant or a Jew. Sadie knew that the librarian was a Catholic and thought perhaps all Catholic women were good-natured but weak enough to be manipulated in accordance with the wishes of a precocious ten-year-old. She decided as a result that she would be a Catholic. Prior to her acceptance she had been asked to attend an interview with the headmistress and Mother Superior of the convent that ran the school.

Sadie had not told the librarian what she was up to but had casually inquired about Catholicism and what, perhaps, a girl of her age would need to know if she were Catholic. Although by now wary of her protégée, the librarian was used to her asking questions about all kinds of things that were unusual and often embarrassing. The answer she gave encouraged Sadie because some of the things she heard were very familiar in the Copt faith her parents practised, though erratically. Sadie went to a Catholic bookshop she often passed by on her endless walks and stole a missal from the church on Barlby Street.

On the day of her interview Sadie sat on a window seat, her thin little legs dangling a good eight inches from the floor, and began to feel her confidence drain away. Hardly any light seemed to penetrate the vast corridor in which she sat, opposite a large and forbidding door. Everything was that strange ecclesiastical brown, known only to the insides of Catholic institutions, a forbidding colour that seemed to give off its own dull and depressing light. It smelt of old polish and cabbage. Sadie was beginning to think that she might not like being a Catholic after all.

Then the door opened in front of her and a woman covered from head to foot in a black and shapeless habit stood looking at her.

'Sadie Boldon?'

She nodded.

'Where are your parents?'

'My mother is very sick and my father had to go to work.'

'At least one of your parents should be here.'

Sadie just looked at her and a small tear, entirely genuine, made its way down her cheek.

The Mother Superior considered. She was not someone who cared for tearful little girls. On the other hand, this particular little girl had passed the eleven-plus with the highest marks she had seen for years. St Mary's had not been doing well academically for some time, not in fact since she had become headmistress. This had been noted by the Diocese and even commented upon by the Bishop. Sadie was simply too valuable an asset to be told to go away.

'Come in,' she said and turned around.

Sadie followed her into a room even browner than the rest, so brown indeed that the colour seemed to have tainted the very air itself. The Mother Superior gestured to one of the three large chairs pulled up in front of her desk. Sadie was obliged to climb into the seat, so tall was it. Again her skinny legs dangled.

'Are you a good girl?' asked the Mother Superior.

'Yes,' said Sadie in a small voice.

'Well, you are certainly a very vain girl.'

Sadie was bemused. She was not used to sarcasm. People almost invariably found her charming. Even her

413

father, bad-tempered and melancholic as he was, found Sadie charming. Cold irony was completely unfamiliar and though she realized the Mother Superior was in some way displeased by her answer, she could not begin to imagine why.

'Do you go to mass on Sundays?'

'When I can,' said the little girl. 'When my mother is well. My father is a very bad man and not a Catholic.'

Despite a temperament that was almost always an even one – that is to say a barely repressed frozen rage – the Mother Superior was taken aback by her reply. She was about to tell the girl off for dishonouring her father but he clearly was a bad man if he was a non-Catholic who refused to accept the prior claim that the church had over his daughter. He had also let the child come here on her own.

'I see,' she said at last, examining the girl if not with more sympathy then at least with a growing sense that she could place her in the scheme of things. 'Do you know your saints?'

'Some of them.'

'When you speak to me you are to say "Yes, Mother Superior" or "No, Mother Superior".' She paused. 'Do you know your saints?'

'Some of them, Mother Superior.'

'Can you say the Hail Mary by heart?'

'Yes, Mother Superior.'

'Let me hear you.'

'Hail Mary, full of grace, the Lord is with thee; blessed art thou amongst women . . .' When Sadie had finished she looked up expecting approval. There was none.

'Recite the Our Father.'

'Our Father who art in Heaven, hallowed be thy name . . .' She rattled it off with as great a degree of accuracy and as little a concern for meaning as any well-brought-up Catholic child.

The Mother Superior did not like girls but even by her own unforgiving standards there was something very odd about this one. She disliked odd children even more than the ordinary kind.

'Do you know the Seven Deadly Sins?'

Neither the librarian nor the stolen *Girl's Book of the Saints* had mentioned these. Something in the Mother Superior's eyes told her to tell the truth.

'No, Mother Superior.'

The nun looked at her for some time. But she was forced to bow to a necessity that she could not fully acknowledge. St Mary's needed a girl like Sadie.

'When you come here, Sadie Boldon, you will learn the Seven Deadly Sins. You must pay particular attention to the sin of Pride.'

Sadie nodded thoughtfully, as if she agreed also that attending especially to the sin of pride would be worth doing, although she had no idea what the Mother Superior meant.

'You may go now.'

When the letter arrived via the librarian to inform her that she had indeed been offered a place, Sadie was less excited than she had expected to be before her interview with the Mother Superior. However, she was stuck with her choice and that was that. There was no going back. That night she took the letter home and explained to her parents that it had been given her by the Headmaster at her primary school and that this was the new school she was being sent to at the beginning of the next term. Neither of her parents understood anything about the English education system and they expected its instructions to be beyond them. Her father knew, however, that it was a Catholic school, but as Catholics were also Christians and had a Pope he reasoned that this was the best that could be done under the circumstances.

Although over the following seven years Sadie came to regret deeply her assumption that all Catholics were amiable but spineless, and to wish she were anywhere but St Mary's, she nevertheless thrived at least in one aspect of her education. If in the Arts there were few really excellent teachers, most were competent if predictable. Compared to those in her past at any rate, these were models of pedagogy. As their brightest pupil they all adored her and also because she had a way of getting people on her side – even the large rump of girls in the school who by the age of fourteen were shaving their hair oddly, wearing Ben Shermans and going around with the emerging local skinheads. Violence between girls was rare in those days but the verbal bullying could be relentless. But people got on with Sadie and those that didn't were wary of her sharp and clever tongue if they tried to give her any grief.

The one person who remained uncharmed by her was the Mother Superior, Sister Mary Frances. Although she kept a cold-weather eye on her, Sadie was not a troublemaker and the number of prizes she won in national essay competitions – Sadie loved competitions – had brought some deeply needed publicity for the school's academic prowess. As long as Sadie kept winning prizes for essays on Nuclear Disarmament, whether or not we should stay in the Common Market, and Shakespearean tragedy, Sister Mary Frances could point to what the school could do with the right material while blaming the school's otherwise mediocre performance on the number of working-class girls in their catchment area.

The school was particularly poor in its approach to

science. This was partly due to the view that girls did not have an aptitude for it and partly because of the deep suspicion that the Catholic Church has always had of science. The nuns did not attack Galileo exactly but the aura that surrounded him was of someone who had offended the Church. Darwin was not mentioned except with repressed disdain. But for this, Sadie would have been a fine scientist and could have been a physicist or a doctor, but the teaching was too poor even for her skills to triumph over. And besides, by the time she was sixteen she had already discovered the love of her life: films.

It started with her visits to the ABC minors on a Saturday morning. She watched everything she could, went to the two films for fifty pence at the local fleapit (though in fact the sounds of scurrying under the piles of old damp seats under the screen were large and four-legged), sometimes watching the same two films twice or even three times in the week. It was *Bullitt* at the Forum or *Night of the Living Dead* at the Premier; *Easy Rider* at the Odeon, *The Wild Bunch* at the Templeton. Then it was the student cinema clubs showing the banned, the freaky and the obscure. By the time it came to choosing a university, there was in fact no choice at all. The girl who could have gone anywhere went to the University of Bangor because in 1979 it was the only university to offer a degree in Film Studies.

There you have it then, all I know, all I am *permitted* to know about Sadie Boldon. I must assume, what else can I do, that what I know is useful in some way, a means out of my current (what can I call it?) predicament. But I'm not so sure I'm getting the point they want me to. I feel, now, like a small boy not getting the answer to a sum and wishing they'd just put me out of my agony. *Just tell me*, I shout. But they don't.

The Inquisition

Do not ask of an organization what function it performs
but of what conflicts is it the scene.

Louis Bris, The Wisdom of Crocodiles

'I'VE HAD ENOUGH of being patient with you. I want an
answer.'

Sadie looked at Farraday with what to an outsider
would have looked like a mixture of fear and hostility. She
turned away. 'Well?' he said. He felt clearer now than for a
long time. He despised this woman and he was not simply
going to allow her to get away with treating him like this.
He did not, he was glad to say, want a reconciliation,
merely a just revenge, a re-balancing of his sense of himself as not the kind of weakling who could be used as an
object of cruelty and malice without cost to the person
who treated him in such a manner. 'I want an explanation
for the way you've behaved and I'm going to get it.'

He liked the sound of himself – menacing, like someone who might do, without mercy, something unpleasant
in order to get his way. Part of him recognized, but did not
acknowledge, that she seemed more miserable than
afraid.

'I . . .' she got no further but then looked down at the table in front of her. He watched impatiently. But still she did not speak.

'You can't just say nothing.'

She looked at him quickly as if shocked by the idea of being obliged to speak, as if such a compulsion was clearly inconceivable and that only perhaps a dangerously violent person would say such a thing.

Again, unacknowledged, underneath his virile demand for justice and respect he could feel the strange fear of her tainting his anger, his fear that there was no engaging with this woman, no possible means of negotiating her inner life. How, you may indeed wonder, could he have fallen in love so passionately with someone he did not understand at all?

What was incomprehensible was that he thought he knew her until, as it were, the moment that he did not. When she was in love with him so intensely, so satisfyingly, so deeply and adoringly, he had only the sense, not least because she so wonderingly referred to it, that he had touched her in ways that she barely realized existed. The intensity of her response to him was so great that it seemed to imprint on him an almost god-like sensitivity to her longings and desires. And in turn he felt that he could communicate everything unspoken in his own heart, just with a touch or a look. How, then, having gone so deep, could he in the space of a day be turned upon? You may regard such ecstasy of feeling as an indulgence, a hyperbole of delusion. After all, look what had become of it. But there's the thing. Look indeed. It had not simply vanished, this mania of theirs, or cooled. She felt as intensely about him, if he had only known, as she had always done, except that this intensity had in a moment turned into an intensity of disappointment and rage.

Why? That was what he needed to know and what you, dear Reader, expect. There is a legend, I understand, about a well in Italy to the effect that if a woman in love drinks from it, it turns that love into a passionate hatred.

He stared at her, anger and exasperation lacerating his soul, but underneath it all a hopeless expectation that if he could get her to speak there would be a sudden revelation. 'Oh, that's it,' he would say, horrified at the misunderstanding that must be at the root of it all. 'Let me explain. It's simple,' he would say. 'You've got it all wrong.' Then she would look at him amazed and it would be all right.

But still she would not answer. Again and again moving from righteous anger to near pleading he tried to get her to talk. But there was nothing, you realize, that she could have told him. Then he grew angry again and she looked at him sensing its power. She held his gaze, not in defiance but with a kind of miserable disappointment.

'What really bothers me', he said at last, 'is that I could have fallen so much in love with such a heartless bitch.'

Then he walked out, not neglecting to slam the door.

A week later all the examiners received a letter sent to their homes by recorded delivery. It was from Nick Berg. With the exception of the name of the person to whom it was addressed, all of them were identical.

For some time I have been concerned about the lack of diversity among the examining staff at the Secretariat. After lengthy discussions with my colleagues there is a uniform agreement that we need a distinct policy to encourage new blood into the organization. As a result the Secretariat has decided to embark on an entirely new way of organizing the role and duties of examiners. I am now writing to inform you with this letter that the entire examining staff will be issued by the end of this month with official redundancy notices. It is intended that the Secretariat will pay a redundancy sum to each examiner according to its legal responsibilities, such sum to vary according to the number of years' service. The period of notice will be three months.

In order to achieve such a considerable change with as little damage as possible to continuity and the quality of service provided by the Secretariat, we have for some time been preparing eight new full-time examiners who will be provided with three-year contracts. After this period these contracts may be extended for a further three years but for no longer.

It is expected that there will be four appointments made from the current examining staff. These appointments will be full-time but will be for three years with no extension. All current examiners may, if they so wish, apply for these four full-time posts.

Yours sincerely,
Nick Berg

Allan Rhys and I had been informed of this coup less than a week before. During the explanations that followed it became clear that Nick's visits to the grubby staircase in Soho that it had taken me so much trouble to photograph, while hardly innocent, had nothing at all to do with Mistress Torment and the sweet pleasures she had to offer. Determined to conceal his actions from the examiners he had hired an entire floor of the building for six months, during which time he had interviewed and hired his eight new examiners and given them three months' training. Once he was satisfied that they were competent enough to do the job he delivered the knockout blow. Rhys and I were to stop doing our completely pointless tasks for the next year and become full-time supervisors to ensure consistency of standards while the replacements for my old colleagues got up to speed.

I think it would be fair to say that when he had finished outlining his plans there was a stunned silence. I was also, of course, rueing the loss of what I had fondly regarded as a hold over Nick, while thanking God that I hadn't had the opportunity to use it prematurely. It was Rhys who spoke first, and very softly so as not to imply in any way that he disapproved of what Nick had done.

'How . . . uh . . . will you select the examiners from the . . . uh,' he searched for the right words, 'present staff?'

Nick's manner was not one fervid with anticipation of humiliating revenge because it would not have been possible for him to accept such a role. Please don't misunderstand, he was not feeling these vindictive things and hiding them under the pose of a manager driven to exercise his obligation to manage the organization for which he was responsible. It was that this was the moral posture that made it possible for him to do what he was about to do, which, after all, was to deprive all of the people who had raised their hands against him of their livelihoods. 'Who destroyeth my living destroyeth me,' as the Bible so simply puts it. The method actor did not exist who could have imagined himself into a role with more depth and conviction. It was not possible for Nick Berg to be vengeful and vindictive; it was only possible to be firm and decisive in the best interests of the Secretariat.

He, of course, expected trouble. There would be weeping, he hoped (without admitting it to himself, of course) and there would be gnashing of teeth and rending of garments. There would be unpleasant and unjustified accusations, personal attacks and vilifications of his motives. But he was armed against them, armour that went all the way into the deepest reaches of his soul. In truth he looked forward to these slurs on his integrity (unconsciously, of course). He would stand against them heroically, armed with the shield of duty and the sword of conviction, both of them forged from his own basic goodness. It would be bracing, like standing on a beach in a storm, testing yourself in the rough winds and driving rain, feeling as the elements fought with you only the power of your strength to resist, a power you know will prevail.

As it turned out, this epic, if subliminal, ambition was to be thwarted. The expected roar of anger and fear from the examiners did not materialize. With my apologies for the grand comparison, it was rather like the fall of the Berlin wall: when it was battered down, there was no reaction at all from those who had everything to lose because they no longer believed in the power of what they were doing; the sense of pointlessness that had lived with them for so long had eroded even self-preservation. It was a reaction that clearly surprised the examiners themselves. When they turned up at the meeting called by Emma as the union rep, they had nearly all, quite independently, decided to take the money and go; the atmosphere had become too hysterical and sour and it was impossible to imagine putting themselves through the humiliation of applying for their own jobs. There was also the fact that being part-time at the Secretariat meant they had other part-time work to tide them over, and mostly in areas they could easily expand to cover a significant amount, if not all, of the income they would lose. The exercise of their integrity was not going to be too costly.

The result was that Nick met only cool disdain at the

The Long Goodbye

Devo punirmi, devo punirmi,
Se troppo amai . . .
[*I must punish myself, I must punish myself,*
if I've loved too much . . .]

Stendhal, *The Red and the Black*

WHEN THE EXAMINERS HEARD what Sadie had done they were all, of course, astonished. The relationship between Sadie and the colleagues who had always liked and admired her was now extremely distant – cold and sour from Sadie, cool and pitying from the examiners. With the exception of Emma Saward she clearly no longer welcomed conversation – all discussions were discussions about work. But what would they have said to her even if she had been more receptive?

However great their amazement at Sadie applying for the new post at the Secretariat they were not at all surprised at Nick's reaction. She was duly interviewed by Nick and Walter for nearly an hour, there was a wait of some two weeks and then she was sent a letter appointing her as a senior full-time examiner.

It was Emma Saward who quietly let it be known what

had happened. By chance she told Farraday when he was with Rob McCarthy. Farraday said nothing but McCarthy made a point that probably represented the view of all the examiners: that, of all the discreditable things that Nick had done, giving Sadie a job was the most unforgivable.

There was deep concern from Walter, as well there might be, about the way the now redundant examiners would react to their replacements. Nick had decided the last three months' employment of the former and the first three months' of the latter should be served side-by-side. Managerially inept to the last, Nick refused to recognize the potential damage to the organization and nothing Walter said would persuade him to change his mind. Somewhat surprisingly the two groups got on pretty well, mostly at any rate. The assumption that the new examiners would be Nick's fervent acolytes, ready to do his bidding, turned out not to be quite the case. They were of another generation, of course, and not really tainted with the peculiar ideals that had ten years before so characterized their predecessors and which had produced so much grief for all concerned. And for what, I asked myself with profound glee.

The replacement examiners brought a very different kind of new blood than that one proselytized for by Nick only a decade before. By and large they had a deep pragmatism about them. Nick had, as it turned out, chosen people who were not less argumentative, less independent, but less, shall we say, sentimental. They wanted the job and they realized better than other equally talented candidates what was required of them by Nick. They were the ones who seemed best able to take the hint that he required if not subservience then tractability. They realized, all of them, that they were here today and gone tomorrow. At the end of each interview Nick had spelt it out. 'You should not take a position at the Secretariat expecting there will be a career for you.' And they did not.

And so the has-beens and the blacklegs got on pretty well; all the former really wanted to do was make it to the end of their notice period and leave. For some time, if the truth were told, the reports had been getting shorter, the thumbs drifting more and more frequently to the fast-forward button. Even before the redundancies the impassioned tracts and fellow examiners' reports pinned up on the notice board had thinned and then stopped altogether. And so it was that the great experiment dribbled to its flaccid conclusion.

Given that they were part-time there was no last day as such. Some finished their final viewing on a Tuesday, some on a Friday. In the past even a secretary of a couple of years' standing would have had a drinks party and a large Hallmark card with good wishes to send them on their way. But there was no ritual of even the meanest kind to mark the passing of the examiners. On their last day each one finished their work, put their red log books back on the shelves on the second floor and cleared off home and that was that.

Farraday had decided to work on the last Friday of all. He told himself that it would be anticlimactic, however lame the whole thing had become, to leave in the middle of the week. He was, of course, deferring the moment when he would have to leave Sadie and never see her again.

His last day's work was dull, old TV series and cartoons, and he was finished writing his reports by four o'clock. As the day had worn on he had become more and more restless and miserable. He kept finding excuses to walk past the viewing room in which Sadie was watching with one of the newcomers. But she did not look away from the screen nor, when she had finished, up from her reports. He had to wait for nearly an hour, edgy and indecisive, before she was on her own. He approached the room slowly, hardly knowing what he felt, nor clear about what he was going to say. He stopped and took a deep miserable breath and then opened the door and went in.

She kept on writing for a second or two and then, merely lifting her head, looked at him with her large deep brown eyes. They gazed at each other for really a very long time. It was more than ten seconds before he spoke.

'Don't you have anything to say to me?'

She did not take her eyes from his and he could feel intense calm from her, a clarity and coolness which he had never before experienced in anyone.

'No,' she said.

exposure and the revelation of how these events came to pass. As they say, in so many of those bloody awful American films for adolescents that I've been forced to watch over the years: Dream on. As it happens, I'm perfectly aware of the limits of my abilities as a Machiavellian. I am no Iago nor could ever be. But, now that I have ploughed the furrow of revenge myself, I find I'm pretty dissatisfied with *Othello* – the play I mean not the character. The thing is that Othello (the character, not the play) is supposed to be a great-souled man with a tragic flaw, a flaw that inevitably takes him to his doom. But there's nothing inevitable about it and it's my humility that speaks here and my experience in these matters which is, of course, rather greater than that of any literary critic pontificating about things of which they know nothing. The reason that I boast of my humility in this is that you have seen, in as much detail as I am able to provide, how these things I have written down here came about. You know my part in them and how central it was that I found and revealed the hidden fax and what my sending it to Sadie set in motion. But you also have to accept that I did nothing else of any real significance, not before and not after. Iago has to dig and delve and winkle and dredge and poke and prod Othello with every kind of brilliant insight. Without Iago's genius for understanding the human heart Othello would have died an old man in Desdemona's arms. How is this, I ask you, then an inevitable flaw? The point I'm trying to make is that it took no such brilliance on my part to cause the ruin, to a greater or lesser extent, of my former colleagues. Rewind the tape of these events a hundred times and while I accept the outcome would have varied it would always have ended badly.

So there I was, then, deeply satisfied with the way things had turned out. I had done what I had set out to do and things had turned out better than I had hoped and, I freely admit this, better than I had planned. I was content. Every day for the next two months I noted that Sadie, somewhat unexpectedly I have to say, was not bitter and angry in her daily work. To be honest I was rather pleased that this was the case. She had about her the air of someone who had been taught a hard lesson and was rebuilding, slowly and carefully, a more satisfactorily modest sense of herself. I did not often speak to her, preferring to keep my distance and observe as she went about her work. That was what pleased me best.

But one Friday we did bump into one another as she was about to leave.

'How's it all going?' I said and I was filled with something almost like compassion as she smiled at me, so achingly did it resonate with the acceptance of defeat.

'Oh fine,' she replied. 'And you?'

'Not at all bad. Though things seem rather dull compared with how they used to be.'

She smiled again, but somewhat blankly this time as if she did not quite see what I meant.

'Doing anything interesting this weekend?'

'Not really. Are you?'

'Taking the kids to Alton Towers.'

'That'll be fun.'

'For them anyway. I'd better get on.'

She smiled again.

'Enjoy yourself,' she said, and she seemed to really mean it.

'See you on Monday.'

But I did not. The next day Sadie Boldon told her husband she was going for a walk and hanged herself in some woods about three miles from her home.

Manchester

Who can measure what has been lost?
White gospel song

EMMA SAWARD SPOKE rather well at Sadie's funeral I thought. Sadie's husband also tried, though he barely made it past his third sentence before a terrible tremor seized his face as if he'd had a stroke and he had to be helped from the lectern by two of his friends. You would not have thought the mood of horror and grief that seemed to create a fog around the people gathered there could deepen. But as her husband howled, bent over in his friend's arms like some stricken toddler, there was a kind of collective groan like one of those deep organ notes you can't hear but seem to feel in the pit of your stomach.

The ceremony was being held in the annexe of a funeral home. She had not wanted a church service apparently. It was a miserable place, built as if someone had tried to reconstruct a chapel in medium density fibreboard from a visit only dimly remembered. At least the ceremony was short. But even after a mere ten minutes I could see that there were people outside waiting to get in for the next funeral. God, it was awful.

432

I had come by train and taken a taxi to the funeral home and was nearly late. I wondered if any of the examiners would be there. But they weren't. Not invited, I suppose. Emma Saward was there, of course. She had supported Sadie right until the end. I wondered how she'd receive me.

When it was finished we all filed out from an exit on the opposite side of the annexe so that we wouldn't have to mix with the mourners for the next funeral waiting to come in. What is it that's wrong with the English? They didn't even wait until we'd all left. It was like being followed by customers at a supermarket checkout.

Almost as soon as I got outside Emma came up to me.

'I had a terrible feeling that Nick was going to come himself.'

'Oh,' I said, 'he wanted to.'

'You're kidding?'

'Not at all. He was entirely mystified when Walter and I said he shouldn't.'

An expression at once bitter and grief-stricken crossed her face. 'It was Nick's fault. This would never have happened but for him.'

This was not, of course, entirely fair but I had no intention of defending Nick. Quite the contrary. Emma was clearly still moderately well disposed to me and I had no intention of antagonizing her.

'He refuses to see any connection. Or claims to.'

'How can that bastard possibly think that?'

'As far as Nick's concerned the fact that Sadie applied for the job meant she'd decided she really was in the wrong – the fact that he gave it to her proved that he was being generous in not holding a grudge. He said at the time that not many employers would have been so generous.'

'I hope', she said, 'he rots in hell.'

I thought it best to change the subject. 'I assumed from the address of this place that she was being cremated but . . .' I stopped in order to let her answer.

'No, she's being buried a couple of miles away. Did you come by car?'

'Train.'

'Do you want a lift?'

'Thanks, that would be very nice.'

It was, I suppose, a reply awkwardly delivered and she looked at me oddly. But if the truth be known I wasn't feeling well and hadn't been for a few days. I never thought that she would have done something like this, do you see.

We barely spoke on the way to the cemetery on the outskirts of Manchester. It was a huge place on the side of a hill and I felt increasingly breathless and ill as we walked up towards the group of people waiting by the grave. Not long after we joined them the hearse arrived. The funeral director opened the hatch at the back and six men in identical cheap black suits carefully lifted out the coffin. They carried it at waist height, I suppose because the grass was damp and it would have been easy to slip. Then they set it down on two flat cords and with some difficulty eased it over the grave and slowly lowered it.

It suddenly struck me, as the coffin slipped irregularly into its place, that this was a body being put into a hole in the ground, the body of someone I knew. An obvious thought but a hard one to grasp when it's happening in front of you. There was a long silence and then a young man I recognized as having helped Sadie's husband down from the lectern moved forward with a piece of paper in his hand. It was windy up there and as he started to speak it was almost blown from his grasp.

'David has asked me to read this.' He held the paper

tightly and then began: ' "Out of the depths I have cried to thee O Lord . . ." '

Within five minutes we were walking back down towards the car park. It was downhill, I know, but I was feeling more and more breathless and I had to stop. Emma, puzzled, stopped with me.

'Are you all right?'

I nodded, although I felt anything but all right. 'Probably got the flu coming on or something.'

After a few deep breaths I did feel better. Slowly breathing in and out and moving around as I did so to avoid Emma's now alarmed stare, I found myself looking back up the hill towards Sadie's grave. There was someone, a man, standing beside it. It was not one of the mourners because Emma and I had been among the last to leave. By now Emma had seen him too.

'My God, isn't that Tom Farraday?'

We had no time to discuss it because we both heard footsteps behind us. It was Sadie's husband.

'Do you know who that is?' he said, nodding at the figure up by his wife's grave.

I couldn't bring myself to tell him but fortunately, though hesitantly and I thought fearfully, Emma replied. 'I think it's Tom – Thomas Farraday. He worked with Sadie,' she added lamely.

'I must talk to him,' he said, after a moment's silence. There was an odd look on Emma's face that I couldn't quite place. Did she know about the affair, I wondered? David Boldon started walking up the hill. For a moment we both just stared, not knowing what to do.

'I think we'd better go with him.'

We had a hard time catching him up as he walked so full of purpose, very different from the distraught man of only a few minutes ago. Between that and my breathless-ness he reached the grave a good thirty yards in front of us. Nevertheless, despite the blood pounding in my ears, I could hear Boldon quite clearly.

'You're Tom Farraday, aren't you?'

'Yes.' Farraday looked as if someone had struck him around the face, white and shocked.

'We met quite a long time ago.' David Boldon's voice was flat and toneless, so much so that it was impossible to tell what he was feeling. Emma and I both stopped and hung back a little.

'Yes, I remember,' said Farraday. And then nothing. They just looked at each other as if they simply didn't know what to say.

'I wanted to say I'm sorry.' Strangely it was not Farraday who said this but Boldon. Farraday looked at him with what I could only call a kind of miserable horror.

'I don't understand,' Farraday said, at last.

'For not inviting you. And the others. I was upset, you understand . . . not really thinking clearly.' He stopped and looked away and there was another agonizing silence, the horror on Farraday's face deepening as I watched utterly transfixed.

'The thing is, Tom, I'm very angry with her.' Boldon looked back at Farraday, as if appealing to him. 'How could she do a thing like that? How could she be so cruel?'

I don't know if he expected an answer but he didn't get one. They just looked at each other. I had never seen such expressions of pain and misery. As I stood on top of the hill in that ghastly place with the cold wind piercing through my coat, the blood started pounding in my ears again and I felt I couldn't breathe. I turned to Emma and touched her on the arm.

'I don't feel very well.'

Something had driven me to come to her funeral,

something so powerful that I couldn't ignore it, try as I did. I didn't know what it was and I didn't want to know. I thought that by coming here it might be satisfied and go away. But nothing was going to drag me into going back to her brother's house with the other mourners (was I a mourner and if not what was I?). I used the long journey back to London as an excuse. At the gates I said goodbye to Emma. She gave me a kiss on the cheek and I remember thinking that it was the first time in the ten years I had known her that we had ever touched.

'Sadie would have been glad that you came,' she said.

I wanted to shout that Sadie wouldn't have given a fuck whether I was there or not. I wanted to call out to her husband and all the other miserable souls whose life that stupid bitch had blighted, to tell them what a selfish, stupid bitch she was. What was the point, what in God's name was the point of killing herself, and over what? In God's name for what? But instead I just looked at Emma as tears filled her eyes. I didn't know what to say so I tried to smile or something, some terrible grimace and walked off down the street. After about ten minutes I found a pub called Help The Poor Struggler. I stared at the sign for a minute and thought I'd walk on. But what did it matter what this Mancunian shithole was called? I went in and called a taxi on the payphone and while I waited I ordered half a pint of lager. It felt like I was drinking sand.

I got home late and fell asleep quickly and when I woke up I felt better – better in the sense that I didn't feel anything much at all. At work the next day I had, of course, to answer awkwardly dutiful queries about how the funeral had been. 'Fucking hilarious, what do you think?' I wanted to shout – but of course I merely shrugged miserably as if it was too painful to discuss. When Nick asked,

I did exactly the same thing and he did exactly the same thing back.

By Friday afternoon the questions had dried up and tired as I was I felt that the worst was over. On the train home I fell asleep and dreamt that I was lying on a beach in about twenty pieces, an arm here, a leg there. A seagull was standing on my forehead and I kept having to purse my lips and blow in order to stop him walking all over my face. When I woke up I had gone past my stop and what with waiting for a train to come back the other way I was an hour later than I should have been. I arrived home shattered and went to bed early, falling into a deep and, thank God, dreamless sleep.

I was woken up the next morning by my youngest daughter jumping on the bed. It was her birthday. 'Daddy! Daddy! Wake up!' I found I was caught up in her delight and with all the preparations for her party that afternoon. Throughout the morning I was kept busy blowing up balloons and helping with the food and also I was soothed by my little girl's pleasure: she was as excited as if she were being visited by a princess. Shortly before they were due to start arriving my wife asked me if I had done the wrapping for a game of pass the parcel. I hadn't and immediately grabbed hold of that morning's paper.

'Don't use the paper,' she said, 'the ink will rub off on their party clothes.'

I ransacked the cupboard under the stairs, found a copy of the *Sunday Times Magazine*, and started ripping out pages to wrap the main prize, a Barbie doll. However, I also had to put a sweet between each layer to stave off the upset of a number of the little monsters who'd have a nervous breakdown if someone else won something and they didn't. So I was in a bit of a rush.

My wife was in the kitchen putting the finishing

touches to the birthday cake when it was time to start the games, so I arranged the children in a circle and started one of them off with the paper-wrapped parcel. Everything was fine for the first few layers, and there was much excitement. Then to my horror I realized what I'd done. I'd wrapped the remainder of the parcel in a photo essay of Lee Miller's pictures of her entry into Dachau in 1945. Squeals of delight greeted each new sweet and each new atrocity as emaciated bodies of dead Jews gave way to a pile of teeth or the camp guards who had been beaten so badly by their former victims that their faces had become a weirdly bulging parody of something human. The most excited shout was for the Barbie doll wrapped in a picture of a dead German floating in the Dachau canal.

Once they'd finished I picked up the pages and quickly threw them back into the cupboard under the stairs before my wife could see them. I could, of course, have said that I did it in a rush and once the kids had started it seemed the best thing to do was to let them finish and not make a fuss. It's plausible I think. It just doesn't happen to be true.

You hear of people falling apart but you never think that it can really happen just the way it sounds, that you can feel bits of you come loose, that odd parts of you fail, and you can feel it happen: a feeling of affection or desire flicker for a moment, come back to life and then die, just like a lightbulb going out. Only inside the heart and mind and soul there is no replacement possible – this bit is dark for ever and you might as well get used to it. But you can't, of course. Somewhere in the rest of the house you can hear the clang of something falling off, you really can become unhinged, screws come loose, and in the dark you can hear them fall, clattering against other things as they drop into the flooded basement of your leaking soul. My

Every Crooked Thought

> Thus endeth this noble and joyous book entitled Le Morte D'Arthur. Notwithstanding it treateth of the birth, life, and acts of the said King Arthur, of his noble knights of the Round Table, their marvellous enquests and adventures, the achieving of the Sangreal, and in the end the dolorous death and departing out of this world of them all.
>
> Sir Thomas Malory, *Le Morte D'Arthur*

> For every crooked thought there is a crooked molecule.
>
> Dr Ray Fuller, discoverer of Prozac

Case 42/173 MD   Dr Steven Pollock
CASE

Duncan Purcell, a 42-year-old married man, was referred to the Beaconsfield Psychiatric Hospital for evaluation and treatment of his psychiatric symptoms. He presented with a one month history of symptoms that included shortness of breath, vomiting and refusal to eat solid food, leading to a weight loss of 12kg. According to his wife he was complaining of constipation, stomach and heart problems, serious insomnia and (she had noticed) self-induced vomiting. Cardiologic and gastrointestinal examinations were performed but revealed no organic pathology.

Mr Purcell underwent a psychiatric outpatient examination here and a preliminary diagnosis of schizophreniform disorder was made. He was prescribed Haloperidol 10mg/d. Unfortunately he escaped from the inpatient unit some three hours after admission while the nurse was closing the secure door. He was 'recaptured' by police officers at a shopping centre in Uxbridge some six miles away from the hospital. He claimed that one of the nurses in the unit was due to go to hell and was trying to send him in her place.

The next morning he again managed to escape, this time through the ventilation area of the lavatories. On this occasion he was again seized by the police three miles away in Bekonscott Model Village. He claimed to the officers that he was dead and was beginning to expand. When they pointed out they were the same size as him and that this was a model village he laughed at them and said that they were also dead and expanding and merely deluding themselves by claiming the town they were in was a model. The Haloperidol dosage was doubled on his return and Zuclopenthixol Acetate 50mg was administered by intramuscular injection.

In his first week Mr Purcell refused solid food and would accept only water and fruit juice. He claimed that he had no stomach and that what was left of his gastrointestinal system was connected directly to his heart, which had no beat because he was dead.

No neurologic or psychiatric disease was present in his family history. He had been academically successful both at school and university. For seven years he had been a civil servant at a fairly high level and ten years ago had become a film censor where he had in the past year been promoted to management level. At the case conference this unusual profession gave rise to some discussion about a possible relationship between his illness and the urge to repress the 'unacceptable' in other people, inherent one presumes in his role as a censor. There was no history of alcohol or drug use. An MRI scan and SPEC tomography of his brain showed central atrophy at the temporal horns of the lateral ventricle and also left parietal hypoperfusion.

After these tests, and over eight hours of conversation with Mr Purcell, a new diagnosis of Cotard's syndrome was agreed on. Cotard's syndrome is an extremely rare condition (no previous cases at this hospital, for example) first described in 1880 by Jules Cotard who called it delusional nihilism. It is characterized by the patient believing that he is dead, a walking corpse. Paradoxically, being 'dead' often gives the patient the notion of being immortal. In Mr Purcell's case he claims that he is facing eternal damnation and can no longer die a natural death. According to the research, extreme levels of guilt about their former behaviour is present in nearly 65 per cent of patients. He also claims that most, though not all, of the people around him are also dead. Whenever his wife visits he expresses astonishment at seeing someone who is alive in this place and anxiously urges her to leave in case she should come to harm.

Some three weeks after his admission he had reluctantly started to drink Proplan and though still seriously underweight, he has now stabilized.

At the same time he began writing copiously in a large red book provided by his wife at his request. Apparently it is of a kind he used on a daily basis during his work as a censor. When I asked him what he was writing he looked at me with considerable apprehension rather as if he were seeing me for the first time. Until this point he had treated me with either mockery or indifference – the former due to my attempts to convince him that he was still alive. His attitude now changed radically and after a few more sessions he said that he wanted to show me what he had written but that he had to 'get it straight first' as he put it. It gradually became clear over the next few months as he began filling these very thick books with astonishing rapidity that he had come to regard me not as a doctor but as some kind of recording angel, who oversaw this place of the dead. He thought that I had the power to let him die but only if his record of what had happened to cause his terrible affliction was completely truthful. Apparently, I had given him the power to see some of what had happened in a way entirely new to him, that he could revisit scenes in the past of which he formerly knew nothing. While it was clearly a good thing that he felt I had some positive role to play in his delivery, his claim that he only had one chance to deliver his account to me was a concern. If I was not satisfied that he had given a truthful account he claimed he would be condemned to be in this state of living death eternally. For this reason he would not discuss the events that were clearly deeply troubling him. I asked his wife if she had any idea of the source of this profound guilt but she could think of nothing.

There was some discussion at the case meeting with Professor Prabhu Gupta as to whether or not my status in the eyes of the patient might be in danger of worsening the problem. On balance he felt that I should remain and that for now, at any rate, we should not read what he has been writing until he is ready to present it to us. At the moment he is writing continuously for up to fourteen hours a day. Another reason to go along with him is that he has agreed to keep eating until he has finished.

God, this is an awful place. It smells and all these noises, voices calling out and the chattering and banging of those people. Why can't they be more careful? I don't sleep much and though I'm so knackered I'm glad of that because I dream such terrible things, things I can't tell you about. But I had another kind of dream last night. I was sitting in my room and for once there wasn't the smell of cabbage water and that other sickly sweet smell you get in these places, you know what I mean. It was so nice, the quiet. Then the door opened and Sadie came into the room. She was smiling.

'Hello, Duncan,' she said.

My heart leapt, it did, it really did.

'My God, Sadie, you're all right.'

'Yes,' she said and sat down on the bed next to me. 'And look,' she said, taking hold of my hand and placing it on her tummy. 'I'm pregnant.'

'Thank God,' I said. 'Thank God.' And she laughed.

And it was only then I realized.

'This is a dream, isn't it?'

She laughed again.

'No, it's not a dream, Duncan. Everything is all right.'

'No,' I said. 'I'm dreaming.'

And then Tom Farraday and Rob McCarthy came in, and they were smiling too. They shook my hand and made fun of me about thinking I was dreaming, though they were kind. Then, of course, I woke up.

I cried for a while, but I must have been making more noise than I thought because they came in and injected me with something. And for a while, as it took effect, I felt wiped out and distant and I liked that a lot; and just before I fell asleep I thought that if I had that dream about Sadie again, this time I'd try to make it last just a little longer.

THE END